Elizabeth, William… and Me

S. Lynn Scott

Copyright © 2017 S. Lynn Scott

The moral right of the author has been asserted.

Cover illustration by Ryan at Monkey Feet Illustration.

Apart from any fair dealing for the purposes of research or private study, or criticism or review, as permitted under the Copyright, Designs and Patents Act 1988, this publication may only be reproduced, stored or transmitted, in any form or by any means, with the prior permission in writing of the publishers, or in the case of reprographic reproduction in accordance with the terms of licences issued by the Copyright Licensing Agency. Enquiries concerning reproduction outside those terms should be sent to the publishers.

This is a work of fiction. Names, characters, businesses, places, events and incidents are either the products of the author's imagination or used in a fictitious manner. Any resemblance to actual persons, living or dead, or actual events is purely coincidental.

Matador
9 Priory Business Park,
Wistow Road, Kibworth Beauchamp,
Leicestershire. LE8 0RX
Tel: 0116 279 2299
Email: books@troubador.co.uk
Web: www.troubador.co.uk/matador
Twitter: @matadorbooks

ISBN 978 1788037 006

British Library Cataloguing in Publication Data.
A catalogue record for this book is available from the British Library.

Printed and bound in the UK by TJ International, Padstow, Cornwall
Typeset in 11pt Minion Pro by Troubador Publishing Ltd, Leicester, UK

Matador is an imprint of Troubador Publishing Ltd

For Nigel, Bryony and Alessandra

CHAPTER ONE

*If this were played upon a stage now
I would condemn it as an improbable fiction.
As You Like It, Act III Sc iii*

It was an ordinary day when Elizabeth came to stay. You would have thought that her arrival would have been heralded by the blare of sackbuts, or crumhorns at the very least, but nothing presaged the great event. Nothing out of the ordinary happened at all.

There was nothing in the post, except junk mail, and nothing on the news, except reports of misery and forecasts of more to come. Nothing in the air, no jarring telephone calls, and nothing foretold in my tea leaves. (Not that I believe in that sort of nonsense.) There was nothing unusual in the way my husband yawned like a hippopotamus, ogled the TV weather girl and left for work, falling over the cat on his way out of the door. Serve him right. Or in the way Grace stayed in bed until the last possible moment and then flung on clothes and make-up with sudden exasperated urgency whilst muttering a couple of four-letter words that she thought I didn't hear.

Definitely nothing unusual in the way that Alex drifted through with his blonde hair tousled, ill-fitting jeans flaunting the waistband and more of his Calvin Klein underpants. Nothing at all unusual in the way he grabbed a piece of burnt toast and grunted a muffled word that might have been 'morning'. Or might not. It was so lovely to have him home again that my anxious 'where are you going?' died on my lips. He had been gone such a long time that to have him with me when he wanted to be with me was enough.

There was nothing at all in this mundane morning business to indicate that something truly extraordinary was about to happen.

Don't get me wrong, I don't hold with prescience or any of that paranormal stuff. I'm an atheist for Christ's sake. Still, looking back, it did seem that something should have heralded Elizabeth's arrival; an otherworldly glow; a hollow voice echoing from the heavens; lightning flashes accompanied by a dull, low roll of thunder, or a swift chorus of The Ride of the Valkyries bouncing off my stainless steel saucepans. But no, I just opened the pantry door and there she was.

I shut it again and drank more coffee.

Hubby's car shot down the driveway scattering gravel and offending the cat yet again. My daughter, Grace, wearing a self-bastardised version of her school uniform that would no doubt get her into trouble at school (again), looked resentfully at me before sloping sleepily out of the front door, brightening as fellow somnambulists called to her from across the street. She always looked at me resentfully these days. I hoped that it was just a phase. I drank more coffee, thinking that we should all get up earlier so that we could have a proper family breakfast of muesli and orange juice like you are supposed to. Like all those families on the television with breakfast bars and 'lifestyles' do. I had been thinking that for years of course but somehow it had remained just an unattainable aspiration and none of us ate breakfast at a table unless we were on holiday and it was served up by the hotel. And the choice then was never orange juice and muesli.

I picked up my keys and left for work.

I got as far as the gate and then I came back into the house, marched up to the pantry door and flung it open fearlessly.

She was still there.

"What," I asked, "are you doing in my pantry?"

It was not an unreasonable question you will agree. She didn't respond, just stared at me with majestically glassy eyes. The full peculiarity of the situation hit me and I took an involuntary step backwards. I was, as my grandmother used to say, 'struck all of a heap'. She took a step forward. I retreated another couple of steps and came into sharp contact with the sink. Unwashed plates and mugs adjusted their position noisily and the leaky tap gurgled. She lifted a small yellowed, glittering hand toward me whilst I, suddenly frightened, did my very best to climb into the sink.

"Who art thou?" She spoke in a harsh, cracked whisper but her manner was commanding.

I froze with one leg resting on a dinner plate. The fingers, thin and crabbed were reaching towards my face, the gleaming dark jewels contrasting and mesmerising with their ageless beauty. I knew who she was of course. I had known instantly. The first moment I opened the pantry door and our eyes met I knew who she was. Considering it was my pantry she had ensconced herself in I had assumed that she must know who I was but apparently not.

"Who art thou?" she repeated.

I told her, not wishing to seem rude.

"Ally," She repeated, with heartfelt disdain. "What earthy name is this?"

"It's short for Alessandra," I stuttered, helpfully.

Whatever she was, this apparition from my pantry, perhaps she would be less intimidating once we had had a chat. "It's Italian."

"Art thou Italian?"

"Oh, no," I was beginning to feel marginally more at ease. "My father found it in a book. It's the name of Mussolini's daughter. Not that he's a fan of Mussolini," I added hastily and then remembered that it was very unlikely that she would know who Mussolini was. "He just liked the name. Mum wanted to call me Ocean Aurora, so I suppose I got off lightly. My sister is Kate but she nearly ended up as Joyful Zephyr except that Dad said it sounded like a budget car, so…"

My companion's eyes rolled heavenwards and she cut across me in what I felt was a very unqueenly manner.

"Thou art much above the middle height." The little old woman was studying me with sharp eyes, bright in her white withered face. "Thou art very large indeed."

"I'm tall," I admitted resentfully. It was my house after all and I wasn't that big. It was just that, by contrast, she was so tiny and shrunken. I didn't quite have the courage to say that to her but I was becoming uncomfortably aware that a spoon laden with last night's bolognese had smudged the seat of my trousers. I decided I had had enough of cowering. If she wanted to suck my brains out or fell me with a thunderbolt, I would just have to take the risk. I slid slowly down off the sink but did grasp the handle of a frying pan just in case. She eyed my cautious movements with contempt and then suddenly stepped out of my pantry and swept past me. She came to a halt in the middle of our small kitchen and looked around. The strange woman was tiny but her dress was huge. Her back was ramrod straight and, when you couldn't see her face, she looked like a gorgeously dressed doll on which the clothes are intended to be the main feature and the body just the frame. I moved with relief from my perch on the sink and the cups rattled and groaned once more. I rubbed the bolognaise sauce off my trousers with a damp tea towel and glared resentfully at her. She stood still, unmoving except for her sharp eyes which roamed freely over the jumbled detritus of my life. I started to speak but was commanded into awed silence by the smallest movement of her withered hand. She certainly had a way with her.

When she had examined my kitchen to her own satisfaction

she twisted slowly around to face me again and any initial impression of lack of stature fled. She was tiny and ugly but even when motionless she emanated an intensity that filled the room. Her unnaturally high forehead glowed whitely in the muted sunlight stealing in through the window. Her thin lips were little more than a cruelly defined line, her cheeks withered and without colour beneath heavy scarlet rouge and her eye sockets were shrunken and darkly shadowed. But her eyes, oh her eyes, held a whole world within them. They were bright, sharp and demanding. Power and command and… Majesty shone from them. They were magnificent, but she said nothing, just held me in her gaze.

I had the uncomfortable sensation that my world was slipping away and I made an effort to break free.

"What are you … where…how did you…?" I started positively enough but ground to a confused halt. The questions were too big for me. "You were in my pantry…" I whined feebly. Perhaps a statement would be safer than a question.

"Whereto tends all this? Whate'er are you? Rude companion, why art thou here?" she demanded at last, revealing a mouthful of very bad teeth. I have quite nice teeth so I felt entitled to be a bit more assertive.

"What do you mean, what am I doing here? I live here. This is my house. The question is what were you doing in my pantry?"

"Ah," she looked about herself again, a touch of bewilderment on her proud face. "I know not. The door didst ope…"

"Yes?" I prompted.

"And thou wast before me." She said 'thou' as if I were something particularly unpleasant that she had found on her shoe.

"Oh …" I digested this and came up with the next logical question. "Where were you before?"

She lifted her hand to her face and the bejewelled fingers

pressed into her loose dry skin. Her eyelids dropped briefly and, robbed of the light of her eyes, she was momentarily weak and ordinary.

"Before my here-approach I was at Richmond. Bed-rid I lay. There was much pain." She stretched her emaciated arms in front of her and looked at them in wonder. "There is no pain here."

"Oh," I said again. We were no further forward and we were, therefore, left regarding each other suspiciously with silence stretching between us. I couldn't think of anything to say that might lead us to a logical conclusion.

"Well, seeing as you are here would you…like a cup of tea?" It was a reasonable offer under the circumstances and I try to be hospitable when I can.

"What say you, child?"

"Tea? Oh. Perhaps it hadn't been invented where, when, you come from? Or is that discovered? You'll like it. We all drink tea when we don't know what else to do. It's a British institution. I'll put the kettle on."

I flicked the switch on the still-warm kettle and the water within shifted and hissed. She started slightly but after a moment her eyes darted sharply back to mine.

"Art thou man or woman?"

"What?" I was offended I don't mind telling you.

"Thine apparel is that of a man. Thou wearest pantaloons. Thy height is much above that of woman and yet thy rounded figure suggests that thou art not a man. Art thou a travesty?"

Bitch, I thought. Then I remembered the teeth, so I flashed mine at her in a brilliant smile. Her Majesty fixed me with an icy stare and didn't smile back. Not surprisingly.

I made the tea whilst she watched my every move. She drew back suspiciously as I held the mug out to her but must have come to the same conclusion that I had, which was essentially that things couldn't get much weirder so she might as well accept whatever was going to happen and just hope for the best. She examined my striped china mug with interest, took one tentative sip and grimaced.

"Foul," she cried, spitting it onto my tiled floor. "Tis poison!"

That was annoying but I swallowed my irritation, added a couple of teaspoons of sugar and, to convince her that I wasn't attempting regicide, sipped from the mug myself. She tasted it again cautiously and then gestured for more sugar. I added one more, then two, three, four and five more teaspoons. It would have been six but she gave up trying to drink it and ate the dissolving sweetness greedily with the spoon. That explained the teeth, I thought with satisfaction.

Either the tea or the massive sugar rush gave her confidence and sparked her curiosity. As she sucked the spoon she moved around the kitchen looking closely at each item. The ceramic cookie jar in the shape of a smiling cow was a particular fascination. Anything shiny also attracted her beady eyes. There wasn't much that fell into that category though. I became uncomfortably aware that I hadn't cleaned or dusted properly in a while. A long while. She didn't touch anything, just studied it closely, came to some conclusion which she did not share, and passed on to the next item. If I made a move to explain or to show her anything I was impatiently hushed. I found myself studying her with the same half-fascinated, half-repelled manner with which she was inspecting my kitchen implements.

Elizabeth's facial skin was white and dusty and her high forehead met curious wisps of rusty, coarse hair thrusting from beneath a cap of fine linen. The ruff was there of course, and the embroidered gown, stiff and heavy with jewels and, one could only imagine, incredibly uncomfortable to wear. The dress was fashioned of a tarnished gold material and the tiny waist that was encompassed by it could have been encircled by my hands with room to spare. That made me feel really overweight and cumbrous I can tell you. She also wore a stand-up collar of fine lace, ribbed and stiff. The whole should have been stunning except that it all looked a little tired. The skirts stood out from the hips but did not fall in clean lines as if the cages beneath were dented and misshapen. That famous stand-up collar, a feature in all our images of this indomitable Queen, drooped where it shouldn't have. The white lace was grubby and there were numerous little holes and tears in the once gorgeous material. Only the many jewels on her bodice, on her fingers and in her hair were unblemished and magnificent.

She paused by the large digital clock on my wall, passed on momentarily to the photos of Grace and Alex, and then returned slowly to the clock. It was a hideous thing. A gift from an uncle of mine. I think he won it playing Bingo. Time moved on and the neon number changed before her eyes.

"Jesu!" she said, clasping her withered breast in horror.

"Mercy o'me, what means this?" she gasped, turning frightened eyes on me.

"It's a clock. It's just the time changing."

"A clock? 'Tis not round. Thou liest, 'tis not a clock."

"It's digital," I explained helpfully.

"Magic…" she whispered in horror.

"No, not magic," I snapped, feeling totally inadequate to tackle an explanation of the inner workings and science of a digital device. "It's digital, you see and it runs off a battery. At least I think it does…It has stored energy, you see, in a little box that…."

It was all getting a bit beyond me so I returned to the crux of the matter before I could reveal the true extent of my ignorance.

"Okay," I said, grimly determined to reclaim some tenuous grasp on reality and to take control of the powers that had deposited into my kitchen, where she had no right to be, this mad little old lady. "I need to know what you were doing in my pantry. I mean where did you come from and why are you here? I mean you of all people! I really have to get to work and… and you have been dead for hundreds of years. It stands to reason that you can't be living in my pantry."

Meatloaf chose that moment to remind me that I was going to be late for work again by shrieking 'Bat Out of Hell' from my handbag. That would have been unnerving for anyone not conversant with the 80's (and probably for some that were), so I wasn't really surprised when Elizabeth pulled the old wooden chair in front of her to act as some sort of protection and moaned in understandable confusion. I rummaged around in my bag and eventually found the mobile phone. It was Blofeld from work.

"I'm on my way," I spat into the mobile. He was shouting angrily, loudly enough for my visitor to hear. He had no man-management skills at all and his vocabulary was limited and monosyllabic at the best of times. In a fit of irritation, I threw the damned phone into the sink with last night's washing up. You will no doubt agree that I had good reason, given what had happened, to feel just a little pissed off. But then I regretted the action and rescued it just before it plunged from a bolognese-covered plate into the cold soapy water.

"Thou art a witch!" Elizabeth screamed, her shrill tones bouncing off pots, pans, and plates and reverberating painfully in my ears. I suppose from her point of view it was a reasonable assumption. I had been shouting into my hand which had, to all intents and purposes, been shouting back. Empty your mind of your twentieth century expectations and you would find that scenario just a little terrifying too. She fell on her knees, clasped her hands and began muttering in a strange language. Latin, I supposed. I learned in time that this was always her recourse in times of stress. It got to be quite wearing after a while.

"I am not a witch," I responded in loud exasperation. "There are no such things as witches and I don't believe in all that supernatural crap. There must be a rational explanation for all this, there just must be."

I rubbed my hand across my eyes but when I opened them she was still there and any rationale eluded me.

"Look, I don't have time to deal with all this. I really, really must get to work or I'll get the sack. Can't you just go back to… where-ever it was that you came from?"

Elizabeth's thin lips continued to move in silent supplication to her God. Her terror was real and I felt a tug of sympathy. She was, after all, just a frightened little old lady on her knees in my kitchen. This tenderer emotion was fleeting though, as, when I offered to help her to her feet, she gave my outstretched hand a stinging slap and spat at me. I retired huffily. Left to her own devices she rose with difficulty, hauling herself up with the aid of the old kitchen chair. She was, no doubt, regretting her impulsive fall to her knees. When she had eventually unfolded her stiff limbs she threw a suspicious, fearful glance at me, another at the clock on the wall and then looked towards the fridge. It was an old fridge. We'd had it for years and inscribed in raised metal letters on the door was the word 'Crown' and a three-pronged logo of the same. I suppose she felt some sort of ownership because, having drawn strength from her prayers, she could not entirely suppress either her natural curiosity or her courage. I could see what was going to happen but there didn't seem to be any way to stop it or any reason why I should. Elizabeth hesitated for one moment only, threw me a proud glance and grasped the handle. She hesitated again and then pulled. You didn't need much effort to open it. Shutting it so that it didn't fly open again was the knack you needed to learn with our fridge.

The heavy door swung wide and light streamed out. Two pots of yoghurt, a soft foul-smelling cucumber, a bag of lettuce that had rotted into liquid and something that even I didn't recognize fell at her feet. Simultaneously the TV remote slipped from its resting place on the top of the fridge and, in hitting the edge of the cupboard on its precipitous fall to the floor, managed to conjure up Jerry Springer, in glorious high definition and surround sound on the kitchen television above her head. Elizabeth, suddenly confronted with the head and shoulders of a living man suspended in mid-air who it transpired was noisily attempting to keep a fat, pudding of a woman from pummelling her equally horrid life partner to a pulp, whilst at the same time being blasted by an inexplicable rush of cold from a large box that had assaulted her with odorous produce was, to say the very least, a little put out. It would be hard to say just what frightened her the most but I strongly suspect it was the less than urbane Jerry Springer.

She uttered a series of piercing screams, put her hands to her eyes and would have fallen on her ancient arthritic knees again if I hadn't decided that enough was enough and caught her. She wasn't heavy but then, by her reckoning, I was huge and manly enough to cope. She remained a dead weight, although unfortunately not a silent one. Once Elizabeth had finished with the screaming, which intermingled unnervingly with the howls of one of Jerry Springer's minders who had been bitten by the she-wolf he was trying to restrain, she instead emitted a high-pitched wailing in Latin as I manhandled her back towards the pantry. Perhaps, considering her distress, I was a little unsympathetic but I was already half an hour late for work and Blofeld was going to make me suffer for every minute of it.

"Look, I'm sorry," I said firmly, if huffily. "I'm sure it would be fascinating to get to know you but I just haven't got the time right now, and I really don't want you to be traumatized by the toaster. If you just go back to wherever it was you came from I think that would be best."

I peered curiously into the pantry whilst propping her up on one shoulder.

"Maybe there's a portal in there somewhere," I mused.

All I could see were numerous cans of haricot beans (can't stand them but they were on offer), a few wizened apples and countless boxes and tins whose best-before-dates would not bear close inspection. If there was a portal into the past it was well hidden. I shrugged impatiently, manoeuvred her, now protesting violently, into a tiny space unencumbered by food stuffs, propped her up against a sack of sprouting King Edward potatoes that didn't smell any too fresh and, deftly avoiding flailing limbs, stepped back with relief. Having failed to physically hurt me she recovered just enough to eye me vigorously with disgust, disdain, and dislike. I slammed the door on her, consigned Jerry Springer to well-deserved oblivion and went to work.

CHAPTER TW0

O, how full of briers is this working-day world!
As You Like It, Act I Sc iii

I don't remember very clearly what happened at work that day. The usual tedium I suppose. I work for the local authority and I'm a Central Optimization Officer. I mean, I ask you! What pretentious birdbrain came up with that patronizing jargon? I'm a clerk. Nothing more and nothing less, and why anyone should think that calling me an 'officer' makes me feel more valued is delusional. They can call me whatever the hell they like, the only thing that would make me feel more valued is a lot more in my pay packet at the end of the month. And more time off. A lot more.

I probably logged on that day, waded through twenty or thirty emails, most of which were complaints because I hadn't done something, or complaints because I had, or demands to do something immediately, or requests to finish something properly, or rude pictures of men from Gloria in Despatch, or polite letters from someone very trusting and godly in Nigeria asking me to look after an unimaginably vast amount of money. I can't say I wasn't tempted once or twice by that last, if only because it would have been nice to deal with someone who was so polite, grateful and appreciative of my time.

Blofeld was my line manager – not his real name obviously but I need to avoid a defamation suit if I can. He was one of those big personalities that filled any room he walked into. Or that's what people said about him. He was a large man and a very loud one and I think his effect on people was more to do with taking up valuable space than possession of any sort of personal magnetism. He certainly repelled me. He was relentlessly jolly but could turn on a sixpence and become thoroughly nasty if you crossed him. I don't know why but I seemed to cross him an awful lot. At first, it was entirely unintentional on my part, but, having received an unjustified (in my view) tongue-lashing on more than one occasion, the rebel in me was awakened and I set out to cross him as often as I could.

Once, he'd rung down and demanded that 'the one with brown hair' go up to his office.

"There are three of us with brown hair," I replied politely, although I knew he knew all our names and he knew that I knew. It was just one of his many patronizing affectations that didn't seem to bother anyone except me.

"Not you. The attractive one," he responded.

Well.

"We're all attractive here," I snapped back (lying through my teeth). "Pamela is drop dead gorgeous, Lorraine is a part-time underwear model and I can stop traffic. You may not have noticed but we have all evolved into intelligent beings with individual personalities that are not reliant on our bra size, so if you want to talk to any one of us I suggest you move your Neolithic backside and get your knuckle dragging carcass down here. You need the exercise." And I put the phone down. His manager having got wind of the episode was panicked into seeing a potential charge of sexism and Blofeld was told to placate me, which fuelled the fire of his hatred even more and was pure torture for me. I much preferred open warfare but we coped, when absolutely unable to avoid each other, by employing a sort of toxic courtesy.

The other girls in the office (I say girls but I mean middle-aged women like me) were a nice enough crowd, some married or divorced and some with young kids. They were all so kind to me when…well, that's got nothing to do with my story. We'd giggle over the rude jokes and emails that Gloria in Despatch sent us (all of them terribly sexist by the way) and laugh like drains whenever Mark from IT Support would come and ask if we'd seen his big package, which he did far too often for it to be remotely funny.

If I am to be totally honest with you, whatever I might once have been, I was now far from a model employee. My heart just wasn't in it anymore. It never really had been but I soldiered on, doing my best, it's just that my best wavered somewhere between adequate and average with the occasional spectacular nosedive into shoddy. Like most people I worked to help pay the mortgage, keep food on the table and for the occasional family holiday. The work was tedious, soulless and mind-numbingly unrewarding but apparently, it had to be done. I had lost sight of exactly why it had to be done some years ago. Part of the problem was that I just didn't have the courage to leave and I'd been employed for so long it was difficult for them to get rid of me. I know that because I'm fairly sure the less than charming Blofeld tried.

So, I was stuck there. Unless I really flipped out one day and stapled my fat boss to the office notice board. Don't think I wasn't tempted.

Anyway, that was work: office politics, minimal socializing, as much skiving as I could get away with and a whole lot of daydreaming. One day, one week, one month, one year much like another and nothing was likely to change anytime soon.

When I got home on that particular day, Hubby and Grace were in the kitchen and the pantry door was wide open. Hubby was hunched over his laptop doing something inconsequential but, apparently, engrossing. Grace was emerging from the pantry with a packet of crisps and Alex was listening to his iPod whilst drumming on the worktop with two balloon whisks. It was a little annoying but Grace and Hubby did not comment so neither did I. I sidled past him and flung a quick look into the pantry. It was empty, of course.

"What's for tea?" Grace asked.

"What do you want?" I replied mechanically.

"I don't know," was the predictably unhelpful answer.

"How about cheese on toast?"

"I hate cheese," said Alex, pulling his ear plugs out.

"Well, if you don't want cheese on toast, I'll see what we've got in the pantry," I said deviously, stepping into the small space to look around me. It was exactly as it had been in the morning only without Elizabeth.

"I'm happy with cheese on toast," muttered Hubby from the depths of Minecraft.

"So'm I," added Grace.

I took a moment to stifle my disappointment over the deserted pantry. It was quiet and cool.

"Mum?" Grace's head appeared around the door. "Are we having cheese on toast then?"

"No," I responded irritably. "I'm not cooking different meals for everyone, tonight. We need to find something that everyone will eat."

"But…" Grace's brows came down and she glowered at me.

"There are chips in the freezer." Hubby interrupted before Grace and I could have a spat. "We could have egg and chips."

"Okay," I agreed absently.

"I hate eggs," said Alex at my shoulder.

"Just have the chips," I snapped.

"But we've got plenty of eggs," Grace protested. "I want fried eggs."

"Whatever," I sighed and Grace rolled her eyes. She hates it when I use modern expressions. Apparently, that's her prerogative.

I really must get them to eat more fruit and veg, I thought. I grabbed a can of haricot beans. No one would want them of course but at least I would have made an effort and it might assuage the guilt of a careless mother who allowed herself to be persuaded that a Bounty Bar and Fruit Pastilles could be counted as one of the required 'Five a Day'. No one commented when I served up the pale, unappetizing beans with the poached (not fried) egg and chips. Nor did they eat them. Hubby, about to say something, caught my eye, changed his mind and instead reached over and ate Alex's eggs from his plate. Everyone sprinkled far too much salt on the chips. Grace rattled on about some boy hacking into the mainframe at school and distributing pornographic photographs into the RE teacher's PowerPoint presentation on the Second Coming. Hubby was outraged. He's not religious but he gets quite passionate about the abuse of the internet. I did venture to ask Grace if she was studying the Elizabethans in history lessons but she said, no, it was women's rights and the development of medicine and it was boring.

The end of the meal came and she went to do her homework. No, that's not true. She went to play music and games on the computer and would probably rush through whatever exercises had been set next day at school. It was another issue that I was going to tackle when I had the time and the energy it would require. Hubby dragged his telescope out of the attic muttering something about a dying star and disappeared down to the bottom of the garden. Alex quietly disappeared as he was wont to do. I washed up and pretended to clean the kitchen and watch the television that had so traumatized my visitor of the morning. As you will have concluded, we have a television on the wall in the kitchen. It makes the place look like a chip shop. The garish parade of murder, mayhem, tawdry relationships and overblown comedy moved noisily across the screen but I saw little and understood less. Hubby reappeared, having tired of trying to find the supernova through obstinate clouds, with his electric guitar strapped to his breast. My dear husband's interests are eclectic and quite often unsuccessful and/or loud. He plays occasionally with a rock and roll group made up of friends of similar age and substance dependence (beer). Individually, they all play quite well. All together, however, they are a bit wayward. He keeps saying that he is going to give it up now that he is over fifty but I don't see why he should. I quite like the noise and we don't get on with the neighbours anyway.

"You okay, Ally?" he asked.

"Yes," I said. "Why?"

"You've been in the pantry for twenty minutes."

"I'm tidying up," I replied absently, moving a box of Oxo onto a jar of Marmite.

"Ah," he said, glancing around at my handiwork, unimpressed.

I slept well that night, relatively speaking of course. I only had to get up once to go to the loo.

When I opened the door, there she was, undeniably regal as she sat upon my toilet glaring at me, her hands folded tightly on her brocaded lap. I stepped inside, shut the door quickly behind me and crossed my legs against the call of nature.

"You're back," I said accusingly, and quite unnecessarily.

She stared at me unblinking, ghoulish and white-faced, and then raised her wasted arm towards the shower. A shiver ran down my back and the hairs on my body stirred. The curtain billowed and a thin bearded face with mild, lost eyes under a very large and floppy hat emerged tentatively from behind the painted plastic goldfish. There was a small man standing in my bath.

"Oh, great," I said, quite loudly. "That's all I need, two Elizabethans following me around! Who the hell are you?"

The little man just looked startled. I might have been more patient if I hadn't needed to wee quite so badly.

"I know who she is," I snapped, "and that is quite weird enough but I really do have to draw the line at strange men appearing out of nowhere in my bath. Who are you?"

No response.

I rounded on Elizabeth. "Did you bring him with you?"

"I did not." She seemed quite offended, but then I had never seen her look anything other than grievously affronted.

"Well, who is he?" I jerked the shower curtain out of his hands and glared at him. He cowered back against the flowered tiles and whimpered. "Who are you?"

"Shakspere," he squeaked, or something very like it.

"Shakespeare?" I repeated, in disbelief. It was my turn to stagger backwards.

"He is nought," chipped in Elizabeth dismissively. "A whoreson scribe of poems, plays and amusements. I know not why he is here. He is naught, a mere wordsmith." Her contempt filled the small room.

"William Shakespeare," I repeated, dumbfounded.

"He said so," Elizabeth said coldly. "I say so too."

"But he is…" I choked, took a breath and began again. "William Shakespeare is the greatest writer the world has ever known. He was a genius."

I remembered the well-thumbed biographies in Alex's room and was momentarily awestruck. I can't say I had ever been particularly interested in either British history or literature but Alex was. It was one of my son's less worrying monomanias and I had therefore picked up enough to be a little star-struck at finding Shakespeare in my bath.

The little man in the doublet and hose stopped whimpering and started listening. Elizabeth, however, after a moment of astonished disbelief, roared with cracked laughter. It was very disturbing.

"Sssh, ssshh!" I hissed, pulling myself together as the harsh notes of cruel merriment bounced off the tiles and porcelain. "My husband is asleep."

She subsided into a hoarse, scathing chuckle.

"So much honour becomes him not. He is a mere actor who hath scribbled some verse and performed on occasion for my pleasure. He hath a turn of phrase, nothing more. I know not why he has imposed himself on my presence thus, any more than I know why I find myself here with you. You interest me not at all and he is not fit to bear me company, a mere court jester."

She stood and moved swiftly towards him. I think she was about to hit him. He shrank from her in entirely understandable terror and inadvertently hit the shower control. The howls he emitted as the cold water spurted over him had to be heard to be believed. Elizabeth, disconcerted by the power shower, retreated to the comparative familiarity of the toilet as William was subsumed by panic and, in his haste to escape the cascade, stepped on the soap. After some truly spectacular flailing, he landed in a wet, bedraggled, noisy, embroidered heap in the basin of the bath. Meanwhile Elizabeth, in backing off, had both managed to flush the toilet and activate the automatic fragrance dispenser. It was quite a lively thirty seconds.

I reached over Williams' still thrashing body and switched the shower off, hissing frantically, "Shhhh, quiet! Please, you are making enough noise to wake the dead."

Even through my frantic anxiety to quell the hubbub that struck me as funny and I started to laugh. There was Elizabeth the First of England, in all her virginal glory, staring in complete astonishment at my fragrantly flushing lavatory and William Shakespeare, the writer, the genius, the bard of Stratford upon Avon, crumpled in a sodden heap in my bath with a look of utter dejection that was positively comical.

And they were both dead. I knew that. Those glorious, incandescent figures of history couldn't possibly be here with me in the 21st century. This proud old woman mystified by the workings of my bathroom appliances and this frightened little man clutching the shower curtain could not be whom they appeared to be.

Elizabeth glared stonily at me as I subsided into helpless

laughter. William, bless him, sat up, wrung his cap out and wriggled uncomfortably as the cloth of his elaborate outfit began to shrink and the dye ran in disconsolate rivulets down the plughole. That made me laugh even more until the tears streamed from my eyes and I was roaring helplessly, holding myself upright only by hanging on to the door handle.

"Mum?" It was Grace. "Mum, what are you doing in there? I can hear you laughing all the way in my bedroom."

That brought me up short.

"Is your Dad awake?"

"No, he's still snoring. The only reason he can't hear you is 'cos he's making such a racket himself."

"All right," I choked back the giggles that still threatened to break forth and glanced back at Elizabeth and William. I made a decision. "I'm going to open the door, Grace. I have something to show you."

"Okay," came slowly, reluctantly from behind the door. I could see her, in my mind's eye, sulkily rolling her eyes heavenward.

"You mustn't be frightened, Grace."

"Yeah, whatever."

"Fine." I flung the door open and looked triumphantly at her. She looked at me. She didn't look behind me. I had expected her eyes to slip past mine and to widen in astonishment and, when they didn't, I turned my head.

They weren't there. There were towels on the floor where they had fallen when William had been thrashing about in the bath and a bottle of shampoo was dripping glutinously on to the floor but they weren't there.

"Mum," said Grace. "Are you okay?" There was something in her eyes that I didn't like. I think it was fear and I wanted to protect her from it.

Of course, I said yes, I was fine, and then I laughed and said that Blofeld had sat on a French Fancy at work and I was just remembering. It was a bit lame, to say the least, and she didn't believe it for a moment but she didn't seem particularly surprised either. I told her to go back to bed as she had school in the morning. She looked at me resentfully again but turned away obediently and in some relief.

I shut the door and remembered that I now needed to wee more than ever. So I did, but it wasn't a comfortable experience. I couldn't see my two new friends but I felt that they might reappear at any moment and that would be embarrassing to say the very least. Anyway, they didn't so I picked up the towels, mopped up the spilled shampoo and went back to bed.

"It's not a canoe," Hubby said positively as I crawled under the all-encompassing duvet, "but, if you want to cook bolognese, I'll need to find a garden gnome." He often said things like that when he was asleep which was funny really because he was a man of very little imagination when he was awake.

CHAPTER THREE

When shall we three meet again
in thunder, lightning, or in rain?
When the hurlyburly's done,
When the battle's lost and won.
Macbeth, Act I Sc iii

The next day passed uneventfully. Grace threw me glowering, suspicious looks when I came out of the bathroom next morning but I greeted her with a bright smile and lulled her into a sense of security by being very normal. Alex appeared briefly and didn't remark on anything out of the ordinary, but then he never did. I checked the pantry and the bathroom and the rest of the rooms in the house and found nothing, not even the hint of a lace ruff or velvet codpiece. At first, I couldn't work out if I was relieved or disappointed. I kept my eyes open all week and expected, every time I opened a door, to find Elizabeth or William or both, but I didn't. By the end of those seven days, I had to admit that what I felt was not relief. I felt strangely bereft. As if I had been promised something very special and was then cheated out of it.

I functioned as usual. Beds were made, papers filed, data inputted, meals cooked and eaten and I even achieved a few hours of dreamless sleep but there was a sense of something missing that was with me constantly. I had known them for only a few minutes and yet a strong sense of loss almost overwhelmed me. There was no question of my sharing the experience with anyone at home or, God forbid, anyone at work and this contributed to a suffocating sense of loneliness. William and Elizabeth had appeared to me and to me alone and, in doing so, had separated me from everyone else in the world.

It was not that I didn't question or try to analyse what had happened. I went through all the plausible explanations I could think of. That didn't take long because I couldn't really think of any. I considered that they must be an illusion conjured up by too much coffee on an empty stomach, or a dream, or that eye condition where people see figures that aren't really there or a fleeting aberration of the mind brought on by who knew what. Or maybe all those years of scoffing at those who believed in ghosts was about to come back and bite me on the bum. But none of those explanations really satisfied me. My visitors had both been pretty solid entities. William, slipping on the soap in the bath, had hit the enamel hard and made a very real mess in the bathroom, and Elizabeth's bony body had been warm and substantial when I dragged her back into the pantry. They were not airy illusions or ghosts or a dream. They just weren't.

So then I started on the even less plausible explanations.

Time travellers perhaps, entering through a portal or a black hole or something along those lines. That was a tempting theory so I trawled the internet in stolen moments at work or at home. You try typing in 'time travel' and see what a disturbing bunch of nutty theories and theorists you find. I went off that idea rapidly when I found myself in a chat room with someone who had seemed intellectual and lucid and genuinely interested in my experiences. But, when he told me he was a Time Lord, advised me to wrap myself in tin foil and then explained how the CIA, MI5 and something called the GONK were taking an interest in his frequent visits for tea and bratwurst to Hitler's bunker and how he had disguised himself as a pig farmer and moved to Norfolk in order to escape a multitude of men in black suits and sunglasses, I lost faith in his complicated and somewhat confused television-inspired theories and decided to look elsewhere for information.

I contacted a host of colourful characters that week.

There was Sarah from somewhere in South Africa who claimed to be in very intimate contact with Elvis Presley and delighted in recounting her somewhat distasteful sexual experiences with the King in lurid detail. I desperately wanted to write her off as barking mad but didn't feel that I was in a particularly strong position to do so. Ed, from somewhere in London, was a sweet young man who expressed interest in my story and questioned me in intelligent detail. I told him all, grateful to share the odd little occurrence in my life with someone who was not quick to judge. But even he was not what he seemed. When I received a detailed questionnaire in the post it became clear that he was a student of psychological illness at the London University and I was destined to become a case study for his Ph.D.

I was pretty discouraged I have to tell you. Then I came across a cheering article in The Times reporting that scientists from Oxford University had proved the parallel universe theory was possible and so was time travel. At least I think that's what they were saying. It was something to do with the formulation of Quantum theory, many worlds, the Hadron Collider, Higgs Boson and Schrodinger's cat. That cat gets everywhere. Apparently, according to Schrodinger, a cat in a box can be both alive and dead at the same time. Now, that theory, accepted by greater intellects than mine, did interest me, so I read everything I could find until my mind was truly boggled. I did my very best to understand but, quite frankly, their explanations, founded in science or not, seemed to be just as unlikely as those of the man who crawled under his sink to fix a leak, slipped into a 'wormhole in the galaxy' and met himself coming the other way. (Oh wake up to yourself – my guess, a combination of alcohol and a mirror!) Or the man who dedicates long hours of his life that he will never get back, no matter how much he travels in time, to spotting mobile phones and laptops in films made in the 1940's. (You need to get out more, start by going to an optician.) Or the man who regularly treats his YouTube groupies to updates on his travels forward in time but gives no more information than that he went – and came back, unfortunately. Or the very persuasive young men who claim to have found modern watches under ancient mummies that have lain undisturbed for thousands of years. Yeah, right, just how stupid do you think we are?

After a while, I found that I just didn't have the heart to struggle through the legions of the misguided or the misguiding on the off chance of stumbling over someone who was still in full possession of all their marbles. The so-called legitimate science was equally impenetrable, so I gave up in despair and went back to endlessly musing over all the details of each encounter and wishing that William and Elizabeth would come to me again.

It had been easy to reveal my story on the anonymous internet, where it would be irretrievably swallowed up in the swirling mass of ill-conceived nonsense that sadly makes up much of the world wide web these days, but there was a palpable barrier to even hinting at what had happened to Hubby or the kids or anyone else in my life. So I just thought and wondered and, after some time, concluded that, after all, I would be better off without apparitions in my bath tub or royalty in my pantry and that it was best to forget all about William and Elizabeth.

It was about three weeks later that Shakespeare appeared again. I was in the supermarket having just bought a birthday cake. I was looking at some frozen pieces of cod. The irony did not strike me at the time. I wasn't thinking about the cod at all; I was churning over a really crappy day at the office in which Blofeld had been particularly pernicious. I really hated him. And then some woman from the Magistrates Office had complained about the tone of one of my emails. I had been 'too polite' and she thought I was being facetious. Actually, she said she thought I was taking the piss and I said, no I was being facetious which riled her even more because she thought I was insulting her face. Perhaps she had her own susceptibilities. The worst of it was that I was beginning to wonder if perhaps it actually was all my fault. Self-doubt is a very uncomfortable sensation.

Anyway, I had been standing there for some time staring at bright blue boxes with jolly fishermen gazing back at me, chewing over what I had said and what I wished I'd said when I became aware of someone at my shoulder.

"Tis cold," William said, transfixed by a bag of scampi. I looked down at him and felt a sudden rush of, well, not happiness exactly, more of interest. Touched with joy. Somehow the day that had been grey and boring up to then promised to get a little brighter.

"It's a fridge," I explained helpfully. "A refrigerator. A machine to keep food cold so that it lasts longer. It's all frozen."

"Ahh," he lifted his eyes from the scampi and looked around him, moving closer to me and grasping my arm.

He was very short, scarcely up to my shoulder, but I remembered reading somewhere that they were all shorter in days of yore. He was slight although there was the suggestion that he might be developing a small paunch. To be honest he didn't look much like Droeshout portrait we all recognise. In fact, he didn't look much like any of the portraits that various people have claimed for him, but that might have been because no artist could ever come close to capturing the humanity of his deep brown eyes. Well, Da Vinci maybe or Michelangelo, but no lesser artist. Sadly, apart from his eyes and his clothes, which did stand out rather, he was quite ordinary. He was about forty years of age and dark haired with a goatee type beard. He had a receding hairline, of course, and wore the remaining hair straight and rather long. His thin nose was almost straight, but not quite. His cheekbones were high but brow bones low, his complexion was pale and he was neatly dressed in a doublet of rusty velvet, with coarse hose, dusty leather shoes with thin legs protruding comically from rounded shorts. I wondered briefly what they were stuffed with. He was still wearing the big floppy hat that should have given him a jaunty air but instead had the effect of making him appear even smaller than he already was and a little vulnerable. He looked ridiculously rustic and out of place against the expanses of melamine and stainless steel.

"So much colour," he whimpered, his eyes wide and staring.

"Colour?" I looked around me and realised what he meant. Everything was stark, vibrant and light. We take it all for granted and I hadn't noticed before just how much is thrust upon us. Colours are everywhere, sharp and hard-edged. From the vast arrangements of garish packaging to the liveried shop fitments, to cars and billboards and clothes, it is a kaleidoscope, a noise of colour with little shading and no restraint. We manufacture life in primary colours these days. To William, used only to the subtleties of nature, it must have been quite shocking.

"Don't forget our AMAZING vegetable slicer promotion today!" A nasal announcement burst abruptly into the air. "Healthy eating is soooo important," the voice which might have been male, female or computer generated droned patronisingly. "And if you want your vegetables chopped, diced and sliced professionally then visit our FREE demonstration and claim your AMAZING VEG MACERATOR, FREE today with every purchase of Norman Ramsey's gourmet periwinkles."

William's jaw dropped open, he shrank even closer and grasped my arm with shaking fingers. I was a bit nonplussed I have to tell you. It was okay in the privacy of your own home but I felt a bit uneasy standing in the freezer aisle of my local supermarket with William Shakespeare, codpiece and all, clamped to my side like a randy whippet.

"Why have you suddenly popped up again here?"

I glanced around as I hissed the words but the closest people were two gay guys engrossed in an argument over the contrasting nutritional merits of salmon and halibut, and a woman on the opposite side of the aisle who was rummaging enthusiastically through discounted products that were perilously close to their sell-by-date and who was oblivious to all but saving pennies.

"Prithee," William whispered, looking fearfully around him. "What is the meaning of thy words, sweet lady? The greatest writer the world hast ever known. Tell me for truth, can this be so?"

You had to love him. Terrified as he was, this mattered more.

"Well, yes." I was beginning to feel my ignorance. I had pored over Alex's history books and looked up some stuff on the internet at work, which was partly why I was in such trouble with Blofeld, but it had begun to dawn on me that I was in exalted company (you couldn't get much more exalted) and that I was, by comparison, untutored and dim-witted.

"If you are the William Shakespeare from Stratford upon Avon who wrote Romeo and Juliet and A Midsummer Night's Dream and all those sonnets and stuff, then yes, it's true."

His pleading brown eyes were fixed on mine and his hands tightened vice-like around my arm as he wrestled with the notion of his own immortality.

"Hamlet?" he gasped, "dost thou know of Hamlet?" I decided that brusqueness might have the effect of masking my intimidation.

"I had to study the wretched thing at school," I grumbled. "It is regarded as your masterpiece, although heaven knows why. I always found it to be long and tedious and Hamlet himself was way too self-absorbed to be anything other than annoying."

"A masterpiece," he muttered, his little face suffused with self-satisfaction. Obviously, my less than enthusiastic evaluation of his work did not register at all. He had me summed up. "I am studied at schools? Like Ovid, Virgil, Aeschylus?"

"Spose so," I said uncertainly. "We don't really bother much with those blokes these days although I do seem to remember that one of them was killed when an eagle dropped a tortoise on his head. That's pretty much the sum total of my classical education."

"Tis meet that maidens too study these works?" He was incredulous that I knew as much as I did and I didn't know whether to be relieved that my minimal knowledge had impressed him or offended that it had. I decided not to care.

"We are all educated, whether we like it or not, up to the age of eighteen or until we refuse to learn anymore, whichever comes first, and we all learn about you and your plays, whether we want to or not. And it is usually 'not'."

He loosened his grip slightly and staggered back under the vastness of this revelation.

"I wouldn't be too pleased with yourself. These days, you are part of the reason that 'the schoolboy creeps snail-like unwillingly to school'."

I was quite proud of my quote even if it wasn't quite accurate.

"And anyway," I mused unthinking, "you have been dead for four hundred years so I can't see what good it is going to do you."

"By the holy rood!" he gasped, crossing himself like a good Catholic and growing several shades paler. "Mercy 'o me."

"I didn't think you were religious." I was a little surprised. You don't equate Shakespeare with any evidence of profound faith. Or at least I, with my sketchy knowledge of the canon did not. On the other hand, it must come as a shock to be told that you are dead if you have been previously unaware of the fact, so poor William had a right to be a little perturbed. "Alex knows more about it than I do and he once told me that you were quite blasphemous in some of your plays but, even so, there are academics who believe you were probably Catholic."

This panicked the poor soul. He didn't know whether to cling to me more tightly or to run from me as far and as fast as his short legs would carry him. I couldn't help but take pity on him.

"Oh, don't get your pantaloons in a twist," I said coarsely, trying to recall some salient facts from my school history lessons, long ago enough now to be consigned to history themselves. "You can believe what you want and worship how you please. The Protestant Catholic thing is long gone. These days that's the least of our worries, believe me. Anyway, you won't be hung, drawn and quartered for any sort of faith. Well, not in England anyway."

"But, thy sovereign...?"

"Oh, we haven't allowed any declared Catholics back on the throne since Bloody Mary but nowadays we don't care what you worship, so long as you don't marry royalty. Are you Catholic then?"

He considered this in silence for a moment whilst regarding a packet of frozen prawns. He didn't trust me and wasn't going to commit himself one way or the other. Given the peculiar set of circumstances, there was very little reason for him to place any faith in me after all. Having pondered my words, he decided to return instead to the crux of the matter.

"In this world I am... dead?"

I sighed. Discussing metaphysics in the freezer aisle of a supermarket is generally to be avoided I felt.

"For four hundred years. It's the same world as your world it's just that this isn't your time and, before you ask, I have no idea how or why you are here. I was rather hoping that you would tell me."

The perplexity on his face told me that wasn't going to

happen anytime soon. He struggled with the concept of being dead for a few moments more and then reverted to the thing that was still uppermost in his mind.

"But... I am in good name and fame with the very best in these times?" I took a moment to work out what he meant and then nodded, smiling at his eagerness and his difficulty in understanding just how great he really was.

The two gay guys, having decided on halibut, were trotting towards us and I waited for their reaction. One would have thought that William's rather gorgeous breeches would have created at least a flicker of excitement, if not quite a furore, but we were passed by without even a glance. I began to feel that this manifestation in this most public of places was going to be a little inconvenient to deal with. I looked in exasperation at William but, although still glued to my side like a limpet, he was clearly in a world of his own, muttering occasionally, "Zounds, my Hamlet! A masterpiece!" or words to that effect. At any rate, he didn't have any concern for my predicament and I couldn't help feeling a bit cross that I had been landed with the inconvenience of an invisible genius. Why me, for heaven's sake?

"I have to go now," I said coldly, disengaging myself from him.

"Don't let me stop you, love."

It was the sell-by-date woman who thought I was talking to her.

"I just want the bargain scampi. It's behind you." She had worked her way up the aisle vacuuming up all the cheap food and had reached the fish course.

"Oh sorry, we'll move." I shoved William quite violently and he sprawled on the floor, a heap of brown velvet and leather.

"Okay." She didn't bat either of her heavily made up eyes as William groped arthritically to his feet and attached himself once more to my arm. I had a foggy, spinning sensation in my head that I didn't like and I felt a bit sick.

"I have to go now," I said again, firmly, to William. He ignored me but the woman glanced up from her forage for cheap crustaceans and said in surprise.

"Oo's stoppin' yer?"

"He is," I said in frustration, fighting a sudden rising panic.

"Oo?"

"Him!" I pointed. I had managed to shake him from my arm only for him to attach himself further down to my leg. It was like one of those hideous nightmares when you are trying to get away from something that just won't let go.

"Oh", she said looking exactly where I pointed and then back at me. "'Im. Look love if you 'ed over to the checkout someone will give you an 'and. You tell 'em that 'e's botherin' you. They'll sort 'im out."

"Will they?" She was reaching around behind me. I think she thought I had designs on the scampi and was determined to wrest it from me if it came to a fight.

"'Course love, they don't put up with no nonsense. You just go and explain it all to them."

She nudged me firmly out of her way and grasped two packets of frozen prawns.

"Oooo! Ninety-nine pence and 60% extra. That'll do. Go on love, go and 'ave a word with them."

Guarding her precious haul, she pointed towards the check-out.

"Do you see him?" I asked curiously.

"Course I do, love. Large as life." She moved closer and whispered confidentially. "I used to 'ave a man following me around too but the pills got rid of 'im. That's what you need if he's bein' a bother, some 'appy pills."

"Oh no!" I exclaimed. "It's not like that at all. He really is there."

She patted my arm, kindly. "Course 'e is love. Do you mind, I just need to reach the turkey dinosaurs? Go and see them at the checkout, they'll call security."

"Perhaps that would be best."

William was regarding the woman's very short skirt and purple legs with great perplexity and was about to move in for a closer look dragging me with him. I stepped back sharply. He, concentrating on the strangely hued legs, was caught off guard, loosened his grip and I grasped my opportunity and headed for the checkout with speed. When I got there and glanced back he was nowhere to be seen. I felt sick and the foggy feeling would not go away. I grasped the stainless-steel counter and tried to steady myself.

"Help with your packing?" The checkout girl asked perkily.

"Yes," I said and she looked at me aghast. Clearly, no one had ever said yes to her before. She gaped hopelessly.

"Never mind, I'll manage."

William was nowhere to be seen and my shopping items found their way past the electronic beeper thing and into my Eco-friendly bags.

"Have you been doing anything nice today?"

"I've been at work."

"Oh…Are you doing anything nice this afternoon?"

"I thought I would invade Poland."

"Mmm…What?"

"No, I'm not doing anything nice, I'm here."

"Ohhh," she breathed, still smiling but uncertain. "Loyalty card?"

I handed it over.

"Cash or card?"

"Card."

"Cash back?"

"No, thanks."

"How many bags?"

"Two."

"Schools vouchers?"

"Yes."

"Trolley Miles?"

"What?"

"Trolley miles."

I was none the wiser but she widened her Hollywood-white smile and was happy to elucidate.

"Look, you have a counter on your trolley see, and we count up all the miles you have walked in the store and give you vouchers to spend on the train or on coach tickets. If you come here enough, you could even fly to Spain. I'm saving to go to Bognor Regis in the summer."

"Oh, how nice." I looked around suspiciously but she gazed back at me with innocent eyes and no one else nearby appeared to be fazed by this odd innovation. For a moment even William's inexplicable presence in a Leicestershire supermarket was no more bizarre than the strange and wonderful machinations of the present day commercial world.

"So…trolley miles?"

I squinted at the counter on my trolley. It said 0000.2.

"Ooo, you won't get far on that." She was still perky but then she didn't look much more than sixteen so life wouldn't have caught up with her yet.

"Tell you what lady," she leaned towards me confidentially. "Next time, just walk around the store a few times before you start to shop. It's what I do. Her, over there," she indicated a chubby woman with a red face, steaming past with an empty trolley, "she's been around seven times already."

"Oh, I'll remember to do that," I said politely, whilst thinking that I'd rather have my eyes poked out with coat hangers than spend any more time than absolutely necessary in any supermarket.

"Don't forget your complimentary Gourmet Periwinkles," she concluded with another perky smile.

I smiled grimly wishing I had been able to resist the AMAZING VEG MACERATOR that the demonstrator had convinced me would solve all my kitchen related problems and instantly, with no discernible effort on my part, create healthy meals that all my family would devour and which would thus render us all clear skinned, slender and able to run marathons with the minimum of training. I also wondered as I grasped the packet of mysterious gourmet periwinkles what the hell they were. I had grave suspicions. I headed for the sliding doors, casting a glance back at the freezer aisle on my way out. It was peopled by the usual pale mums and even paler old people. But no William.

Back in my car I rested my head on the steering wheel and tried to get myself together but the foggy feeling was worse and I began to think that I was going down with bird flu or Ebola or whatever was the latest pandemic. I only intended to close my eyes for a few moments but I must have fallen asleep.

It was more than an hour later that I suddenly jerked awake and, when I had cleared the sleep from my brain, I found that I did feel better. The fogginess in my head had dissipated. The spring sun was low in the sky and I realised that I was going to be late getting home. It also became clear to me that I probably should talk to someone about William and Elizabeth. What had seemed impossible before was now, with new found clarity, the sensible thing to do. The woman in the supermarket had claimed to see William after all, so maybe I was not entirely alone with this thing. I thrust aside the unpleasant thought that she had just said what she knew I wanted to hear in order to safeguard her cut-price scampi.

I would not tell Grace though. I would not burden her and Hubby was just too down to earth. Maybe Alex…

I let in the clutch and moved off feeling much better about everything. In fact, I felt quite jolly and hummed a tune as I trundled along in my little old car. The song I was humming started off as 'I Should Be So Lucky' by Kylie Minogue but somehow turned into 'Greensleeves' along the way. It's amazing how easily Kylie's lyrics fit to 'Greensleeves'. I was just trying to reverse it and sing the words of 'Greensleeves' to the tune of 'I Should Be So Lucky' when I hit the wall.

Well, I hit the wall about two seconds after Elizabeth and William, finding themselves in the back seat of a vehicle moving without the aid of horses, shrieked in unison. Of course, I turned to look at them and that is when I hit the wall. Quite fast too.

CHAPTER FOUR

Out of the jaws of death.
Twelfth Night, Act III Sc iv

I spent that night in hospital. A precaution, they said, in case I was concussed. It seemed likely as I remember involuntarily embracing the airbag with some force. Hubby turned up at casualty looking anxious and very untidy. Not that he was the neatest of men at the best of times but he looked untidier than usual as he shambled in with tousled hair in need of a cut, ill-fitting trousers, dirty trainers and a vast comfortable blue T-shirt. He's a mechanical engineer and does something complicated and technical (at least it seems complicated to me) at a manufacturing plant. Bless him.

"As long as you are all right," he kept saying gruffly, "as long as you are all right." He was unusually jittery and not quite himself but it wasn't until much later that I realised it was because he had been frightened. As I hadn't been at all frightened myself it hadn't occurred to me that he would have been. Between Elizabeth and William and my intimate relations with the airbag there had been no time for fear and, through all the business of the firemen cutting me out and the paramedics being cheerful and comforting, all I had felt was exasperation with myself for being so stupid as to drive into a wall.

Hubby took the first opportunity he could find to go off into a huddle with the young doctor and got quite animated about something although I couldn't hear exactly what. I caught the word 'scan' several times but, from the young doctor's reaction, it seemed I wasn't going to get one no matter how much Hubby waved his arms or how far he chased him up the corridor.

I was then trundled into a room to have blood taken, give urine samples, have my eyes looked at and to be asked inane questions like what day of the week it was, where I lived and various family birthdates. I am not good with numbers so I didn't acquit myself too well with that last and, for some reason, I honestly could not remember the name of the current incumbent of No 10 Downing Street so I shrugged and said "Does it make any difference? They are all the same," and the young doctor immediately recognised that I was at least as sane as he was.

However, I was able to say with confidence that Queen Elizabeth was on the throne. Luckily they didn't ask which one.

I was moved about all over the place and eventually ended up on the Windsor Ward having passed through Balmoral, Buckingham, and Kensington on the way. You had to wonder what warped mind concluded that they were apt names for the soulless pastel rooms of suffering.

I was completely fed up by that time so I said I wanted to go home and decided to get out of bed. Hubby and a nice young porter tried in vain to persuade me that it would be best if I stayed the night but I was determined to escape until an indomitable nurse with a Caribbean accent and huge feet came in and talked to me like I was a naughty three-year-old. Being somewhat distracted by the astonishing size of her feet, I just didn't feel like arguing with her so I gave up and got painfully back into bed.

"Well, there you are," Hubby said vaguely. "At least you've been checked over and they think you are all right." He didn't sound convinced. "You'll feel better in the morning."

He kissed me on the top of my head, which I hate, so I gave

him a filthy look, rolled over in bed and sulked. I heard him sigh as he left.

I spent an uncomfortable night with a thumping head and sore ribs, anxiously wondering what I was going to say when asked to give an explanation of why I had driven into a wall and written off my car. The William and Elizabeth thing just wouldn't wash. Despite my decision to tell someone about these strange visitations it was blindingly clear that, yet again, this was not the time to do it.

Having finally fallen into a deep, unrestful sleep I was immediately awoken by the usual inexplicable bangs and crashes of a hospital ward greeting the day and dragged reluctantly out of oblivion and back into the world. I forced something masquerading as scrambled eggs down my throat so that they would let me go home (or be arrested) later. Then I twiddled my thumbs and worried for a good couple of hours until two policemen appeared at the end of the ward.

The officers bearing down on me in their Day-Glo jackets and stab proof vests did not strike me as being particularly empathetic so I opted for Plan A and decided to say I didn't remember anything that had happened. Retrograde amnesia I think it is called. It is often used as a plot device by the more uninspired script writers of television programmes and is if they are to be believed, difficult to disprove. I thought I could fake the symptoms if need be. They asked me what had happened, notebooks at the ready. I looked as blank as I could and told them that I hadn't a clue. I had just been driving along and that was as much as I could remember. They exchanged glances and I thought, right here it comes, they are going to read me my rights and arrest me for dangerous driving, or without due care and attention, or the abduction of historical characters, or something. I'd never been arrested before and there was a part of me that found the predicament I was in quite interesting but just then Hubby turned up with a big smile and a hideous bunch of green and purple blooms which he thrust at me.

"Oh, lovely", I thought as I looked down at them cradled in my bruised arms, "co-ordinating flora."

"All right, love?" he beamed.

"She doesn't remember anything," the biggest policeman said closing his notebook and, I was convinced, reaching for the handcuffs. In the event, he just scratched his right buttock ruminatively.

"That doesn't matter, though, does it?" said my innocent husband. "You know what happened anyway."

"Do they?" I asked, sitting up in agitation and then, remembering that I was supposed to have amnesia, I fell back on my pillow and tried to look weak and confused. I think I was convincing.

"Yes, love, don't worry. No one was hurt so no harm done. Oh, except for you, of course, and the car. No thanks to those two idiots I have to say."

For a mad moment, I thought he was talking about the police officers and the breath went right out of my body.

"They don't think," the big policeman said scratching his head. "They just don't think and then we have to pick up the pieces."

Despite his hirsute burliness, he had a surprisingly high voice that tended to trail off into an unpleasant whine. I couldn't help but surmise that in the police force he had found a profession that, in reinforcing his superiority to large sections of the population (at least in his own estimation), suited him admirably.

"You think you've seen it all…." He shook his head mournfully and rubbed his nose. "Well, we can make out the report. You will need to put your insurers in touch with us or they won't believe it. No need to bother you anymore."

He then scratched his elbow vigorously, briefly revisited

his left buttock and ran his fingers across his shaven head with an air of intense weariness. He was all for a quick getaway, possibly to alleviate another less accessible itch, but his partner lingered. He was very young, good looking and his voice was smooth and mellow with a hint of a Durham accent.

"It was quite a comedy of errors, wasn't it? You don't remember seeing those two crazy bastards at all then?" he asked with winning charm. I hesitated. He seemed to know all about it and his brown eyes were kind.

"Maybe, for a moment," I admitted, pleadingly.

"It must have given you quite a shock to see them appear out of the blue like that." He laughed and comfortingly patted my hand.

"Yes, it did." I smiled back at him and Hubby, not to be outdone, patted my other hand.

"Well, it's difficult to know how to charge them but they did cause a serious accident so…"

"Oh, we can't charge them!" I exclaimed. "I mean, it was just an accident and it would be impossible to…well, to…"

"Don't you worry. We'll be in touch if we need to be. It was a close call but all's well that ends well," the young policeman said with a wink. I smiled more widely.

"Much ado about nothing," I agreed archly, but he turned away, joined his burly friend and I realised that I had imagined a connection that was not there.

"Much ado about nothing!" exclaimed my husband incredulously. "You could have been killed, I hope you know. And the car is totalled." A note of resentment that I couldn't really blame him for crept in on that last statement.

"Sorry." I was penitent. I liked my little red car and driving into a wall is bound to make you feel a bit stupid.

"You couldn't really have done anything else, though, I suppose."

"No," I agreed cautiously. Then curiosity got the better of me. "So what did happen?"

"You don't remember? But you told the police…"

"I don't remember. What did they say happened?"

"There was a promotional event in the field next to the road and a couple of tandem radishes overshot the drop point and parachuted in front of you. You swerved and hit the wall. Idiots. Not you. The radishes."

"Oh, I see. Well, that explains it I suppose." I felt a sudden spiralling disappointment. The moment of revelation was not now. The rest of the world remained sane and innocent of my secret. I sighed inwardly and gazed at my unknowing husband as his words sank in.

Innocent maybe, sane however was questionable.

"Hold on a moment. Did you just say 'tandem radishes'?"

"It was International Radish Day yesterday, or so I was told, and they are trying to promote them in Leicestershire as we grow particularly fine radishes. Apparently. The event organisers gave me a leaflet and offered us unlimited radishes when in season, by way of an apology."

"Ah."

"I accepted, of course. I like a good radish."

"Oh," I said blankly. Radishes aside it was quite a mundane explanation compared to my version of events.

"Was there anyone in the car with me?"

"No, who should have been in the car with you?"

"Well," I looked at him, my husband of twenty years, his honest grey eyes, gentle mouth and comfortable paunch…and decided that now was not the time. "I'm still a little confused. The kids are ok?"

"The kids?" He patted my hand again and looked serious. "Fine, fine. Grace was here a moment ago. She was very worried of course. At least I think she was, it's difficult to tell what she is thinking these days."

He was right of course. Grace when she reappeared, looked embarrassed and awkward as if I had driven into a wall on purpose to make her look stupid. Alex did not come to the hospital with her but then I hadn't expected him to. He was a young man now and led an independent life, drifting in and out of ours when the mood took him. I understood that of course. We kept a room for him at home but he needed to find his own way in the world. He and I still had a special bond but somehow a separation had developed between him and Grace and Hubby. Families are like that sometimes I suppose. He would come to see me later. We would laugh together at the episode and everything would be all right. I might even tell him about William and Elizabeth. If anyone would understand I had a feeling that he would.

Eventually, I was released and taken home. Initially, I quite enjoyed all the attention. They sent a bunch of flowers from work and told me to look after myself and not come back until I was completely well. "Until you are completely well" was written in a slightly different coloured ink and looked suspiciously as if it had been added later. There could have been a number of reasons for that of course but I thought I detected the dastardly hand of Blofeld in the first part of the message. It would be like him, and like the much kinder women in the office to cover for him. But it didn't worry me too much. I was cosseted at home for about two hours and then Hubby couldn't find his mobile phone and Grace stood on a drawing pin which put me back in charge. I rang his mobile phone number and when 'Rocking All Over the World' echoed from the pocket of a pair of jeans that he had put in the tumble dryer there was that little mystery solved. Grace had been bringing me a cup of tea when she stood on the drawing pin so, whilst she wasn't much hurt, it did take ages to get the tea stains off the ceiling.

She had however felt it necessary to take the day off school to get over the shock. Hubby told me that her teachers had been very understanding and had enthusiastically offered counselling, but a day off school was apparently all the comfort she seemed to need. She dyed her hair red and gave herself a manicure. Alex gave me a warm hug and a grin and disappeared into his room as he usually did so I was fairly confident that my offspring had suffered no lasting trauma by the near-tragic loss of their mother.

The tandem radishes came over, looking sheepish, to say thank you to me for saving their lives by driving into a wall but, as that hadn't been my intention, I ended up looking sheepish too and it was a very uncomfortable half hour. My quick thinking and heroic sacrifice were going to be the lead story in our local weekly newspaper but I got bumped off the front page by the news that a local councillor had claimed her breast enlargement as a deductible expense and so, thankfully, I was spared the ignominy.

After three days of putting shoes away and chasing dust, I was bored and only a little sore in places. Grace went back to school and Alex had drifted away. Even a row with Blofeld at the office began to appeal. Elizabeth and William did not reappear and I concluded that the car accident had frightened them back into whatever dimension they had come from. All things considered, I was not too unhappy about this. Their last appearance had resulted in a fair amount of inconvenience. At least to me. I suppose the tandem radishes had reason to be grateful although they did not know it.

After a few days more I went back to work and time slipped by much as before. Hubby said that even though insurance would cover the replacement of my old rust bucket perhaps it would be better if I caught the bus or walked for a while. We argued about it of course and, even though he agreed with me that driving into the wall was obviously the right thing to do under the circumstances, he still didn't want me behind the wheel of a car just yet. And that was the end of that. I sulked for a while but then I got quite used to the bus and at least I didn't have to worry about things dropping out of the sky in front of me. Or into the back seat behind me.

CHAPTER FIVE

An honest tale speeds best, being plainly told.
King Richard III, Act III Sc iv

I met Nell on the bus. She was always on the same route as me because she worked as a cleaner in my office building. She was a little round dumpy woman somewhere between sixty and compulsory retirement. She had short grey matted hair, an enormous hooked nose, and bright blue eyes. A questionable aroma hung around her and I never saw her wearing anything other than grey leggings, a huge black T-shirt and a dusky violet wool cardigan. Which probably explained the aroma. Somehow, though, she was an attractive, comfortable character and I warmed towards her. For weeks we had just nodded at each other, either as our eyes met on the bus or as we passed on our way into or out of the soulless cavern of our workplace. We eventually progressed to a half smile and a "Hiya" but one evening, as I was on my way home on the Number 127, I looked up to find her blue eyes fixed fiercely on me.

I smiled hello but her eyes met mine with no warm response and shifted deliberately to a point over my left shoulder. I thought that was quite rude so I turned back to the window. It was a filthy day. Grey rain lashed the windows and the dull evening light struggled to make any impression on the sodden atmosphere. The bus lurched and trundled and the old man in front of me coughed loosely. I could still feel Nell's sharp eyes fixed on me. She was on one of the seats set sideways at the front of the bus so I looked towards her again and she met my gaze steadily without acknowledgement before letting her eyes slide deliberately past me once again. I grumpily turned back to the window and watched the passing traffic, mottled through the streaming glass. I was staring for quite a few moments before I became aware of two pale frightened faces reflected beyond my own. Of course, I swung around. There they both were, seated directly behind me, both with their thin fingers clasped on the rail at the back of my seat, both staring panic-stricken at me.

"Oh, bugger!" I gasped. A couple of old women threw me questioning looks. I couldn't blame them. William's be-feathered hat alone was flamboyant enough to evoke scandalised glances.

"What are you doing here?" I hissed, outraged. I had made up my mind to view their previous manifestations as a passing aberration and I was quite disgruntled to find them thrusting themselves back into my life. They had written off my car and hospitalised me with their last visit after all.

"What strange beast is this that holds us within its bowels and bone-shakes and rumbles thus?" William squealed, holding on for dear life. "Lord warrant us! Woman, why hast thou transported us to this hell hole?" His thin face was pale and drops of perspiration stood on his balding forehead as his eyes darted desperately around in search of escape or comfort. Elizabeth looked as if rigor mortis had set in.

"Why have I brought you here?" I sputtered back. "I don't want you here. Go back to where you came from. You are not anything to do with me. Go away."

I turned my back on them childishly but immediately felt guilty. If you put yourself in their seventeenth-century shoes, their terror was entirely understandable. The Number 127 bus into town had cowed more heroic souls than they in its time. Nonetheless, I hunched down in my seat sulkily and refused to meet Nell's eyes. It had not been a good day. I couldn't quite put my finger on why but I felt particularly dreary and directionless and it seemed to me that something wasn't quite right at home. Again I couldn't quite work out what was wrong but, and this might sound a bit paranoid, it seemed to me that Hubby and Grace were…well, watching me. They were trying to be subtle about it but they weren't much good at subtle. Alex wasn't in on their conspiracy of course. In fact, he was increasingly distant, even to me, and we rarely saw him. It was a nagging worry and I determined to tackle him on his withdrawal. Perhaps Grace and Hubby were just feeling a little over protective because of the car accident, although, as I had pointed out to them, the chance of a radish parachuting down on you more than once in a lifetime was fairly slim.

The bus chuntered on its rain-soaked route and people got on and got off. A large woman, in a rain coat that smelt of wet dog, embarked and wheezed herself onto the seat beside me. Elizabeth, who had been prodding me in the back and hissing curses, chose that moment to grasp my shoulder with one hand and insist on my attention with a sharp slap across the back of my head. I yelped and turned furiously on her. The rain-coated woman jerked sideways away from me and, having a rather ample backside, overbalanced and landed in a heap on the chewing gum bespattered aisle.

"What did you do that for?" I screeched at a stony-faced Elizabeth, whilst reaching apologetically to help the felled woman. "How dare you! You don't have the right to hit me."

"I am your sovereign Queen," she said rising regally to her full but not impressive height.

At that moment the bus drew up jerkily in front of the Post Office and she was thrown forward and I was thrown back and the rain coated woman who was just struggling to her feet was thrown down again.

Everyone else in the bus studiously ignored the chaos. An

elderly man with heavy-rimmed glasses gazed at the ceiling as if it were showing a particularly riveting episode of EastEnders and a portly woman rummaged in her capacious handbag for nothing in particular. A young man with red spiky hair and red spiky skin was probably the sole passenger who was honestly unaware of anything out of the ordinary. He was listening to his iPod with all the intensity of lonely youth. Only the two women sitting opposite Nell acknowledged the pandemonium by clasping their handbags tighter on their round stomachs, rolling their eyes and saying 'disgusting' in concert. The unfortunate woman at my feet floundered, fearfully rejecting my flustered attempts to help.

William reached for Elizabeth, possibly with the intention of assisting her but more likely, judging from his terrified air, of attaching himself in a comforting bear hug to the only thing that bore any semblance of normality to him. His hands on her bodice provoked exactly the sort of reaction I was coming to expect from Elizabeth. She boxed him soundly about the ears and when I, for some instinctive reason, began to protest she turned on me. As I flinched from the first blow, which stung surprisingly coming from such a frail hand, I felt other hands tugging at my waist.

"Come on love, time to get off. We can walk the rest of the way."

"But..."

Nell stepped over the legs of the poor damp woman on the floor and manhandled me towards the front of the bus.

"No buts love, come on, off here. Don't keep the man waiting."

I was shoved towards the door and when I glanced back Elizabeth and William were following meekly. I stumbled off, automatically muttering thank you to the driver even though he was shouting at me in wildly expressive Gujarati. William, desperate to escape the monstrous maws of the beast, cannoned into Elizabeth in his haste and so received another slap for his impertinence as she alighted tentatively onto the puddled pavement. He clambered down miserably shivering in the bleak drizzle beneath his increasingly floppy hat. You could see that he wanted to flee but that now the relatively familiar Number 127 offered a safer haven than the bright lights and strange noises of a twenty-first-century town on a rainy night.

Nell gave me a bright smile from beneath her hooked nose and thanked the driver politely. He, mollified by the removal of the dangerous mad woman (me) from his domain, growled exotically as he levered the doors closed. The bus startled us all by emitting a particularly loud roar as it jolted forward, occasioning William and Elizabeth to stagger backward and watch with dread awe as it grumbled away with a row of disapproving faces frowning down through streaming windows.

Nell raised her enormous golfing umbrella serenely. William, having lost all hope of any protection from his sovereign, chose the next best thing and immediately clamped himself to her side while Elizabeth merely gazed at the puddles beneath her feet as if appalled at their temerity.

I looked helplessly at the shabby cleaning woman.

"What am I to do?" I asked miserably. "They won't leave me alone."

"S'all right, love," she said comfortingly. "They can't do you any harm, can they?"

"They made me crash my car!" I retorted petulantly.

"Did they really, bloody ell? Still, seeing as they are here… Are you expected at home?"

"Always."

"Ow about a cuppa? Let's get out of the rain and fink fings frough." I'm not sure where she came from. London, I think. Or maybe Essex. Anyway, I don't think she had ever pronounced a th in her life. They all came out as f's. H's occasionally made an appearance but usually in the wrong place. "Nofink is so bad that it can't be made better with a cup of tea and a natter. Yer mascara's running, love."

Nell started off at her usual brisk waddle, seemingly unaware of William clinging to her side, and I followed, too drained to be anything other than obedient. Elizabeth still stood by the bus stop, staring for all she was worth at anything that moved; the flickering streetlights, the neon shop fronts, the passing headlights beaming into the murk of grey rain, an occasional person passing by hunched against the weather. She viewed all with her stony stare.

"Are you coming?" I asked because I felt I should.

She inclined her head as if to agree but moved not a muscle.

"Come on then," I urged. William and Nell were waiting. She looked at me and then at the streaming pavement and then at me again. I raised an eyebrow.

"If you think I am going to throw my coat over the puddles, you can bloody well think again."

I stomped off after William and Nell who were now headed for one of the most repellent fast food restaurants in the street. There was lots of choice, it has to be said. Nell pushed the glass door open and gestured cheerily for me to follow. William looked daunted but appeared to have developed an attachment to Nell's vulgar charm. He slipped in with her. I threw a quick glance back at Elizabeth who, now standing under a streetlight with her jewels exploding into glittering life, was gazing with awed interest at the bright rays cascading down. I abandoned her to the rain and her astonishment and let the stark neon welcome of the steamy shop embrace me.

The usual sparse suspects populated the tables, predominantly bedraggled youths and their studded girlfriends in leggings that were stretched at the seams to breaking point. An enormous man and his equally enormous wife were devouring portions of lard-laden food. A middle-aged woman with careworn eyes and her sweet-faced disabled son were eating chips and ice cream at the same time.

"Tea love?" Nell bellowed. I nodded. "Are you payin'." It was phrased like a question but said like a statement. I didn't mind anyway.

"Four teas," I said to the glowering young man behind the counter, "with lots of sugar."

Elizabeth was at my elbow again, inquisitively peering over the melamine counter and sniffing the unfamiliar odours of boiling fat and curry sauce.

"Somefink to eat?" Nell was looking longingly at the chips so I ordered four portions and it was all piled up onto a tray. Elizabeth and William trooped after Nell into a corner booth and I followed, searching for a reaction from someone, anyone, to my gorgeously dressed companions. There was none.

Looking around me, though, I began to think that maybe that wasn't too surprising. One of the lads sipping a chocolate milkshake had a mop of shocking pink hair, some of which stood erect to a height of several inches and some of which didn't and his ears had been stretched to accommodate what looked like a couple of Royal Dalton side plates. His girlfriend's clothes, what there were of them, appeared to have been in violent conflict with mud and a pair of scissors and one of the companions was showing a vast expanse of grey-clad bum above his or her waistband and sporting a spiked dog collar and panda eyes. Even the woman with the disabled son was gaily clad in flowing garments that harked back to an indeterminate era somewhere in the region of yesteryear, whilst the large couple had evidently spent a vast amount of money and exercised their powers of imagination, if not of taste, at tattoo parlours regularly over the years. If William and Elizabeth looked odd to me, it was nothing to how modern day humanity must look to them.

"There you are, love." Nell handed around four cardboard cups of something that passed for tea. She slid into the seat opposite to Elizabeth. William followed her in like a puppy dog. I stared at him whilst Elizabeth, next to me, stared at Nell. Nell just sipped her tea with relish.

"That's better," she said smacking her lips. I found myself automatically tearing sugar packets open and pouring them liberally into William and Elizabeth's tea. Nell watched fascinated.

"They like it sweet then?" I nodded. William sniffed his suspiciously and then drank. I added more sugar and he gradually warmed to the taste.

"So," said Nell looking at Elizabeth and then William. "What's the story wiv them then?"

"I don't know," I shrugged. "I opened my pantry door and there she was. Then the next time she was in my bathroom and William was with her, in the bath." Nell looked aghast.

"William was in the bath. Elizabeth was on the toilet. I mean…it wasn't quite how it sounds. Anyway, they have been popping up every now and again ever since. It's getting embarrassing."

"I can see 'ow it would be." Her amused look irritated me.

"Do you see them?" I asked abruptly but without hope. "Please tell me that you see them and that I am not going mad…"

Elizabeth and William both stopped slurping their sugar laden tea and looked enquiringly at her.

"I see what you see love," she patted my hand and shrugged. "I've always bin a bit psychic."

"You see Queen Elizabeth the First of England and William Shakespeare, the Bard of Stratford on Avon, sitting here with us in a fast food restaurant in the year 2016?"

I was deliberately scathing but she didn't bat an eyelid.

"It's a puzzle," she admitted comfortably.

"Thou art rank-scented," said Elizabeth to Nell, her lip curling, and her meaning all too clear. "And thou art marvellous ill-favoured."

"Got a mouth on her, ain't she," Nell responded without much enmity.

I looked at her joyfully. I was no longer alone. My joy was short-lived, however.

"Thou art impertinent, thou art traitorous," snapped Elizabeth. I could see her working up to a sharp slap aimed at the imperturbable cleaning lady. William could see it coming too and shrank away.

Nell didn't flinch, but then she wasn't the sort to cower.

"Take it easy," I pleaded. "Elizabeth, this is not your England, at least not in the way you remember it. A lot has changed in four hundred years. People can say what they think. In fact, it is encouraged, and you are not allowed to slap people whenever they annoy you."

"Oh yeah! I'd like to see the old bat try," chortled Nell, much amused.

"I'll send thee to darkness!" Elizabeth responded with unnerving venom.

"Don't even think abart 'avin' a go at me darlin'." The cleaning woman waved a chip threateningly in her direction. "It won't do you no good."

Elizabeth gave Nell a look that was several degrees below freezing and turned to me. Apparently, I was the lesser of two evils.

"Why hast thou summoned me here yet again? I am Queen and thee and thy devilry and thy devil companions will have no part of me. Begone."

"I haven't summoned you, honestly I haven't. You just appear, usually in the most inconvenient of places. I'm not sure...." I hesitated and looked around me at the world engrossed in its own business and unaware and uncaring of mine. "I'm not sure whether anyone else sees you. Except for Nell." I turned back to her in relief. "Thank God that you see them too. I would think I was going off my trolley otherwise."

William had recovered some of his equilibrium and was tugging my sleeve gingerly.

"Lady, what year of our Lord is this?"

"2016."

"2016! Jesu Maria." He moved his hand in the sign of the cross and started to mutter in Latin but caught Elizabeth's cold eye on him and ceased abruptly with a look of terror in his eyes.

"I wouldn't worry about being Catholic if I were you," I said. "She's not exactly low church herself. I've seen her on her knees crossing herself and praying in Latin."

Elizabeth greeted my rather tart comment with a vicious sideways glance that promised vengeance, if not in this life then in the next.

"Tis a strange and wondrous place," poor William whimpered helplessly, inching towards Nell again for comfort.

"It's still England though. Some things haven't changed," I said, and then couldn't think of any.

William raised his eyes appealingly to mine. "Tis not the world I owe, in this, my many friends lie full low, graved in the hollow ground and I am shipwrecked in a strange-disposed time."

"What?" said Nell.

I put my hand across the table and patted William's small hand, the hand that had penned so many immortal works.

"I keep forgetting how traumatic this must be for them," I mused. "Much worse for them than for me. 'We are such stuff as dreams are made on…'"

"Give over, you're beginning to talk like 'em now," Nell snorted in response.

"Who now reigns in my stead? Sits a king on the English throne?" Elizabeth, it could be said, was supremely self-absorbed and had taken little interest in the previous exchange.

"A queen," I answered. "Your namesake, Elizabeth. The second, of course."

There was a long pause during which Elizabeth considered, William cowered, I held my breath and Nell chewed chips noisily.

"Named for me, tis well done. Hath she issue?" The question came sharply as if pain itself spoke the words.

"Yes," I answered. "Four."

"A male child? An heir?" Even Nell recognised that this cut our Elizabeth to the quick. I nodded but decided not to rub salt into the wound by enumerating.

"I will see her," Elizabeth said graciously and rose, ready to go right then.

"That's not possible," I gasped. Elizabeth viewed me with heavy disdain.

"Nay, but I tell you it is."

"But, she lives in London, if she's not somewhere else in the world which is very likely. And London is miles away, and even if I could get you there she wouldn't just see anyone."

"Dost thou deny me? I am not anyone," she thundered. William nearly disappeared under the table and even Nell looked nonplussed.

"Look, please just sit down for a moment," I begged. "Please."

Elizabeth remained standing and had a look in her eye that threatened immediate and bloody execution.

"Oh sit down, woman," cut in Nell with a command in her voice born of irritation. "You are in our world now. Like it or not. There's fings in this world that you don't understand nor know nothink abaht. There's trains and 'planes and televisions, mobile phones, dishwashers and…" She cast around for something else that would impress. "Them things that exfoliate yer feet. It's the dead skin that causes the smell yer know, so they're quite 'andy. An' talkin' of 'andy, I picked up one of them AMAZING VEG MACERATORS at Shelforpe Tesco. They came wiv free periwinkles – wot are disgusting by the way. You should get one, though. It ain't no good for veg of course but I use it to pare me 'usbands toenails. You 'ave to 'old it right o'course 'cos the blades is quite sharp. But, 'e's diabetic so chances are 'e would 'ave lost them toes anyway."

After this enlightening speech Nell chewed a chip ruminatively whilst Elizabeth, William and myself, in various open-mouthed stages of awe, attempted to make sense of Nell's world.

"Well, wot I'm tryin' to say," Nell continued when she had efficiently disposed of two more chips. "Is that there's lots of fings in this world that will come as a surprise to you Medieval types."

"Tudor."

"What?"

"They're Tudor, not Medieval."

"Yeah, whatever. But my point is that they didn't 'ave things like musical cake slicers or foot massagers."

"There is also democracy and free speech," I suggested hurriedly in a bid to steer Nell away from the purely materialistic aspects of modern life and to distract us all from the unbidden contemplation of her husband's feet. Now presumably toeless.

"Yeah, we're all…what's the word?"

"Emancipated," I suggested again.

"Yeah… Are we? Well, I was going to say digital. Do you know, there's a woman down our street wiv a digital device that flushes 'er loo from the kitchen. Marvellous things they come up wiv, marvellous."

"Stop talking," said Elizabeth at this point. "The eye-offending crow speaks in riddles. You," she pointed at me. "Tell out these marvels of your age."

Thus ordered my mind immediately went blank and I could think no further than the AMAZING VEG MACERATOR, which, Nell was quite right in saying, was totally useless on any kind of vegetable but did mince chicken quite effectively.

"We've been to the moon and back," I stuttered eventually, having caught a glimpse of it gleaming whitely behind the large plastic hamburger stuck to the shop window.

Elizabeth was not impressed but William slowly reappeared from under the table. "Speak thou true words? Thou hast been to the shining moon?"

"No, not us," I interjected quickly.

"She didn't go personally, you prat," Nell chortled. "Astronauts went in the 60's. And there's some Englishman orbitin' up there at the moment, in't there?"

"Why tis fantastical!" William, fear forgotten, was fascinated. "If thou speakest not false then this time is wondrous indeed."

"Tush, tis all tilly-villy, nought but moonshine on the water, and there's an end to it," spat Elizabeth, joining the ranks of the conspiracy theorists with all the arrogance of Tudor majesty.

"Oh, they can believe what they want. We're getting' away from the point." Nell turned back to Elizabeth. "The point is you'd be lost in our world wivout 'er. If you're goin' to keep poppin' up you're goin' to 'ave to accept 'er as a guide. You know, someone to show you around and hexplain things, like a teacher. And you will 'ave to listen to what she says and do what she tells you to do. Uverwise…"

"Otherwise what?" I asked with interest.

"Well, I dunno, do I?" said Nell. "I'm doing me best in a difficult set of circumstances." She sipped her tea glumly.

"Must is not a word to be used to Princes. Howmsoever there is some frame of sense in the base crone's words," Elizabeth said and sat down.

"'Ere watch it," Nell growled. "I 'ave my limits. You ain't no oil painting yourself, duck."

"Much has changed. This I understand." Elizabeth had decided to be gracious so we all relaxed slightly.

William took his chance and piped up with enthusiasm.

"Thou hast said my renown as a writer is great in this world, is it not?"

"I saw a Shakespeare play once," mused Nell. "It was shit."

"Nell!" I protested as William fell back against the plastic backed booth and visibly deflated. "That's just your opinion. Most people believe him to be a very great writer, probably the best ever."

"Nah, Barbara Cartland was the greatest writer ever," she returned with complete confidence. "No one else comes close."

"Well, that's, um… You're certainly entitled to your point of view," I replied weakly.

"Tell me all," cut in Elizabeth impatiently. "Speak true, tell the years. I wish to know the history of these after-times."

"That's four hundred years-worth of history," I protested, without much hope of escape.

"I desire to know who came after me and the birth-right of my kinswoman."

"I don't think she is related to you at all really. Or at least not directly." I looked to Nell for help but she just shrugged. Her disinterest was all encompassing, but Elizabeth demanded an answer so I took the plunge. Most of my knowledge about the kings and queens of England had come from 'A Child's History of England' by Charles Dickens and he didn't like any of them.

"Ok, James took over from you…"

"The whoreson!" exploded Elizabeth with tired venom. "Twas to be expected but I would have given much for a different solution. The Scottish whore triumphed after all."

"Not really." I felt for her. Not much touched her soul but her virginal childlessness was a permanent grief. "The Queen of Scots did not go down in history as well as you did. Her son did better although he had his critics. They said 'Elizabeth was King and now James is Queen,' only they said it in Latin."

Elizabeth chortled, delighting in the terse comparison.

"You seem to know a lot about it," said Nell, accusingly.

She apparently regarded anything remotely intellectual as a personal affront.

"I've been reading," I admitted, guiltily. "I looked up a few things after, well I mean, I needed to know."

"As do I," Elizabeth interjected. "Thus the false Scotch urchin took the throne. Did it go well for him?"

"Not bad, although the Catholics did try to blow parliament up with him in it. They called it the Gunpowder Plot."

"Oh, yeah!' exclaimed Nell gratified to recognise an historical event. "Bonfire Night. Last year me 'usband set off one of them big rockets but the milk bottle fell over and it burned down neighbours shed where 'e kept 'is pet iguana."

Elizabeth cackled in delight at the thought of her kinsman so nearly being blown to smithereens by his loving subjects. She wasn't interested in the exploding shed and the unfortunate incineration of the reptile. In the interests of accuracy, I felt that I should try to redress the balance somewhat as regarded James's legacy.

"James did achieve the union of England and Scotland and gave us the King James Bible and managed to keep the Protestants and the Catholics from killing each other. Well, that is to say not killing each other in huge numbers, although he really only emulated you in that."

Elizabeth nodded magnanimously. "Tis well. Our cousin of Scotland is nobly born and I would have no rascals' son but a king. So, the boy did well, for a whore's son. And thereafter?"

"Then it was his son, Charles the First. He didn't do quite so well."

I felt a bit awkward at this point. I had a feeling that she wouldn't react all that well to Charles's fate. I was right.

"Foul murder!" she screamed leaping to her feet in quite impressive fury. "Thou liest, 'tis an outrage 'gainst all that is sacred. An anointed king most foully murdered."

It was a very Shakespearian outburst.

"T'would not be the first time. Richard the second after all…" William hazarded and had his nose pinched cruelly for his temerity.

"The divine right of kings is god given."

Elizabeth dismissed him with a final twist of his poor nose and he shrank closer to Nell who had happily appropriated his chips and was dipping them in blood-red tomato sauce.

"Proceed, girl. After this most foul and evil assassination, what then?"

"Assassination," mused William rubbing his reddened nose. "'Tis a goodly word. Doth it remain in use for these times?"

"Overused, I would say," I said, handing him a serviette for his nose. "There have been a lot of bloody assassinations over the years. In some countries, it is the national pastime."

"Hah!" trumpeted William, thumping the table with joy. "I have achieved immortality through the lips of men."

"What the hell is the little twerp on about now?" groaned Nell.

"Assassination is one of the words that is supposed to have been invented by Shakespeare," I explained, quite surprised at my own knowledge.

"Well, bugger me backwards," she said, with sarcastic crudity.

"Twerp?" enquired Shakespeare.

Elizabeth impatiently rapped the plastic table with an ostentatiously large ruby.

"Who then was king?"

"We didn't have a king. We had Oliver Cromwell. He was a soldier and a Puritan and was related in some way to the Thomas Cromwell that your father…um…knocked off. He took over after the Civil War. I think they offered him the crown but he refused it."

"Knocked off," mused Shakespeare, quietly.

"A base-born knave offered the crown of England! Is this

woman who now sits on the throne a commoner born of usurpers?"

Elizabeth was appalled at the way things were going so I hurried on with my potted history.

"No, not really. She's pretty much German, mainly. They put Charles' son back on the throne eventually. It seems that the English couldn't do without the monarchy when it really came down to it."

Elizabeth relaxed and her thin lips twisted with momentary satisfaction.

"Thereafter?"

"After Charles II it was James, Charles' brother but he tried to reinstate Catholicism so he didn't last long. His daughter Mary and her Dutch husband threw him out and took over and then Anne, his other daughter. After that, we had four Georges. They were all German, all pretty unpleasant and at least one was completely mad, the others marginally less so. Then we had William who had loads of illegitimate kids but was succeeded by Queen Victoria. She was quite popular, at least as far as Royals go, also married a German and ruled even longer than you did. Then we had a couple more Edwards and a couple more Georges and then this Elizabeth who looks like she'll be on the throne longer than any of you."

"Who is her consort?" It was a predictable question from Elizabeth.

"Phillip. He's Greek."

"Greek!" Elizabeth was appalled once more. "Is he crowned King?"

"No, but he is royal. I think."

"Indeed," she sniffed and ruminated for a moment. "'Tis naught so bad. None who sat on the throne of England were French or," she shuddered, "Spanish. What are these Germans that you speak of?"

"Ah, well, you've got me there. I don't know that a united

Germany existed in your day exactly. I think it was part of the Holy Roman Empire and the Hapsburgs ruled most of it."

"Prussians," Elizabeth muttered, evaluating the information and deciding whether to be outraged by it or not.

"I ain't got no truck with the bloody krauts. Tell 'er about 'itler," said Nell, who had not been interested so far. "Tell 'er about that why don't you? Tell 'er!"

Nell had worked herself into quite a passion and it was quite sweet to see William patting her arm and looking anxiously up at her.

"Bloody Nazis," Nell continued in no mood to be gainsaid. "Evil murdering bastards. I'd give them the final solution, I would."

"Are you Jewish, Nell?" I asked.

"Only on me father's side so I don't fink that counts. I only ever met me father twice. Me mother only met 'im once. I'm fairly sure I'm an agnostic."

"Thou art the bastard of a Jew?" Elizabeth looked down her nose at Nell and even William stopped patting her arm and looked disconcerted.

"And if I am, so what?" she challenged. "There's loads of us in England now. That Oliver Cromwell let us back in after Edward I chucked us all out. And come to that," she added slyly. "You 'ad a Jewish doctor for years. Till you 'anged him."

This William could not take without protest. "He plotted to poison her majesty, the dog had to die!"

"'E were innocent, it were all trumped up!"

"You seem to know a lot about it all of a sudden, Nell? How on earth do you know all that?"

"Oh, I know more than you think." She patted her nose and winked at me.

The world around me shivered and seemed on the point of splintering but the moment passed leaving just a fleeting confusion.

Elizabeth considered.

"Nought, 'tis nothing to our purpose. It seems that much has changed with the passing of the years."

"Yes, yes it has." I was troubled, though. "We are more tolerant, it is true. At least we are supposed to be but…"

"But the hearts of men are ever weak and religion still divides." Of course, she understood without explanation, none better. Elizabeth had herself been Queen of a nation divided and under threat.

"What of parliament? Doth it give proper respect and obedience to your queen? Does it levy taxes as required by the monarch?"

"Hah!" Nell hooted. "No, love. We vote for our government. The monarchy don't 'ave nofink to do with politics no more. Everyone over eighteen 'as a vote and we 'as a choice of which party will get the h'opportunity to make a complete balls up of running the country for four years. Conservative or Labour, it don't make no difference."

"Don't forget the Liberals and the Green Party," I put in, worried that Nell's derisive views were giving a rather negative view of our great democracy. Unfortunately, mentioning the Liberals did not help much.

"Oh yeah, them. And the Monster Raving Loony Party and UKIP 'oo want England for the English. Now, if you ask me, wot needs to be done…"

Nell was all set to expound her foreign and fiscal policies for our edification but Elizabeth interrupted. "England for the English? Whom else should it be for? Who hath challenged the sovereignty of my kingdom?"

"Oh no, lord luv you," said Nell with confidence. "We're wot they call a multicultural society now. Look around you."

We all obediently looked around us. The staff behind the counter consisted of two, one of Asian descent and one African, and one of the youths making rude noises with his milkshake was definitely from points east. I pointed out hurriedly that they were all entirely British and then had to explain about Great Britain, the commonwealth, immigration and the EU, none of which, to my shame, I knew anything about. Alex was the activist in our family and my skimpy knowledge, such as it was, came from him. In common with most British families I suspect, we were only political insofar as policies or events affected us directly, and we trundled through daily life in cosy ignorance of the sufferings and triumphs of the wider world. Alex was different, he knew stuff and could argue his liberal views with passion. I longed for him to be there.

"Moors and Monguls," exclaimed Shakespeare, and I remember thinking that perhaps I should try and explain political correctness to him when I got an opportunity but I need not have worried. His next words proved that he had too big a soul for bigotry. "Tis a… brave new world."

"That has such wonders in it," I finished for him. He looked at me as if I were mad.

"You see," said Nell wisely. "There ain't been no invasion, exactly. They all came 'cos they wanted to."

"Or because we wanted them to," I added in the interests of accuracy.

"Lord knows why, the weather's crap here. It's the flying wot 'as made the big difference, and the internet. If you want to fly around the world you can, if you can afford it. And if you can't you can still reach any part of the world by surfin' on the World Wide Web and then there's blackberries, and News 24 and apps and iPhones and I dunno what else."

"I understand not," Elizabeth pondered. "What is your status? Dost thou attend court? Hast thou land, servants, power?"

Nell snorted. "No, we bleedin' ain't."

"I thought not," Elizabeth sniffed. "And yet thou sayest as if the world was thine to do with what you will."

Nell looked sceptical.

"She's right, Nell," I said. "The world is open to us, I mean us ordinary people, in a way that it wasn't to her subjects. We know so much about the rest of the world now that it does belong to us, in a way."

"Knowing don't put food on the table, though, does it?"

The minimum-waged cleaning lady from Loughborough was not convinced that she held sway in any part of her world and perhaps she was right. Freedom has always been a personal concept and life has many ways of taking it from you.

William had followed all of this with interest but, as Elizabeth leaned back in her seat to digest all that she had learnt, he ventured to broach the one thing that intrigued him above all others.

"Thou fliest and hath been to the moon."

William was looking at us, Nell and me, as if we were goddesses. It felt quite good to bask in the reflected glory of the Wright brothers and NASA.

It didn't last long. One of the hooded youths, the one showing the greatest expanse of underpants above his jeans, lolloped over and lounged across the back of the booth behind William.

"Wotsafukingoingonwiyousinnit?" he said.

We all looked blankly at him.

"Sorry?" I ventured politely.

"Nowothefukyouslikeinnitfukintalkinglikeyousfukincrazee innit – like."

"Oh," I said, none the wiser.

"What tongue speakest he?" William whispered whilst attempting to dive under Nell's arm.

"It is English," I hissed back, smiling and nodding at the young man in an attempt to placate him in case he had a knife.

"But I understand it not." William's muffled voice came from Nell's armpit.

"I don't think they would understand you either."

"Fukyousafreakingfukfreaklikeinnit." I smiled and nodded harder. The young man flicked his wrist contemptuously in my direction and lolloped off swinging his shoulders in sync with his acrylic-clad buttocks as his adolescent followers smirked in uncertain triumph at his cool.

I sneaked a look at Elizabeth expecting her to be ready to order the immediate execution of the impertinent peasant but her eyes were fixed on the young man's bottom with a softer expression than I had hitherto seen from her.

"Ah love 'em. The yoof of today, the 'ope of the nation," said Nell. With sarcasm, I think. "Well, I dunno about you but I'd better get 'ome."

"Your husband will be missing you, I suppose?" I probed, curiously.

"Nah, not he. He's got the telly and the bottle, but I don't want to be out after eight o'clock."

"It's not that bad in this area Nell!"

"Oh no, love, it don't make no never mind to me, it's just that the restraining order takes all the fun out of late night walks."

"You are joking," I said hopefully.

"Oh, don't worry, it was all a put-up job. Even the judge said I was provoked and that if she'adn't put my cat in the wheelie bin I wouldn't 'ave 'ad no cause to dump the slurry on 'er prize petunias. But it does curtail me social life sumfink awful."

I wasn't quite sure what she was telling me but, truth to be told, I didn't want her to leave me alone with William and Elizabeth. Oddly enough she was my connection with reality. Albeit a somewhat surreal reality.

"We'll walk some of the way with you."

As we passed the young disabled man smiled at us with gentle eyes and offered me a chip dipped in ice cream. In marked contrast one of the remaining youths sardonically raised his paper cup of cola and spat "Fukinfreak" as we passed. Elizabeth gave him a hefty wallop across the back of the head, which was a great deal less than he deserved, and he lurched forwards and slopped the entire contents of his cup over the expansive cleavage of one of his girlfriends. It appeared that Royal Displeasure, if nothing else, could make the leap into this world when required. We beat a hasty retreat as the aggrieved young woman viciously attacked her erstwhile lover with a plastic fork and the young man behind the counter reached for the panic alarm.

CHAPTER SIX

*All the world's a stage,
and all the men and women merely players.
They have their exits and their entrances;
And one man in his time plays many parts.
As You Like It, Act II Sc vii*

It had stopped raining and the streets were wet and shining. Nell put up her brolly and trotted off with William under her arm. Elizabeth strode regally by my side. Stopping at the corner, a stream of traffic splashed by and both William and Elizabeth, who had decided to stay close and only to be frightened if Nell or I started screaming, watched in fascinated wonder.

"How ist they roll up hill without horses?"

William, in his thirst for an explanation, tore himself away from the comfort that was Nell and threw himself onto the floor, careless of mud and water, to look underneath as the cars swished by. I think he expected to see running legs underneath.

"Engines," I said. "They are mechanical, like windmills or waterwheels. It's sort of the same principal only these are powered by petrol."

"Pet – rol?" Shakespeare picked himself up.

"It's fuel, and it works like a combustion engine. There's a spark from the spark plug and petrol which is a flammable liquid and it creates a sort of power which turns the wheels and..."

"Tis magic," stated Elizabeth.

"No, it's science." I retorted stubbornly.

As I seemed to have found myself in the position of teacher to two of the greatest minds of the seventeenth century I felt it behooved me to make some sort of effort to enlighten them. My spectacular ignorance, however, was proving to be a bit of a hindrance.

"You see there is ignition, just a spark which starts the engine and, I'm not sure why the whole thing doesn't blow up but it turns cogs and stuff and that turns the wheels."

"And the lights? Are they fire?"

"No, they are electricity. Electricity is…." They were waiting expectantly for my explanation. Even Nell looked interested.

"Well, electricity is when…"

I realised that, despite (or perhaps because of) fifteen years of state-funded education, I had no idea what electricity was.

"Well, it's to do with… It is a sort of magic I suppose." I gave in. "Scientific magic. We don't have witches or sorcerers now. We have scientists instead. They work in laboratories and create all this and then we buy it."

I'm not sure that either Elizabeth or William were entirely convinced by my explanation but Nell certainly was. She nodded emphatically as if I had just given her the answer she had always been searching for.

"That's about it," she said comfortably as a cyclist swished past spattering me with mud but leaving the three of them unsullied. "I'm leaving you here. See you at work, love. And I'll see you," she disengaged herself again from William and nodded curtly at Elizabeth, "whenever."

She waddled off at a surprisingly brisk pace and within seconds had disappeared into the gloom of a misty street. William gazed after her disconsolately. I too watched with regret as my one ally in this strange circumstance left me.

"Come on," I said, wearily. "My husband and my kids will be wondering where the hell I am."

I started off past the old church but hadn't gone more than a few yards when I glanced back to find that Elizabeth had stopped in front of a notice board and was inspecting it curiously.

"I have to get on," I called, impatiently.

William was beside her, bedraggled and disinterested. I realised that I didn't have to wait for them. They had their own bizarre mode of transport and would no doubt find their own way back to me. Or not, and that wouldn't be altogether a bad thing. Nonetheless, as I put a few yards between us, I began to worry that they might get into some sort of terrible trouble if I was not there to protect them, but, thinking of Hubby and the kids, I steeled myself against at least one source of guilt and continued doggedly homewards. I had just turned the corner when I heard running footsteps and a rasping wheeze. I turned to find William haring wildly towards me as fast as his spindly little wool-clad legs would carry him. He was out of breath and even more dishevelled than I had yet seen him. He halted in front of me, grasped my arm and then doubled up with a prolonged racking cough. Eyes watering and face suffused with a sickly hue he tugged at my arm and speechlessly pulled me back towards Elizabeth. Seriously alarmed I lurched into a sprint back the way I had come dragging a gasping William with me. She had not moved. I slowed as I approached and looked enquiringly at William.

An elderly man and a woman skittered past us and, throwing me intensely suspicious looks, scuttled into the church hall a few steps away.

"What on earth is wrong?" I asked exasperated. William, still struggling for breath, pointed at the posters on the noticeboard. I scanned the jumble of soggy papers anxiously. The vicar must have been particularly active amongst his parishioners in that he was offering sexual support and bingo on a Tuesday and inspirational singing and "How to find God on the Internet" on Thursdays. The 'Genital Stretch and Tone' classes on

Wednesdays with Thelma caused me some fleeting concern, though. Let us hope that her physical prowess was greater than her ability to spell correctly.

Then my eyes lit on what was obviously the source of William's excitement. A poster, damp and curled at the corners, exhorted us to pay six pounds fifty to see an amateur performance of Hamlet by William Shakespeare. There was an arty photograph of a slightly overweight young man, wearing a voluminous shirt and gazing soulfully at something out of focus that might have been a skull. Or a pineapple. William's eyes were fixed mutely on me, his emotions barely suppressed, as he waited for confirmation.

"I told you that you were famous. There's nothing unusual about this. Your plays are being performed all over the country, hundreds every night. Thousands across the world, probably."

William clasped his chest, fell to his knees and rolled his eyes up to the heavens gurgling ecstatically. Elizabeth, impatient and probably envious, gave him a sharp wallop across the back of his head and, as a result, his spare figure measured its length across the filthy pavement. Two elderly women hurried past as fast as the Zimmer frame of one of them would allow. I smiled apologetically as I hauled William to his feet but, not surprisingly, they didn't respond likewise.

"So," said Elizabeth taking a few ruminative steps away from us. "This man's works," she indicated William dismissively, "are still performed in playhouses across my realm. It redounds to my credit that I granted thee patronage." She had a remarkable capacity for making everything about her.

William had pulled from his doublet a huge square of rough material and was sobbing uncontrollably into it. I patted his shoulder but Elizabeth, to call an effective halt to a scene in which she was not the main protagonist, snatched the handkerchief from him, wiped his nose and face and stuffed it back into the opening of his jacket.

"We will see it." She folded her hands decisively across her pearled bodice.

"Oh no," I protested. "It probably isn't on tonight," I added hopefully.

Of course, it was. We had five minutes before curtain up and a few (a very few) people were drifting in looking more resigned than expectant.

"They might have sold out," I said, but I knew this was definitely a vain hope.

"I have to get home," I whined as a last resort.

Elizabeth and William were already at the door.

"Leave them," I told myself as they disappeared through the wide wooden doors. "They'll be okay."

I even took a few steps homeward, but of course, I went back. If I am honest it probably wasn't solely concern for them that made me follow. It was curiosity and, more than that, a fascination to experience what they experienced when they looked at my world. I also felt a tug of dismay that poor William's first experience in four hundred years of a performance of his precious work was to be a local amateur production in a midlands town whose only claim to fame in the theatrical world had been to spawn someone who once appeared as a postman on Emmerdale Farm. I had a feeling that William's ecstasy at finding himself and his works to be eternal might well be short-lived when faced with parochial enthusiasts in ill-fitting tights mangling his iambic pentameter.

On entering with trepidation, I found myself in a village hall like any other. Rows of plastic seats were facing a small stage with dilapidated curtains of an indeterminate shade of greenish. Approximately ten grey heads dotted the auditorium, generally in the places where the poor dears thought they would be least conspicuous, except of course for Elizabeth and William who had parked themselves right in the middle. William could barely contain himself but Elizabeth's back was as rigid as ever.

I fell over the feet of a gelatinous young man who was seated across three chairs just inside the entrance. He was enormously corpulent and looked as if he might well be a permanent fixture. He didn't move, probably couldn't, so I hauled myself back onto my feet as he barked, "Six pound fifty." I paid the fee reluctantly and he took a further £1 off me for a raffle ticket that I didn't want. I refused to pay the £4.50 demanded for a programme and thus made an enemy for life of the rapacious Cerberus. I then inched my way along the empty rows until I could fall into the seat next to William. He grasped my arm and turned to me.

"I understand not. These drapes, what do they hide?"

"I hate to think," I grumbled. "Look, you need to understand, this isn't really a theatre, it's a village hall with a very small stage and this isn't a professional production. They are just ordinary people who like to pretend to be actors. I don't think you are going to enjoy this very much and I'll be very much surprised if you recognise any of it as the Hamlet you wrote."

"Hush," snapped Elizabeth. "Tis a theatre of sorts and I wish to be entertained."

"You've come to the wrong place then," I retorted meanly, as I clasped my arms grumpily and settled down for a tortuous evening.

A discarded programme from a previous performance was on the floor beside me. It was decorated with the imprint of a dusty shoe. I moved surreptitiously to pick it up. The minutes ticked by and nothing happened except for the occasional billowing of the stage curtains and a sharply truncated snore from an elderly man who would clearly rather have been in the pub and, when prodded by his embarrassed companion, said as much in a loud voice.

William peered anxiously at the rumpled programme with furrowed brow.

"Canst thou read it?" he asked. "Mine eyes grow dim with the years."

Elizabeth stared steadfastly ahead.

"Hamlet, by William Shakespeare," I obligingly ran my fingers over the letters as I read them.

"Oohoo," burbled the renowned writer expressively, if not articulately. One of the elderly ladies twisted in her seat and gave us a disapproving look as I continued to read aloud.

"Is proudly presented by the Quorndon and Regions Amateur Players directed by Aiden C. Clegg. The cast and crew take great pleasure in offering this, their first foray into the works of the world's greatest playwright."

"Oooohooo!" squealed William, beside himself with glee. I couldn't really blame him. It must have been quite a thrill to find yourself so venerated 400 years after your death.

"After our last immensely successful production of 'What? No Knickers, Vicar!' our director, Aiden C. Clegg, felt that the company was ready to tackle a more challenging piece and Hamlet was chosen. Aiden C. Clegg, who once played 'JoJo Tomato' in a popular television game show and the postman in Emmerdale Farm (two episodes, three lines, and a crowd scene), has wanted to direct this Shakespearian masterpiece for many years, indeed since he played the character of Hamlet himself (to critical acclaim) in Stoke Poges."

"Jo Jo tomato?" interrupted Shakespeare.

"Difficult to explain. Think Dogberry, but without the self-knowledge, nowhere near as amusing and dressed as a Tomato."

I felt momentary sympathy for the sad life of a struggling actor in our throwaway world, and then, noticing that the self-aggrandising Mr. Clegg had included a romantically posed photo of himself alongside the information that he could shortly be viewed as the subject of a reality T.V. programme highlighting intimate bodily dysfunction, my empathy evaporated. I sighed. I am not so naïve as to think that Elizabethan England was graced with more refinement than our own but I could not help thinking that the land that produced Shakespeare should be less desperate to show its bottom (not a metaphor), at every available opportunity for what, surely, could only be the most vacuous of reasons. After that deeply philosophical thought I wearily continued reading.

"Our talented costumier, Dorothy Unwin, threw herself into the task of creating Elizabethan costumes. She had great fun with the codpieces she tells us." I sighed again. "It's humour, William, we don't wear codpieces anymore. Oh, goody, looks like there is going to be a swordfight." I said this with heavy sarcasm. In the last and only production of Hamlet that I had ever seen (a school production) they ditched the swordfights and all shot each other.

The audience, to a man, would far rather they had shot us.

I reluctantly continued reading. "We must not neglect to give our grateful thanks to John Plant who, as many of you will know, is proprietor of Plant Funeral Home ('You Know When You've Been Planted')".

I glanced around at my fellow audience members and thought cynically that, if the aged group wasn't already acquainted with the jolly Mr. Plant, he of the questionable judgement when it came to advertising slogans, they would be fairly soon. "And who has been kind enough to create the impressive weaponry you will see tonight. Also to Doreen and Juanita for providing refreshments." There was much more of the same but I précised mercilessly. "We of the Q.R.A.P. hope that you will enjoy our interpretation of Hamlet, the greatest play penned by the Bard of Stratford on Avon, DIRECTED BY AIDEN C. CLEGG."

"Bard of Stratford on Avon. Who'er be he?" Elizabeth barked.

"That's William," I said turning to him. "They call you that, and sometimes they call you the Swan of Avon as well."

"Wherefore?" asked Elizabeth.

"No idea," I admitted. "I could try looking it up later."

"How wouldst thou look up it?"

"I'd look it up in a book, only we don't use books so much now. I'd Google it."

"Thou wouldst google it?" Elizabeth said this with a raised eyebrow and heavy scepticism.

"Google is a search engine that operates on the World Wide Web which is a bit like a massive library that you can access on a laptop or tablet."

This, not surprisingly, met with quizzical looks from both so I then had to explain the concept of a personal computer. William seized upon the words he understood and worked the rest out for himself.

"Tablet? This tablet is like to a whole library in a table book?"

"Yes, pretty much. You can find out just about anything you need to know on the internet. We can look up the swan thing later."

William however, had his own store of knowledge.

"Mayhap, 'tis because the souls of poets pass after death into the bodies of swans," he mused. "'Tis the Pythagorean notion. Knowst thou the legend of Cycnus?"

I shook my head, although I could not shake a sudden overwhelming reluctance to hear more. William, unaware and with the spark of romance in his dark eyes, continued.

"Cycnus, a boy of much beauty, drowned for love of a friend. His father, the mighty god Apollo changed his shape into a swan and he swims eternally on the lake of his mother's tears. 'Tis a pretty tale."

I shuddered and involuntarily shrank from my little friend. Being an empathetic soul he recognised my revulsion and was immediately concerned.

"The story is not to your liking. It seems thy heart is sorely charged."

"Marry, go to," scoffed the jealous Queen. "More tilly-villy. Enough of swans and gods. How doth they name me?" Elizabeth was not about to let the adulation go all Williams' way.

"Good Queen Bess," I suggested, carelessly. She eyed me with her usual distaste.

"And what more?"

"The Virgin Queen. Gloriana." A smile played briefly at the side of her mouth but it was fleeting.

"Tis not new. Many called me that. Why should he be named a swan? Hath he a swanlike visage, think you?"

I looked at William who gazed anxiously back at me from an ordinary face. He was undeniably balding and, what hair there was, was long and lank and none too clean. His features were nondescript and only his brown eyes were expressive and exceptional. I turned back to Elizabeth, garish by comparison. Neither was remotely swan-like but, in the Cygnus stakes, William was still way out in front.

Luckily I was spared further interrogation by the unheralded appearance on stage of a stocky little man, dapper in a white suit, with a startlingly full head of black hair and one of those little bits of beard in the middle of his chin that is neither use nor ornament. One assumes that it is designed to make some sort of statement about the wearer's character or style. As perhaps it does. At any rate, the little man, bearing a resemblance to the gentleman in the programme who was about to reveal to the viewing public what should probably have remained hidden, 'hemmed' a couple of times as if to attract our attention. Or perhaps to awaken the pub-going snorer two rows in front of us who had once again subsided into peaceful oblivion. When satisfied that we were all transfixed by his presence he began to speak in a breathy drawl that, despite its studied theatricality, couldn't hide the fact that he hailed from Dorset.

"Good evening, ladies and gentlemen. I am Aiden C. Clegg, director. How are you all tonight?"

There was a dreadful pause. He clearly expected a response from us.

"I said, how are you all tonight?" The unease within the

room grew to immense proportions and we all shrank visibly further down into our seats. Eventually, there were one or two indistinct murmurs which the young man greeted as if it were a standing ovation.

"Thank you, thank you. Now I, as director of the play you are to see tonight…." There was another long pause which was eventually brought to a close by a slow hand clap from the back of the hall. It was Cerberus, of course. We all obediently joined in, more to move things along than for any warmth or enthusiasm for what was to come, and managed to produce a reasonable smatter which once again was greeted as if it were thunderous applause.

"Thank you. Thank you. Now I know what you are thinking." He didn't. If he had he wouldn't have been smiling. "Why Shakespeare? What does he mean to us? Is he still relevant?" He gave us a knowing little smile and nodded. "Well, let me say a few words on that subject."

He turned away.

Then he turned back.

"OOOOOOH FOR A MUUUUUSE OF FIRRRRRRRRRRRRRE," he roared, sending William under his seat and the previously sleeping gentleman scrabbling for his asthma inhaler. The rest of us held on to our seats and gazed in shock, which he interpreted as awe. Enjoying himself immensely he ranted on to the end of the speech and then collapsed into an extravagant bow. We all felt a bit sorry for him so we clapped perfunctorily and hoped that he would go away soon.

"Thank you, too kind." Was there an emotional tear in his eye? I think so. "Well, before you enjoy our little offering tonight, directed by me, Aiden C. Clegg, there are one or two housekeeping notices you need to be aware of. The fire exits are to your left and right. If it should become necessary to evacuate, then please move directly to the nearest exit. Kyle there at Front of House," he indicated Cerberus who was blocking one of the said fire exits and looked likely to be more of a hazard than a help. "And of course myself, will be on hand to assist."

Somehow I was not reassured. I suspected that the real reason Kyle/Cerberus was stationed at the door was to keep the audience from escaping back to the world of sanity.

"Please make sure that your mobile phones are all switched off." He then launched into a story about how his friend, Christopher, had left his phone on at the Royal Opera House and had deeply upset a soprano. He seemed to find it all quite funny so I decided not to turn mine off and to leave what might happen to chance. "Please don't take any photographs and the filming of our production is strictly prohibited."

I glanced around at the somnolent audience of the elderly and the misguided and thought to myself that, on present showing, no one in their right minds would want to relive this performance in any way shape or form so he was pretty safe on that score.

"Ah and if any of you feel a bit iffy…" Dear reader, I could not help groaning aloud at that point. "I am a fully trained and qualified first aider so please let our front of house team know and we will look after you." The thought of being ministered to by either the unctuous director or the greasy man mountain at the door made me determined to remain conscious for the rest of the evening no matter what horrors awaited us.

"Ladies and gentlemen, Hamlet by William Shakespeare, directed by me, Aiden C. Clegg."

With what was intended to be a self-deprecating flourish he was swallowed up by the green curtains, sudden darkness fell and a fanfare blared. The timing was good and it would have been impressive except that I was fairly certain that it was a bugle not a trumpet and would have been more apposite for the Alamo than for a parapet in Elsinore. Sadly, this synergy of sound and light was short-lived and the curtains jerked open onto a very small wooden stage decorated with something that closely resembled a cake I had once made for Grace's fifth birthday. That had been pink with machicolations and fairy tale towers too. A couple of over large, heavily be-cloaked figures were hunched in front of it and eventually, once the lighting man had got over the surprise of the play starting, the lights snapped on and everything was flooded in a very threatening shade of red.

William audibly "ooed" beside me and even Elizabeth's firm jaw dropped a little. Bearing in mind that they had never seen stage lights before I decided to open my mind a little and try to see this production as they did. Once Elizabeth and William had grown accustomed to the varied, and frankly random, rainbow of colour that played across the actor's faces, painting them red, blue, green and sallow yellow, they started taking note of the actors themselves. William leaned forward on the seat before him with chin cupped in his hands and gazed fixedly. I doubt he missed a single detail. Elizabeth remained as rigid as ever viewing all through narrowed eyes. I abandoned all critical impulses and tried to immerse myself in my least favourite Shakespearean play. With the dispiriting knowledge that Hamlet was, if uncut, one of the longest evenings of entertainment a playwright had ever felt confident enough in his abilities to inflict on a poor theatregoer, I hunkered down for a tedious evening. And in that expectation, I was somewhat disappointed.

Aiden C. Clegg had taken a pretty hefty pair of scissors to William's masterpiece. Either that or the actors had judiciously forgotten vast tracts of what they should have remembered, which seems more likely. Either way the piece, whilst still too long, and missing some key passages, escaped being agonisingly tedious and was occasionally, inadvertently, entertaining. The actors themselves were an eclectic group. I recognised a couple of female teachers from the local school under unlikely facial hair and a particularly pompous Conservative councillor was playing a particularly pompous Polonius. If you hadn't known that he was that pompous in his everyday life you might have been fooled into thinking it was a fine performance for an amateur. Ophelia was young, a little dumpy and hampered by the most stupendous arrangement of orthodontic braces I have ever seen outside of a James Bond movie. This caused her to spray spittle rather spectacularly every time she spoke, but that she managed any sort of diction at all was to her credit. Gertrude was definitely old enough to know better and Hamlet, well, Hamlet wasn't actually bad at all. He had a good, strong, very Welsh voice and delivered all his lines with conviction and his mad scenes with a touch of pathos. Regrettably, Dorothy Unwin, the esteemed costumier had seen fit to encase the slightly podgy young man in a pair of scarlet, woollen tights and, whilst he appeared at the beginning of each scene quite tidy, with a full complement of manly, scarlet-clad leg on display, the tights would work themselves inexorably floor-wards during the scene until the reinforced crotch was down by his knees and more than a glimpse of grey, well-washed underpants were visible between the waistband and his jacket. It destroyed the illusion rather and made him waddle. But they all soldiered manfully on. The women playing male roles were particularly manful I thought and my respect for William's skills as a playwright soared. The writing was so good that even false beards, hopeless miscasting and manic, misdirected enthusiasm could not entirely destroy its power.

We were staggering thankfully towards the interval when a large community policeman, complete with stab jacket and buzzing radio, suddenly appeared from the wings as Ophelia was throwing plastic daffodils across the stage.

"If the owner of a light blue Vauxhall Visa parked on double yellow lines is present could he or she remove it immediately as it could cause a serious obstruction to emergency vehicles." He gave us all an admonishing glare, rocked once on his heels and exited with aplomb into the rickety wardrobe that was doing service as Gertrude's bedroom. Aiden C. Clegg gave a silent shriek and hurled himself towards the stage mouthing obscenities at the cupboard.

The actors paused momentarily and Ophelia was definitely a little taken aback. Gertrude did look very surprised but that was probably the Botox. Once the policeman had been helped out of the cupboard and ushered into the wings, Ophelia recovered, threw a daffodil or two into the audience and then, with a metallic flash of teeth, descended irretrievably into madness. Mr. Clegg, still wheezing vicious oaths at the plebeian policeman, surreptitiously opened the fire door and slipped noiselessly into the night. To move his Vauxhall Visa no doubt.

Ophelia meanwhile tripped off into the wings still strewing flora as she went. Glamorous Gertrude and the dastardly king, a little grey man with beetling black brows, glowered through the rest of the scene and the interval was indicated by the curtains jerking to a close and the sudden jolly clatter of cups and saucers erupting on a trolley through the door by the ladies' lavatory. Two immensely cheerful women grinned at us through the steam and everyone in the hall perked up enough to create a small stampede, I amongst the first. The women called us all 'me duck', served up darkly strong cups of tea, issued a tray and copious amounts of sugar and demanded £2 with comfortable warmth. I returned to my seat cheered and with circulation restored.

William hadn't moved a muscle. His chin cupped in his hands he stared at the closed curtains as rapt as before. I think he was in shock. Elizabeth, despite her corsets, had managed to slump in her seat but she perked up at the sight of tea and awkwardly inched herself upright again. I perched the tray on one of the many vacant seats and ladled in the sugar whilst glancing in concern at William.

"What do you think of it so far?" I asked with some trepidation. He turned slowly and looked at me. His brown eyes were thoughtful.

"'Tis the same, yet differing. Is't possible that the world should so much differ, and we alive that lived? My Hamlet lives in yet another time and still I know not the answer…"

"The boy is addlepated," snapped Elizabeth, dismissing Hamlet, one of Shakespeare's greatest characters, much as I was inclined to do myself. "The answer is to live."

"There is women on the stage." William, deciding to distract Elizabeth, shook his head in wonderment, sipped his tea and said nothing more.

"Impudent and ill-seeming to our sex. Tis the French way." His sovereign snorted in disgust. I think her bodice was playing her up.

"What do you think of it?" I asked her.

"The apparel is strange but their speech simple and I well understand what they say. I do not understand thy base utterances."

"I shalt attemptest to speakest as thou speakest," I mocked with heavy sarcasm.

"Tis better," she replied with a grudging nod.

"Are you all right, love?" The lady with the Zimmer frame interrupted. She had stopped by in her long trek back from the toilet.

"I'm fine thanks."

"You are welcome to come and sit with us. You look very lonely here all on your own."

I stared back at her in surprise. I was not alone. She was discomfited by my reaction and, already unsteady on her feet, staggered slightly.

"Oh no, I'm fine," I muttered, blushing scarlet and trying to force my features back into a normal expression. "Thank you for asking, though."

"All right, my dear. My grand-daughter is in it. That's the only reason I'm here." She apparently felt obligated to explain but I had already assumed that everyone's reasons for attending must be something of the sort. She rocked off, glancing back once or twice. When she eventually regained her seat she whispered something to her aged companion who glanced back at me with distrust in her watery blue eyes and, pulling her overbalanced friend into her seat, admonished her to ignore us. Or ignore me I suppose.

I leaned back and breathed deeply. Then I stole a glance at my companions. William was still wrapped in reverie but Elizabeth's eyes were on me.

"They think I'm mad," I said. I was probably looking for reassurance from her. Reassurance that I wasn't mad I mean, although I probably was mad to expect it from her. "They think I am talking to myself."

"If thou art mad…" She gazed glassily at me and there was a long pause that was immensely disquieting.

"Though this be madness yet there is method in it," William finished for her without moving a muscle.

"What method?" I whispered irritably through my teeth. I decided that I had made enough of a fool of myself and from now on would be more circumspect, at least vocally, in my conversations with William and Elizabeth.

"What sayest thou?" she demanded.

"Never mind," I breathed, like a ventriloquist.

"What?" she bellowed. "Don't make mouths at me. Speak!"

"Never mind," I yelled. The lady with the Zimmer frame was startled into a nervous jump and the man mountain gave me a suspicious look and grunted. Aiden C. Clegg smiled and waved graciously. He seemed to think everything was a personal accolade and reacted accordingly. It must have been nice to be so self-deluded.

The companion of the Zimmer frame lady pulled her arthritic friend back to face front again and said in an admirably pitched stage whisper. "Don't get involved Vera. It's bad enough having to be here at all without you picking up hard luck cases. You can't help her and she might be …unpredictable."

That was it! I had had enough. I stood up, wilfully scattering polystyrene coffee cups, determined to make my escape, but at that same moment the lights dimmed. At least I think that is what the lighting man intended but, in effect, he plunged the hall into deep, velvety blackness and, with the exception of one emergency exit light reflecting strangely off a skull in the middle distance, we were all blind.

William 'oohed' again. Once my eyes adjusted, I could dimly distinguish the man mountain underneath the glowing exit sign. He was eating a sandwich. At the only other escape route, Aiden C. Clegg was leaning against the door with an expression of artistic concentration on his face. His white suit glowed ethereally. I sat down, defeated by both the darkness and the light.

A further hour and twenty minutes elapsed and in that time virtually everyone on stage died in agony. I watched but, being distracted by my own small drama, absorbed very little. I do know that Mr. Plant's hardware was used mercifully little and the swordplay that might have been very entertaining (and almost certainly lethal) had been judiciously replaced with a bit of dancing around brandishing flexible rubber daggers followed by some chillingly realistic death scenes. The most wooden of the actors turned in an energetic expiration and, such was the appetite for dying gruesomely on stage, that two or three of the bit part players also decided to die for no discernible reason.

Fortinbras and a motley crew of feminine, but heavily bearded ambassadors, picked their way over the bloodied thespians to pronounce their last lines. One misjudged and pierced the dead Hamlet's outstretched fingers with a kitten heel, but he heroically muffled his yelp and the incident might have passed unnoticed if the young lady had not apologised profusely and called for a plaster. This, and Kyle rumbling ponderously down the aisle with a first aid kit and defibrillator, rather destroyed the dramatic effect of Hortensio's declaration of 'carnal, bloody and unnatural acts'. The whole was rounded off by the amateur sound man's equivalent of a twenty-one-gun salute followed by a sudden choking flurry of smoke billowing into the audience that left us in no doubt that the stage manager had at last worked out how to use the smoke machine. At which point all those on stage forgot they were dead and stood up, emerging triumphant through the newly created smog. They grasped hands like the best of friends and basked in relief and self-congratulation.

I clapped loudly feeling obliged to make up for the arthritic patter that was all anyone else in the audience was capable of mustering. Unfortunately, this made me conspicuous and all eyes on stage immediately swivelled gratefully to me. Elizabeth stood and, as she must have done many times before, bestowed on the cast a stiff obeisance and a gracious wave of her jewelled fingers. William rose when she did but stared expressionlessly at the cast as they bowed before him.

I couldn't help it.

"Author!" I yelled. "Author!"

There was a moment of confused silence before everyone decided that I had obviously been educated at a failing comprehensive and the kindest thing would be to ignore me. William turned sad brown eyes on me and I felt wicked. Aiden C. Clegg leapt onto the stage and started kissing all and sundry and I knew it was time to make a run for it before he was inspired to make another speech and before I was compelled by my accursed good manners to listen to it. The house lights came up and I, careless of my two companions, made a dive for the door. Man-mountain was still there but I slickly dodged around a grey-haired fellow-escapee and, with a spry leap over the bloated legs of Cerberus, I gained the freedom of the real world.

CHAPTER SEVEN

Not stepping o'er the bounds of modesty.
Romeo and Juliet, Act IV Sc ii

I had had enough for one night. It was nearly eleven o'clock and I should have been home hours ago. I hurried down the road back towards the town where I knew there was a taxi rank and I did not look back. I fished in my handbag for my mobile phone – it was dead of course. I had never been very good at keeping it charged up. I began to be concerned that Hubby and the kids would be worried about me. The more I worried the faster I walked. I didn't look behind me but I knew William and Elizabeth were there.

I was hurtling past the cinema, still scrabbling in my bag to see if I had money to pay for a taxi when my arm was grasped and a surprised "Mum?" sounded in my ear.

"Mum, what are you doing here?"

It was Alex. I looked up at my tall, blonde, blue-eyed son in surprise.

"I'm, well, I'm going home. What are you doing here?"

"Going to the cinema," he laughed. "It's a late night showing. I'm here with friends." He inclined his shaggy head towards an alarmingly thin young man wearing stockings, suspenders and a miniscule skirt. He was accompanied by a short, voluptuous girl with two black eyes, torn fishnets, a huge expanse of cleavage and a white streak in her hair.

"Oh," I said, mum-like. "How nice."

I glanced around. We were in the midst of a very large group of misfits who were definitely all on drugs and were not the sort of people my son should be associating with.

He grinned at my dismay.

"It's the Rocky Horror Show Mum. Everyone dresses like the characters in the film."

"Oh," I said with undisguised relief. "Oh yes. Believe it or not, I went a couple of times myself when I was younger."

Looking at them in context I could see that they probably weren't perverts on drugs, or at least not all of them, and were just young people out for a good time.

"Why don't you come and see it? You ought to get out a bit more."

"Oh, no, your father won't know where I am."

"Don't worry. I'll text him."

"But you're with your friends. I don't want to cramp your style."

"You won't. Bring your friends. They are dressed for it. They will fit right in."

I looked around. William and Elizabeth were by my side again.

"My friends!" I stammered. "Alex!"

But Alex had turned away and in a moment was swallowed up in the excited crowd. I looked at Elizabeth, stunned. She returned my gaze steadily.

"That was my son," I said. There was a flicker for a moment of something I had not seen in her face before – uncertainty I think – and then she turned to William.

"Tis the woman's son. Her child."

William looked as if he didn't understand at all.

"He saw you and he said that you would fit right in here. Don't you see?" I exclaimed. "If Alex sees you…"

I stepped towards her. I wanted to hug her the relief was so great, but William put a gently restraining hand on my arm and Elizabeth turned away from me.

"Hah!" she exclaimed with intent. She had caught sight of a very young man in black plastic knickers and was moving towards him as if drawn magnetically. William dropped my arm and grasped hers. Risking untold wrath he did his best to pull her back. He didn't stand the ghost of a chance. She gained her objective and, after giving the unconscious young man a very close inspection from the tip of his pointed patent shoes to the top of his jet black mullet, she put out a bony finger and poked him deliberately on his right buttock. He turned sharply and looked right through her. Then, aggrieved and suspicious, he slowly rubbed his bum and turned back to his friends. William, with a heroic effort, pulled Elizabeth back to me.

I put my hand to my head. The fuzzy feeling was back again.

"Art thou unwell?" William's kind eyes were upon me and even Elizabeth looked as if I might be of some small interest to her.

"I am confused," I confessed. "I must speak to Alex. Did you see where he went?"

I looked around. The crowd of ghastly looking young people was ebbing and flowing but I could not distinguish my son from amongst them.

"He must have gone in. I have to speak to him." I pushed my way through and entered the foyer. I was assailed by noisy expectancy, heavy with the smell of popcorn and filter coffee. The young people surrounding me looked threatening but exuded good humour. I edged through the black-garbed throng trying not to get too close to the more outrageously dressed and searched desperately for my mop-headed son. Confusion and panic crept over me although I could not understand why.

"You all right, me duck?"

A busty woman of about my own age with very big blonde hair had taken the opportunity that the event offered to live out one of her more lurid fantasies publicly and was dressed in torn fishnet tights, spiked heels of immense height and a black leotard that culminated in what could only be described as a shelf onto which she had hoisted her not inconsiderable bosom.

"I'm looking for my son," I said helplessly and close to tears. The fuzzy feeling was overwhelming.

"E's probably gone in already. Have you got a ticket?"

"No." I looked around wildly as the ropes dropped and the crowd surged up the stairs towards the cinema doors.

"Look, don't worry, love. 'Ere take this. I ain't goin'in. I've been stood up." She handed me a ticket. "Should've seen it coming. Bastard."

She adjusted her shelf and flung back her hair. I wondered if perhaps her date had seen her coming and executed a quick getaway. Cruel to say but I would have understood if he had. Still, she was a kind woman. She chucked me on the chin in a surprisingly masculine manner, patted my shoulder and thrust the ticket into my hand.

"Go on take it, luv. E's probably inside. You'll find 'im." With another toss of her stiff yellow hair, she was swallowed up by the insistent crowd.

I handed over the ticket to a rather frightened looking young girl at the door and plunged into the semi-darkness of the cinema. I walked up and down the rows of seats looking right and left but with no luck. The crowd was now raucous and restless with expectancy.

"Sit down," someone yelled, possibly not at me, but I scurried obediently to the first seat I could find. I put my handbag on my knee and closed my eyes. I was bone tired and, for a moment in the darkness and the anonymity, peace descended and weariness fell away. The madness swirled around me as I sat there quietly in my ordinary coat and ordinary shoes, clutching my cheap ordinary handbag. The fuzzy feeling in my head slowly subsided and I felt some sort of certainty, of reality, seep back into my consciousness.

I opened my eyes to meet those of William gazing anxiously at me.

"I see thee ill," he said kindly and pressed my hand.

"She is a strong woman, methinks," snapped Elizabeth. "She needs not thy sympathy of woe. Consider thou me. I have made strong proof of woman's abilities. They call me queen but I am as much a king as any who have gone before me."

"Or any that came after," I found myself able to smile at her. She didn't smile back of course. Probably because of the teeth.

At that point, a man in knickers and suspenders leapt on to the low stage in front of the screen and was greeted by a deafening cheer from the crowd. Elizabeth's attention switched immediately from me to him. She devoured him with her eyes. William looked a little disconcerted but he was fairly used to men dressing as women so that once he had accepted the undergarment aspect he began to look more comfortable.

The man in suspenders and a gold corset was whipping the crowd into a frenzy. I remembered being pretty frenzied myself when I had gone along with a group of friends to a midnight showing of the Rocky Horror Show. I'd dressed as a nurse and, at just eighteen, felt myself to be very racy and daring. It all seemed a bit silly now and I couldn't quite work up the energy to be as enthralled by the camaraderie as I had been back then. Elizabeth, on the other hand, was drinking it all in with alacrity and, as the man in tights worked the crowd, eliciting noisy responses, she even attempted a cracked cheer. The Frank-N-Furter wannabe took a flying leap over the footlights. Seeing a six-foot man in suspenders and a gold corset hurtling towards you with legs akimbo is a bit intimidating, to say the least. I shrieked and covered my eyes. William disappeared under my legs but Elizabeth leapt up with her arms outstretched and would, I felt sure, have embraced him with lust, if he hadn't landed in an ignominious heap on several screaming sweet transvestites in the row in front of us. As two faded nymphets and a queen even more flamboyant than Elizabeth herself picked him up and dusted him off, the film burst onto the screen and, not surprisingly, Elizabeth and William jumped to their feet in terror and screamed in concert. Theatre was one thing but this was far too much magic all at once. Such was their panic at the explosion of animated colour that they both turned to flee and, finding their direct route blocked by rows of seats and expectant faces, decided to climb willy-nilly over them in a frantic bid to escape the ten foot high scarlet lips and raucous music that detonated in their ears. I managed to grab William by one thrashing leg and Elizabeth by the hem of her voluminous skirt. With strength borne of irritation and embarrassment, I pulled them both down and back onto their seats. I kept them there by the weight of my body and they sat, horror-struck with mouths wide open and hands clamped to their armrests.

A quarter of an hour into the film neither had moved a muscle and both were still transfixed. I felt it safe to slowly resume my own seat. I was beginning to feel a little guilty. So far, in just one evening, I had subjected William Shakespeare, a literary genius of incomparable standing, and the Virgin Queen, by all accounts one of the greatest minds of her time, to a pretty dreadful amateur performance of Hamlet that had traumatised its author, and to an undeniably bizarre cult film, heavy with transvestism, verging on perversion and with a little pornography thrown in for good measure. It seemed to me that I could have chosen better.

I sat miserably, with Elizabeth on one side of me and William on the other, wishing myself to be anywhere other than where I really was but unable to bring myself to leave. I closed my eyes again and tried to gather strength. For a few moments, I blocked the world out and felt fatigue fall away.

I was brought abruptly back to myself by a sudden stirring beside me. I opened my eyes. Elizabeth and William were no longer by my side. I turned to search the aisles and seats but they were nowhere to be seen. The audience was shifting and several people were leaving their seats and heading to the front of the cinema. 'The Time Warp' blared out and I knew instantly where they both were.

Centre stage. Of course.

Even amongst the wildly weird they shone like the icons they were. "Let's do the time warp again…" Elizabeth, who, so the history books tell us, loved dancing, was bumping and grinding with the best of them. She picked up the steps quickly and her wide skirts billowed provocatively as her jewels glistened and her scant arms flailed. William in his high ruff and with his spindly legs beneath his padded pantaloons wasn't quite as rhythmic but the ferocious concentration on his serious little face suggested that he was determined to give a good performance. Both in their own way were born performers and, bizarrely, they looked more at home gyrating with the misfits than they had in all their previous visits to me. I felt ridiculously proud of them both and, in a moment, was on my feet with the rest of the audience. We were all 'doing the Time Warp,' in a kind of stone cold sober drunkenness. 'And you step to the right…,' the audience roared, '… hands on hips.' Elizabeth, William and I were part of something happening, something inconsequential and joyous precisely because it was carefree and inconsequential.

Wonderful. I felt young again and as if my dreams had never been touched by disillusion and cynicism. Anything was possible and only the best was probable. In a single moment as I glanced back through the eager faces, I glimpsed Alex dancing too. He grinned and gave me a rhythmic thumbs-up before the dancers obscured him once again.

The song ended, the dancers dispersed happily to their original seats and Elizabeth and William clambered down flushed and vibrant. A tight smile adorned Elizabeth's face as she took her seat, queenly once more. William wheezed a bit but his expression had lost the fear that had haunted it for most of our acquaintance. This was theatre as he understood it, loud and raucous, invigorating, immediate, demanding and not a little basic. They didn't know the lines that the audience repeated with gusto but joined in anyway with an Elizabethan approximation. When the music sounded they were on their feet in an instant and, although the strains of rock and whatever it was, must have sounded strangely in their ears (I won't say harshly – have you ever heard a bombard?) they picked up the beat from the music and the abandonment from those around them and we all boogied without thought, without consciousness, without care.

What they really understood of the storyline I don't know but that was never really the point of the film anyway, was it? If it was it had passed me by. It was about freedom, I thought, to be what you were. To acknowledge the dark and wanton side of yourself and to accept it as no really bad thing. I don't think for one moment that Elizabeth saw it that way. She was far too fascinated by the bizarre sexuality on display to analyse anything but I suspect that William found much that was familiar in its theatricality, its raucous enthusiasm for life and its energetic determination to provoke a reaction.

CHAPTER EIGHT

...but it was always yet the trick of our English nation, if they have a good thing, to make it too common.
Henry IV Part II, Act I Sc ii

It had started raining again by the time the cinema disgorged its motley crew back onto the shining pavements. I searched again for Alex but we were held back by the crowd and so were some of the last to reach the exit. I thought he would have waited for me but the young are thoughtless sometimes. The crowds dispersed, Elizabeth and William with them.

I paused for a moment, looked right and left, but they were nowhere to be seen.

There were no taxis around and the town centre was emptying rapidly of my fellow cinema goers, however, home was less than two miles away. I was tired but somehow the lonely walk in the rain appealed to me. The roads were lit and, although I had never walked alone that late at night before, I wasn't frightened. No one bothered me and I reached my door without incident.

I was scrabbling in my bag for the key when the door flew open and there was Hubby with Grace behind him. They both looked frightened. I glanced behind me but Elizabeth and William weren't there.

"My god, Ally, are you all right?" Hubby said.

"Where the hell have you been?" hissed Grace.

"I went to the cinema," I answered surprised, as Hubby ushered me into the sitting room like an anxious mother hen, divesting me of wet coat and bag as we went.

"At this time of night? That's rubbish, it's nearly 3 am," Grace snapped.

"It's all right, Grace. Take it easy, your mother's home now and she's tired."

"No, I'm not," I denied indignantly, but I am intrinsically honest and Hubby was being kind. "Well, yes, I am. But I'm all right."

"Oh, you're all right?" Grace was not going to let it go. "Dad's been worried sick for hours. We were about to call the police, he's already called the hospital and you waltz in here as if nothing has happened."

"But Alex sent you a text message to tell you I was at the cinema with him." I was angry now. "Where's your mobile?" I spotted it on the table as I spoke and made a grab for it. "Look," I said waspishly, thrusting it first at Grace and then at Hubby. "There you are. 'Mum's with me. Seeing a film. Don't wait up.' See!"

I looked up in triumph.

Grace turned away suddenly and stood with her back to me. I couldn't see her face. Hubby just looked at me with that quiet, stricken look that seemed to have been on his face quite a bit recently.

"Don't you ever check the thing?" I ranted. "I can't see the point of having a mobile phone if you never look at it."

I had conveniently forgotten that mine was hardly ever fully operational because I never charged or put credit on it.

"Anyway, I'm tired, I'm going to bed."

I stormed up two stairs but, as usual, my anger evaporated and was immediately replaced with overwhelming guilt. I would give the world to be able to really lose my temper and feel entirely, unquestionably justified. That would be a real liberation.

"Look," I turned back. "I'm sorry, it was a bit thoughtless I know but I was with…" I could now see Grace's face and she was staring at me with something in her eyes that looked like fear…and pain.

"I was with…friends and we all got a bit carried away. It was a late night showing of Rocky Horror. Do you remember?" I touched my husband's arm. "We went together once. I dressed as a nurse and you… I don't think you did dress up, but you had long hair and huge bell bottoms and a tank top so you didn't need to."

I laughed and Hubby smiled gently.

"I remember. Time for bed, love. You must be very tired."

"I am sorry," I repeated, as the tears welled up and slid down my face.

"Night-night, mum," Grace whispered.

Hubby shepherded me up the stairs.

I slept late the next morning. I didn't do that very often and when I woke it was with that delicious, comfy feeling that you get sometimes after a really good night's sleep. I was still somewhere between sleep and waking when Alex brought me a cup of tea and sat for a moment or two on the end of the bed.

"Oh mum," he said, shaking his head with a smile.

I yawned and stretched and snuggled and drifted off again.

When next I woke William was perched nervously on the bed where Alex had sat and Elizabeth was stretched out beside me. She looked like a corpse, but then she always did.

"Good morning," I said sleepily.

"Good morrow," replied William like the polite little man he was.

"Thy bed is soft," Elizabeth commented without opening her eyes. She was taking up most of it with her stiff brocade dress so I sat up.

"Where do you go when you are not here with me?" I asked. Elizabeth opened one eye and looked at William with it.

"Home," they both said in concert.

"Home? Where is that, though?"

"Stratford," William said positively and with something of satisfaction in his eyes. "My house is there."

"And what do you do there when you are not here?"

"Tis another day," said William. "This is the dream."

I pondered that for a moment and then turned to Elizabeth.

"What about you? Is it the same for you?"

"Much the same," she conceded. "And yet..." She sighed. "Here am I free. Whensoe'er I return there is heaviness and pain."

"What year is it? For you, I mean?" I asked without thinking and then could have bitten off my own tongue for asking it.

"The year of our Lord, 1603," she said defiantly as if she had been following my train of thought, and then looked at me with a challenge in her eyes that I was not fool enough to take. I sat and pondered for a moment.

"Why do you come to me?" I asked. "To me, and not to anyone else and why do some people see you and some people don't?"

"That is not the question," William answered with conviction.

"If you say the question is 'To be or not to be', I will...I don't know what I'll do."

"Nay," said William. "The question is how. That is the question. If we knew the how then wouldst we know the why."

He had a point.

"Chut! We knowest nor how nor why," said Elizabeth shortly. "We know not whereuntil this shall continue and therefore say I we shouldst take what we can whilst we can. What is that black box?"

"It's a television," I answered absently.

"Ah." She waited a moment but as an explanation was not forthcoming she rolled herself, with some difficulty, out of the enveloping folds of my bed and onto her feet.

"What are these?" She was at my dressing table and picking up various bottles and pots with her bony, jewelled fingers. "Child, what are these?"

The 'child' surprised me, it was almost a term of endearment, but I suppose it was just that I was young to her. In more ways than one.

"They are face creams," I explained. "Perfumes and what we call make-up."

"For the face? Ah, 'tis the Venetian Ceruse."

"Something like that," I agreed. "Only without the corrosive ingredients."

She sat at my dressing table and grasping a tub attempted to open it. She struggled for a moment then thrust it at William who also struggled. I climbed out of bed and showed them how a screw top worked.

"It has a sweet fragrance."

Before either of us could stop her she had smeared a good dollop of it over her face. The white mass of lead paint caked deep on her face reacted with the kinder lanolin cream and melted into a gooey grey mass. William and I mopped her up as much as possible but she was fascinated by the smells and textures and colours of everything in my little arsenal of beauty products and insisted on trying them all. I found her some foundation and powder, a bright red lipstick and blusher and kohl. We covered her withered, yellow, pockmarked face with ivory base and she took delight in liberally applying the startling red to her lips and cheeks. When primped to her own satisfaction she looked a complete fright but she was delighted and it must be said that the 20th-century cosmetics leant her face a slightly healthier hue than it had had before. She adjusted her wig to show even more of her expansive white forehead and pouted grotesquely into the mirror. There wasn't much we could do about her atrocious teeth but as long as she didn't smile we could look her in the eye without wincing – just. William, not to be outdone, had busied himself with an eyebrow pencil and now sported startlingly blackened facial hair and a pair of quizzical eyebrows.

They were both fascinated by their own reflections in the mirror. I suppose Elizabethan mirrors were not all that efficient. At any rate, they were happy grinning at themselves, so I retired to my bed again and watched in amusement until the door opened and Hubby came in with a cup of tea and a plate of toast.

"Morning, love. Had a good sleep?"

I looked at him and then at Elizabeth and William and then back at him.

"You ok, love?"

"Oh, yes. Fine, much better."

They were behind him now but even so he could not have missed seeing them when he walked into the room. If he had been able to.

"Much, much better. I really needed a good night's sleep," I burbled, over-compensating like mad for the intense disappointment I felt. William shrank back against the curtains but Elizabeth fixed her beady eyes on my husband.

"Good," Hubby said as he bent over to place the coffee and toast on the bedside table. "You have been looking tired and a day in bed won't do you any harm." He leaned forward to kiss me but, moving slightly so that I could see past his generous cheek, I was transfixed by Elizabeth, who, her eyes sparkling with intent, was moving purposefully with a hand outstretched towards my husbands' generous bottom.

I squeaked, Hubby jumped and, if William had not heroically rugby tackled her to the floor at that point, I am not sure what would have happened.

"Something wrong?" asked Hubby, concerned again.

"Hiccups," I said and hiccupped again to prove the lie.

"What the hell has been going on here, Mum?" Grace demanded from the doorway.

Elizabeth and William were in tangled Elizabethan heap on

the floor in the middle of the room so I assumed that this was what she meant and looked at her in joy, but she just marched over to the dressing table. It was a terrible mess with liquid makeup spilt and soiled tissues scattered underneath an all-encompassing fine pink powder.

"What on earth have you been doing, Mum?"

"Just experimenting," I said weakly.

"But you're not wearing any make-up."

"I removed it."

Elizabeth was on her feet again and, with a face like thunder, was shaking William off. I had a wary eye on her but she seemed to have conquered her monomania for the moment and, though disgruntled, was prepared to let William guide her to a corner where she could view the family drama, and presumably my husband's backside, in comfort.

"Honestly, mum. What's got into you?" Grace asked waspishly, as she gathered tissues and wiped up goo. Hubby sat on the bed close to me.

"What?" I asked, irritably as he rubbed my arm and looked gently into my face.

"We're worried about you, love. That's all."

"I'm fine," I protested. "Is this because I was a bit late home last night?"

"Bit late!" snorted Grace.

"It's not like you, love. You haven't been yourself for weeks."

"I'm fine," I repeated scornfully.

Hubby and Grace exchanged glances and I could see that I wasn't going to gain ground by protestations. Perhaps manipulation might be more to the purpose. I changed tack accordingly. Stress was always a good all-encompassing excuse.

"Maybe I have been a bit stressed recently," I conceded with a well-timed sigh. "I could have a rest today. Stay in bed perhaps. Oh, but there is the shopping to do and all the ironing."

"Dad will do the shopping and I'll do the ironing." Grace said firmly. "We can manage."

I was sure she was right and anyway that was two jobs that I hated taken care of. I would have felt triumphant if I hadn't felt so guilty.

"I'll enjoy looking around the supermarket. I haven't been for ages." Hubby had a very annoying manner of finding the bright side to everything, even weekly shopping.

"Ok." It was a bit of a struggle to say that. Inevitably he would buy forty-four frozen tofu burgers on special offer (assuming tofu was a cut of beef), no washing up liquid and a loofah shaped like an elephant, or some other similarly useless object that would catch his eye. Must tell him not to buy AN AMAZING VEG MACERATOR I thought briefly and wondered again what we were going to do with the periwinkles languishing in the freezer. Grace would undoubtedly do a good job of the ironing. All the pairs of jeans would have knife-like creases down the front and the pillow cases would be starched into crispy rigidity. She always did whatever she did to perfection.

"Ok," I said again.

"Good, you have a rest, don't worry about anything and… eat your toast." Hubby stood up.

Grace, still grumbling, gathered up the detritus from the dressing table and stomped out. She was watched carefully by Elizabeth who looked as if she were itching to give her a smart slap but who was distracted by my husband's fabulous posterior on its way to the door. Hubby gave me a kind smile and closed the door quietly.

William bounded over and tucked into the toast without asking. Elizabeth took another long look at herself in the mirror.

"They didn't see you," I said woefully. "I don't understand this at all. Alex saw you. At least I think he did. He said 'bring your friends' and he must have meant you, mustn't he? There wasn't anyone else. And Nell definitely sees you.

Maybe certain people are more...sensitive or something. Like mediums."

Elizabeth had moved on to the television on my chest of drawers and was pushing the buttons with careless curiosity. Inevitably it sprung into noisy life and she staggered backwards landing in a heap on the bed. Of course, it was adverts. It always is when you turn the television on. A pert young woman in very short shorts was wiggling suggestively whilst the voice over exhorted us to buy some sort of pills that would work wonders of weight loss and, presumably, give us all wasp-like waists and enormous bosoms.

"Bawd! Harlot!" screamed Elizabeth in disgust. If it had been male buttocks jigging about on the screen, I think her reaction would have been somewhat different.

William got up and, after gazing open-mouthed at the scantily clad young lady, took a good look behind the box. However, after their experiences at the cinema the previous evening, they were becoming a little more electronically savvy and not quite so easily panicked by the magic of my century.

"Television?" asked William. Like I said, very little got past them without being mentally analysed and filed. "Far off vision..."

"I suppose that is a good way of putting it. It's all to do with pixels, they make up the picture." I said it nonchalantly as if I had a store of further knowledge available on request. Which of course I didn't.

"What is it for?" Elizabeth wanted to know.

I can't say I'd ever really considered that question before.

"It's for entertainment mainly I suppose. Like theatre. A distraction from life. Very occasionally a reflection of it. Your plays have been on it ever so many times in various forms, William, and of course, there are hundreds of films of your plays."

"My plays?" William looked doubtful and took another look behind it.

"They are all the wrong size," snapped Elizabeth who was now studying a field of singing cows. I didn't understand what she meant so she patiently (well, patiently for her) elucidated. "Some time the people are of a littleness extreme and some other of a bigness not true. Thou wilt explain."

An operatic tenor with a waistband as wide as his vocal range was now trying to persuade us that he was a trustworthy character and his insurance was the best by singing excruciatingly bad lyrics and behaving like a lunatic. William put his face right up to the screen again and Elizabeth irritably threw a pillow at him for blocking her view. Without taking his eyes off the television William moved to sit on the floor and, leaning against the bed, made himself comfortable.

"It's filmed with cameras," I attempted to explain, knowing that I was once more way out of my depth. "They take lots and lots of photos…"

"Photos?" queried Elizabeth sharply whilst undoing her bodice for comfort.

"Photos are like…um…paintings only they are created by light." Elizabeth looked disbelieving but William seemed to like the idea.

"Paintings created by light," he echoed.

"They take lots and lots of them in sequence and when they put them all together it sort of creates movement. At least I know that's how they used to do it with film. It's all digital now and I have no idea how that works but it's the same principal I suppose."

"Are these counterfeit people?" William asked as a vacuous blonde tried to sell him toothpaste that would, if the pictures were to be believed, create a tsunami in his mouth and then give him a dazzling smile of such whiteness that he would be able to light his own way on a dark night.

"They're actors, so yes, and no."

"Ahh," William nodded, vastly enlightened. "Actors."

"Bigness, littleness," Elizabeth muttered still struggling for release from her vice like bodice.

"Would you like to borrow a dressing gown?" I asked kindly. She gave me a contemptuous look but I suspected that was because she didn't know what a dressing gown was. I got out of bed, unhooked one from the door and held it out to her. It was yellow towelling. She reached out hesitantly and took it, then ran her hands over it with sensuous delight.

"Tis soft, like thy bed," she said.

"You can put it on." And she did. Over her gown. She then loosened her bodice close to the point of indecency.

"I meant you could take your dress off and then you would be much more comfortable."

She gave me a deeply suspicious look so I thought it best not to pursue the matter. She remained fully dressed, perched on the edge of my bed, stroking the enveloping cheap yellow towelling with sensual joy.

William meanwhile was transfixed by the joys of daytime television. We were now being entertained by a suave man and a perky woman showing us houses in varying states of decay that were being transformed into houses in unvarying hues of neutral magnolia with granite worktops. Elizabeth and William displayed intense irritation if I moved or started to speak. I curled up on the bed and watched them contentedly for over an hour. By the time they had seen the fat man sing for the fourth time, the novelty, not surprisingly, was beginning to pall.

"They prate with o'er repetition and the box brays much with minstrelsy," Elizabeth said in exasperation.

"It's to do with short attention spans, I think, or short term memories, or it might be that they are just trying to beat us into submission."

"Still I see not what it is for," Elizabeth, perched on the end of my bed, was very irritable.

I had to consider that I had given William and Elizabeth a very negative view of mass communication, undeniably one of the greatest advances of the 20th Century. I rescued the remote control from the dust bunnies under the bed and prepared myself to give a lecture. To their astonishment, I ran through the different channels. The abruptly changing pictures fascinated them. William enthusiastically reached for the remote but when it came to control it was inevitable that Elizabeth would demand that as her inalienable right. After an interminable period during which Elizabeth changed the channels over and over again just because she could, I managed to persuade her to settle on the factual channels. A couple of hours later we had exhausted both first and second world wars, warthogs, Nostradamus, had a pretty good idea of the theory of nuclear fission, knew how to make a mushroom paella, an amphibian vehicle and, should there ever be a catastrophic power cut, a battery out of a lasagne. Always supposing you had just made one of course.

William was fascinated by it all, particularly the paella. I thought that the mass destruction depicted in the world war documentaries would appal them but they did not seem to be able to comprehend the immensity and wholesale slaughter of it. I suppose I should not have been too surprised at their apparent indifference. Their times were brutal too and both had lived every day of their lives with death hanging over them.

However, the appearance on the screen of a spitfire bowling along a runway and then taking to the air filled them both with sudden excited awe.

"Is it going to the moon?" asked William, leaping up round-eyed with moustache bristling. "Why, tis a miracle, tis fantastic." Then his face fell. "Tis a forgery of shapes and tricks?" He turned to me crestfallen. "A trick as when the coloured letters move about the screen and when the animals talk."

"No, it's not the same," I assured him. "These days the technicians can make anything you can imagine seem to happen. But planes really do fly."

"Thy world is full of wondrous lies and fearful truths. How ist an honest man to know the truth thereof?" William asked.

I could not think of an answer.

The throaty whine of the spitfire broke in on our thoughts and William returned to the screen with excitement. He watched intently as the planes in a reconstruction of a dog fight danced their deadly steps in the sky. When the titles rolled across the screen there was silence for a moment and then William crept towards me and putting his thin hands on my arm beseeched, "I desire…to fly. Couldst I fly?"

I could see all sorts of potential problems with that one so I took the cowards' way out. "I'll see what I can do." As I didn't have any intention of doing anything it twisted my heart to see the sudden joyous anticipation on his face.

Elizabeth didn't seem too keen on the flying idea but having heard me grant a 'boon' to William she was determined to gain the same.

"Pray, when do we visit my noble kinswoman?"

"I've explained that there are problems getting to her…"

"Chut," she said. "Then she must come here. Send word that I will grant her audience here."

"Here?" I giggled. "You want the Queen to come and visit you here? In my house?"

She looked around with contempt.

"Tis little and ordinary but will suffice me."

"She wouldn't come. I did meet her once, though. Well, not exactly meet. She was opening a new wing at the hospital and my little boy Alex had broken his leg falling out of a tree. She said he was a 'brave boy'… But the Queen wouldn't come here. Would you visit a commoner just because they invited you?" I felt that was the clincher.

"Thou art a thing of naught but I am not. Write thou and command her attendance."

"But..."

"Chut," she said again. "Get me ink and paper. Write."

I decided that it would be politic to comply or at least seem to comply. After all, I didn't have to post the letter. It occurred to me as I looked for paper and a pen that not posting it would probably constitute treason in Elizabeth's time and that they executed people for less but I shook the thought off and sat down to compose a letter to the Queen of England asking her to come and visit my little house in middle England to meet her very, very, very distant and very, very, very dead non-relation. Of course, it wouldn't reach her but whoever in her staff intercepted it would think that I was mad. I couldn't possibly post it.

Elizabeth dictated the letter. I gave William the pen but he had not scrawled more than four words before his queen ripped it from his hand.

"Joithead! Thy clapper-clawed hand makes marks across the vellum likest beetle-crawling. The woman will do it."

She was right. William's writing was illegible at best. Mine is not much better but I bowed to the inevitable and submitted with good grace.

William, slightly shame-faced, once or twice suggested a word or phrase (and I couldn't think of anyone better qualified to do so) but she would have no way but her own.

"*Cousin, thou art one not differing from me in sex, of like rank and degree, of the same stock and allied to me in blood.*"

"She isn't related to you by blood," I protested. "I explained that to you."

Elizabeth peered imperiously at her reflection in the dressing table mirror. "*Allied to me by the blood royal...*" she continued missing hardly a beat.

"*Thou holdst the realm by the like title and right. Time and God hath brought me hither. It is meet that we take such convenient time and leisure as the weightiness of this matter doth require."*

"The weightiness of what matter?" I enquired but Elizabeth did not reply.

The letter went on in a similar flowery vein for some paragraphs. I couldn't make much sense of it at all except that underlying the wordiness lay a determination, almost a desperation that was not characteristic of her.

"I think you should say something about William being here as well. That would strengthen your case," I ventured without thinking.

The suggestion was greeted with icy silence. I glanced across at William who, flattered and frightened, struggled with both emotions until fear gained the upper hand.

"William is very famous in this time," I continued daringly, "and the Queen would be interested to meet him I know."

You could see why Elizabeth had reigned successfully for so long. Her displeasure was paralysing.

Hubby, oblivious to the politics of power playing out in his bedroom, walked in again at that point which was just as well as I think Elizabeth was about to slap me, if not worse. She cuffed William instead who fell to his knees before his yellow-towelling-clad monarch and implored pardon for his presumptuousness in having written works of genius.

Hubby cheerfully served up corned beef sandwiches and tea, plumped up my pillows and reported that Grace was doing a good job with the ironing (of course) and that he had done all the shopping and I wasn't to worry about anything. He then proudly produced his new impulse buy. One of those lap trays with a cushion attached so that I could eat my sandwiches sitting up in bed like an old woman. After he had arranged me and his new purchase to his satisfaction, fussed around a bit more, kissed me on the top of my head (hate it!) and smiled reassuringly, he left the room. I couldn't quite work out whether

I felt very, very old or very, very young. I munched a sandwich and looked resentfully at Elizabeth and William. It was all their fault of course. Exactly how it was their fault I wasn't quite sure but I knew that they were responsible for it. Whatever it was.

They seemed to sense my mood and for a short while even Elizabeth kept respectfully silent. Then William, growing increasingly fidgety and attracted by the television, crept forward and turned the sound back up. An omnibus edition of one of the grittier, and more than usually tawdry, soaps was showing. Within about ten minutes Elizabeth and William were both riveted.

I rarely watch television and soaps even less, so I gave my sandwiches to William, snuggled down under my duvet and left them to it. I had the most unnerving dream. I was the very tall landlady of a pub in Victorian England and all the customers were very, very short. So short in fact that I spent most of the time trying to find them so that I could serve them. Every now and again a woman, tall like me, but who was constructed like a Picasso painting would pop in and ask for a cup of tea but, although I felt that it was very important that I should serve her, somehow I was always too busy to get around to it and just had to keep apologising. The Picasso woman got increasingly disjointed as her search for a cuppa was frustrated at every turn and I got more and more frantic as I tried to keep everyone happy. Then suddenly we were no longer in the pub but in an aeroplane and our destination was the space station. Then the plane started sliding sideways back down to earth and one of the short people grasped my leg and began screaming "We need to talk, we need to talk!"

I woke up to find Elizabeth fast asleep across my bed, using one of my legs as a pillow. William was still watching the television screen with more or less the same expression that he had watched the amateurs performing his masterpiece. I'd like to think that he was using an analytical eye and that he was deconstructing the scenes and coming to a deep and meaningful conclusion but actually I believe he was just trying to work out what the hell it was all about.

A pert young girl with blonde hair and tortured eyes was exhorting a sturdy, middle-aged man with bristly hair, tattoos and the fixed expression of a bulldog to tell her the truth about "me ma". Some things are better left unsaid – except in soap operas apparently where the more said the better.

"I've heard it said that if you were alive today," I mused to William, "you would be writing for these programs."

William considered for a moment.

"I think not." It was the most decisive thing I had yet heard him say.

"Oh?" I enquired, slightly surprised.

"These," he indicated the screen on which the blonde girl continued sobbing, "are very stupid people."

"They do seem to stagger hysterically from one godawful decision to the next without engaging scruples or common sense, I grant you. At least your characters throw in a soul-searching soliloquy every now and again before they decapitate somebody. Hollywood screen-writing would suit you better. I can see you there, under a palm tree, up to your ruff in half-naked starlets and cocaine."

He was about to ask me about cocaine when the girl on the television screamed "but we're faaamily", as if that was the answer to everything, and the big bloke glowered. A woman with a face like a hippopotamus pickled in vinegar hove into camera shot and decked the tattooed bulldog man with a pewter mug. The girl raised mascara smeared eyes to the camera and screeched 'Ma?'

I switched it off.

"Tis passing strange this world," William mused. "The tide of time rushes still and anon and there is no quiet anywhere."

I sighed.

"I haven't shown you the best that our world can offer. I wish I could." Inspired I pulled a pile of books from my bedside table that I had purloined from Alex's room a few days ago. Literature offered a better option. "I've been reading about you."

"Books that tell of me, thou sayest?"

"Most of them will admit that they don't know much about you, so they tend to speculate. There is, of course, the school of thought that believes that because you didn't go to university you probably didn't write many, if any, of your plays and that Christopher Marlow wrote them."

"Kit?" William looked startled. "Kit is dead, these many years, God rest his soul."

"That is a point that tends to discredit the theory. But there are many that maintain that he didn't die and went to live in Italy or somewhere and kept writing under your name."

"Oh. To what purpose?"

"Good question. But there are other candidates to your genius. Here look." I found the page and pointed. "Francis Bacon, Edward de Vere, Mary Sidney, William Stanley. The Earl of Essex is currently a very popular option and quite a few people still hold with the Marlowe theory. You didn't publish much apart from the poems, so it's next to impossible to work out what you did write and what you didn't."

He shrugged. "I owe not the plays."

I looked aghast. Was this an admission that he had not written them?

"I write for the company. The scrips belong to them. Tis the way."

"You must keep copies yourself?" He shook his head.

"They are performed and another is demanded. Sometime I write with others of the company. Sometime they keep'st those scrips that are to be performed again."

"It's no wonder you are such a mystery if you are so careless of your work."

I felt quite cross with him. But he was studying the covers of the books I had placed before him.

"Tell these books the worth of my years?"

"They tell what is known, but that isn't much." I told him what the books said but there is not much is known for certain about my gentle friend so it didn't take long. "You were born in Stratford upon Avon and probably went to school there."

He nodded.

"At eighteen you married Anne Hathaway who was eight years older than you."

He nodded.

"And had, in indecent haste, they say, three children."

He nodded, and the ghost of a smile touched his lips.

"You then disappeared from record for eight years before bursting onto the London theatrical scene as an actor and playwright."

He did not nod. He looked at me quizzically.

"Well, don't blame me. That is just about all that is known about you. Apart from the fact that you made a bit of money and then suddenly gave the theatre up for no known reason and returned to Stratford on Avon."

He had picked up one of the weightier tomes and was studying the handsome cover intently.

"This is the storie of my life," he said raising his eyes to mine, "and certain of my death."

I pulled the book from him, gathered up the others and shoved them willy-nilly into the cupboard of my nightstand. In my enthusiasm to reveal to William his fame I had forgotten that some things are probably best shrouded in mystery. William, wise man, tempted though he must have been to open the cover, knew that.

"Let time shape, and there an end." He always said things so beautifully. I had to give myself a mental shake to stop myself falling desperately in love with him. If he had been just a little less weedy and a whole lot better looking I would have been a lost woman instead of just an impossibly shallow one.

"So where were you for that missing eight years after you left Stratford and before you became famous in London and who was the dark lady of the sonnets, and are you gay and how did you manage to write such fabulous plays without a university education?"

Perhaps I asked too many questions all at once. William pursed his full lips, raised one eyebrow very slightly and said nothing.

"Oh, come on," I said in exasperation. "Academics and historians have agonised over these questions for years. You can answer them now. Have you any idea how awesome that would be?"

"Awesome?" he queried. He was pretty good at deflection himself.

"At least tell me something about the dark lady of the sonnets." William clasped his hands and looked down at his feet.

"You would pluck out the heart of my mystery."

"Oh bum!" I said irritably. "I think you owe me a few answers at least. The books say that you probably had an affair with Wriothsley. You wrote that flowery dedication to him and he was clearly a screamer so he's probably the dark lady you are writing about."

A smile played briefly on William's lips but whether it was of fond memories or a humorous dismissal of a preposterous idea I could not tell.

"So where were you for those years after you married?"

"Mayhap I trod the primrose path." Growing in confidence he had gained control of the remote and the television sprang into life once more.

"Humph!" I muttered. "Now I remember why we all hated you at school. What on earth is that supposed to mean?"

"What you will." A large panda with a New York accent was being amusing about biscuits and William was fleetingly engrossed.

"Tis a marvel." He moved up as close as he could get to the screen. "Awesome!"

The screen blanked and a snake slithered across it. William shrieked and stepped backwards, tripped over my slippers and landed on top of Elizabeth who was still asleep on my legs. We all shrieked in concert and a moment later we heard footsteps thundering up the stairs and the door flew open.

"What's wrong?" panted Hubby.

"Nightmares," I answered. "Terrible."

"Oh, love." Hubby plonked himself down on top of William who was still on top of Elizabeth and grasped my hand. "You know you're not yourself at all these days, do you think…" he hesitated and then forced the words out. "Do you think that perhaps you should talk to someone about all this?"

I was a bit distracted by the agonised look on William's face and more so by the irritation on Elizabeth's. She had wriggled from underneath William and was trying to wrench the towelling robe free but William's and Hubby's combined weight made it immovable.

"Love, did you hear what I said?"

"Absolutely," I said, a little desperately.

"So if I make an appointment you will see someone?"

William was turning blue and Elizabeth was about to hit him, or Hubby or me.

"Could I have a glass of water? I'm ever so thirsty."

"But you will see someone if I make an appointment for Monday?"

"Oh, yes," I said pushing my husband as hard as I could. "Absolutely. Monday, gosh I'm thirsty."

"All right, I'm going."

He stood, William gasped and gulped and Elizabeth,

suddenly released, shot off the end of the bed like a cork out of a bottle.

"I just think it would do you good to talk to someone. Get everything that is worrying you out in the open. You know, have a good heart to heart."

"Brilliant," I said. "I'll do that. Just what I need."

Elizabeth's scrawny hand appeared over William's still supine body as she hauled herself up.

"Well, I'm glad," said Hubby at the door. "I'm glad you've taken it so well. We were a bit worried that you'd be upset by the suggestion."

"Oh no," I said, airily, as he shut the door.

Elizabeth staggered weakly to her feet and adjusted the towelling dressing gown. William wheezed and coughed and realigned himself. Having satisfied myself that neither had been killed the words of the exchange with my husband echoed in my mind.

"What did he just say?" I asked. I looked at William but he was still anoxic and Elizabeth too wrapped up in herself and my towelling gown to have any interest in anything not directly affecting her. "What did I just agree to? Why were they worried I would be upset?"

Elizabeth shrugged.

"What other marvels doth the box present?" she demanded.

Elizabeth pushed William until he rolled off the bed, placed herself comfortably and gestured irritably to me to switch channels. William picked himself up and, although he was still a little woebegone, his interest in the television overrode his discomfort so he curled up on the floor at the bottom of the bed and prepared to be fascinated once again.

I desultorily flicked through the channels. We tried the news channel but some ditzy female celebrity was dominating the headlines by claiming to have been badly used by her overpaid footballer boyfriend and it got very boring after about thirty seconds. Which is about as long as I could have been in their company before I would have had to deck both her and the moronic bozo she was accusing.

The movie channels were offering the usual fare of intense American violence or banal American drama with the odd American disaster thrown in but Elizabeth and William did not have any frame of reference for the passing pictures which held some fascination but no real meaning for them.

We alighted at last on Mr. Bean and they were both immediately entranced. I hadn't heard Elizabeth or William really laugh until then but within moments they were chuckling. William had a surprisingly light titter that developed into a delightful chortle. Elizabeth's laugh started with a sharp 'Ha' that expanded into a series of 'ha's' rapped out with all the intrinsic mirth of a retorting machine gun.

Hubby came in briefly with my glass of water. I pretended to be asleep so he put it on my bedside table and tiptoed over to switch the television off. Through one half-opened eye I saw William's dismay and Elizabeth's fury. She leapt to her feet and would have hurled herself upon him but that he gained the door before her. He unconsciously shut it in her face. I grabbed the remote and restored the picture. In a moment she was content and laughing once more. Luckily for me, it was one of those marathon days and we were therefore treated, if that is the word, to several hours of the tirelessly, some would say tiresomely, inventive Mr. Bean. They loved every moment and resented the advertisement breaks as passionately as any twenty-first-century couch potato could do.

The afternoon programs drifted into evening programs and Hubby came and took me downstairs to eat a shepherd's pie that Grace had made. It was delicious of course.

We sat around the kitchen table and Hubby poured me a glass of wine and then I poured myself one more when he wasn't looking. Alex didn't appear but then, as I have explained, he quite often didn't. He was very popular and had lots of friends. He had quite a lively social life but he was sensible so I didn't worry too much about him. I did worry about Grace, though. She was so serious and so solitary, so much like me when I was her age, and I knew how horrible that had been.

Elizabeth and William drifted down and perched on the radiator whilst we ate and talked. We didn't talk about anything of consequence and Elizabeth and William behaved themselves so the meal passed off uneventfully. I washed up and Grace and Hubby made coffee and we sat in the front room for a while and tried to find something that we all wanted to watch on the television. That was never going to happen of course, so I yawned and said I was going for a bath. Hubby looked anxious and made me drink another cup of coffee. I think he was worried that I would be too pickled to manage a bath without major incident. I was more concerned about keeping Elizabeth and William out of the bathroom, so, when I had eventually shaken off my attentive husband, I activated my twenty-first-century superiority, took them both by the scruff of the neck, metaphorically speaking, sat them on the bed and gave them strict instructions not to move. To make doubly sure I put the television back on so that they could watch the Antiques Roadshow and marvel at the advances of modern technology. Then I got my towel and had a long, long hot bath.

CHAPTER NINE

It is the stars,
The stars above us, govern our conditions.
King Lear, Act iv Sc iii

Elizabeth was pacing when I got back to the room and William was looking frightened again. I assumed Elizabeth had been hitting him. She had the letter to the Queen in her hand and thrust it at me.

"Send this. We waste time."

"It's Saturday night and the post won't go until Monday."

"Post?"

I pulled the wet towel off my head and sighed. It was getting a little tiresome explaining every little thing.

"We have what we call a postal service. We post letters into letter boxes. They get picked up by postmen, they gather them all together in a depot, sort them and send them by road or train or plane or whatever to wherever they need to go and then they are picked up by different postmen and delivered to houses, usually within a day or two, unless it happens to be important in which case it inexplicably takes a lot longer."

"Wherefore do you not just send a man with it?"

"Because I can't," I said irritably. Elizabeth was disgruntled and took another couple of turns around the room. It wasn't a big room so it didn't take long. I amused myself by directing the hair dryer full blast at William. He was enchanted.

"Is the morrow our Lord's Day?" rapped Elizabeth. "The Sabbath?"

"Yes. It is Sunday. And I don't have to go to work, thank God."

"What hour is thy worship?"

"No idea." They both looked at me. "Well, I don't know, I never go."

Expressions of horror crept over their faces. "I don't go because I don't believe in God. Oh, don't look at me like that! Quite a few people are atheists these days. Anyway, even many of those who think they do believe don't bother to go except on special occasions. Or unless they want something."

They both crossed themselves in an instinctive attempt to protect themselves from my corrupting presence and there was silence for a few thought-laden moments.

"Thou dost not worship God?" Elizabeth asked slowly.

"No," I said firmly.

"What dost thou worship then?" William was interested.

"Nothing. I just don't believe in any sort of god. Of course I can't speak for others but there are so many religions and there are so many people claiming that their god is the only god – well, someone has to be wrong and it all seems to boil down to the premise that if you have chosen the right god to believe in then you will go to heaven and if you don't believe in the right god you will go to hell. Except that some believe you are reincarnated on some sort of divine points system. Either way, it all seems suspiciously human and not at all godly."

"What of your eternal soul?" Elizabeth demanded.

"I don't think I have one."

"Thou hast no soul?" They chorused, crossing themselves in horror.

"I don't know what a soul is unless it is the overwhelming need to survive in some form or another."

Elizabeth couldn't work out whether to slap me or not but

I think she was afraid of some sort of contamination if she did, so she didn't and anyway another more pleasing thought had struck her.

"Your people worship thy sovereign," she stated with immense satisfaction at having solved the conundrum.

"Trust me, worship is not the word. We don't really worship anything," I insisted. "Although the occasional footballer gets more adoration than any mortal deserves."

William, who had actually listened to what I had said, suddenly perked up as a thought struck him. "I hath issue," he said. "Susannah and Judith. Hath I kinsmen still living?"

"No, sorry." He looked very crestfallen. "But you, both of you have achieved another sort of immortality so, you haven't been forgotten and probably never will be."

"And so in spite of death, we doth survive," said William slowly.

"Well, it's the way I look at it."

Elizabeth overcame her disgust at my apostasy enough to decide that that particular part of my philosophy, if no other, might be worth embracing.

"My friend Christopher thought as do you," William ventured.

"Speakest thou of the whoreson, Marlow," Elizabeth barked. William shrank back. "He was a traitor and guilty of sedition."

"His was a great spirit," William defended his friend bravely.

"It is believed that he was a sort of spy for you," I countered to deflect her fury at being challenged by William. "That he carried out secret work for you with John Dee, finding out things you needed to know about people."

I got one of her frosty looks for that.

"Pah, the traitorous rascals were useful for a time. We will attend church on the morrow."

"Not me," I said firmly.

"I command you."

"Command all you like." I switched the television off, threw myself on the bed and curled up ready to sleep. She rapped me on the head of course.

"For God's sake," I shouted. "Stop doing that."

"For whose sake?" she asked, one eyebrow raised.

"It's just an expression. Look, I've told you I don't believe in God and I'm not going to church."

"Dost believe in us?" William asked quietly.

"Well, of course, you are here, aren't you? I don't know how but you are, though I still don't understand why most other people don't see you. That doesn't make you any less real though so…" I stopped abruptly. They were both much cleverer than I was. "Ok, I see where you are going with this but perhaps it is just that some things have to be believed to be seen."

Having talked myself into that particular corner I felt obliged to submit to higher intellects than mine, even if it was with an ill-grace.

"All right, I'll take you to church if that's what you really want but right now I need to get some sleep and… Oh hell, my husband is on his way up."

I could hear his step on the stairs.

"Can't you go back to wherever it is you go to and come back in the morning?"

They both gave the Elizabethan equivalent to a shrug.

"We have no power. It will happen or not," William stated without anxiety.

Hubby appeared.

"Who are you talking to love?" he asked.

"Singing," I muttered and gave him a quick chorus of "I Feel Pretty." He didn't look convinced – for any reason.

Elizabeth and William perched back to back on my dressing table stool and watched my dear old Hubby get undressed. Elizabeth watched intently but didn't get excited. I knew how she felt. The big old bed rocked and groaned as he collapsed on to it. I suggested that he turn the bedside lamp off but in all our years of marriage I never knew him sleep in totally dark room. He ignored the suggestion as if he hadn't heard it. That was easier than admitting to me that he was frightened of the dark. I had teased him about it more than once but he claimed that if there was a fire he would need to be able to see to get us all safely out of the house. I said that was what the on switch was for. However, the result that night of his, let's call it a foible, was that, try as I might to forget it, I was constantly aware of the presence of Elizabeth and William. Every time I opened my eyes there they were gazing intently at me.

Inevitably it was one of the very few nights that Hubby felt amorous and I can't begin to describe the utter horror I endured when his hands began to creep towards my breasts. I tried turning over of course but that just made things worse so I groaned a couple of times and that had the desired effect of dampening his ardour, but it must have worried William because I opened my eyes to find him gazing in concern with his face less than two inches from mine. I jumped and screamed and pushed him away and that had the knock on effect of causing Hubby to leap guiltily out of bed.

"What is it? What did I do?"

"Nothing, nothing," I yelped. "Cramp! A nightmare! Sorry, just a nightmare, that's all. With a touch of cramp. Sorry!"

There was a tap on the door.

"Is everything all right," Grace inquired.

"Yes, we're fine. Your mother just had another nightmare that's all. Go back to bed love."

"Ok, if you're sure."

"Sorry," I said again and snuggled back down in bed.

"You must talk to…someone about all this. The nightmares and …. everything."

"I said I would," I agreed, waspishly. "But who did you want me to talk to?"

"Who do you want to talk to about it?" He was hedging of course.

"I don't want to talk to anyone about it."

"You just said you did."

"I said I would, not that I wanted to."

"Well, that's just splitting hairs."

"No, it isn't. I don't know what you are making all the fuss about anyway. I come home a bit late one night and suddenly you are creating all this bother about every little thing I do."

"We're concerned about you. That's all."

"No need to be," I snapped. "Anyway, I'm tired and I don't want to talk about it now."

"All right, all right." Hubby sighed and got back into bed. "You win, as usual."

I resented that of course and spent the next hour resenting it but pretending to be fast asleep. It only rubbed salt into the wound when he started to snore, insensitive sod, scuppering any possibility of slumber on my part. William and Elizabeth, unaffected by the roars emitting from my husband's nose, fell asleep propped up against one another. It was nice to see them so close, even though Elizabeth needed to be unconscious to reach that happy state. Eventually, even angst and nasal rumbling couldn't keep me awake anymore and I subsided into uncomfortable dreams.

CHAPTER TEN

There are no tricks in plain and simple faith.
Julius Caesar, Act IV Sc iii

I awoke to find Elizabeth poking me energetically and pointing through our bedroom window to the rising sun. Unusually for me I snapped out of sleep and was fully awake almost instantly.

"Nice to see you, to see you nice," said William with a touch of pride. It was surreal I grant you and I did stare open mouthed for a moment or two until I remembered the Bruce Forsythe retrospective that we had watched briefly last night. I decided to worry about William's penchant for language and just what he might have picked up at a later date. I had more pressing concerns.

Hubby was spread-eagled on his stomach across the bed with his mouth wide open and his pyjama bottoms revealing a fair proportion of his pale buttocks. I slid out of bed and, with as little rustling as possible, gathered dress, shoes and, as an afterthought and a bit more rummaging, a hat that looked as if it might possibly bear some relation to the shoes. I crept to the bathroom and changed and when I had finished I did not feel like me at all.

We all traipsed down to the kitchen where Grace was making coffee. She took one look at me and yelped.

"What on earth are you doing dressed like that?"

"I'm going to church," I replied calmly.

"To church?" She was incredulous. "What for?"

"I can go to church if I want to, can't I?" I snapped back.

She nodded reluctantly, then sidled past me yelling "Dad!" at the top of her voice.

I didn't want a showdown so I gulped down a cup of coffee and, William and Elizabeth in tow, headed for the door. I was arrested as I reached for the knob by Hubby appearing at the top of the stairs pulling his pyjama bottoms up and calling my name. Grace was peeping over his shoulder.

"Ally, love" he called gently. "Grace tells me you are going to church."

"Yes," I said, defiantly. "So?"

"I'll drive you." The wind was taken right out of my sails by that. I opened the door anyway but it was beginning to drizzle and the hat was not the weather resistant sort.

"Ok," I acquiesced. "But put your trousers on first."

"I'll make you some breakfast if you like," Grace offered sweetly. I suspected she was aiming to delay matters long enough for me to change my mind about going at all.

"Not to worry," I said. "We don't want to be late for the… er…the…"

"Service?"

"That's it."

"We?"

"What?"

"You said 'we' would be late for the service."

"I meant me and….dad."

"Dad won't go in." She had that look of distrust in her eyes again and it hurt me to see it. She was my daughter. Daughters should be able to trust their mothers.

"What time does the service start?" She was buttering toast but she didn't take her eyes off me.

"I'm not exactly sure." I hadn't thought of that but it was Sunday morning so I was bound to catch one somewhere.

"Then why are you going? We've never been to church on a Sunday before. Please don't tell me you've had a revelation and 'got' religion. That would be too weird for words."

"Grace!" Hubby's tone was sharp but his mood was probably irritated by having to get up early on a Sunday morning. And, judging by his stance and pained expression, having caught himself in the zip of his flies. "If your mother wants to go to church that's her choice. I won't have you being so disrespectful."

"I only said it would be weird," Grace sulked. "And it would."

It was nice to know that I was not the only one to have the last word in our family. Grace huffed as only teenagers can and Hubby grabbed the car keys and looked at his watch.

"Come on then or you will miss the...er...the..."

"Service," I said helpfully. "I don't know what time it starts."

"It's nine a.m. at St Bartholomew's," Hubby provided promptly but Grace grasped his arm and gave it a little shake. "That is, if you want to go there. You could go somewhere else?"

"No that's fine," I responded. I had failed religious studies at school so one denomination was as much a mystery as another as far as I was concerned. "How do you know what time it starts?"

"My mate, Oscar, goes with his family every week. He's been trying to get me, us, to go for ages."

We climbed into the car. William and Elizabeth just appeared in the back seat. I don't know how they did that. I never saw them get in or out.

"I won't hang about unless you want me to. I'm not dressed for church and I wouldn't want to raise Oscar's hopes of a convert. You won't need the hat by the way."

We jerked down the driveway and I threw the hat onto the back seat with relief, whereupon Elizabeth immediately appropriated it. She was still wearing the yellow towelling robe and I tried to suggest to William by various winks and pantomime gestures that it would be as well if she could pull up her bodice to hide her withered breasts since we were on our way to church. Hubby pretended not to notice my grimaces as I yanked up an imaginary dress and pushed down imaginary boobs.

"Will you want to talk to the reverend?" He asked as we reached the end of the road and had to wait as a stream of traffic chugged by.

I glanced back at my two friends. Elizabeth was now trying on the hat and nodded vehemently. William having gaged her wishes also nodded. I suspected that Elizabeth wanted to quiz the vicar on his doctrine.

"No," I said.

"Well, it's David Hope. We've met him. He called to see us if you remember?" I didn't answer. "Nice bloke. You liked him and he didn't seem to hold our atheism against us. Oscar told me that he was also really supportive when they were going through a bit of a crisis with one of their family."

"Ok, though I think both our kids have turned out really well. I mean, we are really very lucky. They don't drink or take drugs or stay out all night. Well, Grace doesn't. Alex does sometimes of course. Stay out all night, I mean, and I must admit that it worries me. Quite a bit." I took a deep breath. "But you have to expect that at his age and you have to give them a little freedom… Don't you? So I think we've done well with them both really."

It was Hubby's turn to be silent.

"Well, don't you?" I was grasped by a sudden fear. "Is there something wrong? Is something happening with them that I don't know about?"

"No, no, no, no," Hubby patted my hand reassuringly. "Not at all."

"Are you sure? I know I haven't spent much time with them recently but Grace is doing well at school isn't she? And

Alex told me he's expecting to get that place at university, so what...?"

"Everything is fine," Hubby interrupted, very firmly. "Everything is fine. The only thing wrong right now is you."

I gaped at him.

"What I mean is that wanting to go to church out of the blue like this came as a bit of surprise. Not that I have a problem with it at all. You know best what you need and I think it will be good for you. It's just a bit out of character."

He was right there of course. I couldn't think of a thing to say that could refute that fact so I looked out of the window. The drizzle had decided to make way for a watery sun which was struggling through grey clouds. The roads were surprisingly busy. Even Sundays don't slow things down anymore.

Hubby spotted Oscar and his family arriving at the church and leaned out of the car to hail them. It was almost as if they were expecting us. I felt cold and suddenly reluctant to leave the car and enter the angular grey building. I'd seen it many, many times before but now a chill desolation crept over me as I looked at its harsh modern façade and a blurred memory nagged at my heart.

"You don't have to go in if you don't want to," Hubby said gently. "If it is too painful for you, maybe..."

"No, I'm fine." I chased the nebulous strands of remembrance from my head and climbed determinedly from the car.

Oscar and his wife Em were of Caribbean descent and had four children ranging from five to sixteen years. Hubby looked uncharacteristically embarrassed as they all trotted over.

"My wife, Ally," he introduced me. "She wants to come to the service today if that would be ok?"

"Sure, sure," Oscar opened the door and, gentlemanlike, helped me out. "And what about you, sir? Are you not coming in to hear the Lord's word?"

Oscar handed me off to Em and bent down to talk to Hubby.

"Not today," Hubby said primly, "but if I could ask you the favour of looking after her?"

I bridled a bit at that. Look after me indeed! What on earth did he think could possibly happen to me in a church? I started to walk off in a huff but the five-year-old romped after me and who could resist?

"Sure, sure, she will stay with us. Delighted to have her." Oscar's charm came from saying things like that and meaning them. He clapped Hubby on the shoulder and then linked his arm in mine. Em complimented me on my dress and also sounded like she meant it. The children smiled at me, even the sixteen-year-old and everyone knows that sixteen-year-olds almost never smile at the middle-aged. We all trooped into St Bartholomew's, Elizabeth and William at my shoulder. If I had thought about it more I probably would have taken them to the old Norman church in the next village that hadn't changed in centuries and where they might have felt more at home. St Bart's is a twentieth century construction, all abstract angles and concrete, and they both viewed the church with suspicion. On the other hand, I decided, if they wanted to see protestant religion in action in the twenty-first century then this would fit the bill admirably.

Oscar ensconced me between himself and his wife and scattered his children either side on the long pew. Whilst I did not want to do him a disservice I couldn't help thinking that this was to prevent me making a run for it. I glanced behind. William and Elizabeth had so far separated themselves from me to have a wander around. They were weaving between the other churchgoers, examining both them and the large airy room with equal interest and disappointment. They didn't usually venture far from my side but perhaps, like me, they felt that not much would harm them in a church.

They were not all that impressed by the building. It certainly was rather plain and unadorned, with not a stained-glass window in sight. Even the organ was small and unassuming and the pulpit looked like it might have been delivered in flat pack from Ikea. The people too were simply dressed and ordinary and, as I rubbed the fast forming blisters on my heels from the shoes with high heels that I rarely wore, I thanked heaven that I hadn't worn the hat. Elizabeth was wearing it instead and, if I had wondered at all about anyone else in the congregation being able to see her, I was convinced of the negative by the fact that no one visible wearing jewels, ruff, brocade, yellow towelling, a floppy pink hat and exposing her breasts to such an alarming degree would have gone unremarked.

Em kept up a light conversation about nothing in particular whilst her children, who had been churchgoers since birth, behaved impeccably. Oscar and Em were greeted with warmth by virtually all those who came through the doors. It was an enticing, alluring, gentle, peaceful and friendly place.

Em told me in an undertone that her eldest boy who had always been lively and outgoing had taken to spending solitary hours on the computer and that he wanted to pierce his eyebrows and paint his bedroom black. I told her not to worry, Alex had gone through exactly the same phase but was now a nice, hardworking, gregarious kind of lad.

"Oh, really?" she asked with interest, "I'm sorry, I thought…"

"What do you think of our church then?" Oscar leant over his wife with uncharacteristic brusqueness and clasped my hand. "We have quite a large congregation. At least it is considered large for this day and age. So few people know the word of God these days."

"In Elizabeth's time the people had to attend church or they were regarded as recusants and got fined," I said knowledgeably.

"Elizabeth's time?"

"Tudor England I mean. William is on record as having been fined several times."

"Ah," said Oscar. "Is that so? Well, I bet they had good

congregations in those days, if not necessarily for the right reasons." He chuckled, Em laughed and I smiled. Elizabeth sat herself down in the pew in front of us and turned to scowl at me. If it wasn't Mr. Bean she didn't see the humour. She was fascinated by Oscar though and I couldn't blame her. He had one of those milk and honey voices flavoured with just a hint of Barbados and when he spoke you listened and when he stopped speaking you tried to find a reason to make him speak again.

I wanted to make some explanation of my sudden presence among them but I could not think of one that would ring true. Even the truth wouldn't ring true.

"I'm afraid I haven't been to church myself for years. My family, I mean my Mum and Dad, were never churchgoers. Still aren't. In fact, Mum inclines towards the pagan and Dad is of the opinion that people should worship him."

I giggled.

"That's not true. My Dad's lovely. The last time I was in a church was for a wedding. Most people seem to opt for registry office weddings these days don't they?"

"But you have been to this church before," said Em kindly.

"No, I haven't." Em looked disconcerted at that. I don't know why. Oscar was there though and whatever Em might have said next was replaced with his words.

"It's a shame more people don't open their hearts to the word of God. It is always a great comfort to those who are lost or in pain. Remember that, Ally."

Oscar was only saying what he believed but, despite his kindly intentions, I couldn't quite suppress the faint stirrings of irritation. Which was very unfair of me because what the hell else could I expect to hear in a church?

Elizabeth was poking me in the ribs, and that didn't help either.

"Are these Puritans? No candles, no icons, no Latin, one cross…These are …. recusants, heretics!"

I turned on her. "They are nice people and they have a true faith."

There was a startled silence. Then Oscar's hand covered one of mine and Em's covered the other.

"Ally, we will pray for you. Will you pray with us?"

Oh hell, I thought, desperately.

"Yes, of course," I said, like the hypocrite I am.

We all bowed our heads and Em's and Oscar's friends left us for a few moments in respectful silence. I spent most of the time directing spiteful looks surreptitiously in Elizabeth's direction. It was only when Elizabeth moved slightly that I realised my venomous glances had inadvertently terrified a nervous little woman sitting immediately behind her.

We raised our heads as the service began. A long thin man with a long thin nose and a long thin voice read the lesson. The organ, played by a chubby, middle-aged woman with a mass of salt and pepper hair, wheezed into life. Those things always sound as if they are out of tune to me, but that suits my singing voice to a tee so, when Em handed me a hymn book, I joined in with gusto. It was all new to me but I didn't let that hold me back.

At one point Oscar squeezed past us all and got up to read from the Bible. It was something about Jacob and his son but it could have been the Yellow Pages and I would have hung on every word. Something about his honest beliefs and his passion enlivened the old scriptures so much that I began to feel the yearning that draws you into the comfort that religion offers. Perhaps these gentle people did have the answer to man's fears and hopes and uncertainties. Perhaps they did hold the secret of an afterlife in which there was no unhappiness and you could meet again the ones you had loved and lost. It was compelling.

Em nudged me and as I turned to look at that kind, loving face I realised that my sight was blurred and my face was wet with tears. She put her arm around me and her little girl handed me a handkerchief with a Mr. Happy motif in the corner. I could not suppress a sob. I was excruciatingly embarrassed so I bowed my head, clutched my two hands together and struggled for composure.

An opportunity for light relief came soon enough, when, his reading over, Oscar came back to his seat and a young man with a ponytail and tattoos got up to say how his life had been enriched when he found Jesus and that he was now dedicated to bringing the Word to others through his music. It was a fine and laudable ambition and so when he asked us all to stand and join in with his song, we did, of course. In an instant there was a happy buzz. The first chords were struck and the choir led us all in an enthusiastic meander through a simple melody and some excruciatingly bad lyrics. But it was the spirit that counted. And that was just as well.

A couple of prayers later and it was over.

I turned to look for Elizabeth and William. It was one of the few times I ever saw them hold anything like a conversation. William would have been regarded by Elizabeth as one of the 'low' people and, no doubt, didn't feel he had the right to express his opinions in general to his Queen. In the casual simplicity of modern religion, however, they had found a subject of mutual outrage and their conversation was animated.

"Are you all right now, my dear?" Em whispered as she took my arm and we prepared to vacate the pew.

"Yes, of course, silly of me. I don't know what I was thinking."

"Many are similarly moved when they are touched by the grace of God," Oscar said kindly. "Perhaps that is what has happened to you."

"Oh well," I floundered, not feeling touched by any sort of grace at that particular moment. "Maybe, at least, I'm not sure. It was very kind of you to bring me."

"But we didn't. You found your own way to us."

"Yes, but I really only came because Elizabeth and William were so interested." I could have bitten off my tongue at that.

"Oh, so? And where are they?" I looked back at him blankly but he just smiled as if it didn't matter. "Never mind, Ally, you came today and will come again if it is God's will, and your Elizabeth and William will be welcome too. Now, you wanted to talk to the reverend?"

Of course, Hubby had called him whilst getting dressed. The zip episode served him right.

The reverend was at the door shaking hands with those who were leaving. He looked innocuous and kindly enough but I shook my head vehemently.

"No thank you. Not now, maybe another time." Oscar nodded and, when we reached the reverend, simply introduced me as his friend.

The vicar clasped my hand in both of his and looked into my eyes. He had those very light eyes that always hold a piercing gaze and, though his words were no more than an expression that I would be welcome in his church anytime, I felt that he saw into my soul. Or would have done if I had one. There was something about him though that frightened me. More than frightened. I staggered back slightly and my throat constricted as concern and, something else… Recognition touched his gentle eyes. He opened his mouth to speak again and I pulled away, cannoning into Oscar as I looked for escape. Enclosed in Oscar's arms I was kindly propelled away from the darkness and into the light.

"You are not ready to face it yet, are you my dear?"

Oscar smiled down at me. I pulled away and looked around for Elizabeth and William. They were next to a mini metro talking to Nell of all people.

"Will you excuse me a moment?" I said hurriedly. "There is someone I know from work. I'll just say hello."

"Your husband is waiting," Oscar indicated Hubby who had managed to squeeze our car into a space by the off-licence.

"I won't be a moment," I repeated, "I'll just say hello to Nell." And I hurried away.

"Wotcher," Nell greeted me broadly. She wasn't exactly classy at the best of times but she was looking particularly unkempt that morning. "I 'ear that you've been 'aving fun and games with your two friends."

"You could say that," I laughed. "Did they tell you about the Rocky Horror Show?"

"Well, nice to know you're showing them some culture."

I think she was completely serious when she said that.

"And now you're 'ere at church. What are you goin' to get up to next?"

"They wanted to come. What are you doing here anyway?"

"On me way to the pub, love. They do a Sunday lunch for £3.50 for pensioners. Do you want to come? Bring your 'usband, e' enjoys a good roast."

I glanced back at Hubby and wondered briefly how she knew he was there. And how she knew that he liked a good roast.

"Better not, the kids are at home. Anyway, I'm hardly a pensioner and neither are you come to that."

She patted her nose conspiratorially. "These days you have to do what you can to conserve the pennies. Anyway, our two friends are definitely way over pension age." She cackled loudly and I glanced around. Oscar and Em were talking to Hubby. They were looking in our direction.

"I suppose I had better get home," I sighed and looked appealingly at Nell. "You're still the only one I have found who sees them. Apart from…"

"I wouldn't worry about that, love. It makes you special, don't it?"

"I can do without that sort of special," I muttered. "If I tell them about Elizabeth and William, well, my family already think there is something wrong with me and it is very difficult having them in tow all the time. They are driving me mad. Could you come over and explain that you see them too?"

Nell grinned unhelpfully.

"Please, Nell. I need your help. It won't take a moment."

"Nah, don't fink so, love. I've me own problems to deal with. You know some days it just ain't worth chewin' through the straps. You'll be all right, talk to your old man. 'E's a nice bloke and, like I said, you are special. Not many of us 'ave royalty and genius as 'ouse guests. I'm off. I'll see you on the bus I 'spect."

"Can't you take them with you?" I wailed after her.

She waddled determinedly away and I looked hopelessly at William and Elizabeth.

"I can't talk to you while they're watching me," I hissed. "But if you are going to stay you're going to have to help me keep my family happy and that means you behave yourself and don't get me into trouble. Do you hear me?"

Elizabeth glared back, affronted.

"I'm serious," I snapped. "You are both a damned nuisance and if you don't back off from me a bit I will just have to get rid of you both somehow."

"Stay, goe, doe what thou will. Thou art a dream, a mote, a nothing. The Queen of England doth not haggle with such as thee," Elizabeth thundered.

I stepped back from the sudden onslaught and looked at William but his eyes fell from mine and I realised that I had both angered Elizabeth and hurt William.

"I'm sorry," I said, slightly shamefacedly. "But I can't have my family upset by this, I just can't."

Elizabeth turned expressionless eyes on me.

"Am I bovvered?" she said with supreme gravity.

"Oh dear god," I groaned. "I really have to keep you away from that bloody television. Look, please try to understand, I may be a dream to you but you are in my real life and I need you to help me." I walked away from them because Hubby was coming towards me followed by Oscar and Em.

"Who were you talking to?"

"Just Nell from work," I said airily. "She went to the pub for Sunday lunch. It's £3.50 for pensioners she said."

"Oh right," he looked past me. "I didn't see her. Where was she?"

"She was behind the mini metro," I said. He looked disbelieving. "She's very short." Which was true. Still, it was strange he had not seen her.

"Oh, ok. Em said you seemed upset during the service. I'm sorry, I should not have brought you here. To this church I mean."

"I don't see why." I looked back at the simple square building with the vicar standing at the door and tentacles of blackness reached towards me again, threatening to engulf me in pain. I turned away abruptly, took a deep breath against the panic and decided to change the subject. "I'm starving. Shall I cook a roast? We haven't had a proper Sunday lunch for ages and we could pick up one of those mini-roasts from the supermarket. That won't take long to cook."

"Not necessary," he replied with a barely suppressed grimace. "Your mum's come over with your sister. They were busy cooking when I left. Come and say goodbye to Oscar."

He was playing my game and had timed the last remark to avoid my exclamation of surprise deepening into suspicion. Mum hardly ever came over unannounced and my sister even more rarely. Not that there was any reason why they shouldn't, they were just so wrapped up in their own lives that they didn't. But before I could start to wonder out loud we were plunged into polite thanks and warm good wishes mingled with a sort of tender concern from Em and Oscar. Lord knows what Hubby had been telling them. The family waved cheery goodbyes and Oscar clapped Hubby on the shoulder. I caught the words, "if there is anything I can do to help, let me know," before they all trundled off to their immense and tightly packed car.

Hubby drove in silence for a couple of minutes. I glanced behind, expecting to see William and Elizabeth in the back seat, but they were not there. I was a little worried but I shrugged it off. Provided I had not offended too deeply with my desperation to get rid of them they would, no doubt, appear again soon when least expected. To be honest it was quite a relief. I felt almost normal for a change.

"So why," I asked, "have Mum and Kate decided to come this weekend? Did you invite them?"

"I think Grace did."

"Oh," I thought about that for a moment. "Is she all right?"

"Who? Grace?" Hubby seemed surprised that I was asking.

"Well, yes. She's been quite distant the last few weeks and we used to be so close."

"I don't think it's coming from Grace. The distance I mean. To be honest love, you are the one that seems to be distancing yourself from us. I thought at first that it might have been caused by the car accident but it started before that. We are all worried about you."

"And that's why Kate and Mum have come over," I accused him, "to inspect me and put me back on the straight and narrow."

He smiled at that. "I don't see why anyone would imagine that they could. I'm fairly sure they couldn't find the straight and narrow if it jumped up and bit them on the backside." For a split second, I considered being outraged and insulted by this slight upon my nearest and dearest but then you really would have to be mad not to accept that he had a valid point, so I laughed instead.

"Bless them. My family has always been completely doolally. I'm the sanest one amongst them."

Hubby's smile faded and I felt a burst of guilt. I put my hand briefly on his.

"Look, please don't worry so much. I think," I floundered for an explanation that wasn't a lie. "I think I am living a little too much in my imagination. Some things seem real to me that other people…don't see."

"Like what?" he asked immediately.

I tried to think of a way that I could ease him gently towards the truth.

"Well, I began to wonder what, um, what historical characters might think about the world as it is now. You know, what they would think of cars and televisions and planes and everything. And I am just imagining seeing it through their eyes, that's all."

Hubby turned right at the traffic lights and digested that.

"Historical characters?"

"Elizabethan's for instance," I suggested lightly.

"Why them, particularly?"

"I don't know. Why not?"

"Well, why do you think you are doing this? There must be some reason that you lighted on them."

"They just sort of came to me, that's all." That much was true anyway.

"When you say they came to you…?"

I steeled myself for the inevitable. The time had come.

"Look, if you want the truth, then I will tell you. I opened the pantry door about a month ago and Elizabeth was sitting there."

"Elizabeth? The pantry?" He looked bemused. Understandable I suppose.

"Elizabeth the first, the virgin queen, Good Queen Bess. In our pantry."

"Oh, her." For a moment, from his laconic reaction, I thought that maybe he was used to opening the pantry door to find Elizabeth sitting there but I noticed his knuckles whitening on the steering wheel and knew that he was holding himself in check with an effort.

But in for a penny, in for a pound.

"And then a bit later I went to loo in the middle of the night and William was in the bath."

"William?"

"Shakespeare."

"Oh, of course. Silly of me, I should have known." There was a touch of hysteria in his voice.

"Since then they have been following me around. Or at least, sometimes they ask to go somewhere and I take them. Like church this morning. They were very interested in how religion has developed in the last four hundred years. I don't think they were all that impressed. They are impressed by technology of course but not much else. Actually, I would like to take William to Stratford to see one of his plays performed by professionals. I did take him to that amateur group in the town and he's been depressed ever since. It seems a shame as he is a sweet, quiet little man and it would be nice to do something for him. Elizabeth is a bit of a Tartar to tell the truth. I don't think you will like her much but then, you have to understand, she needed to be tough in her own time to keep her head on her shoulders, so you have to give her a bit of leeway…"

"Are they here now?"

I glanced behind me.

"No, they might have gone with Nell to see what a public house is like." There was silence. I looked across at Hubby. It was a great relief to have unburdened myself. Hubby rarely showed when he was upset. You knew when he was angry but apart from that he didn't express much deep emotion. Alex was like that too and so was my father. A male thing I suppose. I waited a little but he seemed busy with his thoughts and I had no idea what they were.

"Anyway," I said eventually, "they come and go. They don't have any control over it any more than I do. They say that I am like a dream to them. They go back to their everyday lives when they are not with me. William is okay about that but I think Elizabeth is ill as she prefers being here. It's 1603 where they come from, you see, and I looked it up and that's the year that Elizabeth dies. Nell can see them. She says I ought to think myself special because they come to me and no one else. I took them to the Rocky Horror show, you know. That's why I was late back on Friday night and I'm sure that Alex saw them so I need to ask him…"

"For god's sake!" Hubby spat out the words in a manner quite unlike himself as he yanked the car into our driveway. "Have you listened to yourself, Ally? Can't you hear what you are saying? You need to…" He forced out the words as if under some internal labour of massive proportions.

"You need to pull yourself together, for Christ's sake. For all our sakes. Can't you see what you are doing to us? To me. To Grace. Please." He turned towards me and his voice softened. "Please come back to us, Ally."

I gazed at him in astonishment. He stared back, half angry and half something else. Grief-stricken I think. There was a fleeting moment, as we were locked together in that long gaze, when I could have reached towards him, my kind, loved and loving husband, and could have returned to him as he so much wanted me to, but there was something there, something dark and frightening in the shadows that I did not want to move towards.

The moment passed.

CHAPTER ELEVEN

O, that way madness lies; let me shun that;
No more of that.
King Lear, Act III Sc iv

"I knew you wouldn't believe me," I bellowed back at him. "I should never have told you. Forget I said anything. Just forget it all."

I hauled myself out of the car and slammed the door but Mum and Kate were on the porch so my tantrum was brought to an abrupt halt.

"Surprise!" called Mum, cheerily.

You have to understand that my mum has always been as mad as a box of snakes and that my older sister, Kate takes after her big time. Both are wildly artistic – the emphasis being on the wild. My mum studied art in her youth, submerged herself in the Bohemian culture, became an experimental artist and never quite made a name for herself. At least, not as an artist. Her youth had apparently been very free and she had got herself into all sorts of ganja-fuelled scrapes with all sorts of dissolutely artistic people, some of them famous. I don't mean to infer that she was promiscuous, at least as far as any of us are aware, but she was certainly a woman who led a life less ordinary. Somehow, we were never quite sure how, she met my dad who was in the navy, didn't have an artistic bone in his body and was a straight arrow if ever there was one. I'm fairly sure that my

Mum has no idea how or where they met and I'm equally sure that Dad does and that wild horses wouldn't be able to drag it out of him. Anyhow, this very odd couple married, had me and Kate and, to everyone's surprise, lived happily ever after. I was the untalented one. Kate inherited all the artistic genes and now, somehow, makes a living as a potter. She lives in a mobile home in a field and has had a series of fairly long term relationships with a series of kind but stultifying men who bored the pants off all of us including, eventually, Kate. So far the affairs have all ended amicably with Kate leaving the country for an extended and unspecified period. Once her lover's ardour cools or they find someone else to bore rigid she returns. It appears to work for her.

Mum and Kate live in happy, arty, scatty symbiosis, whilst me and Dad, and latterly Hubby, just try not to get in their way. They create bizarre works of art that are usually ugly, invariably unique (because who would want another one) and undeniably exuberant. I love them both dearly but do not tend to go to them for advice in a crisis. Kate is a great believer in art therapy and would, no doubt, put me in a room with clay and paint and encourage me to express myself out of whatever difficulty I was in. If that did not work, then there was always Tai Chi or drinking your own urine. She had tried that for a while and been an enthusiastic advocate for at least three months until a yeast infection put an end to that particular dream of health and happiness.

Mum would take a much more life experience approach and would relate spine-chilling, bone-withering stories about one or other of her vast array of barmy friends who had suffered a similar crisis and she would then amply demonstrate how they had handled it in the wrong way and suffered direful consequences as a result. Then she would tell me exactly what they should have done, which almost always involved running away to live in a hut on Lesbos, rear goats, squeeze olives and dance with abandon to bouzoukis under a Greek moon. Apparently that would cure most ills and there were times when I felt its attractions.

I had feeling that they would both be a bit exercised to find a way out of this one though.

I heard Hubby's car door close and knew he was behind me. I couldn't help feeling a little betrayed so I turned my back and marched jauntily up to my mother and sister.

"Well, this is a surprise. I hear that you have started a roast?"

"Kangaroo," said Kate.

"What?" said I.

"Kangaroo. Had it in Australia when I was there a couple of months ago. Went to study the decline of bees in the Outback due to global warming. Long story. Cut it short, had kangaroo meat under the stars in the bush. Nothing like it. Got back to find they sell it at Tesco's. Brilliant stuff. You'll never look at another lamb."

"So, you're not a vegetarian anymore, then?" I wasn't in the least surprised. She'd eaten locusts in Somalia a couple of years ago and, inevitably, it was a slippery slope from there on.

"Not when it comes to vermin," she said positively, "though I think they might farm them for meat in England. Goes against the grain obviously. Either way though, it's good stuff."

"Lovely," I lied.

"You're looking peaky," Mum said. She might have been right. The thought of vermin on my plate for lunch, farmed or otherwise, had left me slightly queasy. "Have you been taking the ginseng, like I told you?"

"Every day," I lied some more.

"And the aloe vera? What about the gingko beans?"

"Yes, Mum." They were all in the pantry, untouched, but that brought to mind Elizabeth and William so I looked around and up and down the street to see if they were there but there was no sign.

"Who are you looking for?" Kate asked, suspiciously. I met Hubby's eyes as he came towards us swinging the car keys.

"No one," I replied defiantly and went into the house and through to the kitchen. We always congregated in the kitchen even though we had a perfectly good lounge.

Grace was shelling peas and the room smelled of what I had to assume was roasting marsupial.

"Hey, mum. Auntie brought us Kangaroo to roast." She was obviously not at all impressed but was far too polite to say what she really thought with Kate in the room. "What do we do about gravy, Auntie Kate?"

"They roast it over a fire made from aromatic eucalyptus and serve it on flat stones under the southern stars with the sounds of the bush ringing in your ears."

"Use an Oxo cube," suggested Hubby, ever the pragmatist.

"Beef?" Grace asked, without conviction.

"Vegetable might be less…well, maybe the flavours will blend better," I suggested. "We'll use the grey plates, I'll find some fairy lights and we can shake the aspidistra. That will be about the closest we can get to Kate's recipe, I think."

Kate and Mum piled into the kitchen too so I put the kettle on and we all had a cup of tea whilst the meat and vegetables cooked. Hubby soon removed himself to the computer in the living room. He did his best but my family en masse (and even just two of them feels like a mass) is bewildering. Anyway, Grace was there to keep an eye on me.

I parried the expected blow for some time by asking Kate about Australia and the disappearing bees. She expounded on this theme for some time. I then managed to distract Mum for a few minutes by asking how Dad was. She said he had gone to the yacht for the weekend. Well, we call it a yacht. It's actually an old tub called, for some reason lost in the mists of time, Parbuckle. He usually escaped there whenever Mum was getting too arty and the house smelled of linseed oil. He puttered about the river and the estuary and reminisced with some of his old Navy pals who were also escaping back to the closest approximation of their past possible. Mum used to go occasionally but she suffered from sea sickness and though she did her best to soldier manfully on for Dad's sake he felt it was time for her to call it a day when she threw up over his brand new satellite navigation system. He was now planning a jaunt to France and a trip down to Spain through the French canals and wanted Mum to join him on the canal stretch. He was fairly confident that she wouldn't be sea sick on a canal so Mum was trying to work out how much of her art equipment she could squeeze in and Dad was trying to persuade her to limit herself to a pencil. Kate said she would catch up with them somewhere along the route as she was sure the bees needed looking after in France too and Mum suggested that Hubby and I join them for part of it as well.

It was obvious through it all that Grace had asked them to come over and inspect me and that I was under close scrutiny from all three of them. It was very unfair of me, I knew, to resent Grace, whose actions were only born out of concern, so when the subject was broached, characteristically broadly by Kate ("So Sis, what is going on with you? Grace worried, says you've been seeing visions. Expect that nonsense from me. Not from you. Out with it.") I decided that denial would be the best course and a return to normality the safest thing for my family.

Anyway, Elizabeth and William weren't there and might never come back.

"Oh, it's all a storm in a teacup, really."

I laughed and put my arm around Grace.

"You mustn't worry about me, my love. I'm fine. I think I've been under a bit of strain lately, at work, you know and I got a little confused about things and stayed out late one night which was stupid. But I see things more clearly now. I think the day in bed helped."

"What's all this about Church then?" demanded Kate, who inclined towards Druidism but wasn't going to rule out Buddhism either. Mum wasn't saying much – you could never work out whether she was thinking deep thoughts or studying the light playing off your nose.

"Research." It came to me in a blinding flash of inspiration as I looked at my two wildly creative relations. I hoped that the note of surprise in my own voice had not given me away. "I've been thinking of writing a story and I needed some background, about religion and that sort of stuff."

There was silence for a moment so I filled it with a bright smile.

"And what about Shakespeare and the Queen?" Hubby was at the door. He spoke slowly and not unkindly.

"Yes, of course." My own ingenuity took me by surprise again. "It's all part of the same thing, you see." Hubby gave me a look that carried with it more than just a hint of distrust. "What I was talking about earlier, I think you may have misunderstood. It's all part of the story, do you see? My characters, William and Elizabeth sort of time travel to the present day and the story is all about the ….um…. the adventures they have."

Mum clapped her hands together in a sudden burst of glee. "What a wonderful idea. You could write a children's novel. Why stop at a short story?"

Kate was almost as keen. "Sis, brilliant! Knew you had an artistic streak in you somewhere."

"And that's it, is it?" Hubby asked, exchanging glances with Grace.

"It's probably why I have been so distracted you see." I was warming to this story. It had real potential. I could get away with all sorts now and just call it research! Of course, I would eventually have to write something which was a bit of a nuisance but I would climb that mountain when I came to it. Research would be a good excuse for months to come. "You see, I began thinking about their reactions to the modern world, how they would view things and in a way William and Elizabeth have become real to me. That was all I meant."

"I know exactly what you mean," cried Mum. "Hobgoblin Boy was real to me. I saw him everywhere."

I should explain that Mum had once had a commission to illustrate a children's book and Hobgoblin Boy had paid for a holiday in Africa back when we were kids. We all had fond memories of him.

"I've heard that characters in novels do quite often become very real to their authors," Grace said with quiet desperation, spatula in hand.

"So that's all it is," Mum said with her usual gaiety. "Ally's artistic spirit is breaking through."

"Blossoming," agreed Kate.

"All us artistic types have a streak of madness. Just give her a bit of space and time," Mum said to Hubby as if I was not there, "and she'll be fine. She might do something odd every now and again, lord knows I do, but you'll get used to it."

Grace and Hubby looked helplessly at each other across the pink heads of my mum and sister (did I mention that they had both dyed their hair bright pink?) and resigned themselves to exclusion from the normal comprehension of the artistically gifted.

"Kangaroo is burning," sighed Grace, and so the bustle of Sunday lunch commenced.

Kangaroo with Yorkshire pudding, broccoli, carrots and roast potatoes was much as you would expect it to be. Luckily it was a small joint, or possibly a very small kangaroo. We shared a couple of bottles of wine, one Australian, due to Kate's current monomania. It tasted terrible but it was 14% so no one cared. We talked about all sorts. I could see Grace and Hubby slowly relaxing as I played my usual jokey role with Mum and Kate and by the time we got around to arguing about who should make the coffee we were very merry and convivial.

"It's a shame Alex isn't here. He would have really enjoyed the kangaroo!" I joked. Of course, he wouldn't have. He had always been a terribly picky eater. "Where is he?"

I looked around at a sea of frozen faces. Not one of them moved and all eyes were on me.

"What?" I asked, surprised. Grace pushed her chair back violently so that it screamed against the floor and ran out of the room. Hubby's head fell into his hands and Mum whispered my name as if in horror. I looked in bewilderment from one to the other. Kate stood up slowly.

"Better see to Grace," she said and left the room quietly.

"Ally, dear," said Mum, putting her hand on mine, "surely you remember, you can't have forgotten…"

"Forgotten what? I don't understand." I withdrew my hand pettishly. There was silence. Hubby raised his head and shook it at Mum.

"Don't," he said to her in an undertone. "We can't handle this ourselves. We need help."

"What on earth are you going on about?" I exploded in fury. "I ask a simple question and everyone behaves as if I've dropped a bomb. I know you all think that I've been behaving strangely but you should look at yourselves…you're all stark staring bonkers!"

I stood up with as much dignity as I could muster, the kangaroo was not digesting well, and stalked out of the kitchen and upstairs to the bedroom. I closed the door in relief and leant against it. Something was wrong, something was very, very, very wrong in my family and I just couldn't quite put my finger on it.

The fuzzy feeling was back again. I felt a gentle hand on my shoulder. It was William. Elizabeth was at my dressing table scowling at me. At least I think she was. She was still wearing my hat and towelling gown and had the remains of yesterday's makeup smudged across her face so her real expression was unreadable. William patted my arm and manoeuvred me towards the bed. I sat down helplessly.

"I know what it is to lose a son," he said, so very gently.

There were some faint, brief, agonising stirrings of a long-held grief within me. His brown eyes were soft and, funny little man that he was, I felt his compassion and his sorrow and it frightened me more than I have ever been frightened in my life. I stood up abruptly.

"No," I said. "I can't think about that. I won't. I mustn't or I will go mad. I will start screaming and I won't ever stop."

"Methinks," broke in Elizabeth in her cracked, hard voice, "this is a remembrance of things past."

"Time doth not heal all," said William quietly. "Sorrow ebbs to flow again."

"Shut up, both of you," I snapped. "Shut up, shut up, shut up!"

There was a tap on the door and it swung slowly open. Mum was there trying very hard not to cry.

"Ally, sweetheart," she choked, "my love, are you all right. We are all so very worried."

Grief does not sit well on people with pink hair. People with pink hair should always be joyous. William withdrew to the stool by the dressing table and stood next to Elizabeth. She viewed me with ungracious tolerance and William nodded encouragingly. It was such an immense comfort to have them there so I smiled and embraced Mum and comforted her in my turn.

"You must see a doctor, Ally," sobbed Mum. "You know that you are seeing things, people I mean, that just aren't here… anymore. You do know that don't you?"

I stared at my two friends nodding back at me and, feeling entirely like Judas, said, "Yes, I know that Mum. I have funny turns and get a bit confused about things so I will see a doctor."

"And, love, you will try not to, not to mention…" There was a long pause as she struggled with that name. I could not help her. "Please try not to mention Alex, at least not to talk about…

him in front of Grace. She is still…suffering and it brings it all back for her."

"I won't," I cut in, a little too sharply. "I won't Mum, I promise. I'm sure a doctor will sort me out. I'll make an appointment in the morning. They'll give me an hour or so off work to pop along I expect and I can get a prescription for… something or other. It's probably just stress, like I said. Or maybe it's those wretched juju berries you keep giving me," I laughed, "they're giving me hallucinations!" I found that very funny so I laughed some more but, for once Mum, who had a pretty good sense of humour, did not see the joke at all. "Or maybe it's the kangaroo meat," I chortled. "I was doing fine until I ate that!"

Hubby appeared at the door. I think he had been listening.

"Ally should get some sleep," he said very quietly.

Maybe it was the wine because I couldn't help giggling.

"Oh, I'm all right," I said merrily, "really, I am. Let's go and watch a video or something. Where is Grace? I need to see her. Mum said that I upset her. I need to let her know that it's all right now."

I headed for the door but Hubby stepped in front of me.

"Really, Ally," he was quietly obdurate. He is not often like that but you don't get anywhere when he is. "You get to bed. Kate and your mum will look after Grace."

"No, I need to see her," I protested, aghast that I was not to be allowed to comfort my own daughter. I tried to push past him but he stopped me and even Mum put a restraining hand on my arm.

"Please, don't do this Ally," he begged. I was bewildered.

I looked back at William, he had his hand outstretched to me. I went to him. I knew he understood.

"All right," I said calmly. "Mum, tell Grace that I am sorry. I wouldn't hurt her for the world. Will you and Kate look after her for me? I will go have a shower and go to bed early. I am tired." I went to Hubby and kissed him on the cheek. "I'm fine

154

now," I promised. "I won't do it again." He pulled me to him in a warm bear hug of an embrace and then put me gently away from him.

"Is there anything you want, tea, coffee?" I shook my head. "I'll be up again soon to see how you are," he said and Mum and he left shutting the door quietly behind them as if I were already lost in sleep and should not be disturbed.

"Well," I said sitting on the end of the bed, "talk about making a mountain out of a molehill."

"Did thou send the letter as I commanded?" Elizabeth asked, self-absorbed as usual.

"No, and anyway the post won't go today. Stop bothering me about it."

"Thinkest thou I am a pilchard? Obey me, slag."

"Right that's it," I said. "No more television for you. Ever."

Elizabeth's lip curled in contempt and she turned her bony back on me. William stepped forward hesitantly.

"Mayhap, we should carry the missive to London?"

"To London?" The four walls of my small bedroom were closing in on me but, at his words, the chance of escape, of action, of doing something, anything, opened up before me.

Surely it was worth one last effort. One last desperate, agonising effort.

"To London." London was a big place. No one knew that better than I did but…

"To London." I got up purposefully.

I checked my handbag, debit card and, shamefully, took some cash from Hubby's wallet. I put on comfortable shoes. My coat was hanging by the front door. They were all in the kitchen. I could hear the low buzz of concern, so if I was quiet, I could make my escape without them being any the wiser until they checked on me. I would be back, of course.

In a day or two.

CHAPTER TWELVE

Exit, pursued by a bear.
Stage direction from A Winter's Tale
Act III Sc iii

The front door closed noiselessly behind us and after a short walk we picked up a bus and were at the railway station. A ticket for London and we were on our way.

The carriage was quiet to start with and we found ourselves one of those seats with a table. Elizabeth took up two seats with her dress (and hat and dressing gown) and William sat next to me. They looked around with interest but they were adapting very quickly to the different modes of transport I was subjecting them to. They accepted the slow acceleration quite happily to start with but clung to their seats as the dusky world began to speed by at over eighty miles an hour. Houses and factories gave way to the fleeting tapestry of fields and hedgerows, hills and roads, all glowing in the early spring evening and seduced them both into fearful wonder. They asked few questions, preferring to take it all in and assimilate it in their own way.

We weren't bothered by anyone until a sudden influx at Wellingborough when, as we pulled away from the station, a thin man in a hoodie rocked up the aisle singing "I Will Always Love You," tunelessly, at the top of his voice.

"Oh God," I said to Elizabeth. "I just know he's going to sit here. I always attract the nutters."

"'Ello gorgeoush," he leaned over Elizabeth and, ignoring the empty seat adjacent to us, leered at me. I wasn't flattered. He clearly wasn't seeing straight.

"Mind if I shit here?"

"There's someone sitting there," I said firmly.

"No, there ishn't," he said.

"Yes, there is."

"Oh K, shweetheart," he hiccupped, swung a six-pack of lager on to the table, overbalanced and collapsed into the seat on top of most of Elizabeth's dress. She boxed him smartly across the head but he was so inebriated I don't think he felt it at all. I stared intently out of the window in that time-honoured English manner of ignoring the potentially embarrassing. Elizabeth pulled her dress out from under him, gave him another sharp slap and withdrew as far as she could into the corner of her seat. The drunkard burped very loudly a couple of times, liberally dispersing the unpleasant smell of digestion, and leant his elbows on the table and his chin on the six-pack. I considered standing up and moving but the seats had filled up around us and there weren't three together. A prim, elderly woman, struggling with an overnight bag settled herself into one of the seats across the aisle, and, perching her neat little glasses on her nose, peered down that neat little nose at me. I smiled back and received a very slight incline of her head in gracious response. Then she looked at my new companion. Predictably, distaste wrinkled her neat little nose and, a sharp exhalation accompanied by a slight roll of her sunken eyes indicated that she had no patience for weakness or untidiness and was possessed of a particular aversion to inebriation. She furnished herself with a National Heritage guidebook to Hampton Court to hide behind and settled into disapproving silence. My drunken companion, having watched all this with befuddled interest, made up his mind and snorted, with his own brand of disgust, his dismissal of the well behaved, sheltered middle classes. He then laid his head sideways on the six-pack and leered at me through puffy eyes.

"You're gorgeeoush," he repeated smacking his lips.

"I will not let the drunken sot lay hands on you," whispered William in a fine and (and failed) attempt at belligerence.

"Oh, don't worry," I said airily, "I've dealt with worse than him."

"What?" said the drunkard.

"Nothing," I sighed, as six young women in hen party mode, fell through the sliding doors, shrieking with laughter and staggered inexorably towards us.

"'Ello darling!'" The drunkard, spotting a better bet amongst the party girls, abandoned as a bad job his unsubtle wooing of me, stood up unsteadily, put his hands in the air and attempted to wiggle his scant hips suggestively.

Mercifully, perhaps, a sudden jolt caused him to fall sideways and end up with his head buried in Elizabeth's brocaded lap. A woman with long blonde hair and tangerine toned skin recognised him as a fellow inebriate and staggered up the aisle on four-inch heels. Screaming with uncontrolled hilarity she leapt on top of him and, unbeknownst to both, on top of a sovereign queen. A similarly orange woman with even more tinted skin on show followed her and without any shred of what my mother would call reserve, manhandled me over to William's side of the seat and parked her ample backside on my side. William was forced onto my lap and Elizabeth was somewhere underneath two thrashing drunkards. Before I could work up to any sort of protest, two dumpy and but slightly less raucous damsels rocked their way up the aisle and, in the spirit of sharing, balanced their backsides on the seat opposite the prim woman and turned their heavily made-up eyes admiringly on their more extrovert companions.

William was flattened against the window next to me and I was wedged in next to orange lady. Tangerine queen leant over and, still screaming with laughter at her fellow female's bold antics, made some attempt to pull her off the, by now semi-conscious, drunk. Voluptuous arms and legs thrashed about wildly amidst the rise and fall of drunken laughter and the rocking of the train. It was all quite shocking. The one mauling the hooded drunk put a long nailed hand on the table and clawed herself upright. The drunkard reeled himself out from under and Elizabeth, released for a fleeting moment, struggled into a sitting position squashed between them and straightened her hat. Bless her, she looked so crushed and dishevelled.

"Are you all right?" I asked in concern.

"Bawds," she spat, un-crushing her high standing ruff. "Mountains of mad flesh."

"They're just enjoying themselves."

"Oo are you talkin' to?" slurred tangerine queen pulling her elasticated skirt down in a modest but half-hearted, and ultimately unsuccessful attempt, to cover what feigned to do service as a pair of knickers. I suppose we should be grateful for small mercies. At least she was wearing some.

"You're squashing my friend." I was quite concerned. Elizabeth, always frail, looked particularly so, sandwiched as she was between the substantial tangerine queen and the tall skinny drunkard.

"Oo? 'Im? 'E can take it!" and she punched him with some force, narrowly missing Elizabeth's nose in the process. The drunk leered happily back but Elizabeth wasn't taking any more. She released a cascade of slaps and scratches on the tangerine queen who, feeling something of the real queen's displeasure, thought they came from the leering drunk. The affronted woman screamed, in loud protest this time, and her orange friend launched herself heroically over the table to rain heavy blows on the hapless and helpless man. I stood up hurriedly. Elizabeth had disappeared yet again beneath the welter of ochre flesh. Orange woman had leant forward to assist her flailing friend by adding a bit more flailing so I climbed over her back and grabbing William hauled him out bodily by the same route.

I hustled him over the chunky legs of the two fat friends who had decided that the best way to deal with the crisis was to give in to very loud hysteria and throw in a little more flailing for good measure. We reached a breathing space by the luggage rack. I was heading back to attempt a rescue when I saw Elizabeth crawling out from beneath the table whilst aiming some very vicious jabs with the pin of a jewelled brooch at the chunky legs belonging to the hysterical duo. The prim woman was cowering behind her book and stoically attempting to ignore the screaming and thrashing that was all around her. Elizabeth was nearly out of danger and all would have been well, at least as far as we were concerned, except that she caught a glimpse of the front cover of the book the prim woman was sheltering behind and decided to appropriate it for herself. Before I could pull her away she had seized the book, the woman had screamed and covered her face with her hands and a frightened porter, or whatever they are called nowadays, was careering down the aisle towards us and the escalating frenzy. I grasped Elizabeth and hurried her back down the aisle to William, who was clinging to the luggage rack, complete astonishment on his face.

"These maidens are so large, display such flesh, such legs…! Have they an illness?"

"What?" I muttered irritably.

"They are so yellow!"

"No, that's a tan. It's fashionable to look as if you have nothing better to do than lie on a beach all day."

"They lie on a beach all day?" William echoed.

"Actually they probably lie on a sun bed all day, so that they look like they lie on a beach all day. It's a status symbol – like white skin used to be in your day…"

I was distracted by the porter who was attempting to manhandle two of the flailing women off the bewildered and battered drunkard and failing miserably. The two chubby friends had decided that yet another beastly man was attacking their bosom cronies and had waded into the fray with gusto, their not inconsiderable weight improving the odds for the feminine side. Prim lady was still cowering and bleating and several other people in the compartment were about to pitch in on the side of the porter but, in attempting to re-establish order, succeeded only in adding to the mayhem. The language being used was truly atrocious. I slid quietly through the automatic doors taking Elizabeth and William with me by the scruff of each scrawny neck.

We found ourselves in the buffet car. I stowed my confused friends into a corner and perched myself on one of the two high stools provided. A portly gentleman opposite me was reading the Times and clearly did not want to be bothered. That suited me fine. I sighed deeply and closed my eyes for a moment. When I opened them Elizabeth and William were sitting quietly on the floor poring over the pictures in the purloined book. The train rattled on.

At one point the continuing disturbance from the next carriage briefly shattered our peace. One orange maiden and one supportive fat friend flung into our carriage screaming obscenities accompanied by a tough-looking bloke with no hair who might have been an off-duty policeman or a paramedic. He had that calm, detached unflappability that you often see in people who deal with conflict on a regular basis. However, after just a couple of foul-mouthed minutes of colourful abuse from the two hysterical women, the cracks were beginning to show in his professionalism. And when the women pulled away and screamed themselves back to their party buddies he was as vocal and as caught up in noisy outrage as they were.

The door slid shut on them and the man opposite, who hadn't for one moment raised his eyes from the newspaper during the fracas, said quietly, "Birching's too good for 'em." He didn't seem to expect an answer.

"Trollops," said Elizabeth from the corner.

"Churlish harpies," William ventured to concur. For a mild man, he was very good at insults, although it also should be mentioned that his eyes had never left the vast expanse of orange woman's legs.

"They are all drunk," I tried to explain, embarrassed that my countrywomen were showing themselves at less than their best. The gentleman's eyes flickered towards me.

"As you say." He folded his newspaper and walked away. I felt myself summarily dismissed.

Elizabeth and William took the opportunity to re-join me as we perched around the little high table and Elizabeth pointed out in the book all the places she recognised in her father's house. Only the odd person here and there came through for a coffee or a sandwich and, having ordered a coffee myself, I could see why. So, once again, we were quiet and comfortable. A little later the porter staggered through with a slight limp that he hadn't had before and a tissue stuffed up his nose. He asked me for my ticket and then dripped blood on it.

"Country's goin' to the dogs," he growled as I offered him a tissue bung for his other nostril. "I blame reality T.V."

Apart from that, we weren't bothered again until we rolled into St Pancras station. We descended without incident from the buffet car onto the platform and watched for a moment or two as the hen party fell out of the next carriage. Some sort of happy reconciliation appeared to have been brokered for the skinny drunkard leapt out first clutching a can of lager and bellowing his own very personal interpretation of "My Heart Will Go On". This was directed at the blowsier of the two orange ladies who hung out of a carriage door in what she fondly imagined to be a romantic attitude and serenaded him back. The amorous lover must have shared his six-pack, for the rest of the party, also clutching lager cans and managing their six-inch stilettos with varying degrees of success, fell out, and landed in a heap of heaving bosoms and exposed yellow thighs around the inebriated Lothario. They eventually untangled themselves and wove down the platform, the best of raucous friends.

Their good humour was not mirrored by their fellow passengers who disembarked with varying expressions of disgruntlement and huffed off down the platform in disgust. The prim woman stalked up to me in outrage and snatched the book I had forgotten I was holding.

"Thief," she spat at me, very un-primly.

"I didn't take it," I protested.

"Then who did?" she bridled.

"She did," I snapped back, pointing at Elizabeth.

"Pah!" I had forgotten myself in the upset of being accused of dishonesty. The woman looked where I pointed and then took a couple of judicious steps back. "Mad, mad, mad," she said. "This country has gone to the dogs. I blame the namby-pamby liberals."

"Should bring back birching," said the Times gentleman as he passed.

"Too good for 'em," muttered the prim woman sidling nervously past me and disappearing down the platform as fast her sensible shoes would carry her.

"The women here are… strange," mused Elizabeth, straightening her hat and shaking out her ruff.

"Just the women?" I asked. "What about the men?"

"No, they are the same."

I laughed. "I can see that. Come on, let's go."

CHAPTER THIRTEEN

*The common curse of mankind,
folly and ignorance.
Troilus and Cressida Act II Sc iii*

"Whither goest we?" asked William. He had caught sight of the magnificent Victorian glass ceiling and was trying to walk in a straight line whilst looking up at it with awe.

"Hampton Court," said Elizabeth striding out purposefully.

"Maybe tomorrow," I placated. "But I'm heading for the nearest pub. I need a drink."

"A tavern?" William forgot the magnificence of the architecture and hurried forward.

We managed to negotiate the ticket barrier and the party goers safely but it took several attempts to get the timid William on to the escalator. Elizabeth, however, who was nothing if not courageous, stepped on after only a moment's hesitation and descended in regal majesty. Then, after studying the ascending one took an equally delightful ride back up. Having enjoyed it so much she tried it again. Several times. Once I had successfully transported William, clamped to my side like a limpet, down the escalator I could only drag her away by solemn promises that these wonderful machines could be found all over London.

We made our way along the marbled hall flanked by shops selling jewellery, perfume and socks and the restaurants plying tacos, Cornish pasties and coffee and down to the not quite so pretty tunnels that lead to the underground. I had lived in London for a couple of years when I was younger and, not having a better plan, or indeed any plan at all, I decided that the safest thing to do would be to head to Covent Garden where I knew my way around a bit better.

We joined the multicultural morass on the underground, negotiating the long, rounded corridors with the whoosh of warm compressed air as the trains passed through and, to Elizabeth's delight and William's dismay, rode on the long escalators.

"Tis the road to Hades, to the very bowels of hell?" William howled. Even Elizabeth was disconcerted.

"You could say that," I replied flippantly. I had never liked the underground. I realised my mistake when they both started haring back up like wild things.

"No, no," I yelled after them. "It doesn't really take you to hell. I was joking." I ran up after them, struggling past surprised people. "It just takes you to…to wherever you want to go. Not to hell."

"Matter of opinion that," remarked a lugubrious man as I pushed past.

I didn't catch up with them until I reached the top by which time I was much the worse for wear. I wheezed my way over to a wall and tried to feel human again.

It took some coaxing but I managed to get them back on eventually. Luckily William was distracted by the theatrical posters. He had to be discouraged from keeping pace with one for the Reduced Shakespeare Company. Needless to say, the apocalyptic arrival of the tube train threw them both into rigid trauma and I had to struggle on with them both clamped to my sides like, well, like clamps. The ride was remarkably uneventful due to the fact that they both remained petrified and unwieldy extensions to my body.

I concluded that the lift at Covent Garden would be an

adventure too far and so we alighted, somewhat more frazzled and in need of a drink than we had been before, at Leicester Square. Elizabeth gradually thawed out on the long escalator ride upwards to ground level. William took considerably longer and only brightened when we found ourselves beckoned by the warm, yellow glow from a pub window.

"A tavern," he squeaked and loosened his grip on my waist.

"Thank god," I muttered, heading inside with alacrity.

"A large glass of dry white," I said to the elf-like barman with blue eyes who sported green hair, ear lobes stretched around bottle tops, a large diamond through his nostril and who was wearing a skin tight green top and shiny trousers. "A pint of lager and," I glanced back at Elizabeth and considered, "a brandy."

He raised a finely drawn blue eyebrow and asked me how I was going to pay. I pulled out my debit card. He poured the drinks with more far panache than was strictly necessary for a wine, a lager, and a brandy and then processed my card with deep suspicion. I was beginning to wonder if I had perhaps chosen the wrong public house.

We settled into dark comfortable chairs by the window. I felt the weariness drop away and the cheeriness of alcohol lighten my mood. The small pub was stuffy and loud, not shabby exactly but well-worn. We sat quietly as the pub filled up around us. I ordered three bowls of chips with salt and vinegar and three more drinks, the same as the last, and gradually got jollier and jollier. As the wine warmed me I became less circumspect and conversed happily with William about nothing in particular. The tables and booths around us filled up but the three of us were left in peace. I suppose that I knew why but I didn't care.

Eventually, however, a fat old gentleman, untidily dapper in tweed and with a vaguely military air, pottered over and asked to be introduced to my friends. I was quite excited for a moment but his alcohol-laden breath tipped me the wink that, polite and gentlemanly as he was, it was only curiosity that prompted him. That and, as I discovered later, his unerring instinct for a 'soft touch'. He ordered me a drink although he didn't include my companions. He was in his sixties, of very broad girth with abundant grey hair worn rather long, and he was sporting, underneath the dusty tweed suit, a colourful waistcoat adorned with a fob watch and what looked like garlic butter stains. He smelled acridly of pipe tobacco and whiskey although he did not seem to smoke. My judgement was a little impaired, I will admit, but he appeared to me to be warm, gentlemanly and safe. He was certainly an amusing companion and I found myself chattering away in a manner quite unlike my usual self. I told him all about Elizabeth and William, where they had come from and what we had done since they arrived. What harm could it do, I rationalised. No one knew me here and it was a relief to talk without restraint.

William chipped in with the occasional remark or question and even Elizabeth made a few relatively gracious comments which I relayed to the gentleman. He was so interested. Inebriated admittedly, but not obnoxiously so and we were very cosy and convivial. The jovial old gentleman, whose name I learned was John, must have been a regular and was certainly popular because all sorts of people came over to say hello to him. An elegant woman in her late forties, generously endowed with firm prominent bosoms, a mass of untidy jet black hair streaked with silver and wearing a very low cut blouse insinuated herself onto the bench next to John and fixed me with an intimidating glare. Perhaps she felt some proprietorial claim over the old man but I can't believe that she saw me as any sort of competition. Contrasted against her dark fascinations, I was just a pale nonentity. Elizabeth, of course, took an instant and all-encompassing dislike to her, as she did against any woman who threatened the supremacy she felt was hers by right. I mused briefly that it was a shame the two indomitable women could not meet and then, as I glimpsed the dark beauty's glittering glance and met Elizabeth's eyes boring angrily into mine, I realised that not this dimension nor any other could comfortably embrace them both at the same time. I gathered from John's extravagantly gallant introduction that the beauty's name was Cleo. She must have had hollow legs because, whilst remaining ineffably elegant, she knocked back manly pints of Mandragora like there was no tomorrow. Well, perhaps not Mandragora, but you couldn't imagine her drinking anything that wasn't unusual and just a bit dangerous.

Mind you, they weren't all heavy drinkers. A small young man with a haunted air wearing a large khaki combat jacket joined us not long after I bought Cleo and John their drinks, and he drank nothing but a half of Carlsberg all night. He did get up to go to the toilet once and came back much more wide-eyed and even less lucid than when he went, so I suspect that alcohol was not his poison of choice. He had a gaunt look and a confused way of looking at you as if he were always on the point of asking a question of great importance. So much so that on more than one occasion I leant helpfully towards him and said, 'yes?' in full expectation that something worthwhile and interesting would be forthcoming. It never was.

I began to believe myself to be the life and soul of the party as more and more came to say hello to John and stayed to listen to Elizabeth, William and me. We were a bit of a novelty. I don't suppose many of the characters I met that night were particularly well-educated and they were certainly lacking in what my father would call moral fibre. In fact, I am afraid that they were a very motley crew, but, for whatever reason, they grasped the opportunity to socialise with Elizabeth, the Virgin Queen and William Shakespeare and me. I was just the channel of course. They asked the questions and I returned the answers. The crowd around us grew and William and Elizabeth were enjoying themselves. William was clearly at home with tavern life and Elizabeth glowed under all the attention. She still retained the comfort of the soft yellow dressing gown but had straightened her collar, ruff and back, and put the hat back on my head. Her jewels were shown off to magnificent effect in the glow of the subdued lighting and she was every inch the Queen of England, holding court with her subjects. It was a shame that only I could see her. William, cautious as ever, volunteered information reluctantly but watched and absorbed everything. I was very proud of them both.

"So was she a virgin then?" came predictably from a bumptious middle-aged man with a florid complexion, sporting a rude T-shirt that suggested mechanics 'do it better' and who looked like he might be the life and soul of any party that you didn't want to be at. "Don't seem likely. Bet she was a right goer."

My friend John looked down on him and his five coarse attendants with the sort of contempt that only those who recognise the faults of others in themselves can dish out.

"Nick, behave yourself. Ladies present."

"Bet she wasn't," snorted Nick, whilst his rough companions chortled like teenagers at a peep show.

"I was," was the curt answer from Elizabeth. I wouldn't have relayed it if I hadn't been on my fourth glass of wine, and quite intrigued by the question myself. It occurred to me, but probably only me, that, by using the past tense, Elizabeth was certainly telling a truth, but still may not have answered the question as it had been intended. She was a quick and clever woman and most of those around us were neither quick nor clever.

"Ask another," murmured Cleo, who could not be included in the hoy polloi.

"Ask William…" she brushed an invisible speck off her silken stocking and pulled all attention magnetically to her by negligently uncrossing and re-crossing her legs, "why he left poor old Anne Whatsername with his kids and sodded off to London?"

The question was harsh, as it was meant to be, and in no way softened by being voiced in gently accented, but perfect, English.

Poor William. He shot a defiant look at me and shook his head.

"Well?" insisted the woman and when I raised my shoulders in an awkward shrug she smiled in triumph. "Even if he could answer that one, he wouldn't, would he? They're all the same these…men. Only around whilst there's something to be had and then off to pastures new. Some new strumpet to spend their money on, some twenty-year-old with blue eyes and blonde hair and I…she is all forgotten!"

We all knew she was no longer talking about William.

"I would like to know …" began the young man in the khaki jacket. We waited for the conclusion of the sentence but he was staring at the ceiling and nothing more was forthcoming.

"Another round?" asked John, standing. Everyone said yes, including me, and with an expansive smile, he sallied forth to the bar.

"I have a question…" We all waited but the silence fell again.

"Romeo and Juliet was all right," Nick said, knowledgeably, having tired of not hearing his own voice. "And the one about the fairies was a bit of a laugh when me and me mates from the London Transport Social Club did it for the Jubilee a few years back. You remember that don't you Pete?"

Pete nodded less than enthusiastically and was about to speak but Nick had the floor and wasn't going to give it up.

"I was rather good if I say so meself. I played two parts. Obe-something, what was it?"

"Oberonknobe?" John asked innocently, passing me another glass of wine.

"That was it," Nick replied. "Obe-whatsit and Theeusus, or

something like that. Never had an acting lesson in me life and I was pretty bloody good if I say so meself." He pulled on his pint and let out a self-satisfied belch before continuing, oblivious to Pete's groan of remembrance. His four other companions seemed to have had a more positive experience of the said production for they agreed with Nick's estimation of his own talents with a series of nods and quite enthusiastic grunts. "Yes, yes. Nothing much to this acting lark, if you ask me. Once you get the hang of the funny words it's a doddle. 'Course I don't think much to the rest of this Shakespeare's works. Oh, it might 'ave been okay in 'is day but we've moved on since then, 'aven't we?"

"Some of us have certainly," agreed John smoothly. "I mean, who really needs Shakespeare these days when we've got The Sun and EastEnders?"

"I might give it another go, sometime," Nick mused, oblivious to John's sarcasm. "The acting thing, I mean. Not Shakespeare though. Most of the time no one knows what the bloody 'ell he's on about."

"Leonard Dicaprio was very sexy in the film." Cleo was diverted briefly from her bitter campaign against the male sex. She purred the last two words and feigned clawing like a cat. As poor Leonardo was young enough to be her son, if not her grandson, in the said film, I cringed and Elizabeth, who had very little patience with women at the best of times and, despite her own proclivities, even less with the lustful Cleo, leaned over and gave her a sharp shove. The ageing beauty only shuddered in response.

"I have a question…"

"Oh, shut up, moron" snapped the mildly discomfited but wholly inebriated Cleo.

"My personal favourite," said John knocking back his fifth or possibly sixth glass of whisky, whilst inserting himself between the dazed questioner and the disgruntled seductress, "is Henry the Fourth. Both parts one and two. Give the devil his due, the Bard could give life to a character. There is something…" He waved his glass of brandy dreamily in the air as he settled his bulk into a comfortable chair and placed his free hand on Cleo's thigh. "Something in those plays that speaks to me."

"A kindred spirit perhaps," drawled a newcomer from the bar. He was tall and lanky, good looking in a spare humourless way. "John, you old rogue, whose purse are you using tonight to fund your social activities?"

"Oh, hell," I thought. And then "Oh what the hell." I was enjoying myself, after a fashion.

"Jake, I'm offended," the old man responded with a pained glance towards me. "That this lovely lady and her friends should offer to buy me a drink or two shows her warm and friendly nature and who am I to throw it back in her face? It isn't in my heart." He transferred his hand gently to my knee and, with a respectful squeeze and an honest look, repeated himself. "It just isn't in my heart." I patted his hand as if he were doing me the favour and smiled at him as if he were my oldest, dearest friend.

The man at the bar laughed.

"They're all actors you know," he said to me, with a sardonic shake of the head. "Oh, not working actors, the profession wouldn't have them, but they live their lives creating scenes that suit them for the moment and in which they are the major players. If you'll take my advice, lady, I would keep your distance."

"Ha, he jests," chortled my new best friend. "Our Jake is not the life and soul, if you know what I mean. Too sour by half and too ready to make the rest of us miserable. Introduce him to your friends, go on. If anything will brighten him up that will. He claims quite a knowledge of the Bard and he'll get to the truth of the matter, by God he will, if anyone can."

Nick leant towards the man they called Jake and, with his back towards me, gave a brief explanation of my presence. I know that because he circled his finger near his ear in the time-honoured gesture that indicates questionable sanity. I flushed angrily and would have stood up and walked out except that the floor was undulating in quite an alarming fashion and I was afraid I would fall off it.

"I know you don't believe me, I'm not stupid. But they are here, it's just that you can't see them, that's all."

It was a very silly speech to make. Jake's eyes met mine with no hint of either understanding or contempt. Perhaps there was a touch of pity, but I might have imagined that.

Anyway, Cleo chose that moment to cross and uncross her legs again and all eyes, including those of the mordant Jake, immediately switched to them.

"In any case," slurred Cleo, all too willing to claim a derisive alliance with the attractive stranger. "It's all crap, we know that."

"I didn't say that," he said, probably more to annoy her than for any other reason.

"I once saw a ghost," said the young man who couldn't voice his questions. Having uttered a statement instead he seemed as surprised as anyone. "Straight up. It was me dad."

"Not interested," snapped Cleo, aggrieved that she had not immediately fascinated Jake to the required extent. She uncrossed and crossed her legs again, just to affirm her sex appeal. That was, after all, the most important thing. Once we had got over that and the male attention had drifted back to the less enjoyable reality there was an uncomfortable pause.

"They're not ghosts," I said firmly.

"Tell me, then," said Jake quietly. "I am interested to know more about them both."

Elizabeth, who was gunning for her fellow temptress, and could only be kept from flying at Cleo by both William and I sitting on her skirts, was slightly mollified by this attractive man's interest. Another round of drinks appeared, deftly served by the green-garbed barman, whom I began to suspect was in league with jovial John. Even so, I felt that my enjoyment was waning and began to wish for freedom from my new-found friends. Cleo, reluctant to yield the floor to a frump like me, fixated on proving to all present, including Elizabeth and William themselves, that they were both homosexual.

"I read it somewhere," she slurred, confidently. "She never married and he wrote poetry to a man. And he left his poor wife. For another man I bet, twenty years old with blue hair and blonde eyes, I shouldn't wonder. Course they are both gay. They're all gay, the whole bloody world is gay."

She said this accusingly in several directions at once. I think it safe to assume that she had had a chequered love life.

"They say not," I insisted.

"Stands to reason," she repeated, downing in one go pretty much all of another pint of whatever it was she was drinking. "She was a lesbian and William was a raving queen. Tell them what I said."

"They can hear you," I protested, "and they say not."

"Well, they would, wouldn't they? I bet you got beheaded or locked in a dungeon or something if you suddenly told your wife of eight years that you had decided you preferred men. And quite right too, getting beheaded I mean. Though I can understand preferring men. Of course, they were gay."

She was so far gone in alcohol and personal grievances that it didn't seem worth telling her that William had been ogling her cleavage and drooling over her elegant legs for all of two hours and that Elizabeth was getting increasingly frustrated because I wouldn't let her fondle the brown haired, brown eyed youth who was leaning against the cigarette machine behind her.

"Tell me…" Jake, who had totally ignored Cleo's tirade, turned his green eyes on me and laconically sipped his drink. The press around us fell back, as if for royalty, but he made no move to join us. He smiled in private amusement at the circle of expectant faces turned towards him.

"'Tis a Greek invocation, to call fools into a circle," he said, baffling and impressing us all.

Well, all except William who looked cross.

With the uncertain suspicion that we had been insulted we waited with bated breath for his next words.

"Tell me, how was Shakespeare so well versed in Latin, French, science and philosophy? He had little more than a very basic schooling and it is unlikely that he was educated enough to write with such knowledge and experience."

John was right. This Jake knew more than most about William.

John nodded and winked at me. "He knows his stuff. Will get to the bottom of it, he will."

I looked inquiringly at William who did not seem as impressed as I was.

"I told you, William. There are lots of people who think that someone else wrote all your plays and just used your name."

Poor William, he was just getting used to being a worldwide phenomenon and now it must have felt as if it were all being snatched away from him by this ungenial stranger.

"There are even those who maintain that Elizabeth herself could have been the writer," drawled the cynic with an ill-disguised sneer.

There was dead silence at that. My two friends froze and even the dull roar of revelry around us was suddenly muted. Elizabeth, with her usual presence of mind and eye for opportunity, raised the corners of her mouth just enough to let me know that it was, of course, possible. At least she thought it was. William looked crushed.

Cleo and John looked at me with questioning eyes and the tortured young man with so many questions slipped back into conscious presence.

"So all these plays…" For a moment it actually looked as if he was going to get to the end of a question and, although none of us were interested in either the question or the answer, it was a point of some suspenseful interest as to whether he would actually reach a conclusion of some sort. But he didn't so we all turned back to William.

"I learned of noble men," Shakespeare muttered defiantly at my prompting, "and I was made receiver of all the learnings of my time."

Despite his words William, who was always so frank and open, looked distinctly shifty. The stranger shook his head and the hint of a pitying smile curled his handsome mouth.

"That is not possible," he said dismissively. "There are no records of Shakespeare attending any university. He may have been a schoolmaster but even that does not explain his breadth of knowledge."

William appeared to be labouring under some sharp internal conflict but Elizabeth, her eyes narrowed, spoke out impatiently.

"Marry, now it lies on you to speak true. Confess thy sins, lest to thy peril thou aby it dear." Her tone was harsh and I was frightened. William slipped from his seat and knelt at her feet head bowed.

"Gentle Queen, mercy, I beseech."

She sighed impatiently and rolled her eyes.

"Fool," she spat, hitting him sharply on the head. "You think I know naught, but I know all."

William blanched and I felt a bit sick. What dreadful events had I set in motion?

"Yon addle-pated ruffian left England's shores whilst the down was still on his chin and, traitorous rascal, attended the Catholic College at Douai. Campion and Southwell were like to have known him there, Debdale knew him before, and they died for their impudence to my reign." William looked poleaxed. "Fie, you assume a virtue you owest not. Thinkst thou I would have allowed thee success without well knowing what sort of man thou art. Marlowe was your friend but he was secret-false. I knew thee and thy father's plans to make a priest of thee. But thou wast no priest. The playhouse was your heart-blood and you were seduced."

She laughed with harsh enjoyment of her power over him and William shrank, feeling the noose already around his neck.

"Oh, hell," I breathed.

Our drinking companions were clamouring for a response to the question I had all but forgotten in the revelation of poor William's peril. Not Cleo, who was coyly playing with her hair, nor the disinterested Jake who did not expect an intelligent answer anyway but the others, who cared least, demanded an answer. I relayed everything that had passed to the waiting throng. Few really understood the ramifications of my story but the sardonic Jake did and, as he had been automatically accepted as the oracle on these things, all eyes swivelled to him. He looked, for the first time, taken aback and I felt some pleasure in the knowledge that we had shaken him from his complacency. He calmly considered for a moment or so.

"Why was it necessary to keep this secret?" he asked.

"Pah!" said Elizabeth. William flinched.

"It was the Catholic thing, I think," I said.

"And the fool married," spat Elizabeth with worlds of contempt in her voice.

"And he married," I explained.

William put his head in his hands and moaned. "Twas my undoing. I was betrayed by my love."

"Apparently, they weren't supposed to be married whilst at university."

"That is true," the oracle drawled. He turned his handsome eyes on me. "You have studied Elizabethan times in some depth."

I could see Elizabeth smirk but I think that was because it pleased her vanity to have an era named after her.

"No, not at all. This is all new to me too."

"Is that right?" He really did have a meltingly gorgeous voice. "Your theory might have some merit."

"It's not my theory," I protested. "It is what they tell me."

"Indeed." He stood and should have drawn lazily on a cigarette and exited in a cloud of smoke like Humphrey Bogart but instead he just leaned forward and patted my shoulder patronisingly.

"Go home, dear lady. You seem like a nice, educated person who should choose your drinking companions with more care. Take my advice and get yourself home and safely tucked up in bed."

And with that, he ambled off. We were effectively dismissed, the excitement had evaporated, and the others gradually drifted away. I was no longer the centre of attraction, no longer the life and soul of the party, no longer special. I was just a middle-aged woman, more than a little inebriated, sitting in a London pub talking to myself.

A man wearing a wedding ring who was introduced briefly as Mark whisked Cleo surreptitiously away. Nick and his friends dispersed having arranged to meet the next night out of town to discuss some scheme or other and the pale young man said something about having to catch a flight to Denmark first thing in the morning. Good luck with that I thought watching him struggle to remember where the door was.

"Fancy another one, love?"

John, at least, was loyal.

"No thanks," I replied, getting unsteadily to my feet. "I have to go now."

"One for the road?"

"No, really."

He was patting his jacket pocket with a slightly bewildered air.

"Do you know, I think I've had my pocket picked!"

I was just sober enough to realise that John and his cronies had had a very good evening and that I wouldn't be able to get away without paying for it unless I was prepared for a significant tussle.

I straightened my back, took a deep breath, paid the smirking, green haired man at the bar an extortionate sum without comment and exited the pub with dignity. Except for walking into the door jamb, ricocheting off it and into a hunched, spidery figure who was creeping in as I was going out. William picked me up and the dark-visaged man with thin lips and a lank, pageboy hairstyle, was not prevented by injury from calling me a number of picturesque and rather rudely anatomical names.

CHAPTER FOURTEEN

*We are such stuff as dreams are made on,
and our little life is rounded with a sleep.
The Tempest Act IV Sc i*

So, there we were, on the streets of London at nearly eleven o'clock on a cold spring night with nowhere to go.

"Well?" I asked. "What do we do now?"

"He hath belied me," William grumbled. He was still upset that the smooth stranger with the melting voice and the cynical attitude had been so dismissive.

"No, it was me that he didn't believe," I replied with a sigh. "I suppose we had better find somewhere to stay the night."

I looked up and down the cold concrete streets. The traffic was dwindling, the pedestrians were fewer in number and all walked with a purpose towards some home or place of rest. I pulled my bag closer to my body and tried to think. A hotel? I had already spent more in the pub than I spent on food for a week at home and the guilt was terrible. I started to walk. William and Elizabeth followed obediently. I went into Covent Garden tube station and we descended once more into the bowels of the city. I found one of those maps of the underground and looked at it for inspiration. There was none forthcoming, just a jumble of names, none of which, in my ignorance of the city, appeared to offer a comfortable bed at a reasonable price.

'Whitehall," said Elizabeth. "That is one of my palaces. What about Nonsuch? Where is Nonsuch?"

"It's been a few years," I answered acerbically. "Most of them are long gone. The Tower is about the only one in London that I know of."

"The theatres?" ventured William wistfully.

"Burnt down, every one, although they rebuilt the Globe a few years ago."

"Did they?" William brightened visibly. "My lodgings then, in Southwark?"

"Look around you," I snapped irritably. "Everything has changed, nothing is the same."

"We will go to the Tower," Elizabeth said decisively. "Come."

She was heading for an escalator so, in the absence of an alternative plan and resigned to another twenty minutes of riding up and down, we followed her and eventually made it onto the platform. We emerged at Tower Hill and looked across at the Thames. I saw a look on Elizabeth's face that I had not seen before. It was relief. I can't think that she had all that many happy memories connected with the Tower of London so perhaps it was just the fact that something of her time had survived into this. She moved forward with determination and William and I trotted after her.

"We won't get in," I called without much hope of a response. "Or I won't anyway."

My feeble protest was not going to stop this strong-willed Queen. She shed the towelling robe as she hurried towards the tourist entrance, leaving it as a pale yellow splash that was luminous in the moonlight against grey concrete slabs. The area was deserted, the ticket booths silent and the vast wooden gates barred against us. When William and I reached the postern she had already passed through. I looked at William who was gazing longingly towards the first familiar thing he had seen in this strange world of mine.

"It seems that you can go if you want to," I said. "Go, take a look. I can't get in but I won't go far and you'll find me again, you always do."

"Art thou certain, sweet lady?"

I nodded and walked away towards the river bank. When I looked back he was gone.

Old Father Thames snaked by, vastly grey, cold, forbidding. Across the water, the 'shard' rose defiantly against the night sky. A lonely bench beckoned and I sat down wearily. There is something about walking on concrete that saps the energy. Walking on grass or rock is different, less tiring somehow. I sat straight for about two minutes but then the alcohol and the exhaustion took over and I lifted my legs and, pulling my coat closer, stretched my length on the cold metal.

I woke once to find my head cradled in William's lap and the voluminous skirts of Elizabeth's dress spread over me. She wasn't a bad old soul when it really came down to it.

I smiled and drifted off into sleep again.

CHAPTER FIFTEEN

Away! the foul fiend follows me!
Through the sharp hawthorn
blows the cold wind.
Humh! go to thy cold bed, and warm thee.
King Lear Act III Sc iv

I woke. I was consumed with pain. My head felt like it was going to explode at any minute, I swear my eyes creaked when I opened them and every muscle in my body felt like it had been deep frozen. The comforting presence of Elizabeth and William no longer wrapped me in warmth and a very hairy and very dirty man was shouting obscenities whilst doing a jig – or at least that's how it seemed to me. I groaned and inched into a sitting position. I couldn't distinguish any intelligible words but the basic gist seemed to be that he claimed ownership of the bench and felt quite passionately that I had outraged all that was good and decent in the world by planting my backside on it.

"Ok," I groaned, "I'll move, just give me a minute." He harrumphed and spat and then, taking a completely filthy rag from his equally filthy coat, he started cleaning the end of the bench that I had just vacated as if I had contaminated it with something nasty. He muttered to himself incessantly and, if I hadn't felt so stiff and cold, I might have had the wit to be frightened. But I wasn't. He started nudging me. He had cleaned the empty part of the seat to his own satisfaction and he wanted me to stand up so that he could clean the rest. I managed to creak into a standing position but that was as much as I could do. The man assiduously, if ineffectually, polished the rest, nudging away my frozen body. I had thought that he was quite old but he wasn't, probably not more than thirty. He had large brown eyes and the even features of the inherently good looking. Sadly, they were all but obscured by matted hair and an unkempt beard. The enormous knitted hat he sported was so old and so dirty that it had welded into a solid mass and didn't do much to enhance his looks. Nor did the stained trousers or long blackened fingernails. The large luminous brown eyes should have been warm but they weren't. There was something missing – a connection with humanity. He glared at me resentfully as if I were an alien interloper into his world. Give him his due, he probably didn't come across frozen, dishevelled, middle-aged women laying claim to his home at dead of night very often, but he probably looked at everyone like that. I couldn't help maternal feelings flooding over me and I wondered briefly if his mother knew where he was and if she cared. But of course, she did. Mother's always care, even if they make mistakes – dreadful, dreadful mistakes. They still care. I wanted to tell him that but he was not looking for empathy. He just wanted his bench back.

"It's mine, it belongs to poor Tom," he said sitting in the middle of the bench spreading his hands out either side of his body and gazing challengingly at me.

"I know," I replied struggling with the pins and needles that had taken ferocious possession of my feet. I was dimly aware that he might turn violent but at that moment in time, I was in too much discomfort to care. "I just borrowed it for a while, sorry."

"You look like my grandmother," he said.

I went off him rapidly at that. "Thanks," I said with heavy sarcasm, hobbling away, and, I suspect, looking quite a lot like someone's grandmother.

"Where are you going?" he asked. Curiosity, not concern, prompted the question.

"I don't really know."

"Oh," he said, losing interest rapidly. "I've been there."

I turned back but his eyes met mine honestly.

"I need to find a hotel." This enraged him and brought forth a torrent of abuse and another violent jig. He took great exception to my throwing money away on, well, I am not actually sure that he said bourgeois extravagance, but his contempt for my decadent life was abundantly clear. He danced around in front of me yelling Marxist invective at the top of his voice for at least two minutes and then dismissed me with a toss of his dirty hair, flung himself on the bench and crossed his arms. The conversation was over.

I clasped my bourgeois bag to my conformist breast and looked around me. Apart from the young man on the bench, there was no one in sight. The Tower glowered, solid and stark against the neon lights of the city and a low mist drifted across the Thames. I began to think I was in, what my dad would call, 'a bit of a pickle'. What had I been thinking? To leave my family, my home and to run away to London like some desperate teenager, to end sad, cold and destitute on the banks of the Thames.

I started walking. There were bright lights ahead and instinctively I turned towards them. I eventually found myself in front of a large luxury hotel. I lingered for a moment looking longingly at the shiny black windows, golden monograms, and marbled floors. Comfort and warmth beckoned but I had never stayed in a hotel like that in my life and, in the end, it only took a raised eyebrow from a yawning concierge to send me scuttling back to the shadows. If William and Elizabeth had been with me I might have had more courage although I still wouldn't have had the money. It struck me that, having taken them back to a place from their own time, I might not see them again, but I was cold and tired and I didn't want to think about it.

It occurred to me that hotels might be cheaper on the South Bank. I don't know why. Southwark was just a bridge away so, without much further thought than that, I turned my back on the bright lights and crossed the Thames. I walked and walked because there was nowhere to stop. Hard streets, dark alleys, cold dead buildings, lonely roads. It had been a mistake to cross the bridge. The occasional door housed a rag encrusted human but, tired as I was, I couldn't quite bring myself to become one of them.

My feet were killing me and I had stopped at the corner of a dirty building that reached into a blank black sky to ease my shoe off my blistered foot when I heard running feet.

A split second later a violent blow from behind hurled me to my knees. Overcome by shock and pain I could do nothing but lie in the gutter looking up at the stars.

"Shit!" I heard from an unmistakably male voice. Hands were upon me pulling me up, touching me. I froze in terror. Four men, four black men surrounded me forcing me to my feet.

Vast disbelief engulfed me. Rape, murder, suffering, it couldn't happen to me. Not to me, could it? I screamed, clutched my handbag to my chest and shrank back against a cold hard wall. Terror robbed me of further utterance and I mouthed begging words noiselessly at them.

"Wot you doin' out on yer own at this time of night, lady?" The voice came from a faceless, hooded figure to my right.

"You lost?" demanded a lean Rastafarian on my left. The two in front of me were short and muscular with angular designs cut into their hair and a sort of jittery desperation about them. I felt sure they were packing heat. And out of their minds on drugs of course.

I stuttered something, held out my bag and closed my eyes. Something grasped my shoulder and I knew that I was in a desperate plight. I don't know that my life flashed in front of my eyes exactly but I do remember thinking that I really should have cleared my bedroom drawers and chucked out all those pairs of white knickers that had turned a sad, grisly grey in the wash. I would have done if I had known I was going to die before I could get home to do it.

What horrified me more than the conviction that I was going to get raped and murdered and my body left a tangled, bloodied mess on the cruel streets was that Hubby or mum or Kate or, God forbid, Grace would have to go through all my things and would find all the weak, pathetic little disorganisations of what had been my life.

"Lady, we ain't goin' to hurt you." I opened one eye. The Rastafarian's touch on my shoulder was soft and his dark eyes held what might have been a wealth of compassion. Or a drug-fuelled dilation.

"No, no, we ain't gonna hurt you," the three others chorused. I did not trust them. They were lulling me into a false sense of security before dragging me off to use and abuse me, before subjecting me to some sort of unspeakable perversion. I shrank further back into the stone wall, willing it to encompass me, protect me.

"Are you okay? Your knees are bleeding. Did you hit your head?" the Rasta said. I had but I denied it, cringing away from his firm hold on my shoulder. A car approached at speed pinning us in the stabbing headlights. I lunged forward, suddenly brave at this god-sent opportunity to escape, determined to throw myself into its path if that was what it took to escape. But eight arms embraced me and I was flung back against the unyielding wall once more. Someone screamed, a horrifying prehensile howl that cut through the low hum of the sleeping city and turned my blood to ice in my veins. I think it was me.

"Lady, lady, lady," said the lean Rastafarian soothingly. "Don't be frightened, don't be frightened."

"Listen to me," said one from the depths of his hood. I must have looked very wild as I turned my eyes on him for he let me go and pushed his hood from his face. He smiled and I saw a slim possibility of salvation open up before me. "Listen, we won't hurt you. But you shouldn't be out on your own this late. Are you lost?" I stared back at him. Slowly the strong arms that were holding me dropped away.

"Honestly, we didn't mean to knock you over. Are you lost?" he repeated. "Can we take you somewhere? Where do you live?"

I still wasn't sure. Maybe they wanted to murder me in the comfort of my own home. I hugged my bag to my chest and let tears slide down my face. This unsettled them but they were men so that was to be expected. Tears always unsettle men.

"My name is Paul," said the bravest of the four, one of the two with angular hair. He held out his hand as if offering a formal handshake. I looked at it aghast. What new strategy was this, what new horror? "I'm really sorry we knocked you over. It was just an accident. We were running and just didn't see you. What is your name?"

"My name?" I whispered. I wasn't about to give them that. They could take anything they wanted from me, I was not in any position to stop them, but I determined that my name would remain my own.

"Sheila," I answered slyly.

"Well, Sheila, you look like a nice lady who should be safe at home. Don't you have someone who is waitin' for you?"

"Maybe," I said relaxing slightly as I began to think that maybe they weren't too bright and I might be able to outwit them and get away.

"My husband is waiting just around the corner. He's a policeman," I said. And then added for good measure, "he's with the Armed Response Unit."

I realised that I'd overplayed my hand with that. They exchanged glances that held more than a touch of amusement. No one was that stupid.

"Do you want us to take you to him?" Angular Hair Cut number one called my bluff.

"No," I said. "I'm all right. I have to go now."

I sidled away and they let me go. My knee was stiff and painful but I started walking as quickly as I could. After a hundred feet or so I paused to glance back suspiciously. Angular Hair Cut Number Two and the Hoodie nearly cannoned into me again. Rastafarian and Angular Hair Cut Number One were close on their heels.

"What do you want?" I squeaked. "I haven't much money but you can take what I have, just let me go." I held out my bag and tried to position myself so that I could leg it once they had taken it but Rastafarian pushed it back towards me.

"Look, lady, we told you. We don't want to hurt you and we didn't mean to knock you over. We've just finished a late recording session. You're limping and we can't leave you alone in this part of town on your own."

"Recording session?" I muttered. It didn't seem likely.

"Gangster rap," I thought, but didn't say, thank God. In my defence, I was very frightened, my knowledge of modern music is limited and, whilst I consider myself passionately anti-racist, being accosted at night in a strange place by a group of men had apparently awakened deep rooted fears and revealed unconscious prejudice. I was beginning to feel ashamed of myself.

"We're a vocal group, lady." I eyed them narrowly. "We get the studio cheap at night." That sounded plausible so I decided to give them the benefit of the doubt.

"We'll just see you to wherever you are going? The streets ain't all that safe at this time of night."

"No kidding," I could not help saying. They had gathered closely around me, possibly to stop me launching into traffic again.

"I'm not sure where I'm going," I confessed as a couple more cars swished by intent on their destinations.

"You are lost then. We thought so. Do you live in London?" That was the one with the Rastafarian hair. Now that I looked at him he no longer had cruel eyes and harsh features. He had a nice face and a smooth gentle speaking voice. I could visualise him singing gospel so I came to the relieved conclusion that he probably wasn't a gun-toting misogynistic gangster rapper after all and felt thoroughly ashamed of my unwarranted hysteria.

"No, I don't live here," I replied. I felt anchorless and aimless.

"Are you running away from someone?" asked the hooded one, with compassion.

"No," I said positively, then, as I thought about it, "Well, yes, in a way, but I suppose I should go home really."

As the fear-induced adrenalin faded I remembered that my feet were hurting a lot and that I was bone tired.

"And where is home?"

"Loughborough," I replied honestly.

"I know it well, did my engineering degree there. Nice little town."

"Yes, it is," I said, wondering how I could have thought this skinny little soul so terrifying just a few moments ago.

"Do you have any friends in town? In London, I mean," asked Paul.

"No, that is, there is Elizabeth and William but I don't know where they are. I left them at the Tower."

"Tower Hamlets?"

"No, the Tower of London. They wanted to have a look around and see if anything had changed but I couldn't get in because it was closed."

"So, how did they get in?"

"Oh, well, they have their ways." I was too tired to explain. The fuzzy feeling was back and I swayed wearily.

"You're not tellin' us your friends broke into the Tower of

London, are you?" There was a touch of gentle incredulity so I shook my head.

"Do they have a mobile on them? Can you give them a ring or text?"

I giggled at the thought. "No. I don't know if they will come back to me but they will find me if they want to."

"How will they…?" Angular Hair Cut Number One started to ask but was frowned into silence by Paul.

"Ah," he said, and there was a little thinking amongst the four of them. Then "Do you have a mobile on you?"

"Yes," I answered. "Why?"

"Well," he suggested slowly as if he anticipated some objection from me and wanted me to clearly understand what he was saying. "We could call one of your other friends, partner or husband maybe." He was probing for information of course. I knew that.

"Oh, all right," I said scrabbling in my bag. "I ought to let them know where I am I suppose." I fished the phone out. It was completely dead but I had known that it would be. I glanced around while they were discovering this and noticed that there were now only three of them. Angular Hair Cut Number Two was nowhere to be seen.

"It looks like," said Rastafarian, "we need to find you a place to stay for the night and then you can catch a train home in the morning."

"All right," I acquiesced, looking expectantly at them.

They looked at each other helplessly. I think, good hearted as they were, the novelty of having a destitute woman on their hands in the middle of London at the dead of night was beginning to pall. Luckily they were saved the embarrassment of one of their number having to offer me his own settee to crash on by the arrival of a police car. That solved the mystery of where Angular Hair Cut Number Two had been. He climbed out of the back seat and a policewoman climbed out of one of the front seats. I considered running but something told me that it would be undignified and anyway, with the possible exception of the policewoman who looked like she had been poured into her uniform by someone committed to over generous portions, I didn't have a cat in hell's chance of outdistancing any one of them. So, I smiled when she called me 'love', managing to make it sound like more like an insult than a term of endearment, and asked what my name was.

"Shirley," I said confidently.

"You told us Sheila," exclaimed the hoodie, aggrieved.

"And your surname?"

I considered.

"Valentine."

"Uh huh." She viewed me narrowly.

"Your address?"

"She's from Leicestershire," Paul volunteered when I did not answer.

"Do you have friends in London? Is there somewhere we can take you? Someone we can call?"

"I'm all right," I answered, a touch belligerently.

"Where are you going to sleep tonight?"

"I'll go to a hotel."

She raked me with a look.

"Do you have money for a hotel?"

"Yes," I said. "Of course, just point me in the right direction."

The policewoman sighed. I got the feeling that she had already dealt with any number of dramas on her shift that evening and that an apparently homeless woman with a fictional name was not high on her list of priorities just then.

"It's very late and you won't get anyone to take you dressed like that. You look like you sleep rough."

"I do not!" I was outraged and suddenly very aware that I still had that wretched, battered hat perched on my head, that my tights were laddered and my coat was much the worse for the crumpled sleep on the bench by the river.

The policewoman sighed again. "These nice young men are concerned about you. I can take you somewhere you can get something to eat and a bed for what is left of the night. Otherwise, I can take you to a holding cell and let you sleep it off."

"I am not drunk!" I was even more outraged but not, it must be said, entirely truthful. I had downed a fair amount of alcohol earlier in the evening and had still not slept it all off.

"It's up to you."

"The shelter would be the best place for her, officer," said the nice young man Paul. He was a good, caring sort of bloke.

"Do you want to do that?" the policewoman asked.

"It would be best, Sheila, Shirley I mean."

"I'll be all right," I protested, but I'm a pushover when faced with a united front.

The policewoman held the car door open and the four young men willed me to get in, so I did. I'd never been in a police car before. Apart from the vast bank of brightly lit instruments on the consul, it was remarkably ordinary. I waved cheerily to the four nice young men as the policewoman climbed wearily back into the car next to her partner, who, incidentally, never said a word or moved except for the bare minimum required to drive the car. I think the drive only lasted for a few minutes but I fell asleep almost immediately and had to be shaken awake by the ever more disgruntled policewoman.

I was led, blinking and yawning, through wide wooden doors to a small dusty desk in an old dusty building that might have been spectacular once. A spare looking man wearing a brown pinstripe suit, a Rolling Stones T-shirt and bright red plastic sandals was in charge. He had very few teeth but two of them were gold as if to make up for the value of the lost ones.

"Wotcher, Reg," said the policewoman.

"Owzitgoinlove," responded Reg, as he pulled long strands of greasy grey hair over his spare skull and grinned sheepishly. It looked like he quite fancied her but, even though she was no oil painting, I wouldn't have given much for his chances at that point.

"Quietnighttonightgotafewplacesleft."

He handed her a clipboard and gave me an expensive grin.

"Ouserulesnoalcoholdrugsnosmokinginsidenanyviolenceto wardmemembersofstaffandyouwillbeproscutedbuthissisa placeofsafetyandwewillwatchoveryouinthennameofourlord amen."

At least I think that is what he said.

"Shirleyvalentine?"

He read what the policewoman had written.

"Popularnamethat. Mustbethethirdthismonthalready."

The concierge and the policewoman exchanged wry smiles. I began to think that there might be a future for the two of them and that they deserved each other.

They wanted to check my handbag so I gave it to them. I had hidden my debit card and what bits of cash I had in my bra before I left the pub. I'm not stupid.

The policewoman left, ignoring my half-hearted gesture of thanks and Reg led me to a room, or a cubicle would be more accurate really, in what was designated by discreet signage and a heavily fortified door, as the women's area. It didn't actually proclaim that transgressors would be horribly punished but you could see that they were determined to keep the sexes apart and weren't going to rely on self-restraint as the primary means to do so. Before I entered the hallowed portals I saw a couple of men shuffling up to the next floor on a wide staircase but they didn't look as if they felt particularly rampant or deprived of female company so, all in all, I felt quite safe. The pervasive aroma of feet and the resounding hum of not-so-gentle snoring was a little off-putting, but the cubicle was clean, if sparse, and the bed had a mattress, pillow, and blankets. I kicked off my shoes, spread my coat on the blanket for extra warmth, put my handbag under my pillow and, as Reg disappeared down the corridor still muttering unintelligible instructions, I crawled under the blankets, stretched my aching body on the bed and luxuriated in the simple ecstasy of a straight spine and the dissipation of weariness.

Sleep fell heavily and dreamlessly.

CHAPTER SIXTEEN

Misery acquaints a man with strange bedfellows.
The Tempest Act II Sc ii

When I awoke William and Elizabeth had returned. William was poking my shoulder whilst Elizabeth stared coldly down at me, pulling her long string of pearls repeatedly through bony fingers.

I was glad to see them back but decided not to let on. Anyway, I was feeling rough, to say the least.

"I need a bath," I said when I had rolled into a sitting position. "And the loo."

Once in an upright position, I realised that I needed the loo quite desperately so, without further ado, I hurried out of the cubicle and followed the stick lady signs to some very basic toilet and shower facilities.

I emerged from the toilet cubicle, much relieved I might add, to find an elderly woman with short grey hair, pleated plaid skirt, a grey shirt that might once have been white, a wool hat and very thick socks standing in the shower soaping herself all over. I did stare so she was entitled to be a bit cross.

"What're you lookin' at?" she snarled through the froth.

"Nothing," I replied airily. There were three showerheads in a row on a white tiled wall, no privacy, and a stock of worn, thin grey towels. Everything was well used and shabby but it looked relatively clean. And very exposed. While I scrubbed my teeth with my fingers (I would have used one of the stock of brushes that had been thoughtfully provided but a small girl with an amazing number of tattoos on her emaciated body nipped in and took them all) a number of women of varying age and temper hurried through. None of them seemed all that concerned with the opportunities for hygiene but one or two of them leered at me with an interest that I found quite unaccountable and were scarier than any man of my experience so far. I wanted a shower desperately but I had the feeling that if I stripped off I might very well become a spectator sport. Which made the behaviour of the fully dressed lady still lathering herself seem quite sane. Even sensible. I divested myself of my outer layer of clothing, turned on the shower next to the old woman and borrowed her soap.

I then spent a pleasurable ten minutes foaming under hot water and a considerably longer and less comfortable time contorting parts of my body in an attempt to dry myself and my clothes under the hand dryers whilst still wearing most of them. The old woman and I eventually left more than an hour later, damp, pink and gently steaming, the best of bathroom buddies, with our modesty intact if not our dignity.

I returned to my cubicle feeling a lot better. I found a stubby bit of lipstick and a mascara in the bottom of my handbag and was thus able to get my face into some sort of shape but there wasn't much I could do about my hair. It was usually brown and lank but the shower, hard soap and hand drier had had an extraordinary effect on it. It was still brown, with a little grey here and there, but it had developed a life of its own and now floated at right angles to my head. There was a cracked mirror on the wall outside the cubicle and after struggling to tame it for a few minutes I decided that I quite liked the look. It was a little odd maybe but I didn't look ordinary anymore. Elizabeth and William, when asked, approved too. At least William did. Elizabeth had her own agenda for the day and it didn't depend on the vicissitudes of my coiffure.

"Let us go." She walked majestically towards the heavy door that led to the lobby. I collected my shoes, bag, coat and William and followed obediently.

The man with the golden smile wasn't there. Instead, there was a rather large woman with a whole mouthful of large teeth and black rimmed glasses, wearing some sort of Indian tunic over a woollen jumpsuit. She pulled her hand through hair which, whilst very short, still managed to be dishevelled and leapt forward as if she had been waiting all her life to meet us.

"Hullo, hullo," she bellowed. "Did you get a good night's sleep? Feeling much better this morning, no doubt." She probably meant sober. I couldn't help taking a step backwards and hiding behind William who was trying to hide behind me. "Do you want some breakfast? What can we help you with?"

"We're fine," I squeaked. "We were just going out to get some…breakfast I mean, and then we have an appointment."

I thrust William in front of me where he cowered shamelessly.

"Ok," she said slowly, but still loudly. "Who were you going with?"

"Did I say we?" I simpered, sidling past. "I meant me. Me were just going to get some breakfast." I had almost gained the door to freedom but she wasn't the sort to give up without a fight when there was a lost soul to be mothered into conformity.

"Well, why don't we go and get a cup of coffee and talk about what we are going to do for the rest of the day."

"I don't mean to be rude," I replied. "But I don't really need to know what you are going to do for the rest of the day."

She didn't take offence. In fact, she roared with laughter which was even more unsettling. Elizabeth rolled her eyes in frustration and William clasped my arm and pulled me towards the door. Unfortunately, the woman clasped my other arm and started persuading me towards a green door through which glinted an urn and several pairs of curious eyes. I was torn between respect for the work these people did and a desire to escape the label of vagrancy that was being assigned to me. William put up a fight for all of three and a half seconds but he didn't stand a chance. Elizabeth, who, as you know, could sometimes make small dents in this world, weighed in and landed a good kick on the woman's left shin but I think she was wearing boots under the jumpsuit because she didn't flinch. It may have been that Elizabeth's vitriol could not touch the truly worthy, but in any case, the toothy lady had won the battle against my conscience for, before Elizabeth could gather herself for another assault, I was being firmly propelled towards what appeared to be a canteen of sorts. More women of various shapes, sizes, ages and sartorial inelegance were scattered around the room.

The male sex had also been admitted and was represented by two grubby gentlemen. One was spectacularly unkempt with a mass of greying hair framing a purple-hued face. Bushy black eyebrows, sunken eyes, and a jagged red scar disfiguring a worn and weary face, spoke of many eventful years on the streets. His companion was faceless and enigmatic, with a hoodie obscuring all but the rough edges of dirty stubble on his youthful chin. His bowed torso and nervously clenching fist on the table made him shifty and dangerous in my eyes and, although I looked away hurriedly I had the unnerving feeling that he was watching me. I glanced back and caught the impression, no more than that, of clear eyes, blue against white between narrowed lids, their vibrancy at odds with the brown and grey decay that surrounded us. He shifted uneasily in his seat and pulled the loose hood closer – but I knew he still watched me. I shuddered and flinched away. I felt faintly sick and the tendrils of dark fog reached out for me once more. The sight of those two lonely, directionless men unsettled me more than did all the other women in the room.

Most of those partaking of the breakfast were solitary souls, hunched over cups or plates, eating eagerly, prepared to snarl if anyone proved foolhardy enough to snatch a morsel from their dish. They had that 'leave me alone or I'll make you regret it,' look about them. I knew how they felt, so I cultivated the look myself and sat down as far from anyone else in the room as I possibly could. Apart from my toothy friend in the jumpsuit, there were several volunteers in the room, easily identifiable by their cleanliness and air of purpose. A tubby lady was talking earnestly to a diminutive woman who was inscribing swear words upside down in the dirt on the window panes and three other women with kind eyes and comfortable figures were doing their bit, serving coffee, sausages, and beans on toast. A generously loaded plate appeared before me and, despite my determination not to lose myself in the whole homeless thing, I fell upon it ravenously. It felt good not to be constrained by good manners for once and I am sure that the abandoned shovelling I indulged in made it taste better.

The tubby woman had enticed the upside-down writer away from the window with burnt toast and Elizabeth had taken her place. The sharp sounds of the city battered the shaky panes and she looked disdainfully out at the grim, grey buildings of her realm. William was gazing curiously at the fast disappearing mess on my plate. I wiped my mouth on a thoughtfully provided piece of kitchen roll which was doing service as a napkin and offered him a sausage. Elizabeth, immediately losing interest in the dreary view, snatched the other from my plate.

"Manners," I reproved and then laughed at her outrage.

"Who are you talking to?" asked the large woman.

"No one," I replied submissively. It was no use explaining to her. She wouldn't believe it. But to be fair I could see at least two people in the room holding conversations either with themselves or, in the case of one sweet-faced woman, a battered baby doll. I didn't want to think about that too much.

The large woman planted her bottom on the chair next to me and her large bust on the table in front of me and smiled toothily. A much younger woman who looked like nothing so much as a scared rabbit put a notebook decorated with pink daisies down and insinuated herself apologetically into a chair opposite. There was a twitch of her pink lips which I think did service as a smile.

"Well, my dear," boomed the large lady. "Shirley, is it?"

Once I had remembered that was the name I had given I nodded.

"Shirley not!" she said and then laughed a rich full laugh of honest delight at her own very bad joke. I began to like her. "All right, all right, Shirley it is. I am Myra and this is Carla." She indicated the pink lipped rabbit. "Carla is volunteering with us. Did you get a good night's sleep?"

I nodded as I mopped up the last of the beans. Elizabeth had not been won over by Myra's wit and was glaring at her challengingly. William had manoeuvred himself into a position where he could view her generous bust to best advantage.

"Well, now, what more can we do for you?"

"Nothing, really," I sputtered through the last vestiges of the beans. "Though I could drink another cup of tea."

It wasn't what she meant of course but Carla leapt up and bounded off with my tea cup as if relieved to be doing something unchallenging.

"Now, what about contacting your family?" Myra was not going to be an easy woman to say no to.

"I'll do that later," I said firmly.

"Shirley, my dear, look about you." I obediently looked. So did Elizabeth and William. Then we looked back at Myra, none the wiser. "It doesn't look like you have been living on the street for long, a few days only maybe."

That hurt I don't mind telling you. I attempted to smooth my hair down and wriggled uncomfortably. It did feel as if my shirt had changed its shape during its unorthodox laundering.

"Most of these women have been on the street for years. They don't have anywhere to go back to. Something tells me that you do. Call your family, Shirley."

Carla put a fresh cup of tea in front of me and nodded as if she had some intense personal knowledge of my family's distress.

"They will be beside themselves with worry," she whispered. "You should ring them."

"I'll do it later," I muttered again. They exchanged glances and Myra decided to take another tack.

"Is there something you are afraid of? Is there a reason you do not want to go home?"

I looked at her blankly.

"No."

"If anyone has been violent towards you, we can help."

"No!" I said vehemently. "Absolutely not. My family are all…wonderful."

There was silence.

"Look," I decided to be positive and confident and to get the hell out of there. "I'm not living on the street." I stood up and pulled at my skirt which also seemed to be an inch or two shorter than before my novelty shower. "I just left it too late to find a hotel last night, that's all."

Myra was sceptical and Carla was empathising to the point of tears with what she imagined was my sad plight.

"I have money," I protested. "I can pay you for last night."

I started pulling at my jumper and feeling inside my bra. This seemed to alarm them both, not to mention inspiring more than a little interest from one of the scariest women. They weren't to know that I was just trying to find my debit card of course.

"No, no," said Carla as Myra gestured me back down into my chair. "It is not a problem; we just want to be sure…"

She looked helplessly at Myra who finished for her.

"We want to be sure that you have help if you need it."

They were struggling not to overstep the boundaries imposed on them by my rights to privacy and their job descriptions. Carla risked putting a soft hand on mine and poured sympathy from her blue eyes.

"We don't want to pry. We just want to help you."

"Do you drink?" asked Myra with a raised eyebrow. I got the feeling that Myra's personality almost always triumphed over the restrictions of political correctness and basic courtesy and I didn't dislike her for it.

"Yes," I said. "Like a fish."

Carla was startled but Myra eyed me narrowly and came to the conclusion that, because I was so quick to admit to it, it probably wasn't true.

"Perhaps you are not well?" Carla suggested tentatively.

Myra leaned forward and covered my hand with one of her gnarled paws. "You really need to make the call."

"I don't need to. I'm fine," I flashed. "Never better."

I stood up again and looked for William and Elizabeth. They were deep in conversation with the woman with the baby doll. She held the doll up to William and he smiled and said something kind to her. She smiled back and then gave Elizabeth a dirty look.

"Oh, look!" I shouted. "Look, she sees them! She is talking to them."

"Talking to who? Who's talking?" Myra and Carla turned to follow my gaze.

"William and Elizabeth." I was delighted. "Look she is showing William her baby. Elizabeth isn't interested of course; she doesn't like babies. I hope she doesn't hit her."

"She's talking about Molly," whispered Carla to Myra.

"It's not a real baby, Shirley," said Myra.

"I know that," I replied irritably. "Look William is talking to her and she is replying. She sees them. Don't you?"

"Shirley, dear," Myra's tone was soothing. "Molly quite often talks to herself. She has a condition…"

I didn't want to hear.

"Well, she sees them. I need to talk to her." I walked across and joined them with a big smile.

This brought me next to the table where the two vagrant men still hugged their coffees in grubby hands. The younger one was hunched so far over his mug he must have felt the steam rising from it. The other had fallen asleep. Molly pulled her baby to her chest and stared challengingly at me.

"You were talking to my friends," I said.

"Are you from the Social?" Molly was backing off.

"No, I just saw you talking to my friends. To Elizabeth and William and I needed to talk to you about them. You see, you see them and no one else…"

"I won't let you take her… I won't let you take her!" She didn't move but she let out a piercing scream and, when that one was done, followed it with a series of short panting screams that petrified me but galvanised Carla, Myra and several of the women volunteers into action. The young man flinched and those bright blue eyes touched mine for the smallest fraction of a second before he pulled his hood further down with a filthy hand. Motherly women scooped Molly away, surrounding her in soothing sounds and soft comfortable bodies. I was, likewise, woman-handled into a different area by Carla and Myra. Most of the other female inmates didn't turn a hair.

The scary woman did look sideways at me as I was hustled past her chair and growled, "You shouldna upset Mad Molly. Mad Molly is one of us."

"And you shouldn't call her that," flashed back Carla almost aggressively. "We don't use that word. It's not…nice."

"It's 'er name." She picked her well-spaced teeth with a fork. "And she is mad. Barking mad, we all know that."

I sank into a chair, drained and defeated once again. William touched my shoulder which was a comfort and Elizabeth spat contempt, which in my loneliness and fear, was also a strange sort of comfort.

Myra put a mobile phone into my hand. My respect for her increased. She was a clever woman who knew when to press an advantage. I should have refused straight away but I hesitated and was lost. I punched in my landline number and waited. Three rings only. We had one of those silly systems that only rings three times, invariably when you are at the farthest possible point from it, and so your chances of getting to it before it cuts to answerphone are slim in the extreme. It was one of those things that we had meant to get around to sorting out but, well, you know… I could imagine the chaos in my house as everyone scrambled over the furniture and themselves to get to it in time. That is assuming they were waiting for my call. It clicked over to answerphone. I knew that it would. My own voice, cold and uncompromising, said that I wasn't available to take my call but I could leave a message after the tone.

"Hi, it's me," I cried gaily. "I'm fine, don't worry, I will be back in a day or two. Look after yourselves. Bye."

I handed the mobile back to Myra and stood up. I needed to move quickly because I knew what was coming next.

"I have to go now. Can I pay for my breakfast?"

"You can make a donation," said Carla uncertainly, trying to stand in my way. They were stalling of course. Myra disappeared with the mobile. Someone at home would be pressing caller ID and trying to return the call.

I wasn't ready. I had to go. I headed for the door, Carla in desperate but ineffectual pursuit.

"Please let us help you. Do you know where you are going? It can be very dangerous on the streets. Please, Shirley." She put a detaining hand on my arm and then, remembering that she didn't have the right to do that, snatched it back horrified at her own temerity.

"I'm all right really." I thrust a £10 note into the offending hand. William and Elizabeth were outside already waiting for me and I could see Myra through the grimy, glass doors, bearing down on us.

"Thank you but I really have got to go," I muttered, scuttling into bright sunshine.

"We can offer counselling," wailed Carla in a last ditch (and totally misguided) attempt to lure me back to comfort and safety. There was a shadow at her shoulder, a hooded shadow. I legged it down the street.

"You know where we are if you need us." Her words faded as we rounded the corner.

She was a sweet girl.

CHAPTER SEVENTEEN

Lord, what fools these mortals be.
A Midsummer Night's Dream, Act III Sc ii

"Well," I said to William and Elizabeth when we had put what I considered to be a safe distance between the shelter and us. "Now we can talk. How did you get on last night? Did you enjoy visiting your old haunts, if you'll excuse the expression?"

Elizabeth sniffed. "It is all changed and all confusion! Where are the beasts?"

"The beasts?" I echoed weakly.

"The lions, the bears? There is naught as it should be. 'Tis a masque, a travesty!"

Poor Elizabeth. Something in her visit to the Tower had upset her quite a bit. I looked at William inquiringly as Elizabeth stormed ahead to reassure herself with her reflection in the glass front of a coffee shop.

"Her majesty liked the jewels but she hast been overcome by thoughts of mortality. Her majesty knows full well that death approaches."

"She must have known that before surely," I whispered.

"Mayhap the hours here bring sweet remembrance of the fore-end of her time and make the leaving of life a thing of stronger regret. Her visit to the Tower hath put her in mind of pain as much as of triumph."

"Yes, I can see that. She must have seen the place of her

mother's execution. They have marked the spot and made a photo opportunity of it. American tourists and school parties pulling faces and posing in front of the place that her mother suffered such… Well, I don't know what. It is almost unimaginable in our time, in England at least. We just can't conceive that anyone would do that to another person, nor can we really understand how she could have faced that terrible, unjust end with such dignity." I sighed. "Life is so hard at times, isn't it William? In any era, I suppose. The place we were just in…there were so many lost women. I mean lost to this life. I can't help but wonder what their lives have been and if they suffer or…" A new thought struck me. "I wonder what will happen to her, Elizabeth I mean, in this life when she does die in her other life?"

"But she is dead, in your time," William replied.

"I know, and I'm not sure that I've got this right, but she is due to die in her time on 23 March and it is 22 March here today, so I just wondered what is likely to happen tomorrow."

William and I pondered this in silence for a moment or two.

"Mayhap, her majesty will remain with thee."

"For how long do you think?" I gasped in dawning horror.

"For all eternity?" he ventured.

"Oh, crap!" The thought of living the rest of my life locked in an existence with the wilful, crotchety Elizabeth was truly horrifying. "Do you really think that is what's going to happen?"

"I know not."

"I could probably just about cope with you. But her!"

Elizabeth had divined just enough of what had been said to be infuriated anew.

"Come, thou whey-faced fool," she snapped at me. "All our travail must now be turned to good effect."

Her eyes glittered in the sunlight. Her jewels were dull by comparison. Her face was paper white and gaunt in the extreme but there was an undimmed passion and a vigour that I had not seen before.

"I needs must see my kinswoman. I must see thy Queen."

William touched my arm and, speechlessly, gave me to understand that this was something that must be done. My protests died on my lips. Somehow I must get Queen Elizabeth I and Queen Elizabeth II together. It was my mission now. Not one that I understood exactly, or relished, but who was I to question an anointed queen? And I was working to a deadline.

How I was going to achieve this goal was perplexing to say the very least but wandering aimlessly wasn't going to get me any closer so I started off at a smart trot. I didn't know where I was going but the good thing about London is that you are never very far from something that will point you in the right direction to somewhere else. I found a cash machine and a sign that pointed the way to the Millennium Bridge. Elizabeth and William were fascinated by the machine in the wall that gave me money and it took some time to explain that it would only give me the money that I already had and that it wasn't churning out gold like an alchemist. They also couldn't be persuaded that there wasn't a little man hidden in the wall counting it out. Elizabeth was mollified however when I showed her the youthful likeness of her kinswoman on the twenty-pound note.

"She is not beautiful," was Elizabeth's jealous remark, which indicated to me that she thought she was, but I could tell she was pleased that honour was still bestowed on Royalty in this strange world. I restored the money to my purse and then I did something that I had not done before. I took her arm and she let me do it. William happily grasped my other arm and the three of us walked jauntily towards whatever success or failure the day might bring.

Turning a corner, however, my two companions halted abruptly.

"Tis the Globe!" William gasped. "Is this Southwark?"

I must admit that my jaw dropped too. Crossing the river on the previous night had simply been an impulse as my knowledge of the geography of London was sketchy, and yet, here we were, drawn by coincidence or a higher force or a subliminal instinct to this icon of Elizabethan England, nestled smugly under twenty-first-century towers. Whatever had brought us here, the three of us, it was meant to be. With our backs to the river, we stood and stared.

From the exterior, it is a round building, white with black beams as you would expect, and with a sloping roof. It is in fact, in William's own words, a 'wooden O' with the stage itself open to the elements and the stars. The courtyard leading to the building is gated and cobbled and our Globe flaunts a glass fronted ticket office, with café and the obligatory merchandising opportunities. Those modern necessities aside, the building is remarkable in its authenticity. And I can say that with the best possible authority as both William and Elizabeth stated as much.

"They rebuilt it," I explained. "I came once when Alex had a school trip here. The show was great but they made us stand all the way through. Next time I'll pay the extra for a seat. And a cushion."

"Can we enter? Can we see?" William was virtually beside himself with glee.

"It's closed."

"Plague?"

"What? No. It's just too early in the year," I said. "They only open in the warmer months. It's too cold for people to sit and watch shows in the winter."

William looked disgusted. He came from a time when folk were hardier and did not expect central heating and comfort in their theatres. He studied the playbills and gazed in awe at those that bore his name.

"Not marble, nor the gilded monuments of princes, shall

outlive this powerful rime," he muttered as he looked longingly through the gates of The Globe. I could feel his yearning.

"Go," I said. "I'll wait."

"No need to wait." A familiar voice spoke behind me. "I have the keys."

It was Jake. He looked older and craggier in the bright daylight than he had the evening before, but then I did too.

"I would say that it is a coincidence to run into you again, but, given your companions, I suppose you were bound to make your way here sooner or later." He raised an eyebrow and almost smiled. "Nice hairdo by the way. I presume you want to look around the wooden O?"

He turned the key in the lock and we were in the little courtyard. William was torn between thrilling excitement and the revival of his dislike for this undeniably attractive man.

"What do you do here?" I asked as he led us to one of the wooden doors.

"I am an itinerant worker," he replied with a careless shrug. "Sometimes here, sometimes there. At the moment I am here. I am glad to have come across you again. You raised some interesting theories last night."

"They aren't theories," I insisted wearily. "They are true. William and Elizabeth told me and they should know."

He gestured for me to walk forward and we were, in a very few steps, standing in the pit, where the groundlings gathered. William and Elizabeth took to the stage of course.

Jake smiled. It was a bitter, melancholic smile.

"The theatre has been my life's work. I would give a lot for what you say to be true. To be standing here now with William Shakespeare would be…"

"Well, you are," I snapped, rudely. "And ignore Elizabeth at your peril. She has ways of making her displeasure felt even in this world."

He laughed.

"I beg your pardon; I didn't mean to imply…"

"That I am a delusional fool? Well, why not? Everybody else thinks that, but for the first time in years, no, not in years, in ever, I feel that things are right with me. People all over the world believe in different gods, in ghosts, in miracles, in alien abductions…and no one calls them delusional. Well, except for the last one obviously. Anyway, I am tired of it. I just want to spend some time with them, that's all."

"And why not? At the very worst it is just an alternative reality."

I wasn't quite sure how to take that but he said it with the suggestion of a kind smile so I thought I would be gracious.

"So what are your plans?" he climbed onto the stage and stood looking down at me. I got the feeling that he would always aim for the advantage of higher ground, and I don't mean morally.

"Elizabeth wants to see the Queen. I don't know why, but she seems to think it is important so we are going to head to Buckingham Palace."

He roared with laughter at that which was disconcerting as it clashed somewhat with his brittle elegance. I drew myself up with as much dignity as I could muster, gave him a look that could have stripped paint and headed for the door.

"I'm sorry," he said, holding out a hand towards me. "You surprised me, that's all. You have to admit that it is all quite comical."

"I don't see that at all," I snapped back. "And I don't have to explain myself to you. Thank you for letting us in but we want to go now." I looked around for Elizabeth and William but they had disappeared backstage.

"Look, I am sorry, I didn't mean to offend. Please, stay, look around. I have a party of school children arriving in a few minutes but you are welcome to stay as long as you like. All three of you."

"School children?" I asked, partly in token of forgiveness, but more because I was intrigued as to how this mocking and slightly dangerous man had come to be waiting for a group of children. It didn't seem right somehow.

"Educational tours," he shrugged, melancholic once more. "Until next Tuesday. Then I move on."

"What to?"

"That I don't know yet. I will travel I think."

"Have you ever been married, have you children?" I asked curiously.

"Not yet, probably not ever," he replied with a smile. "But either way I have to find the answer first."

"What answer?"

"When I know what the question is I might be able to find the answer. For the present, I'm still searching."

I snorted derisively. I couldn't help it.

"I can't see that there is any particular mystery. Life is crap, get used to it."

"And I thought I was the cynic," he chuckled. "Anyway, it strikes me that we are not so different, you and me." He sat on the edge of the stage. "We're both running. I've been running for years but I suspect that it is a new experience for you."

I would have liked to contradict him again but it didn't seem worthwhile as it was undeniably true.

"What, or who, is it you are searching for?" He had cool green eyes and the lids crinkled at the corners.

"No-one, nothing really, at least not anyone that can be found. Deep down I know that." I shrugged. "I suppose I am running but it's only to get away for a while."

"To Buckingham Palace?"

"Don't laugh at me. Elizabeth wants to go there but I think I do too. It seems to me that I haven't done much with my life up to now. I used to have such dreams… I would plan to do such exciting things. Quite silly a lot of them. I was going to achieve world peace single-handedly."

"And how were you going to achieve that?"

"By extreme violence, of course."

"Of course."

"Don't get me wrong, I have a wonderful family, a nice home, a foul job... but I want, I don't know, total freedom. I want to be reckless, to break out and do outrageous things. I always played it safe. Job, marriage, mortgage... My son wasn't like that, he wanted to live his life, really live it, and I didn't understand. But I think I do now... I'll go back when I'm ready."

He grinned and his eyes twinkled alluringly.

"Sounds to me like you are going to get yourself into trouble."

"I doubt it," I replied glumly. "When it comes right down to it I'm just too ordinary and scared to take risks."

"Tell me about your family?"

"Well," I began. But there it was again that dark surge of blackness that had to be fended off and I knew that Jake too was aiming to catch and return me to stifling safety. I smiled up at him. "Sorry, I have to go now. I just remembered that I need to be somewhere."

"Where?"

"Not here." I turned and walked away.

"Sure you'll be okay?"

"I'm sure." I gave him a half smile and he saluted me with one of those manly waves that say 'so long' rather than goodbye. Past the wooden benches and out through the Elizabethan doors, across the cobblestones and through the metal gates that were ajar ready for the young people to arrive. I never met Jake again but he was someone whose essence lingered all the same and I often wonder if he ever thinks of me.

Once outside I perched on the wall above the river and

waited for William and Elizabeth to return to me. A dark movement caught my eye and I turned my head instinctively towards it. To my left, at the now distant corner we had rounded just a few minutes before, a figure shrank back. My heart started a slow pounding and, as I peered, a hooded head edged cautiously around the building, and seeing that my gaze was fixed in that direction, drew smartly back again. My mind leapt to the younger of the two men from the shelter. Feeling myself to be safe in the open air amongst the early tourists, I watched suspiciously. A moment later three young people, a boy, and two girls, leapt out laughing. All three were wearing the ubiquitous 'hoodies' and I relaxed. Not a stalker then, or a ruffian planning to mug an unsuspecting woman. I smiled at my creeping paranoia and heaved a sigh.

It was still early but the spring sun poured down, tempering the chill breeze. A crocodile of Japanese students wended their way from the Tate Modern further along the river bank towards their Globe experience with Jake. I wondered what they would think of him. Their bright youthful faces shone with enthusiasm for life – if not necessarily for the landmarks that were remorselessly paraded in front of them.

"Hi Mum," said Alex beside me.

I was very pleased to see him, of course.

"Your two friends are getting you into quite a bit of trouble one way or another." He leant against the wall next to me and tucked my hand under his arm.

"They are, aren't they?" I replied happily. "Do you know what they want me to do next? Take them to see the Queen!"

He chuckled, his fair hair shining in the sun and his blue eyes full of fun.

"Well, why not? It's about time you ran a bit wild. Mind you, I didn't expect to find you in such exalted company."

"I know," I agreed. "I still don't know why they chose me."

"Don't you? Well, I expect you'll find out, but don't leave it too long Mum. You need to be able to find your way back and the longer you're away the harder it will be."

He squeezed my hand and laid his warm cheek against mine. Joy flooded over me.

"Dad and Grace need you, so don't leave it too long."

He was gone but the joy remained. I hugged it to me like a warm blanket and shut my eyes to keep him close.

"Miss?" I opened my eyes reluctantly to find that two of the Japanese students had hung back from their friends and were gazing at me quizzically. They were both about fifteen. The boy with thick shiny hair had his arm draped casually over the slim shoulders of his pretty girlfriend. "Photo please?"

The crocodile had disappeared through the gates that led into The Globe and Romeo and Juliet had separated themselves from it. Having recently absented myself from order and habit, I felt an immediate affinity with these teenage rebels, particularly as they disdained selfies in favour of the old-fashioned camera. I nodded and took the electronic contraption he handed me. Their assumption that I knew what to do with it was flattering but the young man was charming and patient and we eventually, between the three of us, managed to create a photo that encompassed both young people in focus, arms and legs and all, smilingly frozen against the backdrop of The Globe.

"Now you, Miss." The young man positioned me, I smiled awkwardly and the photo was taken. The two young lovers, with polite smiles and bows, went off with my image and a brief, inconsequential memory of the English woman they had met on the banks of the Thames. That might have been all except that the day was still young and a certain amount of celebrity was about to attach itself to me. A copy of that photograph eventually found its way to me and I treasure it still for the happy memories it evokes.

Not long after that, I espied Elizabeth steaming towards me pulling poor William by the ear. Not surprisingly he had wanted to stay a little longer but this his sovereign queen would not allow. Despite his discomfort, I could see that whatever he had seen had pleased him.

"Time is wasting and we hunt-counter," snapped Elizabeth. "Abate the hours to my audience with your Queen."

"All right, but let William go and stop bullying him or I won't help." Elizabeth's high drawn brows arched even higher at my temerity but she released William's ear after a last vindictive tweak. Tears rolled down his brown cheeks and his lower lip trembled. It may have been the pain of course, but I think William had been, understandably, very moved by the working monument to his life and works that is The Globe. I squeezed his shoulder and he smiled up at me.

"Tis marvellous to me that my renown lives on through so many ages to this day."

CHAPTER EIGHTEEN

What hempen home-spuns have we swagg'ring here,
So near the cradle of the fairy queen?
A Midsummer Night's Dream, Act III Sc i

Hunched against the chill river breeze that had sprung up, we crossed the Millennium Bridge. I thought the magnificent St Paul's cathedral rising over the City of London would have impressed but, when I drew their attention to Wren's masterpiece, Elizabeth merely expressed irritation that the spire had not been rebuilt after being destroyed by lightning. She had paid out of her own purse to have it re-erected, she told me with ireful wrath and was profoundly annoyed that it had never been done. Elizabeth, therefore, found the magnificent dome, built much later and with no credit due to herself, offensive. William was more interested in taking backward glances towards the theatre we had left behind.

I could not shake an impression that a formless shadow kept pace with us but, even though I glanced back several times, I saw no lurking figures. The moving humanity streamed past intent on personal business, anonymous and remote.

Persuading William away from his last lingering look at The Globe, we left the bridge and I paused to consider our next move.

Perhaps to those not privy to the fact that I was accompanied, I appeared lost, maybe even vulnerable. At any rate, it looked as if my luck was about to run out. A young woman cannoned into me and then grasped my arm, apologising profusely in a language I did not recognise. At the same moment, I felt a sharp tug and my bag, which had been hooked negligently over my shoulder, began to slide away from me. I didn't have much, but what I had I was going to hold on to and I reacted instinctively. I reached wildly for the strap and hung on while the woman held me in her grasp chattering urgently. A sudden wrench and I lost my grip. I remember opening my mouth to shout (something really original like 'stop, thief', no doubt) when the bag was unaccountably thrust flat into my stomach and I grasped it in surprise. I looked up to find that the unsuccessful bag snatcher had legged it into an oblivious crowd followed by a lithe figure in grey. The woman had melted from my side and I was left staring about me and wondering if I hadn't imagined the whole incident.

'I wouldn't put it past her', I hear you thinking.

Neither William nor Elizabeth or indeed anyone else around me had been in the least bit aware of the little drama and I was left feeling shaky but mostly foolish. After gazing around in astonishment for a moment or two I gave myself a mental shake and walked quickly away.

London had shown me only it's smiling, compassionate side up to that point. You could argue that whoever had rescued my bag and returned it to me was just such another of the majority who aim to help not hinder their fellow men, and therefore my brief brush with the criminal element should not be held as the measure of the city. Still, I was shaken and looked about me with more suspicion and less confidence as I led my two friends down into the rumbling confusion of the underground. I felt dazed and unhappy and my earlier determination had dissolved into uncertainty. I reached a platform and, not caring much where I went, boarded the first train that drew to a halt in front of me. William and Elizabeth were beside me, unusually silent and wraithlike, and the fuzzy feeling was back again. I sat dispiritedly as the sliding doors closed.

There was Alex. He was framed in the window of the door, one hand on the glass, calling to me. "Mum…" The train gathered speed and he fell away.

I looked at William and Elizabeth and sighed.

We emerged, for no good reason that I could give you, at Trafalgar Square.

The city was just getting into its stride for the day. The watery sun fought its way through grey clouds and raised the spirits of tourists massed across the concrete. Mine too. William was so impressed by Nelson's column that he overbalanced whilst staring up at it, but that didn't dampen his spirits in the least. He darted from one plinth to another, delighting in the lions and revelling in the majesty of the cold stone statues.

Elizabeth, in contrast, planted her feet in one spot and efficiently and methodically viewed the whole scene, turning slowly and taking in each area as if she were cataloguing and filing her impressions for a treatise under the title 'Wonders of the Modern World to be Considered for their True Worth at a Later Date.' Knowing her it would probably be written in perfect Latin. Her dignity was somewhat deflated when a single brave pigeon landed on her head. I say brave because years have passed since Trafalgar Square was host to thousands of marauding pigeons. A ban on feeding them and the introduction of regular early morning visits from a Harris hawk have effectively chased them away to other more welcoming areas. The monuments are cleaner admittedly and the proud men on them can now maintain a pristine dignity. Loyal William came to the rescue of Elizabeth's dignity and, in a series of short runs with lots of arm waving, he persuaded the maverick pigeon to keep a respectful distance.

I caught sight of one of those open-top tour buses and it struck me that, if nothing else, riding on one of those would save us a bit of walk to Buckingham Palace, and might give me an opportunity to reconnoitre the area. Tourists were piling on already so I told William and Elizabeth to follow, bought my ticket and clambered up the winding stairs to the top deck. I chose seats at the back, mainly because the ones at the front were filled with five strangely dressed young Korean men and their entourage. They were, presumably, some sort of embryonic boy band as they kept singing and gyrating. There was another not quite so young man with the most enormous camera I had ever seen taking photos of every lithesome move. The other seats filled up, more or less, with a motley crew of Spaniards, Dutch and, the most bewildered of all, British. I looked around for Elizabeth and William but they had not followed me. I leant over the rails at the back and scanned the crowds anxiously.

"Nice hairstyle," cried a flamboyant young Dutchman who had just taken the seat in front of me. He wore purple trousers, a yellow T-shirt with huge white flowers emblazoned on it and clasped his hands to his face with an excitement that I could hardly feel was warranted, even by my unconventional hairdo. "Vat product do you use on it?"

"Ah," I said to gain time whilst I thought of something less embarrassing than the truth. But I couldn't so I said, "Soap."

"Ja?"

"Yes, I'm worth it." He didn't understand the rather weak joke which was just as well.

He reached out to touch, took a handful of wayward tresses and rubbed them between his fingers in wonder.

"Soap. Zo soft and it floats in the air." He flung his arms up with infectious enthusiasm. I felt quite good about myself for a few moments even though he was, it has to be said, so much more feminine than I was.

"Thank you," I said and turned back to my search.

"Who do you look for?" He was next to me, scanning the crowds as assiduously as I was.

"Oh, my friends," I faltered. "I don't know where they have got to."

"Vat are zey wearink?" He intended to help me find them and I could see that would be awkward. I toyed with the idea of describing my companion's sartorial ensemble and then rejected it for obvious reasons.

"Oh, well, it doesn't really matter. They will find me when they need to," I muttered and, with a last desperate look around, I sat down just as the bus started.

"Are you alone zen?" I smiled and shrugged but, for some reason, this skinny young man with white-blonde hair, who seemed to live his life as if it were a non-stop party, had decided that I was interesting. I couldn't for the life of me think why. "You vill join Erich and me, we vill have much fun, no?"

"Oh, I..." but my British reserve was no match for this Dutchman's joie de vivre.

"Zis is Erich. I am Karl. I am hairdresser and I haff just come out of the wardrobe."

"Oh, really?" I said, feigning equanimity with some difficulty. He was in his late twenties so it must have been an interesting wardrobe and it can't possibly have fooled any but the most determined fantasist.

"Erich vas married."

"Ah," I said feeling like a traitor to my sex.

"To a man, off corse." Somehow I didn't feel quite so traitorous. And then I felt outraged with myself for being so contrary. If infidelity was bad one way, surely it was just as bad the other?

I squirmed whilst smiling politely. I did feel that the exuberant Karl was going to give me much more personal information than I had any business knowing. Erich, a mild looking middle-aged man with thinning hair, wearing what could only be described as slacks and a pink crew neck, nodded speechlessly as Karl leaned towards me and spoke in lowered tones.

"He does not speak the good English like me." He grasped Erich's white manicured hand in his own and brought it to his lips. "Ve are in luff. He leaf his husband for me."

I smiled and nodded to Erich and Erich smiled wanly and nodded back. I was sure that he understood more English than Karl thought he did. He certainly indulged his vibrant partners' excesses rather more than he should have. Perhaps he loved him for them. Opposites do attract after all and there was something very endearing, if a little wearing, in Karl's enthusiasm for, well, pretty much everything.

Perhaps because of our Korean visitors, there was a tour guide attached to our group, a nervous young man in a smart blue and yellow jacket. He was introducing himself and London. Karl fell into rapt attention so I twisted around and looked again for William and Elizabeth. It didn't take long to find them. We were just turning off Trafalgar Square and heading down Whitehall towards Big Ben. We weren't moving at much more than a fast snail's pace which was just as well because I looked over the back of the bus just in time to see Elizabeth, skirts flying, take quite an astonishing leap onto the open platform at the back of the bus. William was a few paces behind her, running as fast as his spindly legs could carry him, his padded breeches pumping comically from side to side, as the bus increased speed. I couldn't help an exclamation of concern and Karl, sensing excitement like a bloodhound, was by my side in an instant.

"Vat is it? Is it accident?"

"No, just my friends, oh my goodness!"

William, running hard, had made a desperate grab for a bar on the rear of the bus with one hand and Elizabeth's withered outstretched hand with the other and had then fallen. I leant over the railings and could just see his upturned bottom on the floor of the bus and his leather boots pounding the tarmac as he struggled to climb aboard.

"Pull him on, Elizabeth!" I bellowed. "Pull him on!"

Karl, next to me, also hurled himself as far over as his tight trousers would let him and joined in.

"Pull! Pull," he yelled, as urgently as I, although without as much conviction.

I was just about to rush down the stairs and pull William on myself when the boots, with a final spurt of speed, gathered enough momentum to leave the road and force the rest of his body safely onto the bus. I sat down with a sigh, no, a gush of relief, and met Karl's broad questioning smile and the 'health and safety' scowl of the young man in the blue and yellow jacket.

"Sorry," I muttered. "I was just…sorry."

"Ja, sorry," Karl echoed winningly and the young man turned back to his microphone with a roll of his eyes and a forced smile. "Did your friend catch ze bus?" Karl asked innocently.

"Yes, I think so. They are probably waiting for me downstairs." I got up and so did he, grasping the compliant Erich by the arm and hauling him to his feet. Mr. Blue Jacket gave us all a warning look. At that moment William's floppy hat appeared at the top of the stairs and I relaxed back into my chair. "They'll be all right, I'll see them later."

"Zat is good, you stay with us, yes?"

"Yes."

William was flushed as his head appeared jerkily over the hand rail and he was wincing in some distress. The reason transpired to be Elizabeth prodding him mercilessly from the steps below. He staggered onto the top deck and fell, almost sobbing, to his knees at my feet. Elizabeth, by contrast, ascended majestic as ever, and, with the wind on her face, surveyed the moving scene that was magnificent London with calm satisfaction.

William's head was on my lap and his arms clamped like a vice around my legs. Bless him. He was a sensitive soul and, between his fearless Queen and this fast moving, unforgiving new world, it was not surprising that he needed a little comforting every now and again.

To hell with it, I thought with a sidelong glance at Karl. Why should I be worried what a man in a shirt like that thinks of me?

"It's all right, William," I said, patting his hat. "You're safe now. Where on earth did you get to?"

Karl was disconcerted for all of twenty seconds but even a shabby woman talking to her own lap, was not going to faze him completely.

"Is your friends?" he whispered.

"Yes," I said boldly. "This is William and that," I indicated the windblown Elizabeth, standing like the figurehead on a galleon in full sail, "is Elizabeth."

"Ah." He clearly couldn't see them. Erich, even though I believe he understood my words, didn't quite grasp the situation. Karl turned to him and said something incomprehensible in Dutch. I would imagine it was along the lines of 'the woman is mad but she is English so we'll humour her until she gets annoying…or boring.' At any rate, Erich nodded and smiled at me, so I nodded and smiled back. In fact, this was pretty nearly the sum total of our relationship so I needn't mention it again. Just imagine that every few minutes we would have occasion to nod and smile at each other and you have the entire scope of our interaction for most of the day.

Karl should have been interested in the tour guide's spiel. The young lad was growing in confidence and it was, judging by the hilarity of the Korean boy band's reaction, very entertaining, but my new best friend couldn't take his eyes off me. It had been a very long time since I had inspired that sort of interest from anyone. Shame he wasn't straight.

"Vat is your name?"

"Juliet," I said, not quite randomly as I was looking at William at the time and thinking that the accepted image of him as being quite a tough character with a penchant for boozy evenings clashed with my experience of him. My William was a sensitive soul and that it was he who created some of the most delicate scenes and characters in the English language was more believable.

"Haf you known your friends long?" Karl asked, hooking his elegant hands over his crossed knees.

"About two months, I think," I replied honestly. "They come and go."

"Und you bring zem to zee the wunnerful zights of London."

"She wants to see the Queen," I indicated Elizabeth who was inspecting the Houses of Parliament with approval. "She has a special interest."

"Zo? And Villiam?" He glanced at my lap. I was still patting Williams head comfortingly but Karl's undeniably salacious look made me feel very uncomfortable so I pushed William away abruptly. "He's a writer and he gets very nervous."

"Ah, ze artistic type. I know, I too am artistic. My hair creations are vorks of genius. Everyvun says so. In Amsterdam I am famous. I take inspiration for ze hair from ze air. Und from you. Your hair is like…vat is ze word…eh…Gorgonzola."

"Like cheese?"

"No, no, no, like ze lady with snake hair."

"Oh, like a gorgon." On the whole, I think I preferred the cheese comparison.

"So Villiam is a writer? Is he famous? Is he rich?"

"Well, he is famous."

"Not rich?"

"I don't think so. But not poor."

He leaned forward and whispered naughtily, "Is he good looking?" Erich and I exchanged one of those glances and William gave me an anxious look.

"Yes," I said. "At least he has very special eyes. They are dark and brown and you can see the whole world reflected in them." William smiled at me. He got to his feet and wedged his little body into the space next to my seat. We understood each other perfectly.

Elizabeth who had surveyed this little interchange with contempt leant over and cuffed William about the head. She just couldn't help herself. She recognised empathy when she saw it but was rarely capable of it herself and it irritated her to see closeness between anyone if she was not the object of it.

"Und ze lady? Is she beautiful?"

William's face froze and so did mine. Elizabeth's was pretty much always frozen but her eyes fastened on mine and developed that piercing look that I took as a warning of violence to come. It wasn't that she didn't know that her days of beauty had owed everything to youth and that with the passing of the years she had lost all claim to any sort of bodily appeal. She could spot flattery and sycophancy with the efficiency of a hawk but wanted to hear it anyway.

"She, well..." I floundered.

"Her eternal summer shall not fade," said William in one of his many moments of inspiration. I grasped it like a drowning man grasps a straw.

Elizabeth's eyes tightened slightly with suspicion and she glanced dismissively at William but she did not object to the compliment. Who would?

"Ok...nice." Karl was bemused and almost completely uncomprehending. I think he was quite happy to accept that I was speaking to thin air but a mad woman quoting poetry was far less interesting. "So....your friend is not beautiful."

The wonders of London were passing him by but his attention remained riveted on me.

"Vere do you lif? Haf you place in London? Haf you husband, lover? You vill come to lunch with us? Ve vill haf dinner. Ve haf billets, ah, tickets you say for real Old Time cockeney dinner wif the singing and the dancing of the Pearly Kings. It will be much fun."

It sounded awful to me but he didn't seem to require any answers to his questions and was happy in his gregarious planning so I let him talk. He occasionally glanced up at a landmark as the tour bus chuntered purposefully along but, on the whole, he preferred to chatter on, and was an entertaining conversationalist, if a bitchy one. Karl was unashamedly, gloriously, loudly shallow and would have been entirely obnoxious if he hadn't also had a comical charm about him. An elderly English couple in front of us were becoming increasingly irate as Karl leapt up and, pointing at a large man trying to squeeze himself into one of those new minis, screamed with laughter. They did what the English often do, threw disapproving glances at him, huffed and puffed, and muttered grumpily to each other. This only had the effect of encouraging him to be even more outrageous. He plugged in his iPod and, despite the fact that only he could hear whatever disco dream was drumming in his ears, he treated us to a very sinuous, hip thrusting, and possibly, if you were attracted by a young man doing that sort of thing, a very sexy dance. William, nothing if not broadminded, loved it but only I think because Karl was an entertaining oddity. The young Dutchman was not, by any stretch of the imagination, masculine, so Elizabeth regarded him as an annoying irrelevance. The two examples of repressed middle England seated in front of us were appalled and disgusted. And I knew that because they turned to me and said so.

"Appalling," whispered the woman.

"Disgusting," grunted the man.

The Korean boy band giggled and applauded but I think they were a bit peeved that someone else was more outrageous than they were aiming to be. They gathered Karl up though and posed for a succession of frantic photos with him whilst the blue and yellow jacketed tour guide smiled through very white teeth and tried in vain to regain control. Erich watched with quiet enjoyment and immense dignity and the indignant couple was discouraged from following up their remarks to me by one look at him.

We chugged on, around the various landmarks. Some people got off and some got on. Apart from a few churches not much had survived that was familiar to my Tudor friends, but tourist London on a sunny spring morning is an impressive and beautiful city with endless interest for those of a mind to enjoy it. William and Elizabeth were of that mind.

At last Buckingham Palace drew near. This was my goal. If my Elizabeth was to have any chance of a meeting with the current incumbent, then this was likely to be the only place in England that we might have half a chance of finding her. If she was in residence, which she probably wasn't. If not, I had no doubt that my Elizabeth would drag me around every other royal residence in England and that didn't bear thinking about.

Karl was excited by Buckingham Palace. He found its opulent grandeur attractive. At any rate, he was busy waxing lyrical, as far as it was possible to do so in guttural Dutch, to Erich, when I stood up and, climbing down to the lower floor, got off the bus with some relief.

The cool March sun had come out and the area was bright and bustling. Every nationality on planet earth must have been represented in some shape or form. There were large groups of young people and many small groups of older people as well as couples and children of all ages. There were no single people as far as I could see. Tourism isn't the sort of thing that you do solo. I plunged into the crowd and aimed for the majestic main gates. There wasn't much chance that I could get in that way but I planned to reconnoitre. I managed to fight my way past some surprisingly muscular amateur photographers who were determined to capture on film every second of the changing of the sentry and pressed my face up against the bars. Elizabeth and William squeezed in beside me.

"Funny bonnets," commented William in surprise. Elizabeth cocked her head on one side and just enjoyed the spectacle of young men marching.

"Youliette, Youliette…" Someone behind us was yodelling the name repetitively and it took a few minutes before I realised that the someone was Karl. He was po-going above the crowd in search of me, Juliet. I tried to wriggle past the slim Teutonic woman with long blonde hair and her two boisterous boys but the look I got was none too encouraging so I wriggled the other way but then came up against three South African women wearing rugby shirts. It didn't seem a good idea to upset them so I stayed put and braced myself for the flowery onslaught.

"Youliette, Youliette!" Karl, with Erich in complacent tow, fought his way through the press, undaunted by the ferocious women who gave way to him although they had not to me, and reached my side with a scream and a giggle. "Vere did you go? Ve vas looking for you."

"Sorry," I said, though I wasn't. The changing of the sentry had been achieved and the crowd loosened and disintegrated into distinct drifting groups. "I wanted to see the changing of the guard," I said, though I didn't.

Karl took my arm and began sauntering along parallel to the iron railings whilst chattering on about how effective the colours of red and black with touches of gold were and that he could see a stunning new hairstyle based on those colours and the shape of the bearskins. It certainly sounded striking, if a bit disturbing, but Elizabeth was hissing in my ear.

"Child, I must speak with my kinswoman."

"Well, why don't you just go in," I exclaimed exasperated.

Karl was delighted.

"Ah! You are talking to zem? Vat do zey say?"

"It's just Elizabeth," I said, impatiently shaking her bony, persistent fingers from my arm. "She wants to go inside."

"Ok, ve go," Karl said expansively, steering me purposefully back towards the palace.

"It's not going to be that easy," I replied testily, pulling back from his grasp. I was getting a bit fed up with people pushing me around. "They aren't just going to let me walk in."

"Oh, I haf billet, uh, you say ticket. You use the ticket of Erich. He vill not mind."

"You have tickets?" I don't know why I was quite so surprised. The way the day was shaping up I was beginning to think that anything could and probably would happen.

"Oh, yes, is special tour, not for ze whole palace, it is too zoon, ziz iz only for zummer time. But ve see the small bit viz ze 'orses, you know. Erich vas given ze tickets special. See, here is naam. Zpecial guest. Ve haf the time of vun pm so is time to get some lunch, yes, then you say you are Erich und zere is no problem."

"Well, I think there might be," I pointed out acerbically. "I am not a man and Erich is." It was Karl's turn to look surprised as this didn't seem to have occurred to him. "In any case, it doesn't really matter, they can get in without me. I don't know why they haven't just gone on their own." I glared at William and Elizabeth who were deep in animated discussion. I freed myself from Karl and marched over to them.

"Her majesty wilt not go without thee," William said mournfully.

"Why on earth not?" I snapped. "I cannot get in and if I tried I'd probably be shot. Those are real soldiers you know and real guns. They don't mess around these days."

"I command thee," Elizabeth stamped her foot and slapped me across the back of the head. Her eyes flashed. "I desire it. This weighty business will not brook delay."

I appealed helplessly to William who was always the voice of reason but he shook his head gently at me.

"Reason not the need."

"Well, that's helpful," I snapped irritably.

"Come, ve go to lunch," Karl was skipping up the Mall and this time it was Erich who beckoned to me to follow. Once again there wasn't much choice left to me so I followed obediently, if resentfully.

Lunch consisted of hotdogs and crisps bought at a kiosk and eaten on a park bench under a tree. It was very pleasant. Erich and Karl sat next to me and talked long and hard in guttural Dutch. Karl laughed often but Erich not at all. Elizabeth and William were also deep in conversation. They drifted away and, as I sat on the bench vaguely wondering how and why I was there, the heaviness of sleep beckoned. I laid my arm over the back of the bench and rested my head on it. I pulled my legs up onto the bench and closed my suddenly heavy eyes. The voices grew musical and dim and I slipped comfortably into a gentle dream of Grace and Hubby and Alex. We were all together by a lake, wrapped in an Elysian haze, happy, relaxed, content, as the swans slipped by on the glassy water. "Where are you going?" I called as my fair-haired son ran down to the cold-edged lake.

"I'll be back soon," he replied, laughing as the white tendrils of mist closed around him.

CHAPTER NINETEEN

Here's a maze trod indeed,
through forth-rights and meanders!
The Tempest, Act III Sc iii

I jerked fully awake gasping, reaching for Alex, with my heart aching and a scream dying on my lips. The reality I returned to wasn't quite Elysium but it was comforting by comparison. William was sitting on the grass with Karl and Erich. Erich was stretched out flat under the chilly sun and Karl, looking very pretty in the sunbeams slanting through the trees, had a plastic water bottle and several cans of hair products. He appeared to be brewing some sort of cocktail whilst William watched fascinated. I stretched and stood, staggering slightly under my own weight. I walked over to Elizabeth and she gave me one of her usual cold looks.

"Time gallops apace," she repeated. William looked up at her words, leapt to his feet and bounded over to us. He grasped my hand and pulled it to his lips in a most uncharacteristic expression of affection.

"Tcha," was Elizabeth's disgusted response.

"Youliette!" Karl was gathering his potions together and nudging Erich with his foot. "It is time. Time to go." I was still dazed and confused by my recent absence. "Time to see the Queenie Queen."

Elizabeth's expression spoke volumes at that.

Karl threw his arms wide and practically crowed with delight. There really was something very Peter Pan-ish about him.

"I hav vurked it out, you leaf it to me. Come, come, come…" He aimed another playful kick at Erich who rolled over and got up obediently. Karl slung his man-bag over his shoulder and tripped over to take my arm. "Come ve go."

"I still can't see how we are going to get in," I protested one more time.

"You take Erich's ticket, here it is, see. If they ask I vill say zat Erich would not come and you are my muther." I balked at that but of course, I was more than old enough if not quite crazy enough. "Vunce ve are in I haf a plan."

Erich stepped forward and put a restraining hand on Karl's arm. He then spoke at some length and with the first traces of exasperation that I had seen from him but Karl just laughed and when I protested once more that I could not take Erich's ticket, he turned to his lover and rapped out a guttural question. Erich shrugged and then nodded pleasantly at me with a smile.

"You see," Karl said triumphantly. "He is happy not to go. He is, vat you call her, he does not like der Kings und der Qveens."

"He's a republican?"

"He is ignorant," he said with a satisfied flourish. I was appalled but foreign languages don't always translate exactly, I suppose. "He is not interested in your history."

"Oh, I see!"

Erich got a scathing look from Elizabeth for that of course.

"He says it is boring. Me I sink zis also but I like der palaces. I get much inspiration."

I could visualise his next extravagant hair design and it was chilling but he was bustling us all along back through the park and towards the grand facade of Buckingham Palace. Past the grand gates we trouped, Karl, Erich, me, Elizabeth and William.

A motley crew if ever there was one - two gay hairdressers, a middle-aged woman, a literary genius and a Tudor monarch.

A group of tourists were gathered at the entrance to the Royal Mews stables. Erich peeled off after what appeared to be a final warning to Karl not to get into trouble. He gave me a quick smile but I caught him rolling his eyes as he turned away. I felt trepidation grasp me by the throat but Karl had me by the arm and Elizabeth was right behind me. There was no escape.

Karl tucked his arm through mine and launched into a very physical pantomime to indicate to any watchers that he was looking after his aged and decrepit mother. If he'd been subtle about it there probably wouldn't have been any watchers but, as it was, Karl was so flamboyant that all eyes were focussed on us and people stepped aside to make a clear path through the throng. No one dared to raise a murmur against Karl's blatant queue jumping.

We were brought to an abrupt halt in front of a very tall, thickset man and a small efficient looking young woman brandishing some sort of metal detecting implement who was regarding us with deep and entirely warranted suspicion. Karl turned on what he imagined was charm and simultaneously lost the ability to speak any English whatsoever. After a remarkably entertaining dumb show in which he was asked for his tickets and pretended not to understand, handing over instead passports, airline tickets, a packet of condoms (black and liquorice flavoured), a bottle of water and a coffee shop loyalty card, he successfully created generalised havoc. I adopted what I hoped was an expression of harmless stupidity and remained mute and horribly embarrassed. Unfortunately for Karl, a bilingual lady materialised from the gift shop and insisted on translating every word very slowly. She eventually succeeded in getting him to take back all his belongings including the condoms, despite his reluctance to reclaim them, and in wresting his two tickets from him. By this time everyone was frazzled and we were definitely unpopular. Karl's bag and my battered handbag went through the metal detector without a murmur except that the hairspray was confiscated. This triggered another display of very camp histrionics and caused us both to be subjected to a brief but humiliating body search. By this time, however, there was so much chaos and Karl had proved himself to be such a drama queen that no one in their right minds could have viewed either him or me as being anything other than damned annoying.

We were dismissed to join the rest of our group who were cowering in a corner, devoutly wishing that they had chosen some other day for their visit to the palace – or that we had. The tour guide nonetheless smiled brightly and gave Karl and me the once over as if she had been pre-warned about us. Then she gathered us up and led us into the Mews. Elizabeth and William kept close to me at first although the magnificent sight of the golden state coach held an attraction that, understandably, could not be resisted by a woman such as Elizabeth. She had gone from my side in an instant and taken her seat by right.

The group moved on but Karl held me back.

"Come ve haf some fun now," he chortled. "Over there, you see, it zays 'ztaff only'? I make the, vat do you call it, the trouble, the big trouble and you go in. Perhaps zat iss the way to the Qveen."

"Are you mad?" I hissed. "This place must be covered with cameras, and the guns the guards are holding aren't toys. I could be shot. You could be shot!"

Karl shrugged. I had no reason to expect any great concern for my life, freedom or well-being from him but even so, it seemed a bit callous. Elizabeth in her determination to reach the current British monarch was prepared to do it at any cost and was likewise careless of my safety.

"Time passes," she muttered once again in my ear and at that moment I gave up and abandoned myself to whatever insanity the rest of the day had to offer.

We had been led into a corridor to look at some bridles or something. Karl cased the area rather too expertly, established the position of a discreetly placed security camera, placed me between it and him, brought his man-bag down from his shoulders and, whilst everyone else's attention was directed towards some sort of fascinating harness, he slickly emptied the contents of the water bottle into an upturned bucket without seeming to move a muscle, and then squeezed the contents of a tiny tube after it. He then took my arm casually and we moved off to the other side of the room to gaze with rapt attention at a picture of a very oddly proportioned horse.

It wasn't long before a few noses started twitching and a sense of embarrassment, along with a particularly noxious odour, began to pervade the air. Expressions of suppressed consciousness crept over various faces and there was a definite fragmentation of the little group as one by one they sought to distance themselves from whoever was closest to them and whom they thought was the source of the increasingly foul emission. Karl nudged me towards the staff door and the last thing I saw was him working up suggestively from a ripple of small coughs to a full-blown hacking choke with accompanying dramatic flailing. Panic took hold amongst the greying tourists and several more clutched their throats and started staggering towards the various exits. Even the supercilious tour guide looked panic-stricken and was sucking frantically on an inhaler as she shepherded her gagging charges towards fresh air. Karl lifted his head once to wink at me and shoo me through the door so that, whilst I had been momentarily appalled by the possibility that I had perhaps harboured, and unwittingly assisted, a bona fide terrorist in his nefarious plan to gas innocent tourists, I was reassured enough to see that all he could be legitimately accused of would be of creating a nasty smell and using the power of suggestion very effectively. Perhaps he was cleverer than I had given him credit for, and then again perhaps not. He would have to work very hard to get away from this little episode with anything less than deportation and permanent exclusion from our fair shores.

Elizabeth and William and I slipped through the door, closed it on the coughing and retching behind us and found ourselves in a long corridor. I raced along it with absolutely no idea where I was heading or how to get through to the main part of the palace where, presumably, the Queen's apartments would be. As we reached the end of the corridor a loud persistent ringing started somewhere and I realised that the fire alarms had been activated. This was probably to our advantage as the heavy door we had reached opened to my touch which it certainly would not have done under other circumstances. I instinctively took advantage of the opportunity to move through two more slightly shorter corridors that might likewise have been barred against us before the alarm ceased to sound. Our luck held. We saw no one.

We were now in an area of offices. People, in various stages of disgruntlement, were being herded down the corridor away from us, by a large lady with a clipboard. I took the opportunity to, with duck and a dive, get myself unseen into a small uninhabited office. By this time, I was thoroughly winded, not to say terrified, but William and Elizabeth were crestfallen. The outside of the wonderful building had promised so much but they found the interior disappointingly mundane. They poked and pried and Elizabeth prodded the keyboard of a computer, searching for Benny Hill or Downtown Abbey probably. Draped over a polystyrene cup and a half-eaten salad sandwich next to the computer was a security pass on a red lanyard. The photo on it was of a woman about my age with a sharp nose and pink cheeks. Her hair was tied back in a tight bun but it was the same colour as mine and in my terror, I felt very little compunction in 'borrowing' it. I really was very far gone down the road of criminality. So far gone now that there was no chance of turning back. William had discovered piles of paper stacked up by a photocopier, white, pristine and full of promise (which was extremely unlikely to be fulfilled) and he practically drooled over it. I moved over to the open door and peered down the now deserted corridor. The alarm had been silenced. They could return at any time. I stood trying to control my heartbeat and my breathing, whilst muttering "what the fuck have I gotten myself into". You will know by now that I don't normally swear but I felt that my usual curses ("knickers", "oh bum", "hell's bells" and, in extremity, "bugger it") couldn't possibly do justice to the situation. As I did so, a door to my right opened and a tall immaculate gentleman in black tails, high collared shirt, and spotless white gloves made an entrance that would have done credit to Jeeves. He swept smartly and efficiently down the corridor and, equally smartly and efficiently, walked straight past me.

I had flinched back against the door jamb and then, in a belated effort to look as if I was supposed to be there, I changed my stance to lean nonchalantly against it. It cannot have been in the least convincing but, for some reason, he either didn't see me or, as was more likely, he was so self-absorbed that I did not register as worth noticing. I caught Elizabeth's eye and indicated the slowly closing door he had come through with a jerk of my head. She grasped William by his ruff and hauled him away from the photocopier. I reached the door milliseconds before the lock clicked and we plunged through willy-nilly. Parallel to the administrative corridor was a corridor of a very different sort. High ceiling, rich red carpet, sweeping white plaster walls punctuated with grand portraits and gorgeous moulding, glittering crystal chandeliers and extravagantly Rococo furniture. Elizabeth's sigh was one of relief and homecoming. It wasn't the style she was used to of course. It was too light and detailed but it was royal and it was rich and impressive and that she understood. William had been more enthralled with the vast amount of smooth white paper available in this new world but even he nodded with satisfaction.

"There are bound to be security cameras," I muttered to myself, looking about surreptitiously. Then it struck me that if I looked as if I was supposed to be there I might just get away with actually being there for a few minutes longer. I hung the purloined security tag around my neck, fished in my bag and pulled out a pen that didn't write and a crumpled piece of paper. Then I sauntered positively into the centre of the sumptuous corridor and moved confidently up it, ostentatiously making the odd note as I went. My companions kept pace with me but Elizabeth paused often to view with interest, if not always approval, the cumbersome artwork that adorned the walls. Once or twice William skipped from my side to take a closer look. An alabaster bust caught his eye and he spent several moments nose to nose with the Duke of Wellington. A few feet further on he passed by a sculpture of himself without a second glance. I was about to point his likeness out to him when a door to our left flew open and a young man hurtled out. He drew himself up in a skid when he saw me and, amazingly, bowed briefly.

"Good afternoon, madam," he said politely. "Spot of bother in the Mews. All over now, could you let them know that Her Majesty is not to be disturbed?"

"Yes, of course," I said helpfully and, I thought, with admirable aplomb. I inclined my head slightly for good measure. He adjusted his jacket and set off again at a smart trot. I, feeling that my luck couldn't hold much longer, also set off at an equally smart pace in the opposite direction in order to put as much space between us as possible. A door at the very end of the grand corridor was slightly ajar and I put my eye to it. As far as could be discerned, it led to another shorter, wider corridor at right angles with several more doors. I glimpsed a pair of high heels and immaculate legs under a knee-length skirt disappearing into one of the rooms on my left.

"Why dost thou tarry?" Elizabeth hissed in my ear. "Go forth, go forth…"

She gave me a sharp push and I lurched forward into the corridor just as the legs came back out of the door they had just gone in to. I turned smartly away and headed purposefully towards the door at the further end of what was actually just a very large room that led into various other rooms. I was playing a sort of desperate game of Russian roulette in my head trying to decide which of the doors I should risk entering with the least chance of being shot by the occupant when the owner of the smart legs called after me.

"Excuse me?" I tried ignoring her but she just spoke louder, quite a bit louder. "EXCUSE ME?"

I braced myself and turned. She wasn't pointing a gun at me which was good but I felt that my days as a free woman were about to be curtailed for an indefinite period.

"I'm sorry to bother you," she said.

My spirits lifted slightly.

"I'm new here, only started today." My spirits soared. "I was asked to get a ream of paper for the printer from the…" she consulted a paper in her hand squinting through geek-chic black rimmed glasses, "the Mews Administrative offices?" My spirits could not have soared any higher.

"Of course, dear," I replied kindly. "It is such a maze, so easy to lose yourself. I've been here a surprisingly long time myself, and I'm still quite lost. Let me see, the quickest way will be…" and I directed her confidently back the way Elizabeth, William and I had come.

"Through there?" she looked young and doubtful. "Would I be allowed? Ought I to be in there?"

"Don't worry," I patted her shoulder reassuringly, "I've just been through myself. We use it as a shortcut." I gave her a gentle push and closed the door on her.

I still had no idea where we were or where we were going,

but to press on and hope for the best appeared to be the best option. I chose one door and entered confidently only to find myself in a large cupboard that held the most immaculately clean cleaning equipment I had ever seen outside of a Kleeneze catalogue. Another, however, led to a flight of wide stone steps accessing all the floors of the grand building and, with a quick glance to ensure that no one else was using them, I hurried up. One floor, two. There were another two flights but terror and exertion left me struggling for breath and I had to sit down and lean my head against cool marble balustrades for a moment or so.

Elizabeth, increasingly excited as she scented the close proximity of her quarry, scowled at me.

"Go to, go to, why do we tarry when we are nigh?"

"For God's sake," I snapped through laboured puffs. "Just go and find her yourself. Do you have any idea how much trouble I am in if they find me here? That is if I live long enough to find out what the penalties are for breaking and entering a Royal Palace."

"Execution?" William was deeply concerned, bless him.

"Worse," I replied bitterly. "Much, much worse. My family and I will be splattered all over the tabloids and made ridiculous. And then we will be tempted by vast amounts of money, that we can't possibly refuse, to sell our story to the highest bidder and will be made contemptible."

I sobbed and he winced, with full understanding I think, and patted my arm compassionately whilst turning wistful eyes towards the unmoved Elizabeth.

"She must take me," she insisted. "I know not…" She paused. I doubt whether she used those three words together in that order on many occasions and hearing herself say them had come as a bit of a surprise. "I know not if the new woman will hear me. You must be with me, make haste to find her."

"I don't know where to look," I rapped back exasperated.

"It's a huge building and I am not even sure if she is here at all! She could be at Balmoral or launching a ship or visiting the great-grandkids or something."

Elizabeth cocked her old head slightly on one side and slapped me hard across the back of mine. That had the effect of shocking me into silence. William, brave soul, jumped up and put himself nervously between us but Elizabeth had already moved off in disgust.

It was at that moment that I heard from far off a sharp bell sound twice, three times and then it seemed there were running feet everywhere. I got up shakily and looked cautiously down the stairwell. Men in uniform, soldiers were running effortlessly up towards us, their shiny black boots ringing on the marble steps. Above a man in a morning suit was running down towards us. I whipped smartly through the first door I could find to a galleried landing overlooking the vast sweep of a magnificent carmine carpeted stairway.

Immediately in front of me were three booted and suited butlers, their backs towards me, who were leaning over the rail of a sumptuously carved balcony.

"Wot's goin' on?" one shouted down to someone below.

"Security alert," drifted back the reply, "I bet it's that new girl. She set the damned alarm off this morning by opening her window and throwing her yoghurt pot into the guard house."

"Silly mare," muttered one of the butlers under his breath.

"Nice legs though," muttered another. It seemed she would be forgiven a great deal for that.

"Bloody 'ell," groaned a world-weary butler with a bald head and handlebar moustache. "That'll be the third friggin' time this week. Wot wuz it yesterday? Some foreign dignitary bloke getting caught short and making a dash for the toilet. Someone should have warned him that anyone wearing white robes and running in this place is asking to be brought down by a rugby tackle. Poor bloke. That didn't end well."

"Twice before that it was old Ernie getting a bit energetic wiv 'is feather duster on the ormolu. Mind you we did 'ave an explosion last week."

"That was just some prat's spotted dick exploding in the microwave. They are all just too bloody jittery if you ask me. They're seein' terrorists under every bed. Afternoon, ma'am."

This was directed at me as they turned sanguinely back to their various duties. I smiled a half smile and nodded graciously. My heart had stopped some time ago. In fact, I couldn't feel it beating at all anymore. I took a couple of steps forward to the space they had vacated and peered over the balcony. Several people were moving around hurriedly and with purpose and, despite my incredible luck so far, I could not help but feel the teeth of the trap closing in on me. I had an overwhelming urge to hide, and not in plain sight either.

Panic, only slightly submerged for the last half hour or so, took hold. I wanted to squeal with fear and, when a whole regiment of soldiers (or so it seemed, I didn't stop to count) appeared at the far end of the corridor behind me, I wheeled, pulled open the first door I came to, tumbled in regardless of William and Elizabeth and almost slammed it behind me, only collecting myself in just enough time to pull the last few centimetres gently.

Elizabeth screeched in outrage and William yelped but as far as I was concerned they were on their own. Like an animal at bay, I turned panting, the door at my back, and looked around desperately for some refuge from my own folly. My heart was pounding again as if it would take flight from my rib cage and the fuzzy confused feeling was overpowering.

I was in a large room. Well, I say large, it was probably one of the smallest the palace had to offer but it was large to me who had spent nearly all my life in a three-bedroom semi. Sweeping blue curtains obscured the high sash windows and the room was calm and comfortably furnished. Expensively I would say but with more of an eye to comfort than opulence. There was a grand desk of shiny mahogany, heavy high-backed cushioned chairs and a low table strewn with newspapers. Bookcases lined the walls but encased, not the heavy leather clad tomes that were to be expected, but modern books with bright dust jackets and even a few garish paperbacks. There were the ubiquitous portraits of grim looking Victorians and plenty of ornate plaster work, tinted white and gold. Nonetheless, it was clearly an office of some sort, a working office, probably one of the many administrative offices required to run the Palace and the business of monarchy, but for a much more important administrator than those who inhabited the workaday offices below.

It was empty but I could hear heavy marching steps approaching. I tiptoed across the deep carpet and, as the footsteps stopped abruptly and a knock sounded at the door, I flung myself down head first behind a stuffed leather sofa.

An insistent but polite knock sounded again at the door. It was a gentle knock, at odds with the heavy fall of military boots in the background. No response was forthcoming however and the door swung slowly open with a very un-palatial creak to reveal, to me at floor level, a pair of the shiniest, roundest boots I had ever seen in my life. Obviously, more of the boots' owner existed but, flat on the floor, breathless and in agony from my precipitous head long dive, the shiny footwear was all I could see and all I wanted to see. Ever.

"Sir?" A very deep voice came from the direction of the boots. There was still no answer of course because there was no one in the room. Except me and I couldn't speak even if I had wanted to.

"Sir?" I bit my knuckles and prayed to the God I didn't believe in that they wouldn't search the room. They would, of course, it was inevitable.

"Go away, go away, there's no one here," I said very loudly

in my head as if I might be able to subliminally dissuade them, which was silly because I didn't believe in that sort of thing either.

"SIR!"

This was said very loudly.

"Yes? What?"

My previously quiescent heart suddenly exploded against my rib cage and began to pound very loudly so that my eardrums rattled. Conversely, my breathing stopped entirely.

There was someone in the room and that someone must have seen me.

"I'm sorry to wake you, sir."

"Wake me!" came the indignant protest in a cultured male voice. "I wasn't asleep."

My breath came back in a gasp.

"Just a bit of a doze, nothing more. I don't sleep in the day. Bad form that."

"Yes, sir." The response was unemotional. "I just need to inform you that we have another security alert."

"What is it this time?" The deep, soft voice was weary. "Has one of those damn dogs chewed through the wires again?"

"Probably, sir. The men will stay in the corridor until we have ascertained the situation."

"Hrrrmmm, as you say." I glimpsed a thin gnarled hand wave in a gesture that encompassed both weary agreement and dismissal from behind one of the high-backed chairs. The soldier didn't exactly click his heels before he departed but there was a definite movement that suggested it. The door closed respectfully behind him and I was left prostrate on the floor behind the leather settee with my knuckles jammed firmly between my clenched teeth, the gentleman comfortably ensconced out of my sight behind the high-backed chair and a contingent of burly men armed to the teeth behind the door.

Elizabeth marched over to the chair and took a long look

at the figure there. William, timid soul, had decided that discretion was the better part of valour, even for the invisible, and was crouching with me behind the settee. A strange, strangulated sound erupted from behind the chair and for a moment I wondered if it was the gentleman's vocal reaction to discovering the Virgin Queen examining him, but he was just yawning prior to stretching and standing. From my restricted viewpoint I could only see a pair of very expensively-trousered legs and yet another pair of very well-polished shoes. Elizabeth was inspecting him in detail and with interest and what she saw obviously pleased her. She liked her men younger overall but, even so, she approved the look and the bearing of this man. She gave three sharp nods and then sat down majestically on another of the high-backed chairs opposite to him, folded her hands expectantly on her lap and watched the gentleman intently. He stood and the legs took a couple of slow, stiff turns around the coffee table and then moved towards the window. I was just wondering if I could risk squeezing myself under the settee and then just staying there until I died. It seemed to me to be the only possible way of ever getting out of this terrible predicament. I cautiously pulled my knuckles from my face, placed my hands flat on the floor in front of me and lifted my head very slightly. No sound, and I couldn't see the feet at the window. I could, very faintly, hear voices intermittently behind the door and, somewhere far off, the bell was still ringing.

The door opened again but no one came in although I thought I heard a woman's voice. A small squat little beast, however, whiffled across the carpet and came for me like an arrow. I froze in sheer terror even though in the general scheme of things I quite like dogs. The wet nose hit mine and enquiring canine eyes looked at me with little intellect and a whole lot of suspicion. The fuzzy feeling was back in my head and I was either going to scream or faint. Probably both. The barest growl started low in the creatures' throat. It was working up to one of those ear shattering bouts of hysterical high-pitched yelping that are one good reason of many that you should never choose small dogs, when William, seeing the danger, leapt from my side and smartly pulled the little stump that did service as a tail. Animals at least appeared to have an awareness of this altered state of being. Having gained the outraged creature's attention, he effectively managed by means of several other well-timed pulls to get the creature to chase his own tail in the middle of the room.

"I'm fine, I'm reading. Can you take the dog with you?"

A quiet exchange was taking place between the woman at the door and the expensive trousers but, in my fright at my discovery by the yappy dog, I had not heard any of it until the last few words. A quiet command came from behind the door and the dog snapped twice at the air, threw me a filthy look and pattered out.

The door was all but closed when Elizabeth rose and drifted silently through. William threw me a questioning look and I shrugged. I was far from caring what Elizabeth was up to. I shut my eyes and tried to think. How the bloody hell was I going to get out of this one? I thought longingly of normality, of Hubby and Grace, of our comfortable, safe, cosy house and of our comfortable, safe, cosy life and I began, not for the first time, to wish devoutly that I had never set eyes on Elizabeth and William. There was absolutely no way out that did not involve disgrace, notoriety, and a prison sentence. Even that might be a relief if it had not been for the horror that it would cause Grace and Hubby and my mum and dad and my sister. No, perhaps not my sister – she would be inclined to think of it all as a slightly anarchic escapade and would revel in her association with such an infamous rebel.

A tear slid down my cheek and I covered my face to suppress a sob. But crying would get me nowhere so I took hold of myself and tried to think, to formulate a plan. If I just hunkered down where I was and stayed put the alert would be called off. Eventually. I hoped. It looked like the security system, fine-tuned as it undoubtedly was, had a bit of a hair trigger and the household was rather fed up with false alarms. We'd had a computerised fire alarm system fitted at work that had similarly gone off at the drop of a hat (Or if a mouse farted as Cynthia from despatch put it). In the beginning, it went off so many times for such a variety of inconsequential reasons that, after the first twenty or so unnecessary evacuations, we tended to ignore it and when Blofeld made a toasted baked bean sandwich and burnt down the kitchen none of us moved until the firemen ran through the office with hose and hatchet. So, that's what I decided to do. Not run around with a hose and hatchet but sit tight and wait until the gentleman left the room and things settled down. Then I would try to find my way back to the offices. I should be able to bluff my way out when the office staff left, much as I had managed to bluff my way this far, I reasoned desperately.

Feeling more secure now that I had a plan of sorts, I took a couple of long slow breaths wiped the tears from my cheeks and opened my eyes.

CHAPTER TWENTY

Strong reasons make strong actions: let us go:
If you say ay, the king will not say no.
    King John, Act III Sc iv

"Hello," said the gentleman.

He was leaning nonchalantly on the arm of the settee, looking down at me quizzically. He was of medium height but looked tall, at least from ground level, and of slender, spare build, with only the suggestion of a stoop and much less stiffness than you would credit for a man of his advanced years. The rest of his clothes, grey cardigan, shirt, and tie were as refined and expensive as the trousers. His straight white hair, worn short and immaculately cut, was sparse. He had a slim, lined face with thin, aged skin stretched over high cheekbones and a strong, aristocratic nose. His watery blue eyes under tufted grey eyebrows retained the twinkle of a very far distant youth. He raised one gnarled, but still elegant, hand, ran it over his mouth and gave me a calm considering look. He was not in the least bit fazed at finding a dishevelled woman with red eyes prostrate under his settee, but then he had a military bearing and you felt immediately that it would take a great deal more than that to alarm this man.

I gaped at him speechlessly, afraid to move a muscle. William grasped my hand comfortingly.

"I will not let him hurt thee." William had taken the man's

measure and, bearing in mind his own comparative youth, he felt he could probably thrash this man without too much trouble if it came to a tussle, although how he expected to achieve that in his altered state I had no idea. I suspected that he was overconfident after his recent success with the Corgi.

"It's all right William," I said quickly as he began to flex his muscles. "This had to happen. It's all over." I sat up slowly and smiled at William in brave defeat. "Where did Elizabeth go?"

"I know not. She saw the woman at the door and followed her."

"Perhaps she discovered that she did not need me after all. Typical!" I snorted. "If she had found that out before I wouldn't be in this mess."

"Who are you talking to, young woman? Not to me I think." The question was asked serenely and with no surprise.

"Oh, it's a long story," I replied sadly. "And you wouldn't believe it. No one does. But I didn't mean any harm, honestly, I didn't."

"Then what are you doing here?" I looked at him dumbly. He cocked an eyebrow and suddenly there was a look of frightening severity that sent my over-worked heart plummeting.

"You are in a very great deal of trouble. I would like to hear what you have to say before I call the guard. The truth if you please, and no nonsense."

"I came with William and Elizabeth," I replied obediently. This was going to be difficult but there was no doubt that only the truth would do. "Elizabeth wanted to see the Queen."

His eyes never wavered from mine but his demeanour tensed at my words and his gaze sharpened.

"And where are this Elizabeth and William now?"

"They are here. At least William is. Elizabeth left when the dog went out."

"I did not see her."

"No, you wouldn't. No one does, except me. And Nell but

she's in…well, Loughborough, I think. William is here. Beside me." I indicated William who was kneeling beside me with his fists ready and poised to do pugilistic damage if any threatening moves were made.

The gentleman just cocked another disbelieving eyebrow at me but his body relaxed slightly. He was coming to the inevitable conclusion of course. "Mad but harmless," I could hear him thinking. He had no doubt spent some moments appraising me as I lay with my eyes shut and had already decided that I was not an immediate threat to his person or property. His concern about my accomplices was evaporating with the knowledge that they were invisible. Why he had not called the soldiers at the door though was a mystery.

"William and Elizabeth are your children?"

I grimaced. "It feels like that sometimes but no; they are…" I sighed deeply. "You will think I am mad. Everyone does."

"I find that 'everyone' generally has an opinion that they are all too keen to express and 'everyone' is usually wide of the mark. I have been a target of 'everyone' for as long as I can remember so I will listen to your story. Come," he said, as I bit my lip and no doubt looked a bit sheepish. "I've had a very boring day and you look interesting. Who is this William character who appears to be sitting on the magazine rack?"

I glanced at William, who was indeed now perched precariously on the walnut magazine rack and took another deep breath.

"It's Shakespeare," I said boldly. "William Shakespeare."

The gentleman was looking at the magazine rack, not at me, but not a flicker of surprise or even disbelief crossed his aristocratic features.

"Ahh," he said. There was a pause. "He's very welcome. I've enjoyed his works."

William looked pleased as he always did when people in this world recognised his name. It was pretty mind blowing if you thought about it, that the little man from Stratford who had gained such a small amount of recognition in his own lifetime should gain such universal fame after it.

The gentleman was deep in thought.

"And Elizabeth?" he asked at length.

"Oh, well." I was even more reluctant to spill the beans on this one than on William, but his gravity was compelling and, as he wanted an answer, I didn't feel that all things considered, I had much of a choice but to give him one.

"That would be Elizabeth…Tudor." He nodded with superb aplomb. "I know it's hard to believe. I just opened my pantry door one day and there she was sitting on a sack of potatoes. King Edward's as it happens. William turned up a couple of days later and they have been with me, on and off, ever since."

"Hrrrhm," he looked at me with a touch of humour in his eyes. "They get you into all sorts of trouble I imagine."

"You could say that. They got me here. Well, with a bit of help from a gay Dutch hairdresser." He raised another patrician eyebrow at that. "Another long story. Oh, the hairdresser was real. I mean he is a real person. Not that William and Elizabeth aren't real. They are, they really are. It's just that not everybody sees them. I wish…that you could see them." I let that pathetic thought hang unhappily in the air between us.

"Hrrrhm," he said again. "Let me see if I have got this right. You have come here because Elizabeth the First wants to see the Queen?"

"Yes, I don't really know why but she has not got much time left and she is desperate to talk to her."

"Not much time left? Do you mean she has not much time left with you?"

"I think she has not got much time left in this world or in her world."

"I see. And she wishes to talk with the Queen. No doubt they would have much in common."

I wasn't too sure about that. Queening had changed over the years. He moved back towards the high-backed chair and indicated the one opposite, the one Elizabeth had briefly occupied. I hauled myself up off the floor and, pulling my skirt down and smoothing my flyaway hair, I walked apologetically over to the chair and sat down obediently. There was a little footstool at the side and William perched comfortably on this and leant, as if for reassurance, against my legs.

"Tell me your story." Like I said, he was very compelling, so I told him pretty much everything. Well, I missed out the trip to the Rocky Horror Show. He was most interested in what William thought about things. He sat, his whole frame relaxed, but his eyes piercing with an intensity rare in one so, well, let's face it, old.

"Describe him. Describe your Mr. Shakespeare to me," he commanded at length. I looked at William perched on the stool at my knee, his fingers linked across his knees and his liquid brown eyes fixed on the lanky, old gentleman.

"He's quite, well, small and very..." I was going to say ordinary looking, but that seemed unfair. "...he is well-looking and he has beautiful brown eyes and a pointy beard that needs a trim and an unremarkable nose, but his lips are quite full and he has quite dark skin. Dark hair of course, longish, and he's dressed pretty much as you would expect him to be."

"And what does he think of this world of ours?"

I turned to William.

"He says it is full of miracles," I reported back, "and that he has seen the impossible made possible. He wants to fly in an aeroplane and to see all the wonders of our modern world. He says that he is ashamed to come from a time of ignorance and wishes more than life itself that he could live in this time."

"And, yet, if the great Shakespeare had never lived in his time, the world of today would be a much poorer place, don't you think?"

"That is very true," I agreed. "You were meant for your time and I was meant for mine and that's it, that is all there is."

William looked heavily crestfallen, perhaps he hoped that 21st-century royalty had evolved into wizards who could grant his wishes. If you looked at it from his perspective, it wasn't unreasonable. Our modern world had already offered him so many 'miracles' that William's timid suggestion that he might be able to transfer permanently to our world wasn't entirely ridiculous. At least not in his eyes.

I began to understand Elizabeth's desire to see our Queen. She would only deign to make the request from an equal, and there was only one.

The tall man's eyes twinkled and he smiled at me.

"You are not religious then? You do not have a faith to sustain you?"

"No," I sighed. William's hand pressed mine.

"God hast delivered me to you, and you to me," he whispered. "And to her. He means something by this though I know not what. And thou hast shown us immortality tho' we wander in illusions. We learn from this although we cannot share it. I see in your experience what mine shall be were I to tell too much."

I laughed, bleakly. "Yeah, I'd keep it under your hat if I were you."

"Tell me something. Who was the Dark Lady?" the tall man asked suddenly. "I was reading something recently about the various theories and I would be interested to hear the truth from the…horses' mouth as it were." He leaned forward, prodded my knee and chuckled.

"The dark lady of the sonnets," I turned to William. It was a test of sorts, I recognised that, even though it was so gently phrased, but, although my knowledge was limited, I was confident that my source was impeccable. "It is believed that the dark lady was your lover but that she ran off with one of your friends."

"Dark lady?" queried William, nonplussed. My heart plummeted but he knit his brows and presently a thought touched him. "Ah, my sonnets written in the green years. Thou speakst of Emelia?"

"Probably," I muttered.

"The Lanier woman was faithless indeed." William let my hand go and pressed both of his own together. His dark eyes fell from mine. "She betrayed far more than I. She hath been the mistress of many whom she thought might grant her advancement. But for me, she and I…" He sighed slightly. "I could give her nothing but myself and for a while that was enough."

I repeated William's words for the benefit of our companion.

"Ah," he considered. "Emilia Lanier is the favourite with the academics at the moment I believe, although there have been others. Well, that would explain both the passion and the pain of the sonnets. It has long been speculated that Lanier was the woman but it is good to have this confirmation, even if none but ourselves will ever know it."

William smiled a small bitter smile. "Our love was ever under the rose."

"Bit hard on poor old Anne though," I couldn't help saying, with a touch of bitterness, on behalf of my sex.

William gave me one of his wounded looks.

"Don't give me that look," I snapped back forgetting that he and I were not alone. "You left her alone in Stratford with your kids for months, possibly years and then, by your own admission, went off with the Lanier woman. What did she have that your wife didn't? Youth and beauty I suppose, if not actually enormous knockers."

I suddenly recollected the old man in the chair opposite and an uncomfortable heat crept over my whole body.

"Sorry," I stuttered.

William, predictably, enquired, "Knockers? What is knockers?"

The old man smiled. It might have been a humorous smile, but it might also have been contemptuous. I was too flustered to be sure.

"Knockers?" persisted the ever-curious William. I indicated my breasts as subtly as I could.

"Ahh, dugs." He was enlightened but my other companion was confused.

"Something wrong?"

"No, it's just that I have to explain a lot of things that William doesn't understand."

"Like 'knockers'?" He let out a shout of laughter at my discomfort, William chortled in concert and I felt that I had let the cause of feminism down dreadfully. "Be fair to Mr. Shakespeare though. From what I have read Emelia Lanier was an exceptional woman, a musician and a poet, so perhaps it was as much a meeting of the minds as of the bodies."

"Maybe," I conceded grudgingly.

"And," he responded comfortably. "She became a published poet herself, I believe. She was quite the feminist and lived to a ripe old age."

"I am glad," said William, softly. "I am glad."

The old man continued.

"And tell me the solution to another mystery. Why did your friend stop writing at the height of his powers and return to obscurity in Stratford?"

"He won't know that," I said. "He's not a ghost. That hasn't happened yet."

The gentleman nodded slowly but William spoke.

"My eyes grow dim. I seek relief but doctors give me few years in the light and no hope."

"A tragedy indeed," our kindly companion commented, as I grasped William's hand more tightly and tears sprang once more to my eyes.

There was a polite knock on the door. I jumped.

"Come in," the gentleman said calmly.

I shrank back into my chair. The knock was repeated, and once again "Come in," was the elderly gentleman's laconic, but slightly louder, response. The door remained closed. Our elderly friend sighed and, despite my strangled remonstrance, got to his feet. I flinched back into the encompassing arms of my chair and threw him an imploring look. He returned a kind smile, went to the door and opened it.

The next thing I knew he was engulfed by about ten enormous men, bristling with guns, and I was staring down, or should that be up, the barrel of a fearsome looking automatic weapon. William was on my lap with his arms around my head and the room was full to bursting with khaki and testosterone. I'm pretty sure I whimpered pathetically. I know William did.

"No, no, no," came the gruff voice of our mutual friend from behind the impressive wall of muscle. "This is unnecessary. The lady means no harm. She has wandered this way by mistake. You are frightening her. Give the command to stand easy, she is no threat."

"Sir," said one of the biggest who seemed to be in charge. "We need to be sure. These people can be devious."

The tough soldier stood, immovable as rock, eyeing me over his gun grey automatic. Me, a wide-eyed, petrified, middle-aged woman, clothed entirely by British Home Stores. He wavered of course. I could almost see the image of his own mother rising before him. The muzzle of the gun drooped slightly and, though not a muscle moved under any of the khaki jackets, you could feel that the situation was not quite as highly charged anymore. William relaxed enough to realise how ridiculous he looked and to release his arms from their stranglehold on my head.

"Stand up!" barked the soldier in charge, reluctant to give in to the mundane without one last grasp at heroic action. Both William and I jumped to our feet obediently whilst the gentleman made a pained sound of protestation. He was old school and didn't like to see women bullied. Neither, for that matter, did I.

"Turn around." I did of course (and so did William). Without a doubt, I would have been ignominiously searched from head to foot for knives or explosives right there and then if the kind old gentleman had not interfered once again. As it was, I was just divested of my coat and cardigan, which were briefly inspected. My handbag was taken to one side and, without even a by your leave, was emptied on to the magnificent mahogany desk, where my cheap pink lipstick and Peppa Pig purse looked diabolically incongruous when directly contrasted with the weighty importance of royal furniture. Grace had thought it funny to give me the purse for my last birthday. I had thought it funny to use it to embarrass her in front of her friends. The kind old gentleman had taken the opportunity to say something aside to the soldier, who looked respectfully pissed off but inclined for the first time to regard me as an outrageous nuisance rather than a threat to national security.

"The lady is just lost," my friend remonstrated mildly. The soldiers, having rummaged through my meagre possessions and not found anything more lethal than a fluff-covered Fisherman's Friend, fell back obediently and my old friend calmly joined William and myself between the chairs. "She got separated from her group when that damned alarm went off and found her way here, nothing more than that."

I found the confidence to nod in agreement. I still hadn't said a word and was quite happy to keep it that way.

"There is a letter here, sir." One of the men held out Elizabeth's letter that I had never posted, and the atmosphere was charged once more. "It is addressed to Her Majesty."

The senior officer viewed it with deep suspicion and I could see him thinking 'anthrax'. My friend, however, was made of sterner stuff. He reached out and, before any of us could move, had flipped it open and was reading the contents. He smiled and, in the absence of a cloud of white powder, the muscles in the room relaxed once more.

"I'll make sure Her Majesty receives this. She will be very interested in your…erhm, story." It was folded and in his pocket before the military gentleman had time to protest.

"She's probably the mother of the Dutchman, sir," muttered a particularly determined young recruit who had been waiting patiently for his moment.

"Dutchman? What Dutchman?" The officer raised one hand and suddenly the room was clear of armed men except for the determined young recruit and the officer himself. I might have been the object of their investigation but I was not to take part in it.

"There was a tour in the Mews this afternoon. The Dutchman said he got separated from his mother when the alarm went off. He said that his mother was not…er, not quite…"

He had caught my eye by accident and all the military training in the world couldn't save him from this landmine. I wasn't going to let him off so I stared back, challenging him to call me mentally deranged. He floundered in confusion and retreated into silence.

"There you are then," the gentleman yawned slightly as if to impress on the muscle-bound young men just how mundane it all was. Or perhaps just because he really was a very elderly gentleman. "The lady should be reunited with her son."

"We'll take her into custody, sir."

"Not necessary," snapped the gentleman beginning to get crotchety on my behalf. I don't know why, but perhaps it was because he knew something of restriction and of not always being free to make your own decisions.

"It isn't as easy as that, sir," protested the officer.

"Yes, it is," my friend insisted. "She has done nothing, sat with me for a quarter of an hour or so…"

"Quarter of an hour!" the officer protested in horror.

"Quarter of an hour or so, at my invitation. We chatted."

"You should have called us sir. We have had a number of security alerts and we need…"

"Pshaw," he interrupted, seating himself once more on his high-backed chair. "Security alerts every five minutes for the last two weeks. What set the damned alarm off this time?"

A smartly suited civilian had entered the room and came respectfully forward.

"It seems we had a group of school boys in earlier and we believe that one of them left a…hrrmm…a stink bomb in one of the buckets in the Mews. No one noticed until the second tour came in when it seems to have ruptured. It was assumed to be some sort of gas and caused quite a panic, sir. This does look like the woman the gentleman from Holland described."

"Did you not pick her up on the CCTV?" the soldier asked, exasperated.

"Yes, actually we did, but she looks very similar to Mrs. Benson who is a member of the administrative staff so we didn't take much notice, I'm afraid."

I thanked God that the purloined security pass had slipped comfortably into my cleavage and out of sight. If found in my possession it would disprove any innocent reason for my presence in the Royal Apartments and condemn me as the deliberate trespasser I undoubtedly was.

The smart suit turned to my gentleman friend.

"I can only apologise most profoundly, sir. This should never have happened. You should not have been disturbed."

"Humph," the old man said, looking disgruntled.

What I had told him didn't quite match up with this much more mundane story and I think he liked my version better. I, however, glimpsed the possibility that I might just get away with my mad adventure. It seemed as if the Fates, with a little help from Karl, Mrs. Benson and the wonderful fallibility of human beings, had conspired to provide me with a get out of jail free card. If looking a little spaced and accepting the mundane, not to mention the aspersions cast on my mental acuity, would gain me my freedom I was all for it.

"You had better take her back to her son," said the smart suit.

"Yes, sir," the soldier acquiesced reluctantly.

I think he would have liked to have caught a bloodthirsty terrorist. I was a bit of a disappointment.

"Mind you do," said the gentleman.

I was in the process of being bundled unceremoniously out of the room when he spoke again. I was allowed to turn around briefly to face him although restraining hands were kept on me in case I should suddenly run amok.

"I wish you and your friends well, young woman. I enjoyed our conversation."

"Thank you," I whispered. "You've been very kind, sir."

He leaned forward and tapped his nose confidentially.

"Tell your friend William I shall be reading his work again with new eyes."

"I will," I replied with half a smile. It was so nice that he believed. I was whipped smartly around and marched out of the door. William gave the old gentleman a wide smile (which he didn't see of course) and scampered after me.

Back through the wonderful rooms we tramped. No one spoke to me except for the occasional "This way, madam". They weren't taking any chances. Two soldiers walked either side of me, and two behind. I felt quite important. It was very strange, though. We passed the three butlers who gaped guiltily at me and decided that if they weren't asked they wouldn't tell. The young woman with the smart legs turned a corner and came upon us suddenly. Taking in the situation at a glance she squealed with horror, rushed off to have hysterics and then, I imagined, to tender her immediate resignation on the grounds that her nerves wouldn't stand the rigours of palace life.

Whilst descending a flight of stairs I glanced back and saw that Elizabeth had re-joined us and was following regally with an air of intense self-satisfaction.

I was hustled down corridors and through such a multitude of doors that it came as a shock to be suddenly regurgitated into the cold grey exterior with only a short walk before me to the iron gates, behind which I could see the wild hair and wide smile belonging to Karl. Erich, the faithful shadow, was at his shoulder.

"Youliette," Karl yelled, waving his arms like a windmill and jumping up and down. "Youliette, ve are here."

"Your son is over there. Do not talk to the press," said the officer. "See her to the gate," he ordered one of his men. "And off the property permanently," was sternly implied.

A different hand grasped my elbow and I was guided firmly and quickly across the short space, past one soldier, three more guards and two waiting policemen.

I was ejected with no more ceremony through the iron gates and into the fond embrace of my 'son' Karl.

CHAPTER TWENTY-ONE

*I had rather have a fool make me happy
than experience make me sad.
As You Like It, Act IV Sc ii*

"Ah, Youliette, I vas so vurried."

"Juliette?" came an interrogating voice from a petite woman with sharp features, a prominent nose, and highly coiffured blonde hair. Behind her stood a scruffy looking man with lank hair and weary eyes. He was operating some sort of oversized camera. Behind them were crowds of curious tourists sensing something scandalous and preparing to relay it by iPhone and Twitter to family, friends and anyone else who had nothing better to do but eavesdrop into lives they assumed were more interesting than their own.

"You call your mother Juliette?" the blonde journalist asked suspiciously.

"It is her name," Karl replied airily, hugging me enthusiastically, more to keep me quiet I think, than from any excess of affection. "She is my little muther. How do you call it, my muther off the birth? My long-lost birth muther. I come to London to find her and haf wunnerful day together, wunnerful, und zen..!" He threw up his hands and pantomimed despair. "Und zen, disaster, alarms are going off, dring, dring, dring..."

He tucked my head under his arm to keep me from protesting and gave us a very loud and a very creditable impression of the palace's alarm system. The woman was too hard-bitten to be impressed, but her interest was piqued and some of the crowd closest to us were enjoying Karl's performance.

"Dring dring! Disaster! Alarms are going off and my beloved muther is, pouf, vanished."

I realised with a sudden thrill of horror that the camera was pointed in my direction. I was being filmed. The woman sensed a story and Karl, revelling in every fantasy fuelled moment, was well on the way to giving her one. He had a great many good points but a sense of decorum wasn't one of them.

"Can I ask your name, please?" The woman's mascara laden eyes turned sharply to me. Her instincts told her that, despite Karl's energetic play acting, there was a story and it lay with me. I shrank back and Karl came to my rescue. Sort of.

"It is Youliette…Minnelli," he said boldly. "She has have difficult day. I take her to hotel now. She rest."

Sadly, I don't think he was particularly solicitous as to my wellbeing. I think he was playing hard to get.

"Mrs. Minnelli….or is that Ms?" The reporter persisted. It must have been a slow day and I was her last chance for a tawdry story. She obviously got her stories through persistence. She certainly didn't get them through charm.

"Did you breach security in the Palace? Did you get through to the Royal Apartments?"

Karl opened his mouth with every intention, I believe, of embroidering my little story with the most astonishing events his over active imagination could come up with, but at that moment Erich decided that things had gone far enough. I don't know what he said. It was only one word but Karl shut his mouth, put his arm around my shoulders and turned me away.

"My muther has no comment," he said firmly. Well, firmly for him anyway. Erich took up the rear and we walked away.

"Mrs. Minnelli, Juliette, my bosses would be prepared to pay a substantial sum for an exclusive on your adventures in the palace. Did you see any members of the Royal Family? Did you get into the Queen's apartments? What do you think of the security arrangements at the palace? Are you a terrorist?"

"No comment, no comment," Karl airily waved them all aside. "My muther haz no comment."

"Have you been threatened, or paid to keep silent?"

I don't know who she worked for but being possessed of a modicum of scruples was not a requirement of the job.

"Were you mistreated or manhandled by any of the guards? If you have any allegations of mistreatment by the military, we could pay you a very substantial sum?"

Karl hesitated momentarily and glanced inquiringly down at me but another sharp word from Erich decided him and he hustled me across the road and out of reach of the curious crowd. The reporter and her camcorder friend dogged our footsteps for another few hundred yards but, tiring in the face of my obstinate determination not to be the next desperate, disposable celebrity, fell back to go in search of some other tawdry tale of unhappiness or outrage.

"Ve leaf zem behind," Karl said at length, with a touch of regret in his voice. "Vat ve do now?"

We were half way down the long, wide sweep of the Mall and dusk was falling. I stopped and waited. William and Elizabeth joined us.

"Well," I asked. "Did you see her?"

"Ahh," breathed Karl, brightening at the prospect of more excitement. "Did you see her?" He asked, facing the wrong way and speaking to thin air.

Elizabeth gave him a despairing look and me one of exasperation.

"Well, did you?" I snapped. She was unmoved and annoyingly enigmatic. "After all I went through to get you into that place," I pointed back up the Mall to illustrate my point, "the very least you can do is to tell me whether you saw her."

"Yess!" agreed Karl vehemently. Elizabeth remained stony-faced. She never reacted well to direct questions. Or any other sort of questions come to think of it. William touched her arm lightly and gave her a pleading look.

"Psha!" she spat. "I did all that I needed to do. Ask me no more!"

"After all I went through, that is all you are going to tell me," I sputtered. The tension of the last few hours was beginning to weigh on me and I felt my reason beginning to fray into strands of hysteria. "Did you speak with her? Did she hear you? Did she see you?"

"Patience, wench!" she spat. "My service will make a good account to Almighty God and leave some comfort to our posterity on earth. This I have learned and it is enough. Question not princes, we answer only to God."

"Well, I'm so glad you got something out of this afternoon's work," I stormed, sarcastically, "because all I got was an hour of sheer terror followed by post-traumatic stress."

"Still you do not see what is before you," she glowered, impatiently.

William hastily interposed himself between us.

"Light seeking light doth light of light beguile," he uttered earnestly in impenetrable explanation. I don't know if Elizabeth understood what he was on about but I sure as hell didn't.

"What?" I snapped, irritably.

"I mean only that in seeking for the truth thou art blinded by it."

I groaned in exasperation. "I have no idea what you are talking about. I just wanted to know if Her Majesty over there," I indicated Elizabeth, "saw Her Majesty in there."

Once more I indicated the Palace behind us.

"My friend," William said patiently, "believe that all is as it should be and that thou hast advanced from this day's work, though thou seest not the gain."

"No, I do not see the gain," I moaned. "All I see is…Oh, hell, hell and crap!"

The security badge that I had purloined earlier had worked its way out of my cleavage so that the bright red lanyard lay accusingly across my chest. I pulled it around and looked into eyes that stared back accusingly. The name under the photo was Mrs. Helen Benson.

"And what am I going to do about this?" I was close to tears yet again but, before you become impatient with my weakness, remember that I had been through a great deal that day and it was beginning to look to me like the nightmare would never end. "We can't let it fall into the wrong hands. We'll have to take it back but there will be all sorts of trouble when they realise I took it."

I had even taken a couple of guilty steps back towards the palace with the honest intention of returning the badge and confessing all if necessary, but our two media friends, having witnessed our movements from behind a distant tree, were once more intrigued by the tired-looking woman who, having been ejected from a royal palace by armed guard, was now having an animated conversation with thin air. The camera was pointing in our direction yet again and Blondie was steaming up the Mall as fast as her five-inch heels would carry her.

"Lady, lady," she purred breathlessly, reaching out to me with a huge furry microphone. "I am sure you have a story to tell. Was there anything sexual going on?"

"Er, no," I stuttered, hiding the security pass behind my back and looking guilty as sin, although for a different reason than the one she hoped for.

"If you expose any…er… thing going on inside the palace it will be in the public interest…"

My red face had piqued her interest even more and now she was convinced that I had a lurid story to tell. She moved even closer and tried a friendly smile but Karl, never at a loss, easily gained her attention by adopting a serious pose, staring at her hair and tutting with deep concern.

"Is something wrong?" she asked, looking away from me and fearfully patting her hair.

"But yes!" cried Karl, reaching to feel a blonde curl and then dropping it in disgust. "You commit crime, yes! This is peroxide. In two years you will be smooth, you understand. Smooth, no not smooth, bold. Yes, bold!"

Erich meanwhile had grasped my arm, pulled the offending security badge from my hand and transferred it slickly into Blondie's coat pocket. She didn't notice a thing. In the same movement, he turned me away from the woman's grasping red fingernails and propelled me several feet away. It was impressive and I had no time to consider the moral implications of Erich's actions.

Blondie, however, would not have been shallow enough to allow either Erich's manoeuvrings or Karl's dire predictions to deter her from a good story except that at that moment an expensive black car whispered up The Mall and drew into the kerb.

A manly hand beckoned. Blondie recalculated; pursue this strange red-faced woman who didn't want to talk and who may very well not have anything interesting to say anyway, or find out who and what this new angle to the story was. Not wanting to burn either of her bridges, she gestured for us to wait (which we didn't) and hurried over to speak to whoever was inside the sleek car. She wavered for a moment and then, with one last suspicious glance at my rapidly receding back, obediently got in and the car drove off. The camera man was abandoned on the side of the road. Perplexed, he looked after her for a moment or two, then inquiringly after us and then pointed his camera at a pair of squirrels and went off to indulge in a bit of wildlife photography. I suspected, from the much happier expression on his face, that he was a country boy at heart.

Karl, Erich and I looked at each other. There could have been any number of reasons for the little rescue scene that had been played out but I suspected that the Palace Public Relations officers were working overtime to downplay suggestions of Royal vulnerability after my little escapade and that the more voracious of the reporters would be tempted away from publishing half-stories by promises of certain exclusivity in the future.

That is, of course, pure conjecture on my part.

Whether she was caught with the security pass, or what she did with it if not, I never discovered.

A year or so later, I saw a news report, in which she appeared prominently, having been accused of electronically bugging a politician and a film star in search of scandal. It was unclear if she found any, scandal that is, but I suspect the odds were quite high. Anyway, I took a malicious, if unworthy, delight in watching her being chased up the street and in and out of court buildings by her erstwhile colleagues. I was probably not the only one.

As the car continued its stately way up the Mall, we all looked around guiltily, but no one else appeared to be watching us. Erich said one word directed at Karl which was probably along the lines of "pillock" and then we turned, as if of one mind, and walked across Green Park as fast as we could.

CHAPTER TWENTY-TWO

When you do dance, I wish you
A wave o' th' sea, that you might ever do
Nothing but that.
The Winter's Tale, Act IV Sc iv

Dusk was falling from a rosy sky as we hit the concrete streets once more. So many people. It was gone five o'clock and businessmen and women and shop workers were spilling onto the streets in search of time that belonged to them alone. Buses, trains and taxis, were operating at maximum capacity and the restaurants were filling up exponentially as the shops and offices emptied.

"Come, ve go to Covent Garden," said Karl ebulliently.

So we did.

The old fruit and flower market, transformed now for many years into a Mecca for tourists, filthy lucre, and white-faced loonies, was, of course, a seething mass of shifting humanity. Expectant theatre goers rubbed shoulders with students, buskers, and trendy Londoners drinking Pimms next to the leaping lights of burners set out by the cafes to take the chill off the early evening air.

A musician with a battered guitar, amplifier and microphone took the soul of a song and, with nothing more than raw talent and heart, breathed life into the very air. Karl and I, with one accord, pushed to the front of the desultory crowd who listened, clapping half-heartedly to the pounding beat.

One lone woman had the courage to shed her inhibitions and to dance as her soul urged her to. She was elderly and awkward and, luckily, lost in her own world. I say luckily because in this world she was subjected to pitying glances and sniggers from those who imagined themselves superior because they did not dance. I wasn't one of them. I gave my bag to Erich and stepped right out. And then there were two of us, two happy women, moving to the rhythm, free from care and of concern, free from all those phrases that start with should or shouldn't and not touched by opinion, fear or embarrassment. Elizabeth and William were there in a trice of course and Karl joined us, and then another and another. The singer played on and the number of dancers grew and were added to and expanded once more as wives pulled in husbands, young people danced to their own beat, children to yet another and the old people danced to their memories. At one point I looked up and people were dancing as far as the music reached on the night air and beyond. Those that weren't dancing were smiling. In the cafes and the restaurants, they raised their arms and moved them in time to the music, and waiters and cooks came up from the kitchens to view the anomaly and to snap pictures and video on mobile phones. Watchful policemen were pulled in and good humour prevailed. It was joyous. That is the word. Joyous. The young man played on until he couldn't in all conscience continue and, when he stopped, the crowd stamped and cried for more. Bemused he played again and again. When we left he was still playing and people were still dancing.

Erich handed me my bag and gave me an approving smile. He led us to a café and we sat outside in the chill evening air and drank steaming mugs of over-priced coffee whilst listening to a woman sing opera and a string quartet who danced whilst playing. William hung over the railings above us and stared in awe at the beautiful woman whose voice soared in golden triumph up and above us poor mortals who are eternally tethered to mediocrity.

I think I have the soul of an artiste.

Unfortunately, I am not blessed with the body, voice, brains or talent of one. It must be wonderful to create something, even just one moment of something, that is eternal. William, was a showman, an actor, writer and creator and when the lovely singer bowed out and the comic string quartet took her place he was at first interested, then mystified and then entranced all over again by their astonishing antics. I could almost see the wheels of genius working as he laughed at this, filed that for reference later and decided that he would use that in his next production. It's well known that he wasn't averse to a little plagiarism. Eventually, the acts all went off to their evening engagements (surely none could be anything less than fully employed?) and there was an appearance of a lull as the theatres around us filled up. My stomach rumbled. I glanced at the prices on the chalkboard by the door of the little restaurant and stood up.

Karl stood up too. Erich likewise.

"Ach, ve go now. Ve be late."

"Well, it was very nice of you to look after me," I said politely. "It was fun...really."

"Come, come..." Karl looked surprised as I held my hand out to him. "Vere you go? You come with us, no?"

"Oh, no, I really must go..." I floundered. "I have to..."

I really didn't have anything to do or anywhere to go of course, and I was a lousy liar, so suffice it to say that, after a little more protest, and after being persuaded that, for some unfathomable reason they really did want me, I went with them.

Karl hailed a taxi, gave the driver a crumpled leaflet and we all climbed in. Karl laughed like a drain when I told him he was sitting on William. He was lucky it wasn't Elizabeth or he might not have found it so amusing. We tumbled out of the taxi in front of a slightly dilapidated theatre.

"Ziz is the place."

"Where are we? What are we here for?" I asked. Despite their kindness, I was getting a little weary of being directionless and not knowing what was going to happen next.

"It iss the Cockeney Club," Karl said triumphantly pointing to the dog-eared leaflet. "It is the real London music hall. Look they haff here the faggots and the Queens."

"Ah," I said, somewhat alarmed.

I caught Erich's eye. He just smiled. We all trooped in. I thrust a twenty-pound note at Erich as he bought tickets but I found it back in my pocket not ten minutes later. He was very good at that. I began to speculate about his previous career.

We were admitted into the packed stalls of a small Victorian galleried theatre and seated not in rows but at large sturdy wooden tables. Karl, Erich and I were shoehorned onto the end of a row. The rest of the table was made up of middle-aged Americans, who were good-humoured, welcoming and much, much louder than middle-aged English people would have been. Karl was quite right. Faggots (with peas) were on the menu and there were Pearly Queens aplenty, most of them rather elderly, but in good voice. They called us all ducky, or luv or darlin'. Good hearty English food, steak and kidney pudding, fish and chips or faggots, was served up haphazardly, and somewhat messily, by singing serving-wenches whose skills in performance were better developed than their skills in waitressing. It was tourist London at its best. Or worst, depending on how you prefer London to be represented. The whole place was stuffed to the rafters with raucous good-humour and our middle-aged Americans were up for everything. Audience participation was meat and drink to them, which was just as well because you should have heard what they said about the food.

William and Elizabeth drifted through the throng, William as fascinated as ever, but Elizabeth was somehow distant. She had always been aloof of course, but this was different. She had been scathing and irritable but always sharp. Now she viewed the unconscious melee as if we were not the real entities but rather faded figures in a gentle dream. I wouldn't go so far as to say that she regarded us all, the Pearly Kings and Queens, the raucous waiters and the rowdy Americans, fondly, but she did appear to be more likely to forgive us our vulgarity. She didn't even join in with the inevitable knees up but stood smiling graciously and beating time on William's head.

I think Karl was disappointed that the show wasn't a little more extreme. All the same, he joined in and sang very loudly when we were exhorted to greater effort by the performers who pointed out the words displayed on a screen and who would brook no excuse for non-participation. He also sang very loudly when we weren't supposed to, making up the words and I suspect a whole new language when he didn't know them - which was all the time of course. We were not the most popular people in the room but Karl was irrepressible. Erich just watched indulgently. He only intervened when life or limb was in danger, or, because he was a kind man, when he saw that Karl's exuberance was causing distress to others. Suffering from Karl's appalling singing did not fall into either of those categories apparently.

He did move uneasily in his seat when Karl volunteered me to go on stage as the magician's assistant, but it was a done deal before I knew what was happening, and Karl, in gales of laughter, was pulling and pushing me up the steps and onto the stage, which had seemed small and insignificant before, but was now revealed to be vast and exposed. The audience, when I reluctantly turned to face them, numbered in their thousands, or so it seemed and were packed in like grinning sardines.

I have no idea what trick the magician performed on me. It involved wearing a ridiculous hat and pigeons being magically produced out of my armpits and various other orifices. It was hilarious, judging from the audience reaction. Even Erich was chuckling heartily. Karl was rolling on the floor. Literally, of course.

In one of my few pigeon-free moments, I glimpsed Elizabeth at the back of the auditorium.

She was leaving.

William, with an appealing look back at me over the heads of the multitude, was leaving with her. They had done this before of course, but something in that backward look from William told me that this was different. I thrust a brown pigeon back at the magician, managed to extricate another that was squawking in the nether regions of my cardigan, and muttering 'sorry', made a dash for the steps down from the stage. The magician recovered from his surprise at being deserted before the climax of his act and said something very amusing as I made my dash, causing the audience to erupt once more into laughter.

I fought my way through, climbing over legs and bags, pushing past people and tables, shoving disgruntled waiters out of my path, and even avoiding a couple of kind-faced women who were concerned my mad dash indicated that I had been upset by the rough and tumble of show business. Panic was certainly taking hold of me and when I, at last, stumbled out onto the cold streets to find no sign of William or Elizabeth, I was stunned by the sudden sense of loss that overwhelmed me.

I ran one way and then the other, straining to see over and around the people, the cars, the objects, but they were not to be found. They had vanished. I grasped the cold railings at the edge of the road and felt the tears slip down my face. Surely they could not be gone. Not without a goodbye? Not without some sort of warning, some sort of sign. But then, they had arrived without fanfare so it was fair to assume that they might leave the same way. The fuzzy feeling was back in my head, competing with my grief. I held on to the cold railings and fought to stay standing. Soft arms crept around my waist and gripped and two bodies were there supporting me. Karl and Erich of course.

Perhaps I have not given Karl his due up until now. I have painted him as self-absorbed, self-centred, shallow and even a little vacuous. He was all of these things of course, but he was not without empathy. He had connected with something in me and although our relationship, if it were to continue in any form, would be volatile and centred almost entirely on his needs, he would not willingly see me unhappy without trying to alleviate it.

They both spoke soothingly and called a taxi and, although I knew I should protest, I obeyed them meekly, as I was whisked through the London streets and into a vast, marbled, golden palace on the edge of the river.

The fuzziness only subsided completely when I found myself seated on a leather easy chair, in front of an expanse of glass that presented to me the glittering panorama of London overlooking the Thames. A cup of coffee was placed in my hand and Karl squatted on a matching leather footstool and looked at me quizzically.

"This is nice," I said inadequately. "Where are we?"

"Iss our suite in hotel," he shrugged dismissively.

"It must cost a fortune to stay here!" I exclaimed, suddenly feeling awkward in my cheap scuffed shoes and stretched cardigan. My bag, which they must have rescued from the Music Hall, looked very woeful against a striped rug that appeared to be made of tiger-skin. I sincerely hope it was fake but given the decadence of the place I would not be too sure. I looked around anxiously. Erich was seated at a vast glass table on which was a laptop. He nodded encouragingly at me.

"Erich is very rich," Karl whispered. "He is businessman."

"I thought he was a hairdresser like you?"

"Yess, of course. He has many, many salons."

"Oh," I said inadequately. It looked like I had fallen in with very rich hairdressers, a species I had not come across before. That came as a surprise. "Well, I feel better now. I ought to be going. Thank you for looking after me. I really appreciate it."

I stood up without wobbling, which surprised me again, and determined to leave. However, I hadn't taken much notice of my surroundings when we had come in and, now that I looked around me, I couldn't see anything that looked like a door. It was very much as if we were entombed in marble and mirrored panels accented with zebra and ocelot.

"No, no, no," wailed Karl.

Erich said something quietly without taking his eyes from the screen of the laptop, and I took that to mean that he also felt that it was time that I leave. I shouldered my bag and looked again for a door. Any door.

"No, no, no, you stay. Look, William and Elisabeth, they want you to stay also. See!"

I looked around sharply but they were not there. I shook my head sadly and Karl bit his pink lips and, for a split second, looked shamefaced.

"Thank you again." I went over to Erich. "You have been very kind and I really want to pay for the meal…at the Music Hall."

I laid the dog-eared twenty-pound note on the shining glass of the table and smiled down at him. He smiled back and shook his head.

"I must go now."

"But where?" wailed Karl. "It is too late. You stay here, look you can sleep on …. zer couch." He pronounced it 'cooch'. "And tomorrow we take you home, yes?"

There it was. Bless them.

I shook my head, said "thank you, goodbye" and, taking a flyer at something that looked like it might open if pushed, walked determinedly into the most stunning bathroom I had ever seen.

"Blimey!" I exclaimed. It was black and silver and smelt of jasmine and luxury. It didn't seem to have anything at all to do with the usual functions and requirements of a bathroom. Taking a pee or anything else so base in there was unimaginable. Still, when I looked at the deep black bath and imagined it full of hot fragranced water, I was fairly sure I would be able to overcome my scruples.

"You want to use bathroom?" Karl was at the door looking at me quizzically. Erich was behind him.

"You will stay." Erich only ever said those three words directly to me and there was never any question that I would obey them. It was immediately clear how he had made his millions. It would take an exceptional person to withstand the force of his will, and I was not exceptional. Karl clapped his hands joyfully, pulled a fluffy bathrobe from the door and threw it at me.

"Have nice bath," he ordered and shut the door.

I spent a deep and dreamless night on the sofa, wrapped in the fluffy bathrobe with the darkly glittering panorama of London spread before me.

CHAPTER TWENTY-THREE

O Death, made proud with pure and princely beauty!
King John, Act IV Sc iii

I opened my eyes in the very early morning, whilst the sky still clung to a darkness pierced by a myriad of man-made lights. The city was moving inexorably towards the bustle of morning and, as I watched, a dull grey began to stain the sky and the glint of yellowing lights faded into the whiteness of day.

I stretched into emptiness and thought. It must be time to go home. What I was going to say when I got there was the big problem. No doubt I would think of something. It didn't matter much anyway.

Nothing really mattered.

I dressed back into my clothes, visited the bathroom to scrub my teeth and then looked around doubtfully. There was no sign from the bedroom of Erich and Karl so I sat down to wait politely until I could thank them in person and say goodbye.

"Come, good friend."

It was William of course. I squealed with delight and hugged him. He looked pleased and patted my hand but there was a sense of urgency about him as he pulled me to my feet. "Come, we must attend our queen. She desires thy presence, for the..."

"For the last time." I finished for him.

"Aye."

I smiled sadly.

"Ok, but I will just scribble a note for Karl and Erich. They were so kind."

"It is good, I think, that people can be what they are in this world."

"There are some who would argue that point, even in this world," I said. "But Karl certainly brightens up a room."

"He is joyful."

I sighed remembering a few moments at the glass table that had taken place the previous night, and the white powder and the knowledge that Karl and Erich, rich and careless as they were, had their own demons that would, like as not, sooner or later, darken even the brightness of their world.

'Dear Karl, Dear Erich,' I wrote. 'I have to go now but I want to thank you so much for your kindness to me. I hope that we will meet again.'

That didn't seem to say it all but William was anxious to go so I signed, 'Love, Juliette.' Then I crossed the lie out and wrote instead 'lots of love, Ally'. I put the pen down, picked up my bag and left the room quietly.

The corridors were silent and the lift empty. The atrium was virtually deserted and looked more like an art gallery specialising in works of the inscrutable variety. They were very ugly. The lone desk clerk glanced suspiciously at me. I think it crossed his mind that I might be a lady of ill repute, but I don't think that idea stayed with him long. Anyway, he suffered me to walk the length of the echoing lobby and exit the vast glass doors unchallenged.

Once in the chill morning air, William took my hand, said "Hie, gentle lady, hie!" and we ran together.

A low mist rolled across the river and the sky was tinged with shades of apricot and gold. Breathless and tingling from the bright, damp chill we reached the road that led across the river and I saw her ahead of us. She was on the bridge, about half way along, and looked entirely as if she belonged there.

Tower Bridge is a Victorian construction of course, but it has the quality of historical oddity, much like Elizabeth herself. A jewelled hand rested on a railing and she was looking back towards the Tower. William and I hurried to her. My grief of losing them last night had been softened by my joy of Williams' return this morning and now, as I looked at Elizabeth, magnificent under the rising March sun, I realised that there should be no sadness in this last goodbye. Her features were ravaged, as they always had been in our brief acquaintance, and they were set in her usual expression of severity, but still there was something beautiful about her. I smiled as we drew near. She didn't smile back of course, but there was a softness in her eyes that told me she was quite pleased that I was there.

"The wheel hath turned full circle and I am here. The time has come, child."

"I know," I said. "I will miss you."

"Hrrumph," she dismissed my affection with a wave of her jewelled hand. "Thou wilt have William with thee for a while longer yet, I think."

I was inordinately pleased about that but, knowing her as I did, I felt it judicious not to be too effusive, so I just bowed my head and squeezed William's hand. It came as something of a shock then to suddenly feel the dry, withered hand of a Queen laid gently on my cheek.

She ran her fingers gently down to my chin and raised my face to look into hers.

"My child, thou hast suffered much," she said simply, honestly. "The time is near when thee must suffer again. You will find the strength."

I pulled away from her angrily. She had no right. I turned my back on her and grasped the railing.

"I wish you well my child, for all time." She did wish me well.

I knew that of course and so I turned back to say my goodbye... but too late. She was there for a brief moment but only as a whisper, a transient wraith, like a breath of mist dispersed by a breeze. And then nothing.

I cried of course. I'm just that sort of person. I turned to look out across the river and sobbed a few gut-wrenching sobs. William patted my shoulder. He must have felt it too of course. He'd known her a lot longer than I had after all.

The police car skidded to a halt behind us and a very big policeman got out gingerly and edged towards us.

"You all right love?"

"Yes." I said gulping sobs and backing away, closer to the railings which was exactly the wrong thing to do.

"You don't want to do that, love," he said. "Come away from the edge and, whatever it is, I am sure we can sort it all out. It's never as bad as it can't be made better, as my old mum used to say."

"Oh," I said glancing down to the brown murky waters of the Thames. You would have to be very far gone to find the thought of plunging into them inviting. "No, I'm not going to jump. Honest."

"Good, good, glad to hear it." He didn't believe me but it wasn't the response he expected either and now he was at a bit of a loss. "Well, that's all right then."

"Yes," I said, then, "thank you," for no apparent reason. "Well, goodbye then."

I wiped my face with my hand, pulled my misshapen coat around me and walked purposefully away, back the way I had come. He stood for a moment or two, deflated by our odd little encounter, then rolled his eyes and climbed back into his car. He kept an eye on us, well me, until I was off the bridge and then presumably found some other public service to perform.

CHAPTER TWENTY-FOUR

*Why, but there's many a man
hath more hair than wit.
The Comedy of Errors, Act II Sc ii*

There was a little café on the corner at the end of the bridge with metal tables and chairs outside. It was closed and managed to look both sad and inviting. I sat down wearily and William sat next to me. We gazed out at the wakening city and the slow river.

"Should I go home now?" I asked. There was no answer forthcoming but I didn't expect one. Elizabeth would have told me what to do but William wasn't like that. Actually, Elizabeth would just have told me what she wanted me to do and I would have felt obliged to do it.

"I wish I knew what this was all about. Why me? And why you? And why Elizabeth? And why not anyone else – except Nell. I refuse to believe that you are not real. You are real. You have to be real."

"If I am not real..." said William kindly, "then what?"

"You are," I cut in. "And I don't think I am ready to go home yet."

"Mayhap, I am." I looked at him in surprise. He met my eyes with a gentle smile.

"You can't leave me. Don't leave me."

"We cannot read the book of fate, but methinks the time is near when thou will choose to leave me."

"I don't think so," I scoffed, to hide the fear that had grasped my throat.

"Sorrow not for me. We must take the current when it serves."

"Hello," said a bright girl, who had somehow materialised just behind William. "Who are you talking to?"

"Oh no one in particular," I lied.

"Don't be embarrassed, I talk to myself all the time. I'm Marley."

Marley smiled through moist scarlet lips and her nose stud glinted in the morning sun. She had long black hair streaked with electric blue dye and wore Doc Martin style boots and a black skeleton T-shirt over a loose pink skirt. The whole was covered by a voluminous black coat. This interesting apparition held out a tattooed hand with shiny black nails and I had no hesitation in offering my own less interesting hand. It was grasped firmly.

"Are you here for the march?"

"Oh no," I replied. "What march?"

She perched herself on the metal table in front of me and offered me a cigarette. When I shook my head, somewhat surprised I have to say, I mean, it has been years since anyone thought that there was the remotest possibility that I was a smoker, she placed one between her red lips and lit it with a sophisticated flourish. I liked her for her lack of assumption.

"We're marching on poverty," she said with a careless air, pulling in the smoke and exhaling it upwards in an acrid cloud that dispersed slowly into the cold air. "We're protesting against the immoral and indefensible misuse of public money. Against globalisation and... all that sort of thing. We are for the people. We are for action. You should join us."

"Should I?" I didn't want to, but I knew I would. It was inevitable.

"Yes, you should." It was decided. I was now a protester. I

felt the faint stirrings of rebellion within me. "You're one of the oppressed, aren't you?"

"Am I?"

"We all are. Crushed by big business, robbed of our individuality by the unelected men in suits who exploit the world's poor. Did you know that globally speaking, the richest ten percent control more than half of the total wealth? That just isn't right, is it? Wealth is power and the power is in the wrong hands. We are for redistributing the wealth of the world more equally."

"Isn't that communism?" I asked tentatively, with the confused idea that becoming a communist might be a step too far, even for me.

"I don't like labels," she replied. I considered pointing out that she had just labelled me as one of the downtrodden, but she was young, probably not more than eighteen, and her ideology was worthy, if a little confused. Anyway, she was sure of her ground and I wasn't at all sure of mine.

She drew another long breath of nicotine laden smoke and said dreamily, "We're taking action," whilst indicating the lonely road behind her as if it were packed with warring hoards.

William was looking at me with several questions in his eyes.

"It's democracy in action," I tried to explain, careless of Marley's reaction. "A protest against the things we disagree with. If a group of people feels that something is wrong, they band together and protest against it. It even works sometimes."

"What a precious comfort 'tis to have so many brothers commanding one another's fortunes." William smiled a melancholy smile. "But yet, 'tis not new-begot. A thousand and more apprentices of my time partook of general riot to force perforce the price of bread. 'Twas noble but aimed awry."

"I hardly dare ask what happened to them."

"The leaders among them were hanged, drawn and

quartered," was the predictable response. And then he added with much more emotion, "and the theatres were closed."

William, for all his understanding of humanity, had a disturbingly mercenary streak at times.

"Bummer," I muttered, unable to think of a more intelligent reaction.

"But the burning stick in her mouth?" William was regarding Marley's cigarette with curiosity.

"You can blame Elizabeth for that," I said. "Sir Walter Raleigh is responsible for killing millions by popularising tobacco. Although, you could argue that he fed millions with his potatoes. But there again you could counter that with the invention of chips that also kill millions so, either way, old Raleigh has killed more people than anyone else in the whole of history – ever."

William was horrified and, it must be said, that perhaps I was condemning this historical hero a little unfairly.

"Are you speaking to your angel?" Marley was watching me through narrowed eyes.

"William is not an angel. He just is."

"But you do have an angel. I see him, or it could be a her, there is no difference. There is an aura around you. It's a yellow glow mainly over your left shoulder. I have one too, can you see him?"

My new friend was a fascinating mix of the sublime and the earthy, but William wasn't anywhere near my left shoulder and all I could see behind Marley was one of those street cleaning cars working its way noisily through the gutters of London. It wasn't remotely celestial. I shook my head apologetically.

"Oh, well, it doesn't matter. Take it from me though that you do have a guardian angel that watches over you and protects you from danger."

"Could you ask him to be a bit more vigilant when it comes to avoiding humiliation too?"

That wasn't quite kind of me but Marley laughed, although I had a feeling that she was one of those happy people that rarely embarrass themselves, at least in their own eyes. I felt that I could ignore the elephant in the room (or lack of) no longer so I added casually, "Are you marching on your own?"

"Oh no, my phalanx will be along in a minute. They stopped at McDonald's to pick up breakfast. That'll upset the hard-liners of course, and not many of us do agree with that sort of global capitalism but there is nothing else open yet and an army has to eat."

"Fair enough," I concurred. "Are there many of you?"

"Millions. Worldwide, that is. It might even be billions but about thirty today for sure. Thirty-one if you join us."

"Thirty-one it is then."

"They'll all be along in a minute and there might be others joining us on the way."

I hoped so, I rather wanted to lose myself in the crowd. I'd never struck a revolutionary blow before and I was beginning to feel a bit nervous.

"What is your name by the way?"

"Joan," I replied, in hopes that the crusading saint would inspire me. She frowned with displeasure and I wondered how she could possibly take offence at a name, but then I realized that someone else had joined us.

"I'm completely friggin' knackered."

A diminutive man, who looked about sixteen but was probably older, stepped from behind my chair and collapsed into another.

"Why did we have to start so friggin' early? I didn't go to bed last night or I would never have friggin' made it." (He didn't say friggin' of course. You know what he said.)

Marley, after a single contemptuous glance, did not look at him. Her eyes were fixed on the corner, around which a motley group of young people was beginning to straggle.

"This is Joan. She is joining us. And you know why we have to start now, Henry. He's arriving early and we have to be there."

"Yeah, yeah. And don't friggin' call me Henry, Marlene." He drawled her name in a tone of pure spite. Marley threw him a look of wary hatred which he shrugged off before fixing his pale, blue eyes on me. "They call me Biker."

"They call you a lot of things but Biker isn't one of them," snapped Marley who had put all her charm aside to deal with this sullen young man. "You'd better not start anything today. We can't stop you coming with us but Guy and the others will have their eyes on you so control yourself or you will get more than you bargain for."

He leaned back in his chair and grinned a gap-toothed smile at me. "Can't 'elp it if I'm friggin' passionate to the friggin' cause," he drawled through a yawn.

For all his relaxed pose and assumed ennui he had the suppressed energy of a wound spring. His pale sparse hair stood in short spikes all over his head and his face was small-featured and would have been pretty except that it was pasty and pock-marked. He looked like he hadn't seen a decent meal or a toothbrush for some considerable time. He carried a leather bag slung over his stooped shoulders that looked suspiciously expensive against his worn jeans and grubby jacket. His watery, light blue eyes flickered over me more than once and I couldn't help thinking that, despite his apparent youth, he was dangerous. Which was, of course, exactly what he wanted me to think.

"Where do I know you from then?" He prodded my elbow and squinted at me.

"We've not met. I'd have remembered."

"Oh yeah, unforgettable me. 'Spose it's just 'cos you remind me of someone."

"Not a close family member, I hope," I replied, waspishly.

"Come on, Joan," Marley grasped my arm, hauled me

to my feet and chivvied me towards the crocodile of assorted youngsters stretched out along the pavement. "We'll join the others, but stay away from him, he's only along to cause trouble if he can."

"I don't want to get caught up in any trouble," I moaned, like the boring, unadventurous middle-aged woman that I was.

"You won't, just stick with me."

"Where are we going and what are we going to do?"

"We're heading to the Bank of England first. We have a tip off that someone we have an interest in is visiting. Small groups like us turn up whenever we can. We keep the pressure on that way and every now and again there is a really big rally. Don't worry Joan, we're for peaceful protest only."

Looking around, it did all seem quite innocuous. We were walking in ones, twos or threes either side of the pavement, crossing the roads courteously and there was not a placard in sight or a chant in earshot. Even Biker who had joined the rear guard gave no hint of the real purpose of this pleasant stroll through the London morning. William, trotting by my side, was beginning to look a little bored. We wandered along Lower Thames Street and up towards Pudding Lane where the Great Fire of London started. I pointed out the monument and gave William a potted version of the events that instigated it, but the most interesting fact I could remember was that Samuel Pepys buried his Parmesan cheese in his garden to protect it from the flames. I couldn't confirm if he ever retrieved it or in what condition. William was not impressed. There was then a very tedious trek up King William Street and it was only as we approached our destination that an air of suppressed excitement finally gripped the little group.

Marley had attached herself to a very tall, rotund young man with an enormous torso carried on surprisingly slender legs encased in the tightest jeans I had ever seen. On his feet, which might have been of a normal size and shape for all I could tell, were shiny, black, inordinately long winkle-picker shoes, that were not as stylish as presumably intended due to the gentleman being somewhat pigeon-toed. He was pleasant, though, with shaggy brown hair and a gentle manner. Four or five others had swelled the ranks during our trek and the tall young man moved between the small groups giving instruction like a battle commander. Marley and I (and William of course) found ourselves in a brigade that included three well-made and sensible looking young men and, eventually, after a brief altercation with his leader, Biker. He gave me a sly smile as he found himself so disposed of and I had the distinct feeling that the three young men of the group would have their work cut out to keep him in line.

The imposing many-colonnaded façade of the Old Lady of Threadneedle Street was before us. William cocked a critical eye.

"What palace is this?"

"It's more of a place of business. The Bank of England. And a fortress I suppose as it keeps the countries gold reserves."

"Where are the guards?" he asked in surprise.

I considered.

"I'd rather not find out. I'm beginning to think this was a bad idea, perhaps we should go."

"Nay, nay, stay a little. I wish t'observe this strange event when commoners lay siege to the Queen's gold." I should have known that the mention of unimaginable wealth within spitting distance would have intrigued him.

"Oh, please stay," interposed Marley. "Having you is…well, it, sort of, helps."

I must have looked as bewildered as I felt for Biker laughed and threw an arm over my shoulder to give me a very unpleasant hug.

"It's 'cos you're old love. You give us a bit of credibility, you know, like representing the old fogies of the world."

I pulled away and looked resentfully at them all. They were all young. I could give twenty years to the oldest, but even so, I was outraged at being described as an old fogie. I should have walked away then but, as usual, I did the opposite to what I should have done and decided to be the best damn revolutionary that my aching feet and middle-class principles would allow me to be.

At that point the large pigeon-toed man joined us and the plan of action was explained. He instructed us to fragment into much smaller groups around the building and to be as inconspicuous as possible. Good luck with that I thought. He really did stand out in a crowd. We were to watch for the arrival of the filthy capitalist (not their words exactly) and to signal at which entrance he was to alight. Then we were all to hare like mad things to the common point and chant "No to Globalisation! Human Need, Not Capitalist Greed!" Once I'd got my tongue around that I was stationed about halfway down Lothbury Street next to a forbidding metal door that looked like it hadn't opened to welcome any visitors, important or otherwise, in either of the last two centuries.

About one hundred yards to my right Marley guarded a much more ornate (and therefore more likely I would have thought) entrance, and to my left, two of the young men of our group stood watch over another door - and the unsavoury Biker. Other revolutionaries were stationed on the corners with a view of others who, armed with walkie-talkies, had been deployed in Bartholomew Lane, Princes Street and at the main entrance in Threadneedle Street.

As instructed I stayed at my lonely post and attempted to look inconspicuous. My plain, boring door was so unlikely to be the entrance chosen for the great one, whoever he was, that I felt quite secure and, my revolutionary spirit having dissipated by this time, I planned, once the signal was given, to wander around and watch the shenanigans from a comfortable distance. I was, however, uncomfortably aware that there were certainly security cameras covering the whole area so I pulled that wretched hat over my eyes, clamped my useless mobile phone to my ear and held a conversation with William.

I don't know why I hadn't thought of that before! A few purposeful people passed us by without a glance as I chatted happily with William, and I began to feel quite light-hearted. An affectionate young couple smiled at me as they passed into Tokenhouse Yard and, for the first time, no one glanced askance at the sad woman talking animatedly to herself.

"Wilt thou be stock-punished," William asked, with a touch of honest concern. "Or whipped shouldst thou be apprehended?"

I gave him a brief run-down of the British justice system. It was necessarily brief as my only experience of the law in action had been going with my dad to bail out my sister when she was going through her graffiti phase.

She would be so proud if she could see me now, I thought fleetingly.

I was brought abruptly back to immediacy by the realization that a gleaming limousine had whispered towards me and that the previously impregnable door close on my right was now standing wide open. Four smartly dressed men and one woman issued from the building as the car drew to a supercilious halt.

From that point, everything happened so fast and so much of it simultaneously that it is very difficult to explain exactly how the egg got into my hand and then into the American's famous comb-over.

I remember seeing Marley in the distance steaming towards me, white-faced and red-lipped, with the large young man behind her running as fast as his tight jeans and directionally-challenged feet would allow. Others with placards followed but, more alarmingly, the affectionate couple who had passed by so innocuously earlier, now swept towards me absolutely bristling with cameras, microphones, and journalistic determination.

I stepped smartly to one side so that they could achieve their objective of thrusting a microphone into the ochre-hued face that was emerging from the limo, only to be shoved violently and very nearly knocked off my feet by Biker who had misjudged the velocity of his arrival. I steadied myself against the concrete wall whilst he slid the leather bag from his shoulder onto the floor and reached into it.

"'Old this a moment," he muttered, handing me an egg and descending back into the bag for who knew what.

I stood for a long moment, holding the egg before me and gazing at it in disbelief whilst Biker rummaged at my feet. Marley and several of the others had reached the little group from their side and were, a little out of breath, chanting and waving magically produced placards with gusto.

Just as I raised my eyes to a wide-eyed William for some sort of inspiration to extricate myself from this predicament, Biker's minders bundled in with the clear aim of preventing the loose cannon from going off. One bent over to wrest the bag from him and the other two threw their arms around him and held him down by my feet. William, for some reason best known to himself, leapt in with gusto and began ineffectually pounding any body part that was immediately accessible.

The sudden short, deafening scream of a siren announced that the police were now also on the scene and all three, plus Biker, lurched upwards.

Biker's head hit the back of my hand with some force and the egg curved upwards in a long beautiful arc.

Up, up, up. I watched it, mesmerized, as it took graceful flight.

Around me, all was chaos as Biker and the young men tussled, while Marley and her cohorts chanted and jostled and whilst the smartly suited people both welcomed and protected their distinguished visitor from potential unpleasantness. All were unconscious of the egg arcing high over their heads towards them. It reached the apex of its climb and started on the downward trajectory and I prayed that it would fall harmlessly somewhere, unnoticed. But, of course, it was one of those accidental things that are perfect in every way and that you could not achieve in a month of Sundays if you had any intention of the sort.

It landed, an impeccable golden yellow bullseye, on the crown of the head of the American and shattered, as eggs do, in the straw-coloured thatch of what some maintain to be a very badly conceived transplant. Inevitably it drew all eyes and an eerie silence descended onto Threadneedle Street.

"Ohhh shit," I said very, very quietly and then, as two policemen grasped Biker's minders by the shoulder and pulled them away, as the blood of fury and assaulted dignity rose to the face of the outraged visitor, as a half-suppressed cheer broke from the peaceful demonstrators and as confusion, anger or horror took hold of all those present, I found myself ejected from the melee and pushed firmly away. I hesitated, just for a moment, before I casually crossed the road and strolled into Tokenhouse Yard.

So ended my only participation in direct action. Unintentional admittedly but quite startlingly effective none the less. I didn't suffer too many pangs of guilt with regard to the recipient of the egg wash. The arrogant so-and-so was not a person I had any time for, but, given the choice, I would have wished to make my point by more intelligent means.

CHAPTER TWENTY-FIVE

Art thou base, common, and popular?
Henry V, Act IV Sc i

Biker caught up with me just as I was debating whether it would be right to descend into Moorgate Station, make my getaway and leave the whole sorry mess behind.

"Friggin' brilliant!" he chortled, as he threw an arm around my neck. "Freakin' marvellous! Couldn't 'ave done it better myself."

"It was an accident," I protested. "It was your fault."

"Don't matter oo it was, we got the job done. It'll be 'eadline news!"

"That's all I need. Will Marley and her friends get into trouble?" I didn't bother to ask how he had managed to evade capture. He was the sort that usually would.

"Nah, nothing serious and anyway they couldn't friggin' work out where the friggin' egg came from. It came straight down. What a friggin' shot!"

"Accident!" I hissed at him. "Well, if you are sure no one else is going to get into trouble, I need to get going. I've had quite enough excitement for one morning, thank you."

With that, I spun smartly around intending to walk away with dignity from this unpleasant little man but found myself instead with my face buried in a patrolling police officer's stab vest.

"Oh," I said, inadequately.

"Take it easy, Mummy," Biker grasped my arm and revealed his un-brushed teeth to the tall policeman. "We'll get a taxi over 'ere. Sorry about that officer. Touch of the Alzheimer's, you know. This way, Mummy. I'll 'ail a cab."

The policeman and his partner were watching us with expressions that gave nothing away.

"'Op in mummy. Mind the step. Comfy?"

I was efficiently deposited on the slippery seat of a London cab and Biker climbed in beside me. The policeman said something amusing to his companion and they turned away as the cab lurched with supreme confidence into the city traffic.

I turned on Biker. "Mummy? Seriously?"

"Yeah, well, anyone 'oo calls 'is old woman Mummy ain't goin' to be arrested is 'e? Where we 'eading anyway? You're paying so the choice is yours."

"Oxford Street," I said randomly. "I want to…shop."

What I actually wanted was to rid myself of the horrid little man as soon as I could, which probably wasn't very fair of me but the truth was that William had disappeared just after the egg incident and I was terrified that he wasn't going to come back. I needn't have worried because he was on the roof of the cab. I glimpsed his reflection in the shiny metallic windows of an office block. He seemed quite happy and secure, sitting cross-legged and looking around him with interest. I relaxed back in my seat and viewed my other companion with distrust.

"You don't like me, do you?" he said, stating the obvious.

As with most people who are unexpectedly challenged with a similar statement, I was taken aback and my first instinct was to vigorously deny it, either from ingrained politeness or a reluctance to hurt his feelings, which was ridiculous because it was clear that the same consideration would not be extended to me.

"I just think you are a bit… wild and…and untrustworthy. And I think you are one of those people who cause trouble."

Perhaps honesty was the best policy. In this instance, it might well have been for he roared with laughter.

"Ha, ha, you're a fine one to talk. That's freakin' 'ilarious, that is."

"I don't see why," I snapped, aware that, unnervingly, the cab driver had taken his eye off the moving traffic to check what was happening, and that William's face had appeared upside down in the window for the same purpose.

"I remembered where I'd seen you before. You're the woman what broke into Bucking'am Palace yesterday, weren't you?"

"No, I didn't…Break in I mean. That's not exactly what happened. It was sort of accidental… How did you know anyway?" I gasped, suspecting some nefarious otherworldly interference, but it wasn't that. It was all quite simple and I should have seen it coming.

"'Oo doesn't? You've gone viral and that's all before the egg incident 'its the fan, which it will be doing any time now. You're an online celebrity!"

It was inevitable. With the amount of mobile phone cameras around and the high-profile spectacle I had made of myself, it would have been a miracle if I hadn't shown up somewhere in the ether.

"Oh, crap."

I slumped back into the chair and William somehow transferred himself from the roof to the seat beside me.

"I am in so much trouble."

"Yeah, you are," Biker chortled. "But look on the bright side, we could make some real money out of this. 'Ere, mate." As this happy thought struck him Biker rattled on the window separating us from the long-suffering cab driver. "Change of plan, we're 'eading to Fleet Street." He turned back to me with enthusiasm in his eyes. "Take you into one of the tabloids and they'll pay a bundle for your story. Thousands, 'undreds of thousands maybe. Story like yours could be even more than I… than you imagine. We… you could be rollin' in it, love."

The cab driver hadn't heard the last lines but he met my eye with a silent question and I shook my head. From then on he kept his eye on me, didn't change his route and we were in silent collaboration.

"Don't call me love, and I'm not selling my story to some muck-raking rag."

"Suit yourself, we'll make it one of the others then. The poncy newspapers. Or a magazine. Some of them will pay a fair whack for a juicy story."

I had to get rid of him.

"All right then," I shrugged. "But I'm not going into any media offices without some make-up on. There's a Boots. I'll pop out and grab a lipstick, you wait in the cab."

He wasn't going to do that of course and, although I slipped out as quickly as I could, he was on my heels before I could shake him. I took a few steps towards the shop and then stopped.

"I'd better pay off the taxi as I am not sure how long we will be."

I went back, purse in hand, and, after a very brief word with the driver, wrenched open the door, threw myself in, slammed it behind me and fell to my knees as the driver put the pedal to the metal and we screamed out into a stream of moving traffic. Amidst the outraged blare of many horns, I pulled myself onto the seat just in time to glimpse an outraged Biker come into collision with a real biker as he dodged into traffic in vain pursuit. I don't think he was much hurt. The real biker that is. I was not above wishing Biker himself some painfully grazed knees and a mild concussion.

William was on the roof again for some reason and when I tried to express my gratitude to the kindly cabbie I was met with monosyllabic gruffness that either hid a self-effacing heart of gold or a "I have to do this all the time and I find the everyday depravity of the human soul annoying and ridiculous" sort of attitude. I can't help thinking that it was probably the latter.

Left to myself en route to Oxford Circus I reviewed what I had learnt from Biker. It wasn't much. I was apparently some sort of internet sensation. I had to see what I could find out. What were they saying about it all? Were Karl and Erich in custody, deported, worse? As we swung up and down increasingly busy side and back streets I chewed a fingernail and worried. I had to get access to the internet. Of course! A department store with an IT department. They usually had computers up and running. I had been dragged around countless electronic shops displaying their wares by Hubby who always hankered after the latest device even though we could not afford any of them. I felt a sudden pang at that thought. If Biker was correct in his estimation of my newsworthiness I had just turned my back on the means to return to my family as a Lady Bountiful, showering gifts and humiliation in equal measure. On balance, I thought I had made the right decision.

The taxi driver ignored me for the rest of the journey and, when we reached our busy destination, acknowledged payment and a generous tip with no more than a grunt. My hero then chuntered off down Oxford Street, as if the moments of conspiracy and excitement we had shared had never happened.

"Come on," I said to William. "You will never have seen a shop like this and I have to check something out before we do anything else."

We entered the department store and, having hurried, gasping for pure air, through the perfumed aisles, rode the escalators up and up, past the glittering floors laden with stuff and more stuff, to the highest floor where the electronic paraphernalia was displayed. We hurried past the washers, cookers, vacuums and microwaves and I, for once, ignored

William's pleas for enlightenment, heading instead for the laptops and televisions in the distance. Televisions are vast these days. In fact, I think they call them home cinemas and you can see why. Thin as a postage stamp and the size of a self-respecting wall some of them. William was immediately captivated of course and, forgetting the mysterious household implements, began studying the 3D gyrations of a rap star and his numerous scantily clad female companions. He had an innate rhythm as I think I have said before and his little hips, made emphatically bigger by his padded round hose, jiggled away enthusiastically to the pounding music. I would have watched him in amusement but I had more important things to do.

I began to browse nonchalantly. My clothes and hair were tidier since my sojourn with Karl and Erich but still a little ragged around the edges and I wanted to keep a low profile. I paused by a medium range laptop and considered, walked on a little looking at others and then drifted back. It all seemed connected and live. If only it wasn't in demonstration mode. It was of course. They all were. I was just swearing under my breath when William hurried over and started jiggling my arm. I glanced up but there wasn't anything to be concerned about that I could see. There were a very few people dotted about and a bit of a queue at the tills behind me, the televisions were still blaring their multi-coloured images and only a couple of kids, about five and eight years of age seemed to be paying me any attention at all. Even their attention was split between gazing open-mouthed at me (or maybe at William?) and at one of the most enormous screens in the room. But no security guards.

"Stupid, stupid, stupid," I muttered to myself. "I should have gone straight to an internet café. Oh, what is it?" I asked William irritably. The kids were still staring at me and one was giggling. I checked that my skirt wasn't caught in my knickers. William didn't answer. His eyes were rounded in astonishment and darting here there and everywhere.

I glanced around again. Nothing.

Well, nothing except an absolutely huge bloody digital image of my face plastered over every single bloody one of the massive screens in that cavernous bloody department.

You've probably had the experience of unexpectedly catching sight of yourself in a mirror or on a screen and wondering who that person, who looks vaguely familiar, is. Well, when the penny eventually dropped, I looked around me and let me tell you that you have never experienced total horror until without warning you have suddenly seen your own face repeated in cruel and minute detail ad infinitum on screen after screen after screen after screen. Small, large and ginormous there were moving duplicates of my face on almost every one. In my confusion, I looked around for the camera trained on me but the ticker tape at the bottom of the screens told the story and jolted me into a very surreal realisation of my predicament. It was the footage taken outside Buckingham Palace on the previous day and there was I, revealed to the world as the 'mystery intruder at the palace'.

I was not only an internet sensation; I was on the news channels.

I was the news.

I was petrified.

There I was in a bear hug with Karl being claimed as his long-lost birth mother, Juliette Minnelli, before the whole world.

And there was I again, being forcibly (well, politely would be more accurate but the T.V. coverage intimated otherwise), ejected from Buckingham Palace by six soldiers and a policeman.

'Terrorist or Royal Stalker?' the text screamed excitedly. 'Who is this mystery woman?'

The muck-raking blonde reporter was there excitedly gabbling as much as she knew of the incident and more that she wildly conjectured. She obviously viewed me as a career maker.

Jake appeared briefly, framed against the Globe, suave and good-looking and with so much natural stage presence that even the story he was telling about me paled into insignificance against his own fascinations. He wasn't above milking the incident to his own advantage either. Erich and Karl did not appear, at least not in the long frozen minutes that I stood in petrified dismay. That, I was convinced, was either down to the quiet diffidence of Erich who would have worked out some clever way to keep Karl under the radar or because they were being intensively interrogated by MI5.

But the horror did not end there. Viewers having seen this footage had sent in more candid shots of me; exuberantly leading the dancers at Covent Garden; leaning over the back of the tour bus and yelling at invisible people; having pigeons pulled out of my cardigan on the stage at the cabaret club. Even the pub and the shelter for the homeless featured briefly and some enterprising journalist, who should have had better things to do, had been assigned to trace my route and create an unnecessarily magnificent 3D map of my wanderings…

Good god, they had turned me into a city-wide game of Where's Wally!

"BREAKING NEWS!" screamed the ticker tape.

The impeccably groomed female newsreader leant forward over her shiny desk, raised one thin eyebrow and crooned, "We are just receiving reports, and I must point out that these are unconfirmed at this point, that the mystery woman has been involved in a violent demonstration in which a visiting dignitary has been assaulted. Stay with us and we will bring you more details as they develop in this fast-moving story. Looks like you'll have to add another location to that wonderful map, Ken," she added brightly with a smirk and just the acceptable amount of superciliousness. Ken smiled weakly and looked as if he would much prefer to be under fire in a war zone.

The two children had run up one of the aisles and were

pulling at their father's sleeve. He, in deep conversation about an iPad, brushed them aside, but it was only a matter of time. The assistant with him, less invested in the iPad discussion, threw me a curious look before turning his eyes to one of the screens closest to him. An elderly couple of browsers further away had already made the connection and were presumably discussing whether to approach me out of curiosity or to exit the potential scene of explosion or gunfire as fast as their arthritic legs would carry them.

Only one thought came into my head – run! I grabbed the open-mouthed William and legged it out of the department.

Together we hurried down the endless escalators as inconspicuously as we could. Given her propensity for long escalator rides it was just as well Elizabeth wasn't still with us. We reached the ground floor and dodged busy customers through the islands of the handbag department, squeezed past elegant and not so elegant women at the scarf counter and took a deep breath before plunging into the perfumery. Someone yelled 'Inspirational Muse' at me but it sounded to my panicked ears like 'it's the mad woman from the news', which actually would have made a great deal more sense. As I stepped back in shock she squirted eau de cologne over me in an all-enveloping cloud and shoved a fragrant leaflet into my hand.

"Thank you, not now," I muttered as I saw recognition spark in her heavily made-up eyes.

Despite this, we gained the revolving doors without being accosted further. William, not understanding the concept, went around three times but even so we eventually managed to gain comparative obscurity in the crowded streets.

CHAPTER TWENTY-SIX

With mirth and laughter let old wrinkles come.
The Merchant of Venice, Act I Sc i

"Where to now?" I asked, at a complete loss. I pulled out the mobile phone and turned my face to the window displays. I felt like a fugitive, like an animal at bay.

"Home," said William. He probably meant my home. In fact, I know he did but I wilfully misunderstood him.

"Why not. It should be quieter there."

I scrabbled in my bag for an elastic band and, as we walked, pulled my hair into a messy bun, squashed that awful hat into my handbag and bought a very cheap scarf from one of the tourist kiosks which I layered over my coat to disguise its most recognisable features. I also made a concerted effort to wipe the lost, somewhat gentle expression that I seemed to have in all those dreadful images of me and replaced it with the most ferocious I could muster. I had a pair of black-rimmed reading glasses in my bag so I put those on too. They were only those cheap ones that you buy at pharmacists or on the market and I had mistakenly bought ones that magnified much more than I needed so, of course, the result was that the whole world was severely out of focus and I was a menace to others and to myself. I also looked like a demented owl, but even that was preferable to being recognised, so I blundered on and only nearly killed myself in traffic once.

We struggled through the anonymous crowds on the streets and down to the underground and, as you will know if you have ever been to London, no one ever looks anyone in the face. I did have a nasty moment on the Jubilee Line when I sat down and discovered (after a full two minutes of staring at it) that my face was plastered over the front page of a free paper and that every person on the train seemed to be reading it. Still, no one took any notice of me. Perhaps the glasses really were an effective disguise. Maybe Superman wasn't such a dork after all.

We reached pretty Victorian Marylebone Station without further incident and I bought a ticket for Stratford upon Avon. William grasped my arm and looked questioningly at me but I shrugged him aside.

"You said you wanted to go home."

That was unfair of me, I know. I was suddenly tired and dispirited. I pulled the scarf over my head and bought a hot coffee and a sandwich from one of the kiosks. I probably looked quite odd but then there are a lot of odd-looking people in London so I went unnoticed through the various transactions. For once William didn't seem that interested in food so I found a quiet corner and ate whilst we waited. He wandered around looking closely at people and things much as we do when leaving a particularly beautiful or a precious place with no expectations of a swift return. There was a distance between us that hadn't been there before but I was feeling just a little cranky so I figured he was giving me some space.

We climbed aboard a train that had plenty of room and no drunkards. I settled back in my seat, William opposite me, and fell asleep almost instantly. I woke several times, as you do when travelling on trains, because my head had fallen forward or because the ticket collector shook my arm or because I realised that my mouth was wide open and I was dribbling, but I was too tired to be aware of very much else, apart from the fact that whenever I opened my eyes William was there, quiet and watchful. The scarf and people's lack of curiosity with regard to their fellow travellers did the business and no one recognised me. We arrived in Stratford upon Avon, William's place of birth and of death at nearly 3 pm. The day was still fine and, once I had shaken the heavy sleep from my body, I felt brighter myself.

We got directions from the station staff and walked into Stratford. William held my arm tightly but said not a word. You will know that there is much of Stratford that was built in William's time that has been preserved, albeit more by luck than by judgement. The house that William worked so hard for, and the one he died in, was demolished by a clergyman who got fed up with people peering in at his windows and asking to see the house where the playwright lived. I suppose we can all have some sympathy with that, but what a missed opportunity for commercialism. And our heritage, of course. The house in which William was born and lived much of his early life survives intact, next to a shiny purpose-built museum. There were knots of tourists here, there and everywhere of course. He was astonished – well who wouldn't be? Imagine finding yourself in the future and having your own rather ordinary life, as you are experiencing it now, turned into a theme park.

Just as we reached his childhood home I turned to speak to William and he was not there. I bought another coffee and sat next to a group of Indian students whilst I waited. My head-scarf allowed me even more anonymity amongst them. A couple of policemen wandered by without glancing my way and the rest was hustle and bustle in the souvenir shops or queuing for The Shakespeare Experience. If only they knew, I thought.

I had just finished my coffee when I realised that William was with me again. Well, not exactly with me. He was standing a few yards away facing the snaking line that queued to enter his home to do homage to his genius…and he was laughing. Very loudly. I jumped up, clamped the defunct mobile phone to my head and hurried over. Tears of mirth were streaming down his dear little face, making his beard hair glisten, and he grasped my arm to steady himself as the gales of laughter wracked his body and rendered him helpless.

"What's so funny?" I asked. I had expected him to be touched, awed even, by the reverence accorded to his works and life, but it seemed he found it hilarious.

"Lord, what fools we mortals be," he chortled at length, wiping the tears from his eyes with his velvet sleeve. "Indeed, I had not thought it possible, for glory is like a circle in the water which never ceaseth to enlarge itself till by broad spreading it disperses to naught, and yet I was wrong for it seems I still live in fame though not in life. These people are like to pilgrims, to see the relics of my life. Of my life! My ordinary, base, sinful life of labour and strife. I know not why exactly, but tis a wonderful jest."

"You are too modest," I replied, a little annoyed that he found our veneration for his work, and for him, a thing of so little moment.

"Not so neither," he took my arm again and smiled up at me. "Present mirth hath present laughter, no doubt, and there is much in both our worlds' that is hidden from us. But yet…tis still a fine joke!" His eyes twinkled and I began to understand. It was quite funny when you looked at it from his point of view.

"The theatre," I said firmly. "I doubt you'll dismiss your fame so easily when you see the bricks and mortar built in your name. Come on."

Down to the river, past the canal boats and across the expanse of grass and walkways.

He viewed the vast, concrete structure for long moments, then he hesitated and threw me a sideways glance.

"Tis…"

"Ugly," I finished for him. "Afraid so. Sorry about that."

"No, 'tis big. Tis strange and yet marvellous in my eyes."

"Let's get something to eat and then see if we can get in for the evening show."

The emptiness of hunger was gnawing at my stomach and the sandwich I had eaten at Marylebone was but a distant memory. I was also desperate for a cup of tea. William, catching sight of a caricature of himself on a tea towel was distracted by the RSC gift shop. I left him staring open-mouthed at a plastic wind-up Shakespeare that bore him a quite unsettling resemblance, not least in its rather odd gait. I could understand that that sort of tribute to his life and works probably took a fair amount of processing.

Purchasing a scone and a cup of tea with the last of my dwindling cash I looked around to find somewhere to sit. Several coach tours had arrived and the limited seating inside was packed with elderly ladies. One or two gentlemen stood gallantly, balancing tea cups on palsied hands. I was just contemplating going outside to the empty and uninviting benches there when I was gathered up and, before I could protest, was forcibly ushered on to a small two-seater settee. Two women then squeezed themselves either side of me and I was wedged and immovable. One of my captors took my plate of scones and placed them on the low table in front of me whilst the other asked "Sugar?" and then tore the little white bags open and stirred them into my tea.

"We've been watching you," whispered one.

"You're that woman they're all looking for," hissed the other.

"FROM THE NEWS," concluded the one who sat opposite, very loudly.

"Shsshss!"

About six others gathered around shushing her. One leaned over and adjusted her hearing aid while the two gentlemen 'hurrumphed' and shifted their weight uncomfortably. I peered at them through my magnifying spectacles and realized that the cat was out of the bag. I sighed, pushed back the head scarf and removed those horrible reading glasses. I was surrounded by nine elderly women, all in their seventies at least. The two spare gentlemen (and I mean spare in both senses) were also part of the party although somewhat divorced from the main energy which was definitely female.

"I said it was her," rasped a sharp-faced, sharp-voiced woman next to the deaf lady. In case anyone had missed it, she rapped her walking stick sharply three times on the floor to get her point home. "Didn't I say. Didn't I?"

"Yes, you did," said the much kinder lady on my right. "Now be quiet or you'll frighten her away."

Fat chance I thought. Situated as I was it was unlikely that anything short of a mechanical winch would ever release the three of us from that wretched settee.

"So, dear." The lady on my left, who was very large, dressed in pink and white and looked like a huge marshmallow, addressed me kindly. "What has brought you here and is there anything we can do for you?"

Eleven pairs of eyes were on me.

"Could I…would you mind if I ate my scone. I'm awfully hungry."

This created a wave of motherly concern that would have knocked me backwards had I not been wedged so tightly. Three of them fought to hand the scone to me, one of them rushed to the counter to demand a refill in my tea cup even though I had only taken two sips and two others were scandalised to discover that no jam or cream had been supplied with the scone. All concurred that the scones were very dry and really not up to standard. Would I like anything else? A sandwich? Jean still had some coronation chicken sandwiches and there was a piece of Hazel's famous fruit cake left from their packed lunch on the coach.

"No, no, please. This is fine," I sputtered through scone crumbs. They were right, it was very dry.

"Are you here to see the play?" a diminutive lady enquired, whilst helpfully brushing crumbs from my lap with a lace handkerchief. "We've heard that it's very good. Jean's nephew is the director, you know."

"How would she know that?" demanded Jean. "She couldn't possibly know that. But," she turned to me proudly, "it is very good indeed. It's a sell-out. You'll like it."

"I'm afraid I haven't got a ticket."

"WHAT DID SHE SAY?" asked the deaf lady.

Having cleared my lap of crumbs, taken my plate from me and replaced it with a refreshed cup of tea, the diminutive woman adjusted the woman's hearing aid again.

"She says she hasn't got a ticket."

"Well, that's all right, she can have Doreen's ticket," was the deaf lady's better-modulated response. An awkward silence fell. "Well, Doreen can't use it, can she? And it said on the news that the girl was obsessed with Shakespeare so she'll enjoy it more than Doreen would have because she only ever came for the company and the interval drinks. I can't see why you're being so bloody daft just because the woman's dead."

"It's only been a couple of days," ventured the lady on my right.

"Oh, give over, none of us can afford to waste an hour, let alone days, and if we stop doing stuff every time one of us pops our clogs we'll never do anything. Give the girl the ticket."

"That's very kind of you but I…"

"Stuff and nonsense, unless you want us to hand you over to the police."

I shook my head like a naughty school girl.

"Didn't think so."

"She hasn't done anything wrong," remonstrated the marshmallow lady. "Well, not really wrong anyway."

"She did break into Buckingham Palace."

"That nice lady on the BBC explained all that. She just got separated from her group when the alarm went off and wandered about for a bit. No harm was done."

"They said she assaulted that awful American."

"It was only an egg. I'd have thrown a lot more than that at the horrid man if I got the chance."

The lady with the stick brandished it threateningly and took out three tea cups and marshmallow lady's handbag in the process.

"Jolly good show that," volunteered one of the gentlemen. His sole comrade against the monstrous regiment of women patted him approvingly on the shoulder. The females ignored him.

"We'll call your family dear, and you can watch the play with us while we wait for them to get here."

The marshmallow lady stated this calmly and was backed up by vigorous nodding from the others and several approving raps from the walking stick. The game was up. There was no gainsaying the nine old ladies.

"That way you can avoid the media circus," said Jean, demonstrating, presumably courtesy of her media savvy nephew, a knowledge of the ways of the world. "Once you get safely home you can get a lawyer to deal with any unpleasantness."

"And in the meantime, you will be safe with us."

I smiled at the circle of kind ladies and agreed. I toyed with the idea of making a dash for it but, always supposing I could extricate myself from the settee, I had a feeling that these redoubtable ladies would not be as easy to fool or to escape as Biker had been. Nimble they may not be but determined and resourceful they definitely were. Quite aside from that, they were also very kind and sensible and I could do worse than have them on my side.

"Write down your home telephone number dear."

The marshmallow lady gave me a pen and a pretty pink notebook with Grandma inscribed in glitter on the front and they all watched as I wrote my number down. She then waved the little book at arms-length and said "David!"

One of the gentlemen leant forward obediently and took it from her. He then looked about for somewhere to put down his cup and saucer and was rescued from this dilemma by the other gentleman who took it from him. The first gentleman then pulled out a mobile phone looked at it in confusion for a moment or two, found his glasses, put them on upside down, removed them and put them on the right way up, discovered he still could not see well enough, moved towards the light at the window, tapped ineffectually with his thumb at the device for a moment, took in good part the tentative suggestion from the other gentleman that it might not be switched on, switched it on, considered for a few moments more, turned the phone the right way up, politely asked his friend if he would also hold the notebook while he dialled, waited whilst his friend looked around for somewhere to deposit both his and his friends cup and saucer, waited whilst this was achieved, handed over the pink sparkly book, squinted at it, asked his friend to read the number out and then waited whilst the second gentleman went through the rigmarole of finding his glasses. Not a single woman offered to help although they all watched with interest. At this point, a coronation chicken sandwich was thrust into my hands to distract me and another cup of sweet tea demanded of the young girl behind the café counter. I ate and drank, two of the ladies took out knitting and one crochet-work and the others regarded me indulgently, like a favourite grandchild.

"Did you see the Queen, dear?"

"Oh, no, not at all. I did not get that far."

"What a shame."

All murmured their sympathy.

"Did you see any other members of The Family?"

Here I took a big bite of the sandwich and chewed ostentatiously whilst I considered what to admit to.

"I was found in a sort of office."

The lady with the stick gave me a sharp look but the others

chorused "what a shame" again and so I managed to side-step the question. I'm not sure why I needed to but I felt that the kind gentleman at the palace would probably prefer it that way.

What was it like inside? Were the soldiers kind to you dear? Were there many servants around? Another cup of tea dear? Did you see any of the private apartments? What do you think the Queen is really like? Have another cup, dear. Does she knit do you know?

Over the next few minutes, the ladies shot these and many other questions at me. I answered them all as honestly as I could. They were less interested in my anti-globalisation activities because they had been covered quite extensively on the news with photos and video and because Buckingham Palace held greater domestic mysteries.

"Is it sorted out, David?" Marshmallow lady spoke softly but I had been watching the two gentlemen throughout and I knew that it was.

"On their way," he said.

"Good, well, come on ladies, time to go in. Have you all got your tickets?"

It was at this point that my two bookends came to the realisation that we were in danger of becoming a permanent fixture in the café. I wriggled, they heaved, we all strained but three substantial sets of hips attached to aged knees could gain no leverage against the floor and the rest of our party had almost disappeared into the theatre before the lady with the stick realised we were not with them. She hobbled back, gave me her hand over the low coffee table and assisted by a remarkably robust pull I burst from between the two well-covered ladies like a cork from a shaken champagne bottle.

"If you didn't stuff your faces with cake you wouldn't have these problems," the lady with the stick grumbled, turning her back on us. "Now, move your backsides."

Our seats were in the stalls and quite close to the stage.

William was already there, pottering about the stage. I waved but he was too caught up in wonder to respond. He looked right at home. Which of course he was. He stepped into the wings and I imagined him wandering past actors and costumes and stage managers, taking note and absorbing everything. I was very happy for him. The play was The Tempest and from my limited store of knowledge, I knew that it was believed to be one of the last that Shakespeare ever wrote and viewed by some as a conscious farewell to the stage before his retirement to Stratford. As a play that my William had not yet written it would have been all new to its own writer that evening and it laid open the prospect of a very odd sort of plagiarism. But, as William and Elizabeth had said, their time with me was simply a shadow in a dream, misty vestiges of images that slipped from the memory like quicksilver as soon as an attempt to reach out to them was made.

William stayed on stage throughout the magic hours when the shipwreck and the island were created, whilst Miranda and Ferdinand fell in love, the drunkards caroused and poor Caliban lowered and plotted. He followed Prospero step by step and word by word.

> *Our revels now are ended. These our actors,*
> *As I foretold you, were all spirits, and*
> *Are melted into air, into thin air:*
> *And like the baseless fabric of this vision,*
> *The cloud-capp'd tow'rs, the gorgeous palaces,*
> *The solemn temples, the great globe itself,*
> *Yea, all which it inherit, shall dissolve,*
> *And, like this insubstantial pageant faded,*
> *Leave not a rack behind. We are such stuff*
> *As dreams are made on; and our little life*
> *Is rounded with a sleep.*

The tears slipped down my cheeks and once again William was by my side. He put his hand on mine and smiled.

"Our parting is near. I would that it twere joyous."

"Oh yes," I said.

"What? Do you need the lavatory, dear?" hissed marshmallow lady her eyes still on the stage.

"Yes, it's all that tea I drank. I'll just slip out…"

My new friends were all more or less engrossed in the play, although one of the gentlemen was nodding off, so I was able to slide easily from my seat on the end of the row and, making apologetic faces to the usher, escape to the foyer with very little disturbance. As it happens all the tea I had drunk did occasion a short trip to the lavatory and after that, we slipped through the doors and out into a star-lit night.

CHAPTER TWENTY-SEVEN

Farewell, my dearest sister, fare thee well.
The elements be kind to thee, and make
Thy spirits all of comfort! fare thee well.
Antony and Cleopatra, Act III Sc ii

We didn't decide where to go next, we didn't need to, we just walked. It wasn't far.

The church had closed for the evening but as we hung over the gate a ghostly figure appeared from amongst the tombstones. The priest smiled gently at us, almost as if we were expected, and, without a word, lifted the latch, led us up the path and into the ancient church.

"I have one or two things to do," he said quietly. "If you would like a few moments alone here then you are welcome, of course."

"Thank you," I said. It was a lovely building. We turned left and there in the apse were the three tombstones, the one on the far left with fresh white flowers laid carefully below the name.

William Shakespeare.

It was journey's end. Perhaps it would be more accurate to say that it was the end of the road trip, the end of my escape, the beginning of reality. The dark swirling fog was beckoning, offering nothing but fear and pain and all I had to do was to find the courage to embrace it. Whether I would ever come out the other side to live in a bright world was a question that no one, not even William or Elizabeth, could answer.

For a long time, we sat quietly together, William and I, gazing at the delicate white flowers on the grave stone, our hands clasped. When exactly the right amount of time had passed I turned to look at my friend and smiled. There he sat, a little man with neatly trimmed beard, warm eyes, wrinkled tights and that silly floppy hat.

"I've heard it said that you're good with words," I quipped lightly, in an attempt to fight the rising tears. "You should say something."

He smiled.

"Sweet lady, the world holds many truths, you must seek yours."

There were long minutes of silence before I spoke again.

"I have lost my son."

William touched my hand and spoke softly.

"For he being dead, with him is beauty slain,
And, beauty dead, black chaos comes again."

"That is it, exactly," I replied. "But you, you and Elizabeth… you lightened the black chaos. For a time. I'm not sure, if I enter it again, that I will ever come out the other side?"

"Give sorrow words, gentle lady, and fare you well."

"Must you go?"

But I knew the answer. I gazed at the empty space beside me as if I could bring him back by force of will long after he had slowly faded into nothing.

"Ally?" The voice seemed vaguely familiar but I couldn't quite remember why. Then there was Hubby sitting down beside me taking my hand in his, with all the despair of the last few days written all too clearly on his dear face.

I looked back for William but he was gone and would not return.

"Ally, it's time to go home, love."

The kindly priest was there behind my husband smiling and nodding at me.

"Will you come?" Hubby asked tentatively.

He held my hand as if he was frightened. Not frightened of me exactly but frightened of what I might do. As if there was something immensely fragile about me and as if the wrong move or the wrong word might shatter me. It was very unlike him. And unlike me. I wasn't the fragile sort.

"Yes, of course," I said, standing up with determination. "It is quite late, isn't it? We'd better get home. How are Grace and…" I paused and took a long breath. "How is Grace?"

Hubby put his arm around me, the priest stepped back, and he steered me towards the door as if I were a piece of precious china.

"I must just say thank you…" I pulled away for a moment, ostensibly to grasp the priest's hand and say thank you, but really to glance back for William. He was not there. If he had been I would have run to him and to hell with the consequences. As it was I took one last look at his resting place with the fresh flowers on it and then turned back to life.

"Is Grace all right?" I asked, suddenly overcome with the guilt of a careless mother.

"She's here."

"Is she? Why?"

Of course, she was there. Of course, they had been looking for me frantically for days. All of them. And all of them were there, standing in a little loving knot outside in the darkened churchyard, Grace, Mum, Dad and Kate. All bore signs of strain and all had the same look as Hubby - restrained and fearful. Except for Kate, of course.

"Been worried about you, love," said Dad, gruffly.

"Enyerussnfum," said my mum, reaching blindly for me, choked by tears.

Grace just hugged me as if she would never let me go.

"Bugger it all Ally!" exclaimed my sister angrily punching my shoulder. "Have you any idea what you have put us all through? If you want to go chasing fairies all over Britain, you should…well you just bloody shouldn't."

Actually, she didn't say bloody, she said something much worse and I am fairly sure the kind vicar heard.

At any rate, it effectively broke the figurative ice and we were pretty much back to our usual family state. I laughed because I find the absurd quite funny, my father was outraged and told her not to fucking swear in a churchyard. He can be surprisingly coarse at times. My mother, glancing at the vicar, shushed my father and blew her nose very loudly. Grace released me, rolled her eyes and flounced off in teenage disgust, feigned to disguise emotion, and Hubby muttered effusive apologies to the vicar whilst darting looks that could kill at my recalcitrant sister who was making elaborate preparations to light up a cigarette.

Knowing my sister as I did, it probably wasn't exactly a cigarette so, seeing that no one else was clear headed enough to salvage the situation, I grasped her arm and pushed her back down the churchyard and through the gate. Unfortunately, there was a police car there. Kate came to realisation just in time to put the joint down her cleavage and Hubby and Dad bustled past us to reassure the policeman about something or other.

I wanted to know what they were talking about but Kate's cleavage was beginning to smoke fragrantly so I marched her down the pavement at a smart pace. Mum and Grace chased after us, concerned that I was going to do another runner. Kate retrieved the smouldering butt from her bra and spent the next few minutes alternately dragging on it in desperation and blowing down the front of her dress. Dad and Hubby joined us after having convinced the policeman that they were fit and proper persons to look after me. I'm really not sure how they did that.

And that was that. The end of my adventure and the beginning of what those around me called my recovery.

CHAPTER TWENTY-EIGHT

Cure her of that!
Canst thou not minister to a mind diseased,
pluck from the memory a rooted sorrow,
raze out the written troubles of the brain,
and with some sweet oblivious antidote
cleanse the stuffed bosom of that perilous stuff
which weighs upon her heart.
Macbeth, Act V Sc ii

Some time later I found myself in a square, white room, set in an angular grey building surrounded by oblong green spaces. It was felt to be best that I take 'a complete rest', as it was put to me. I saw through that of course. I had been put in a psychiatric ward, a nut house, a loony bin, a Bedlam.

The outrage I felt at that betrayal cannot be adequately expressed even now, but I had faced an almost unanimously united front at home. Hubby, Mum, Dad and even Grace all joined in their efforts to persuade me to agree. Only Kate was on my side and eventually, conversely, that was what decided me. My sister wasn't the most reliable judge of sanity, if you know what I mean.

Anyway, I had agreed to come into the hospital for a couple of days and some counselling. It was all rubbish of course. I refused to take any drugs so the treatment consisted of sitting around and talking about myself with doctors and sometimes in groups of people who were far barmier than I was. Apart from that, it was just a lot of sleeping. At first, I refused to talk at all, despite William's advice, but that got quite boring, so I started talking a lot and at least had the satisfaction of getting my own back by boring other people rigid.

Then, after a few days, something got lost. I don't mean just time. I mean something inside of me. All I remember after that is a spiral of blackness.

It was all confusion. It may have been just a few days after William left me, or it may have been many months. I found it difficult to keep track of time. I do know that I never had the opportunity to ditch my dressing gown and put proper clothes on and that people fed me and walked me round and spoke kindly, and I probably was given some drugs at that time and probably took them willingly. I was quite happy in the fog. Somewhere beyond the fog was realisation and reality. Oh yes, on the whole, I preferred the fog.

Grace and Hubby and Mum and Dad came to see me often. Every day I think. Kate was discouraged from coming because they might have kept her in. Every now and again someone would join with my family to try and jolly me along, but I would turn my face to the wall and they had to give up sooner or later. I knew I shouldn't do that, it was selfish and rude and I wasn't usually either, but I just couldn't help myself. The fear was always greater when Hubby or Grace were near and I knew I should fight to hide my terror but to shut down and turn away was the only way I knew.

I saw Alex too, of course. He came often to stand silently at the end of my bed, but this Alex was not the golden lad that was my son. This Alex was gaunt, hollow-eyed and grey, a ragged shadow of what he had been. That was when I was at my worst. That was when the blood rushed around my head and I wanted to scream and scream and scream and scream and just never stop screaming. Because he wasn't really there. He was dead.

After a while, he stopped coming.

The fog began to dissipate slowly, despite my struggles to remain hidden and safe within it, and then despair crept in and brought with it hours of endless, helpless crying. Grace didn't visit much during that period but Hubby was there all the time. After that came exhaustion and not wanting to do anything except lie staring at the ceiling.

One morning the comfortable grey cocoon that surrounded me, shifted and swirled and all but evaporated as a great commotion erupted in the white corridor outside my quiet room and "Youliette, Youliette!" bounced off the doors and windows. Karl, taking no notice of protest or expostulation from the bemused staff, burst into the room, closely followed by the faithful Erich. I turned my face towards him and smiled wanly for the first time in…well, I don't know how long. He, on the other hand, took one look at me, clasped his manicured hands to his feminine face and screamed in honestly felt horror. By the time he and Erich left, I, and most of the nursing staff had startling new hair do's. Brooking no protest, Karl dunked reluctant heads into the small sink in my room, washed, cut, primped and blow dried and would have coloured and permed if Erich hadn't indicated that, in this particular instance, less might be quite enough. He was certainly a talented hairdresser but more used to models and the drop dead gorgeous than dumpy health workers and housewives from middle England. We may have been (briefly) high fashion from the hairline up but we were definitely low fashion from there on down. I didn't talk much, but then no one could ever get a word in edgewise when Karl was in full flow. Erich and I smiled and nodded speechlessly at each other as Karl attended to my neglected tresses, chattering away about nothing and everything. I felt that they were very kind to come and see me, and I began to discern a very small ray of light flickering weakly through the heaviness. They did not mention William or Elizabeth, but my hair looked great. Or would have done on somebody else.

Another little break in the sad monotony was occasioned by the arrival one morning of a simple little card and a spray of red roses. With understated elegance, the glorious blooms screamed good taste. On the card were the hand-written words "I am sorry to hear that you are not well. I hope that you feel better soon". The signature was a simple 'P'. I think Hubby was a bit suspicious. I might tell him all about my conversation with the old gentleman one day. Of course, he won't believe any of it, and maybe he would be right not to, but the flowers were real. At least I think they were.

I was staring at the ceiling on another dark morning when someone else appeared and made me lose count. I should have mentioned that I counted whilst I looked at the ceiling. I reached 21,002 one day. Not that day though because a woman's ugly face appeared above mine.

"You all right love?"

"I'm counting."

"What are you counting?" She looked up at the blank ceiling.

"Nothing. I'm just counting."

"Fair enough. Are you coming to the community room? They're putting that ballroom dancing show on."

"God, no," I said.

"Don't blame you," and she ambled off. I'd lost count so I had to start all over again.

She was back the next day.

"How far have you got?" she asked

"5,257," I replied.

"That's good," and she would have ambled off again.

"What are you doing here?" I asked. I had been dully wondering since the day before.

"Wot else would I be doin'? Bloody workin' as usual. S'all I ever do, work and watch telly."

"Oh, okay, but why here?"

"They need cleaners 'ere too." Nell spat on her finger and rubbed at a stain on my bedside table. "Mucky lot. So what about you then? 'Ow's it goin' in 'ere?"

"I don't know, I'm asleep most of the time."

"Sounds bloody good to me."

After a moment I said sadly, "They've gone. William and Elizabeth have gone."

"Probably just as well, don't ya think?" She shrugged and waddled out.

I only got to 1,470 the next day.

"Still counting?"

"No," I said. "Where are you going?"

"To the community room, they're showing that cooking programme today. Want to go?"

"Yeah, ok," I stood up, weakly of course, because lying on your back for days on end does nothing for your core muscles, and followed her to the community room which was peopled with lots of pyjama's and dressing gowns. The assortment of men and women all looked quite normal to me, but then perhaps, like my sister, I wasn't much of a judge.

I sat down and watched three celebrities battling good-humouredly to cook the best soufflé. It was bizarre but bland, and unlikely to arouse strong feelings of any sort, even amongst chefs. Dinner was next. To provide the evening with a nice contrast they served up a glutinous shepherd's pie masquerading as something edible, but which fooled no-one, and a pudding so heavy and tasteless that, loaded into a cannon, it could have felled a regiment. Whoever was responsible for these culinary delights had missed his or her vocation and should have been laying tarmac. Nell returned and sat down beside me.

"Fancy a cup of tea?"

"Do you think they've got anything stronger?"

"Strong tea, strong coffee, strong orange juice."

"I've got to get the hell out of here. The food is terrible."

I sighed. She chewed a dirty fingernail and regarded me with no sympathy whatsoever. I decided to be combative.

"You know Nell... I'm beginning to think that I didn't really see them at all. And, if I didn't, then you didn't see them either."

"Did, didn't, 'oo knows? Point is they was real to you."

"The problem is...I'm not sure what is real anymore. You for instance." I glanced around to see if anyone had noted that I was sitting on a settee talking to myself, but I would have had to strip naked, cover myself in gravy and swing from the light fittings before it would occur to anyone there that perhaps I was behaving a little oddly. They were a very broadminded and accepting group of people. "You were my link to reality but, if you did see them then you can't be real either, and yet here you are."

Nell had progressed to picking shepherd's pie out of her teeth with the said fingernail. Once she had dislodged the offending morsel she spat it across the room. She then leant back in her chair, balanced her flabby arms on her drooping bosoms and said with great aplomb.

"Maybe that should tell you something?"

"What? What should it tell me?"

"Oh, bugger, now you've got me confused. I don't bleedin' know, do I? I'm not one of them trick cyclists. I'm not up to this psychological stuff."

"But you were talking to them," I interrupted, impatiently. "You had a conversation with them. With Elizabeth and William. You and Elizabeth hated each other. Don't you remember her calling you a rank-scented, eye-offending crow?"

Her brows lowered.

"Look luv, I'm just a cleaning woman from Luffbra 'oo once spent a very interestin' evening wiv ya in a greasy spoon...'Old onto that an' you'll be all right."

She got up and walked away.

"Oh."

William and Elizabeth slipped further and further away from me, taking certainty with them and leaving only confusion and loneliness. There had been no external or supernatural forces at work.

No spanning of time or universe.

No divine miracle or scientific phenomenon.

No William, no Elizabeth.

Everything that had been created had been created internally…Created by me, an ordinary woman, broken down by long-held grief, desperately reaching for the wraith of her lost son.

CHAPTER TWENTY-NINE

Grief fills the room up of my absent child,
Lies in his bed, walks up and down with me
Puts on his pretty looks, repeats his words
Remembers me of all his gracious parts
Stuffs out his vacant garments with his form
Then, have I reason to be fond of grief?
King John, Act III Sc iv

I was called into a private session the next day with Doctor Pinch. I didn't want to go. We'd had several sessions before and I found them profoundly annoying. Doctor Pinch knew my story, knew all about William and Elizabeth and my adventures with them. I had related it all to him in minute detail, more for something to do than anything else, but he had refused to be moved or entertained by any of it. He was impassive and profoundly un-shockable, but then, in his profession, he had probably heard it all before. He was a tall, spare man with thinning hair and watery grey eyes, in his fifties at a guess and always immaculate in well-fitting suits and muted ties. He wore rimless glasses which he never removed and which, at certain angles, caught the light, blanked out his eyes and left the man with even less definition than he ordinarily possessed.

"How are you feeling today?" he asked, sitting opposite to me on a horrible orange NHS chair.

"Much better," I said firmly. "Quite like my old self and I think it is time for me to go home."

"Do you?" He never made a statement or expressed an opinion. I'd learned that. He was a walking question mark.

"Yes, I do. Don't you?" I gazed challengingly at him, my arms folded against my stomach. This was a game we played. Question for question and it wasn't easy at times.

"What makes you think that?"

"Are you saying that I am not well enough?" I countered.

He considered for a moment.

"Have you had any visitors recently?" I knew what he meant of course. He meant, had I been visited by any of my invisible friends. His questions could never be taken at face value.

"No. Have you?"

"Can you remember the date that Elizabeth the first died?"

This was something new. An entirely new tack.

"Of course I can," I replied dismissively. "23 March 1603."

"And William Shakespeare?"

"24 April 1616."

"Wasn't that his birthdate also?"

"So they say."

"Why do you think you remember those dates so well?"

"Good memory," I snapped, irritated.

"Didn't your son go missing on 23 March?"

"You know he did, so why ask? Anyway, he didn't 'go missing' then. That was the date he left home."

"And what happened on 24 April last year?"

I stood up abruptly and considered walking out and returning to my square white bedroom. But I would only have to go through it all again next time, so I determined to stay and brazen it out, even though the cold hand of fear had closed around my heart once more. I sat down.

"You know that too," I said, staring at the ceiling and beginning to count.

"What was your relationship with your son? Would you say it was good?"

"Of course it was good. Of course it was. We were very close. Very."

There was silence in the square room and Doctor Pinch said nothing. The silence stretched on, accusing me of the lie I had just told.

I tried to start counting again but it was no good. I sighed and submitted.

"No, it wasn't. It wasn't good. At least not for the last few months. He was growing up, becoming independent… and I could not bear to let him go. He left school before A levels, didn't want to go to university, got a job stacking boxes, for god's sake. He wanted to travel. He was a bright boy, top of the class. He could have done anything, been anything but he threw it all away. He wouldn't listen. I couldn't bear it."

"So that triggered the breakdown of relations between you?"

"I've just told you. He was throwing his life away. He wanted to backpack around the world. He was only seventeen. I said no. I said no again and again. He said he was going anyway. He went."

"Why do you think you were so angry with him?"

"I wasn't angry. I was never angry. I was frightened."

"Frightened?"

"Of losing him. I wanted to keep him close. I wanted to keep him safe. I was so frightened…"

The white room receded and I was watching Alex running down the garden path, leaping over that damn cat, a heavy backpack carried lightly on his shoulder. I watched him with my own bitter words of fury echoing in my ears, with the certain knowledge that Alex was as slow to forgive an injury as I was and that Hubby and Grace would be broken-hearted when they came home to find him gone.

"I should have stopped him. If I'd stopped him, it would

have been different. If I'd found another way to hold him back…"

"What then? Would he have been happy?"

"He would have been alive."

Now I was angry. Angry with the simplistic crap that Dr. Pinch was spewing, and I told him so. He was characteristically unmoved by my diatribe but I felt marginally better after it.

"Do you think…" There was a long pause during which the doctor stared at the ceiling. Maybe he was counting too. I pulled my knees up to my chest, chewed my lip and tried not to dissolve into tears.

"Do you think the outcome would have been different if you had supported him? If you had let him go?"

That I did not know. If I had given in and let him go with my blessing would his actions have been different? Would the timing have been crucially different by a month, a week, a day or a minute? Might he not have caught that particular ferry in Thailand but a later or an earlier one? Might his friend not have called for his help in the drowning waters and might he not have gone to his aid? Might he have given a thought to his shattered mother and saved himself instead?

I did not know, could never know, but one thing would have been different.

"There would have been a good-bye," I said.

"What happened on 24 April last year?"

That day, that terrible day. Alex's birthday and the day we lost him forever.

"You know what happened. Why ask?"

There was a long pause and he looked at his wrist watch. I prepared myself to leave but it wasn't time. He settled himself more firmly in his chair and considered for a moment.

"Your husband told me that Alex stole money from you."

"No," I said angrily. "He didn't. The money was his. It was always intended to be his."

"How did you feel about that? Your son stealing from you?"

"I told you, he didn't. It wasn't theft, I would have given it to him. It was his. I just didn't want to give him the money because then he would have left."

"How do you think Alex would have felt about stealing from his mother? Do you think he would have felt guilty? Ashamed?"

"How many times?" I exploded. "It was his. I should have given it to him when he asked, for Christ's sake. It is my fault. All my fault, not his. He was a good boy. He was so brave and…I was…proud of him."

Alex had saved his friend that dreadful day. He had dragged him through drowning corridors and out through the ferry's shattered sides. He, like his friend, could have struggled through the storm waves to the lonely dinghy, but he turned back to help others. He could not have survived, his grateful friend told us, amidst honest tears and fearful anguish.

And then the days and weeks went by with no word from our boy and the little spark of hope that lingered against all odds was eventually quenched forever.

"What about Grace?" Dr. Pinch asked. It felt very much as if, having plunged the knife into my heart, he was now setting about twisting it with some gusto. "How do you get on with her?"

"Fine," I replied. "I won't make the same mistake."

"The same mistake?"

"I mean, that I won't…smother her. She blames me, though. So does my husband."

"So you feel guilt, as well as grief?"

Time for another rant. He really knew how to needle me.

"I can't think why you lot get paid such enormous amounts of money. All you do is ask endless questions and then state the bleedin' obvious! Of course, I feel guilty. I drove him away, it's my fault that we lost him and now Grace hates me and I have no idea why my husband stays with me and, if you think about it, it's no wonder that I ditched this shitty world and created one of my own. Probably the most sensible thing I've done in years."

There was a long pause after that. Doctor Pinch stared down at the sharp crease in his trousers and thought. I don't for one moment believe that he was thinking about me and my mental state. I think it was much more likely that he was thinking about himself. People that well-groomed are usually narcissistic…or obsessive compulsive.

"Shall we finish there for today? Are you ready for lunch?"

My time was up. Some other poor sod would be waiting outside for their session.

"Is anybody ever ready for lunch here?"

"Don't you like the food?"

"Obviously you don't eat it or you wouldn't ask."

CHAPTER THIRTY

I pray you, in your letters,
When you shall these unlucky deeds relate,
Speak of me as I am; nothing extenuate,
Nor set down aught in malice. Then must you speak
Of one that lov'd not wisely but too well.
Othello, Act V Sc ii

The next session with Doctor Pinch started much the same as all the others.

"How are you today?"

"Just peachy. How are you?"

"Did you sleep well?"

"Like a log. What about you?"

"I believe that Nell spent some time with you the other day. Is that right?"

"Oh! Yes." Once again he had surprised me. "I didn't know that you knew her. She told me that she works here."

He nodded, but I wasn't entirely convinced.

"She's quite attractive, don't you think?" I continued demurely. "With all that long red hair and those big blue eyes?"

He raised his neat eyebrows mockingly.

"Is that how you would describe her? Not as short, round, loudmouthed and a bit common?"

"Ok, you do know her. Or did I describe her to you?"

Perhaps I had.

"Shall we talk again about you?"

"No," I snapped. "I'm sick of talking about me, let's talk about you instead. But you won't will you? So I will tell you what I think. Firstly, you are gay, obviously. I can tell that because your nails are manicured, amongst other things. And you own a dog because there are sometimes coarse hairs on your trousers. You live with your mother…," I had a quick think here. "Because, someone makes the sandwiches you bring to avoid eating the swill they serve here. I've seen you throw them in the bin and visit the vending machine instead. And it isn't you making them because you'd make something you knew you were going to like. So would a partner. So I will bet that it's your mother. And, that it's your mother's dog because you're too immaculate to let some slobbery dog leave hairs on your clothes through choice."

I was quite triumphant, even though I'd come up with it all randomly on the spot, but the good doctor only inclined his head very slightly.

"Am I right?"

"Isn't it also possible that I am happily married to a wonderful woman who just makes lousy sandwiches, have polo ponies which I ride in matches at the weekend and a daughter studying beauty therapy who needs to practise her manicurist skills?"

"Oh bum," I puffed my cheeks out on a sigh.

"So," he continued. "As it is my turn now, I can perhaps deduce from your comments that your mother makes terrible sandwiches?"

I surrendered. He was cleverer than me.

"Well, as it happens, when I think of sandwiches I do tend to think of Mum. She puts things like corned beef and strawberry jam together. It's not usually intentional, just the result of artistic distraction. I suppose I was sort of …what's the word?"

"Projecting?"

"Yes. I suppose so. I was sort of projecting the experience of my mother on to yours. If that's not too disturbing an image."

"Is that something you do often, do you think?"

I sighed. He was determined to make everything about me.

"Yes, I'm really good at it, brilliant in fact, but you already know that."

"Shall we talk about your two friends?"

"If we must."

"Why Elizabeth and William, do you think?"

"How the hell should I know?"

"Why do you think those dates we were talking about in our last session might be significant to you?"

"I don't think they are." He was going to ask another question so I jumped in quickly. "Well, all right, if we follow your convoluted train of thought, it is just, remotely, possible that the dates have something to do with why I fixed on William. Alex was born on 24th April and we always joked about it being Shakespeare's birthday. Alex was a good writer and he loved history. I used to help him with his homework and I got interested. Those dates being the same as when we lost him... it was all just a fluke but the coincidence played on my mind. I see that now. And I know that Elizabeth and William were just a part of me. A projection, if you like. Listen to me!" I smiled drearily. "An expert in self-analysis and Elizabethan history. I had no idea that I was so clever."

"How would you describe your life to me?"

"Wasted." I had spoken without thought and wanted to take back the word even as I spoke.

"Perhaps unfulfilled might be a better way to put it, don't you think?" If he hadn't been so lacking in empathy I might have thought that he was being kind. "Will William and Elizabeth visit you again, do you think?"

"No, I don't think so, but..." I looked at him defiantly. "I can't help being sorry for that. They were...spectacular. And they were my friends."

CHAPTER THIRTY-ONE

So there's my riddle: one that's dead is quick.
All's Well That Ends Well Act V Sc iii

Alex came to me again the next morning just as I was struggling into consciousness of the day. I saw him standing at the door. He hovered there, not wholly in the room or wholly out of it. The sun streamed in through my one window and the spring leaves on the trees waved in the wind.

"Mum," he said, in a voice I did not recognise.

"Go away," I replied. "Just go away, leave me alone. Please don't come back."

I turned away from him, pulled the blankets over my head and tried to fight my way back into nothingness. When the nurse bustled in some time later and insisted that I get up and go for a walk before it rained, he was not there. I tried to rouse myself when Grace and Hubby joined me in the windy gardens but I could not. They talked of inconsequential things. Things that could not upset or challenge me and I smiled and nodded but felt no interest and could not feign that I did. I felt myself slipping back into that dreadful state where nothing was clear and all was pain. I had put illusions behind me and needed to keep them there.

My session with Dr. Pinch was much later that day and by then I had recovered some of my determination to seem as sane as I possibly could. Maybe then they would let me go home. At home, I could at least get something decent to eat. I had roused myself enough to extract some interesting information from one of the nurses, so that, when the time came for our session, I was fired up and ready to run rings around good old Dr. Pinch.

"You bastard!" I commenced, as soon I entered the room. He didn't flinch. He was probably used to much worse. "You are gay, you do live with your mother and you do have a dog. Two, in fact, both of them Schnauzers."

He almost smiled.

"Sit down Ally."

A good start, I thought to myself. A command, not a question, that's new.

"Did you sleep well?"

Well, that didn't last long.

"Yes."

"But you had a visitor this morning I understand?"

My hopes of going home faded. They would never let me go if I were still seeing visions of Alex.

I made no answer, but slumped down into my seat and wrapped my disappointment around me.

"I would like you to take me back to the morning when you had breakfast in the shelter in London. Would you do that please?"

Now I was really annoyed.

"Oh, what the hell? You've heard it all before."

"Who was there? In the room when you arrived for breakfast."

"What does it matter?"

"Who was there?"

"Myra and Carly and various other women. Most of them were from the streets and the others were volunteers. So what?"

"Anyone else?"

I sighed noisily to demonstrate my exasperation.

"Just a couple of men. One quite young, the other old-ish with a purple nose."

"Anything unusual about either of them?"

"You mean apart from the purple nose? No."

I bounced angrily in my chair and huffed again.

"They were street people. And I didn't see the young one's face clearly."

"You told me that you thought he was watching you?"

'Well, yes but, most of them in the room were watching me. I had William and Elizabeth in tow and, at one point, I created quite a kerfuffle."

"You also thought that he followed you, didn't you?"

"Well, even the paranoid must be right some of the time."

"Let's leave that for a moment then."

"Oh, yes, let's," I said sarcastically.

"And go back to this morning."

"What about this morning?"

"Your visitor."

"What about my visitor?"

"I think you should tell me."

I stared at him. A low hum began somewhere in the world and swelled and increased and hit my ears and I felt as if my brain was vibrating against my skull. All blood drained to my feet. All strength left me. The world slipped sideways and my mouth was dry. I licked my lips and forced words through the thick air around me.

"How…how did you know about him? About Alex? How… did you know that he came to me this morning?"

"How do you think I knew, Ally?"

"I didn't tell anyone," I tried to think but I could not work it out. "No-one at all. I know I didn't tell anyone."

He waited whilst the room wheeled around me. Faintness pressed and my heart started pounding as if I should know something…as if I should have been able to work out something very important…I just couldn't quite put my finger on what it was.

"Then if you told no-one," he said very gently, "but if I know that he visited you in your room this morning…there can only be one explanation, don't you think?"

I sat very still. Not daring to move a muscle. Not able to move. But I knew that they were there behind me in the doorway. Hubby, Grace and…Alex.

CHAPTER THIRTY-TWO

The lunatic, the lover, and the poet, are of imagination all compact.
A Midsummer Night's Dream, Act V Sc i

The web of our life is of a mingled yarn,
good and ill together.
All's Well That Ends Well, Act IV Sc iii

It is now many months since I came home with my family. With Hubby, Grace and Alex.

The hospital staff had been quite exercised as to how to deal with the whole situation as it turned their normal procedure on its head and played havoc with their treatment routine. Dr. Pinch decided that it would be best if I found my own way, slowly, to the truth. I had to learn to distinguish what was real from what was imagination and that is, sometimes, very difficult to do. I needed to accept my grief and my guilt before I could recover from them, and Alex needed to learn that shame or anger should never keep you from those who love you.

But his return was hard for any of us to believe at first. I wake sometimes at night believing him still drowned in that distant sea and even his presence at breakfast cannot completely reassure me. So few of the lost are ever found. So few of those who choose to be lost to their families ever return and even less are the chances of the dead being restored to those who love them. This we know all too well and so our reality seems very fragile at times.

That he had lived rough and with the rough we began to understand, and, knew too, that when he eventually made his way back to England, brown and gaunt, he was uncertain, adrift and laden with the sort of experiences that are the stuff of nightmares. He should have come home but he drifted a while longer, both ashamed and defiant, until that day in London when he found his mother as lost as he was himself.

But he is home now, for a while, and is my... our...Alex again. We both still have some healing to do but having lost him once I know better now how to keep him and know that I will always have a place in his future, wherever, whatever, that might be. Grace and Hubby and I are happy once more.

When the dust had settled I went in search of Nell, but I was not able to find her or anyone who knew anything about her. Perhaps she was, is, just another part of me. (Which isn't a particularly comfortable thought, I have to say.)

But, what of my good friends Elizabeth and William? Well, I will admit to you that I could not relinquish them completely.

I go into my son's room often and they are always there, where they were before, waiting for me.

Elizabeth stares down, imperious as ever, from the bookshelf where she resides next to Henry and Mary and little Edward. I can spend time with her in her world anytime I open the cover and pore over the glossy illustrations and detailed text. I can feel her bony fingers prodding me and hear her cracked sardonic laugh.

The well-thumbed Complete Works of Shakespeare lying on the bedside table brings dear William to my side and we chuckle together over the absurdities of Dogberry and Bottom, we weep for sad Ophelia and doomed Richard, and marvel at the limited wisdom and the infinite stupidity of kings and men.

I don't go there in sickness of spirit. I go to visit old and very dear friends.

Author website   www.s.lynnscott.com
Email   slynnscott17@gmail.com